MW01259465

Knife in the Back

TITLES BY KAREN ROSE

DIRTY SECRETS (enovella)

Baltimore Novels

YOU BELONG TO ME

NO ONE LEFT TO TELL

DID YOU MISS ME?

BROKEN SILENCE (enovella)

WATCH YOUR BACK

MONSTER IN THE CLOSET

DEATH IS NOT ENOUGH

Cincinnati Novels

CLOSER THAN YOU THINK

ALONE IN THE DARK

EVERY DARK CORNER

EDGE OF DARKNESS

INTO THE DARK

Sacramento Novels

SAY YOU'RE SORRY

SAY NO MORE

SAY GOODBYE

New Orleans Novels

QUARTER TO MIDNIGHT

BENEATH DARK WATERS

BURIED TOO DEEP

KNIFE IN THE BACK

San Diego Case Files

COLD-BLOODED LIAR

CHEATER

DEAD MAN'S LIST

Knife in the Back

KAREN ROSE

Berkley
New York

BERKLEY
An imprint of Penguin Random House LLC
1745 Broadway, New York, NY 10019
penguinrandomhouse.com

Book design by Alison Cnockaert

Library of Congress Cataloging-in-Publication Data

Names: Rose, Karen, 1964- author.
Title: Knife in the back / Karen Rose.
Description: New York: Berkley, 2025. | Series: New Orleans Novels; 4
Identifiers: LCCN 2024059980 (print) | LCCN 2024059981 (ebook) |
ISBN 9780593638613 (hardcover) | ISBN 9780593638620 (ebook)
Subjects: LCGFT: Thrillers (Fiction) | Detective and mystery fiction. | Novels.
Classification: LCC PS3618.O7844 K65 2025 (print) |
LCC PS3618.O7844 (ebook) | DDC 813/.6—dc22/eng/2041220
LC record available at https://lccn.loc.gov/2024059980
LC ebook record available at https://lccn.loc.gov/2024059981

Printed in the United States of America
1st Printing

The authorized representative in the EU for product safety and compliance is Penguin Random House Ireland, Morrison Chambers, 32 Nassau Street, Dublin D02 YH68, Ireland, https://eu-contact.penguin.ie.

To Kay. It's so hard to believe that we've known each other for forty-six years. I cherish your friendship, the CoosDay photos every Tuesday, the math memes, and all the thoughtful articles on murder that you send when your insomnia strikes. And, of course, the "small" matter of introducing me to Martin. You knew we'd hit it off, and forty-three years later, I guess you were right! You've changed my life for good. Love you, my friend.

And, as always, to my sweet Martin. I love you.

Knife in the Back

PROLOGUE

Kenner, Louisiana

FRIDAY, FEBRUARY 21, 5:05 P.M.

"SEE YOU TOMORROW!" Naomi Cranston waved to her boss as she left the flower shop. Pausing on the sidewalk, she drew in a deep breath of fresh air and tilted her face to what was left of the sun.

The warmth on her skin felt so good.

So free.

After five years of incarceration, Naomi would never take the sun for granted again. After five years of incarceration, Naomi would never take *life* for granted again.

She certainly would never trust the system to protect her again. Her innocence had never once entered into the equation. NOPD had wanted a scapegoat and they'd chosen her.

She'd never be anyone's scapegoat again.

But at least I'm out of that place. She still bore the scars of prison, both on her skin and on her soul. A year of freedom hadn't changed that.

Shaking off the lingering bitterness, Naomi headed to the fifteen-year-old Volvo that had seen better days. It wasn't the nice car she'd driven before, but it got her to work and back home.

Home wasn't the nice house she'd had before, either, but her new place was in a decent neighborhood and had a bedroom for Everett.

Her heart hurt at the thought of her son. He hated the weekends he spent with her, retreating to his room and only emerging for food after she'd gone to bed.

He hated her now. And, based on the lies his father had told about her, Naomi couldn't blame him. It broke her heart, but she understood.

An overturned conviction wasn't the same as a statement of innocence.

But at least I'm out of that place.

Chin lifted, shoulders back, steps measured, she strode to her car with faked confidence. It was how she got through each day.

Eye contact was the hardest, because she knew what she'd see in the expressions of others. Hardly anyone believed she hadn't done it.

Her mother believed in her innocence, as did her new boss.

But not Everett.

Her shoulders sagged as she reached her car. He wouldn't be home when she got there. He'd find a friend to go home with. Sometimes she got a text telling her where he was, but that was rare.

Her heart ached at being shut out of his life.

She opened the car door, only to have it shoved closed.

She froze, now aware of the man standing behind her. She could see his face reflected in the car's window and her aching heart skipped a beat.

No. It couldn't be.

But it was.

He'd paid her a visit six years ago, changing the course of her life. Because of this man she was an ex-con.

Slowly she turned. Chin up, shoulders back. "Yes?"

"Mrs. Haywood?"

"No." She'd changed her name after her divorce. Had gone back to her maiden name. Which would make no difference to the man giving her a leering appraisal.

Her skin crawled, but she held her ground. *Don't let them see your fear.*

She'd learned that on day one inside. She still had the jagged scars to prove it.

He shrugged. To him, she was a tool. A toy. A convenient scapegoat.

His face was imprinted in her memory. He'd lied so smoothly when he'd taken the witness stand against her.

The jury had believed every word.

That she hadn't taken the stand in her own defense had sealed her fate. She'd known it at the time, but . . .

She swallowed but said nothing. It was a power play she now knew well. *Make them speak first.*

He huffed a labored sigh. "We have a job for you," he finally said.

She had no interest in anything this man was selling. "No."

He looked amused. "No?"

Bile burned her throat. "*No.*"

He smiled broadly. "He goes to school at St. Basil."

Her heart skipped another hard beat. *No. No, no, no. Not again. Please. Not again. Not Everett.*

But no one was listening to her prayers. Not six years ago and not now.

"He leaves to catch the bus at seven thirty every morning," he went on, chuckling at the fear she could no longer suppress. "Unless he drives himself, and then he leaves at eight fifteen. After school, he plays basketball at the Y. His friends are Gerry, Caden, and Steven. Usually he goes home with one of them. Has dinner with their families. Not with you. Not even on his weekends with you."

She started to retreat, but her back hit her car door. There was nowhere to run. Nowhere she could hide.

"All we want is for you to carry a few packages in your flower van. You're making a ton of deliveries right now—to hotels, party venues, everywhere people gather to celebrate. Flowers are so nice, don't you agree?"

She said nothing. Her throat had closed and no words would come.

He frowned. "I said, don't you agree, Mrs. Haywood?"

"No," she said, but more quietly. "I won't do your bidding."

"Then your son will suffer." He put on a sad face that was as fake as her confidence had been. "Hasn't he suffered enough? What with his mama going to jail for stealing from the NOPD?"

"You know I didn't."

"Everyone believes you did."

And that was true. Everyone but her mother and her new boss.

He winked at her. "And if you tell your ex that your son is in danger, he'll have grounds to yank your custody faster'n you can say 'You're guilty.'"

That was also true. Her ex would be calling his attorney seconds after her call, were she to tell him.

But she wasn't going to do this man's dirty work. She'd die first.

And she just might if she denied him.

She wouldn't be missed by too many if she turned up dead.

"Why?" she whispered. "Why me?"

His fake jocularity disappeared as he leaned closer, his face only an inch from hers. "Because you *never* should have gotten out." The words dripped with venom. "We had a deal, Mrs. Haywood. You cheated us. We don't abide cheaters."

She might have laughed at his hypocrisy had she not been so damn scared of him.

"We'll drop off your first package on Monday." He took a step back, tipped his ball cap. "Always a pleasure doing business with you, Mrs. Haywood."

It's Miss Cranston, you sonofabitch, she wanted to snarl.

But she didn't. She didn't say a word as she watched him saunter away.

She didn't say a word as she got into her car and drove to her little house. Her empty little house. Because Everett wasn't home. He would slide in around nine and go right to his room.

Maybe he'd be better off without me.

Maybe I should just let Jimmy have full custody.

But that wouldn't stop them from hurting her son. It wouldn't matter where Everett was or who he was living with. They'd make good on their threat. Of that she had no doubt.

And then Everett would hate her even more than he already did.

Woodenly she got out of her car and went inside. It smelled like the peanut butter cookies she'd made for Everett the night before.

Cookies he'd left on the kitchen counter, untouched.

She dropped her purse on a chair and went straight to the bathroom, where she sank to her knees in front of the toilet and vomited up everything she'd eaten that day.

She had a Glock in the gun safe in her bedroom. It was loaded. She could just end her life on her own terms. It was tempting.

Because if she did what they wanted, Everett would be safe, but she'd end up back in prison. Prison was a given. But Everett's safety was not. They might still hurt him.

She couldn't let that happen.

There had to be *something* she could do. Someone she could go to for help.

But there wasn't.

She was on her own.

And she was terrified.

1

The Quarter, New Orleans, Louisiana
MONDAY, FEBRUARY 24, 8:45 A.M.

BURKE BROUSSARD PLACED the papers he'd just reviewed into a drawer in his desk at Broussard Investigations. Business completed, he wanted to spend a few minutes with the man he'd called brother since they were teenagers.

"Everything looks good, as usual, Kaleb. Thank you."

Kaleb accepted the thanks with a nod and the smile Burke had grown up seeing. It was a bittersweet connection to better times, because he and Kaleb were the only ones left now.

Burke's mother, his uncle Larry. And Kyra, of course. All gone these twenty-five years. Even Kaleb's father, Uncle Larry's dear friend and business partner, was gone now. It was just Burke and Kaleb.

"Now that the business is out of the way," Kaleb said, "how the hell are you?"

The "business" was Kaleb's quarterly presentation of their company's profit and loss statement, along with the new initiatives that kept Fontenot Industries at the top of its game. Burke didn't always understand the software that the engineers were designing, but he could read a P&L. Their company was doing very well.

Kaleb Marchand was the genius behind all the tech. As the owner, Burke mostly just signed the checks. The profits he made from Fontenot allowed him to fund the work he really loved—getting justice for those who'd been let down by the law. Some of the people he aided didn't have the money to pay them. Because of Uncle Larry and his gift that kept on giving year after year, Burke could do a lot of pro bono work.

"Oh, you know," Burke said with a shrug. "Same old, same old."

Kaleb shook his head fondly. "Meaning you have loads of cases you can't tell me anything about." He looked over his shoulder to the closed office door. "Glad to see Joy looking so healthy."

"You and me both." Burke's office administrator had been shot two years before and had taken eighteen months to come back to her job full-time. Rehab took a lot longer with age. Joy wasn't all that old—only thirteen years older than Burke's forty-three—but her body had taken a real beating.

She'd nearly died.

However, she was back at her desk, and he couldn't be happier.

"How are Juliette and the kids?"

"Juliette's got the house and the office decorated for Mardi Gras," Kaleb said with a grin. "You should come over for supper."

"I will. And those godsons of mine?" Braden was fifteen, Trent thirteen. It seemed like yesterday that he'd held them at their christenings, and now they were teenagers.

Kaleb rolled his eyes. "Braden's got a girlfriend."

Burke barely controlled his wince. "Another one?"

"Yep," Kaleb said dolefully, and then his smile was back. "But

Trent's getting an award in two weeks. He developed a robot in his after-school program. Did it all on his own, without my help." Kaleb's pride was clear. "It's extremely well-done."

"Apple didn't fall far from the tree," Burke drawled. "If there's a ceremony, send me the details, and I'll be there."

"You always are."

Burke's desk phone buzzed and he checked the time. "That's Joy telling me that my nine o'clock is here."

He didn't know who the appointment was with, and that had his hackles rising. Joy normally gave him all the details on clients. That she hadn't done so this morning was both intriguing and concerning.

Kaleb rose and Burke came around his desk to give him a bear hug. Kaleb grunted, then laughed, hugging him back.

"Don't break my ribs," Kaleb said. "I might need them someday."

Burke slapped his back, then let him go. "Sorry."

Kaleb looked up at him with a smirk. Kaleb was tall, around six feet, but Burke was taller. And bigger. It had been that way since they were teenagers.

"You need to find a woman who'll appreciate those bear hugs of yours," Kaleb said. "Juliette has a new list of ladies for you."

Burke opened his office door with a good-natured groan, because Juliette never tired of trying to set him up with her friends. "Can you tell her to stop?"

"I can and I have, but you know Jules."

Burke did, and he loved her. She was the sister he'd never had. "I'll figure out a way to weasel out of anything she sets up."

Kaleb chuckled. "You can try." He walked into the lobby, leaning down to kiss Joy's cheek. "I missed you, J-Bird. Glad you're back full-time."

Joy beamed up at him. "Me too. Give my love to that wife of yours."

"I will. Thank you for rescheduling me on short notice. This trip came up last minute. I fly out in a few hours."

"Safe travels," Joy said. "Bring me something from Chicago."

Kaleb smiled at her. "Chocolate?"

Joy nodded. "You've always been a smart one."

Burke waited until Kaleb had gone before leaning against Joy's desk. "Where is my nine o'clock?"

Because the lobby was empty.

"Chilling with Antoine in the computer room. She and her friend didn't want to be out in the open."

Burke nodded. "Skittish, huh?"

"One of them is." Joy's expression became troubled. "Don't say no right away, Burke."

Burke's eyes went wide. "Why would I say no?"

"Promise me," Joy pressed. "Hear her out."

Now Burke was even more intrigued. "Okay." He turned for his office door. "Send in my appointment—and her friend—when they're done 'chilling' with Antoine.'"

"We're done," a familiar woman's voice said. "And we're ready."

Burke turned, puzzled to see Sylvi Kristiansen walking up to Joy's desk. "Sylvi? What are you doing here?"

"I need your help."

Sylvi's sister Val was one of Burke's inner circle. He'd gotten to know Sylvi over the last two years, since she and Val had healed a family rift that had kept them estranged. He and Sylvi had become friends. If she needed his help, how could he possibly say no?

Then he looked over Sylvi's head to the woman standing behind her, and the smile he'd been prepared to give disappeared like mist. Rage bubbled up, and his fists clenched.

He knew this woman, too.

Naomi Cranston.

He'd met her only once, when he was a detective and she worked in the evidence room. While he'd fought to remain honest, to retain his integrity, others took the easy way. The illegal way.

Which Naomi Cranston had done.

"No," he said, then turned on his heel and walked back into his office, shutting the door hard enough that everyone would know it was his final word.

The Quarter, New Orleans, Louisiana
MONDAY, FEBRUARY 24, 9:03 A.M.

"Burke Broussard!" Sylvi shouted, her anger clear as day. "You come back out here!"

"It's okay." Naomi had known this would be Broussard's response. She'd hoped for a miracle, but . . . she'd known.

"No, it's not okay." Sylvi marched to Broussard's office door, her fist lifted and ready to knock, but the soft whir of the admin's electric wheelchair stopped her.

Joy Thomas had placed herself in front of Broussard's door. "Simmer down, Sylvi. Let me talk to him."

Sylvi swallowed hard. "Okay. Thank you."

Joy squeezed Sylvi's hand. "Good girl." Then she entered Broussard's office, closing the door behind her far more gently than Broussard had.

Naomi started for the elevator. "It's no use. I told you that."

She'd been saying that ever since Sylvi had knocked on her front door Friday evening, shortly after Naomi had gotten home, shaken and terrified. Sylvi had seen Gaffney approach, and while she didn't know the man, she'd seen Naomi's expression. Worried, Sylvi had come by to check on her.

Possibly saving my life.

Naomi hadn't opened the door, but Sylvi had a key for emergencies. The petite florist had used that key, storming in on Naomi as she'd sat on the edge of her bed, staring at her loaded Glock.

Had it not been for Sylvi's arrival, Naomi wasn't sure what she might have done. Now she wasn't sure what she'd do. Burke Broussard had been her only hope.

Sylvi grabbed her hand before she had a chance to press the elevator button. "Just wait. Burke will help you. Give him a few minutes."

"He said no, Syl. I have to respect that. I might say the same thing in his place."

"No, you wouldn't. You'd bend over backward to help."

She probably would, even now. Even after her willingness to help another person had contributed to her downfall. "Well, he's not me. And he said no."

"Let Joy convince him."

"I didn't come here to cause trouble."

The door opened and the whir of Joy's wheelchair had them both turning.

Joy was pointing to the open door. "Go in, Miss Cranston. He'll listen."

"And then he'll help," Sylvi said with a confidence that Naomi did not feel.

But she followed her boss into the lion's den, flinching when Joy shut the door behind them. The admin remained in the lobby, giving them privacy.

She didn't look at Broussard, who sat behind a large mahogany desk. She merely followed Sylvi to a set of visitor chairs, lowering herself into one of them as Sylvi did the same.

Broussard said nothing. Naomi kept her eyes on her hands, clutched together in her lap. She didn't need to look at the man to know this was hopeless.

Sylvi sighed. "Burke . . ." She reached out and gently separated Naomi's hands, holding one tight. "You're going to hurt yourself," she murmured.

Yes, she would. In the end, she would.

Not with the Glock, because Sylvi had locked it away. And not with any other instrument of suicide.

She truly didn't think she had it in her. Although the alternative—prison—was a compelling argument to the contrary.

But she didn't have many choices. If Broussard turned her away, she'd accept Gaffney's drugs—but not in Sylvi's van, and she'd not take them to the address that she was sure she'd be given. She'd use her own car so that Sylvi wouldn't be implicated. And then she'd call 911 and anonymously report herself.

She'd be arrested and sent back to prison. She'd tell her ex to protect their son.

Maybe Broussard could be convinced to do so as well. Protection for Everett.

Yes. That was what she'd ask for.

"What?" Broussard finally said irritably.

Naomi glanced up to find Sylvi staring Broussard down, a tiny five-foot woman glaring defiantly at a brickhouse of a man. He had to be six-five. His dark hair was cut short, his handsome face tanned, despite it being winter.

She glanced at the bicycle leaning against one wall. Biking to work would explain it. She had the brief, insane desire to grab his bike and escape the man's hawklike gaze.

"Sylvi," she whispered. "You don't need to do this."

"Yes, I do," Sylvi snapped. "Burke, you might think you know about Naomi's situation, but I can assure you that you do not."

"I know enough," Broussard said, his deep Cajun drawl rumbling out of his chest. It was a broad chest. A strong one.

He'd be able to protect Everett. And he had the reputation for taking on hard cases. Once she was back in prison, Everett would need all the help he could get.

"Did you know she was out?" Sylvi demanded.

"I'd heard."

"Her sentence was overturned."

"On a technicality," Broussard said mildly, his Cajun accent thick. "An overturned conviction is not a declaration of innocence."

And there was the rub. Naomi would never be looked at with anything other than derision again, and that hurt. However, Everett was more important than her hurt feelings.

"I want to hire you," Naomi blurted out. "To protect my son."

Sylvi and Broussard both turned to stare at her. Sylvi was stunned. Broussard looked . . . curious.

Curiosity was better than derision.

"Naomi, *no*." Sylvi's eyes filled with tears. "You *can't*."

"I don't have a choice." Tugging her hand free of Sylvi's grip, she faced Broussard head-on. "I've been given an ultimatum. Transport illegal drugs or my son will be harmed. If I don't do what they say, they will hurt him. He's only sixteen. He's innocent of all this."

Broussard glanced at Sylvi, who was now openly crying.

Her boss had a tender heart. Which, Naomi supposed, was the reason Sylvi had given her a job to begin with.

"Why not take this to the cops?" he asked.

Naomi laughed bitterly. "Because they *are* the cops."

Broussard's body language abruptly changed. His arms had been locked across his chest, but he lowered them to his desk and leaned forward with narrowed eyes. "Who?"

"Do you know a cop named John Gaffney?"

Broussard nodded, his expression giving nothing away. "I do."

Naomi wanted to look away but forced herself to hold firm. Broussard wouldn't respect her if she flinched. And if he didn't respect her, he wouldn't believe her.

Do this for Everett.

"He used to report to Captain Cresswell." If she hadn't been watching, she would have missed the small twitch of Broussard's jaw. That was good. He didn't like Cresswell. They had at least that in common. "I know you worked in Cresswell's department for a few years. I know you . . . left."

"Escaped," Sylvi muttered, drying her eyes with the sleeve of her jacket. "Some people weren't as lucky."

"Sylvi." Broussard's voice softened. "Let me listen."

"She shouldn't have needed to invoke the name of Gaffney or Cresswell to get you to listen," Sylvi snapped.

Naomi laid a hand on her boss's arm. "He only knows what the media covered. He doesn't know the truth."

Broussard sat back in his chair. "Then tell me the truth."

Naomi squared her shoulders. She didn't have anything to lose. "I was an honest cop. I worked in the evidence room."

"Until you stole a kilo of cocaine."

Naomi shook her head. "I never did. They hid it in my car. It was found when I stopped at a traffic accident."

"To supposedly help a woman whose car had been wrecked."

Naomi remembered it all in sharp detail. "Her flashers were on and her car had been damaged. The front bumper was crushed and the driver's-side windows were broken. She looked so young and scared when she ran into the road, motioning me to stop. So I stopped. I wasn't on duty at the time, so I called it in as a hit-and-run and waited with her until the police arrived."

"And then?" Broussard asked.

"She'd asked to put her book bag in my back seat, because it was pouring down rain and her windows were broken. I let her stow it back there without another thought. The cops arrived, took her statement, then told her to get her book bag from my back seat. That's when she saw the evidence bag. Her exclamation was so believable. Even I believed her for a moment. Until I realized what was happening. It was an evidence bag full of cocaine I'd processed." She lifted her chin again. "I was *careful,* Mr. Broussard. I was *meticulous,* for all the years I did that job. There were two bags of cocaine confiscated in an arrest, but there was no record of the second bag being delivered to Evidence."

"Did you take it?" he asked.

She met his gaze. "I did not."

"And the young woman?"

"I'll never forget her little smirk when the officer cuffed me. She was in on the frame."

"She was questioned."

"She was. She stuck to her story—and her prints weren't on the bag. I didn't see her put it there, but I don't know how else it could have happened. The bag was stashed under the seat and the cop picked it up."

"That was Gaffney?"

"No. That was Officer Morrell. He seemed genuinely shocked to find the drugs in my car."

"All right," Broussard said calmly. "Where does Gaffney come in?"

"I kept saying I was innocent. I didn't know how the coke got into my car, only that I didn't put it there. I got an attorney and was ready to fight it. And then I got a visit from John Gaffney. I'd been released on bail and was at home. I wish I'd had cameras."

"You do now?" he asked.

"I sure do. Gaffney walked into my house like he owned it. Told me that I wouldn't fight the charges. Showed me photos of my son at school." Her voice broke. "He was only ten. Gaffney said that my son would be sent to me 'in pieces' if I fought the charges. To just 'let it happen.'"

Broussard was watching her closely. "So you said nothing in your own defense."

"I went silent. My mother kept begging me to *say* something. To *do* something. But I was afraid. I was sure they would have followed through on the threat, Gaffney and Cresswell."

"So you were sentenced to prison."

She nodded, her throat tight. "Spent five years inside."

He didn't offer condolences and that was somehow better. This man was all business and she appreciated it.

"You got released on a technicality. How did that happen?"

"My mother never believed I was guilty. She got me a new attorney. Mortgaged her house to pay the woman." And for that alone, Naomi would love her mother forever. "The attorney told Mom going in that it was a long shot. She filed a request for a lab test of the evidence—the bag of cocaine I supposedly stole. My first attorney hadn't requested it. I think Gaffney got to him. Made him do a shoddy job. I could see a difference between one visit and the next. The man couldn't meet my eyes. Changed his mind about me testifying in my own defense."

"But the second attorney was better."

"The second attorney was lucky," Naomi corrected. "The test on the coke came back as zero cocaine at all. It was ground-up Sheetrock."

"So the stolen evidence got stolen again?" he asked.

"Maybe. I don't know. All I know is that my second attorney filed an immediate appeal. That Cresswell was somehow involved got it pushed through."

He tilted his head to one side. "How did Cresswell factor in?"

"He was Gaffney's boss at the time. Captain Cresswell getting arrested got the DA to back off trying me a second time when the first conviction was overturned." Two and a half years before, the former NOPD captain had murdered a suspect and was now serving life. "Anything Cresswell touched is tainted now. So, like I said, my attorney got lucky. By extension, so did I."

Broussard laced his fingers together, resting his joined hands on his stomach. "What brings you here today?"

"I was leaving my job on Friday. I work for Sylvi."

"I wondered," Broussard said, glancing at Sylvi. "Hire a lot of ex-cons?"

"Only innocent ones," Sylvi said, her glare not having faded an iota.

Broussard's mouth kicked up into an almost-smile. "What happened on Friday, Miss Cranston?"

"Gaffney approached me as I was getting into my car. Told me I was to transport packages for them in Sylvi's florist van because we're making so many deliveries right now."

"Mardi Gras parties," he murmured.

"Exactly. I told him no. If I did something like that, I'd go back to prison. He started telling me my son's schedule. He knew the names of his friends. He knew that Everett doesn't come home for dinner most of the nights he's with me."

"Joint custody?" he asked.

"I get weekends."

"Her son believes she's guilty," Sylvi inserted. "Naomi's ex poisoned the boy's mind. Everett hangs with his friends so he doesn't have to come home."

Naomi shrugged, ignoring her broken heart. "As you said, Mr. Broussard, an overturned conviction is not a declaration of innocence."

"True enough. Why do you think they've targeted you, Miss Cranston?"

"I've racked my brain for six years, and I still don't know. When I asked him why on Friday, all Gaffney said was that I wasn't supposed to get out, that we had a deal but that I'd cheated them. I truly don't know why he picked me, now or six years ago."

"Okay. What do you plan to do?"

She opened her mouth, suddenly unsure. She'd been sure just moments before, but now the plan that had seemed so clear was . . . not.

"I won't be their drug runner. Of that I'm certain. At least the last time, I knew I was innocent, despite what everyone else thought. If I do their bidding, I'll be guilty. But if I don't, they'll hurt my son."

Broussard was watching her thoughtfully, but he said nothing, so she soldiered on.

"I can't let them touch Everett," she said, hearing her own desperation.

"I agree. So what do you plan to do?" he asked again.

"If I refuse to take their package, they'll plant drugs in my car like last time. And if I do take their package, they'll eventually arrange for a routine stop and I'll be framed again."

"So what do you plan to do?" he asked for a third time.

Her eyes were suddenly burning. "If you can assure me that my son will be safe, I'll take their package and anonymously report myself to the police. I'll . . ." She exhaled shakily, panic rising despite her best efforts to beat it back. "I'll go back to prison. I don't want to, but I'll do it to keep them away from Everett. As long as Everett will be safe once I'm out of the way."

Sylvi leaned forward in her chair, her expression beseeching. "Please, Burke. Say that you can help her. Say that you can keep her *and* her son safe." New tears rolled down her cheeks. "Please. I'll beg you if I have to."

"Sylvi," Broussard said quietly. "Stop. I don't know exactly what I can do, but I'll look into it. And, for now, I'll put eyes on the boy."

Relief rushed over Naomi like a wave. "You won't let them hurt him?"

"No, ma'am."

"My son won't be cooperative," she warned.

Broussard smiled, revealing a deep dimple in one cheek. "He won't be our first reluctant charge."

"My ex-husband won't be pleased."

"I'll deal with him, too, if need be."

"If you tell him that I'm being targeted, he'll apply to have my custody revoked." Her shoulders sagged. "Although that might be safer for Everett."

"Does he love your son?" Burke asked.

"Yes," Naomi said, without hesitation. "He'll want to keep Everett safe. But Jimmy hates me. He testified against me at my trial. He wanted me out of the way, too, so that he didn't have to share custody."

Broussard frowned. "I'll try to make sure he understands the reality of the situation. Did you have any indication that he was involved in your arrest?"

Naomi slowly shook her head, because she'd wondered the same thing. "He cheated on me with a younger woman—who's his new wife—and fought the reinstatement of my alimony when I was released. That is the other reason I think he testified against me. He didn't want to have to pay alimony."

"I see," Broussard murmured.

"And Naomi?" Sylvi pushed. "What about her? She can't go back to prison, Burke. They'll kill her in there. And I'm not being dramatic. Someone nearly did kill her the first time."

Burke lifted one hand, halting Sylvi's argument. "I didn't think you were being dramatic, Sylvi. I can only imagine what happens to a former cop in prison."

It had been far worse than he could imagine.

Naomi fought the urge to touch her neck. Her scar wasn't visible if her hair hung the right way. She didn't want to draw attention to it. Didn't want Burke Broussard to know.

She didn't want his pity.

"I can pay you," Naomi said. "I have a little money put away. I don't know if I can afford you, but I'll figure something out."

"We'll deal with that later." He glanced at Sylvi. "We'll protect Miss Cranston as well. For now, I want you to go back to work and try to act as if everything is normal. I'll put someone on your security detail." He quickly checked his computer. "Val's back in town. I'll assign her. She's a frequent visitor to the flower shop, so she won't draw too much attention."

Naomi had met Sylvi's sister, Val, and trusted her. "Thank you."

"Don't accept any packages, and if you get one, call me immediately. Don't even touch it, either of you."

For the first time in six years, hope bloomed in her heart. "Do you think you can help me avoid going back to prison, Mr. Broussard?"

His gaze was serious. "I'm going to do my damnedest, ma'am."

She shuddered as the tears finally fell. "Thank you."

2

The Quarter, New Orleans, Louisiana
MONDAY, FEBRUARY 24, 10:15 A.M.

DAMN, THAT CRESSWELL keeps coming back like a bad penny," Antoine Holmes said grimly after Burke had briefed his assembled crew in the conference room.

Burke had the feeling that Naomi Cranston and her son would need all the guarding his people could provide. Molly Sutton and Lucien Farrow were his top investigators, but they were also both capable bodyguards. Sometimes the job required both sets of skills. Antoine was Burke's computer wizard. If anything needed doing—or hacking—in a computer network, Antoine was the man.

"You've got Val at Sylvi's shop now?" Molly asked.

"I do. I've asked Joy to schedule a protection detail for both Miss Cranston and her son. She'll probably schedule you, Val, and Lucien, depending on how long the danger lasts."

"What do we know about her?" Lucien asked.

She's sad. Beautiful and sad, her brown eyes full of pain. Her dark hair was cut in a sleek bob that he guessed was intended to hide the scar on her throat, but it didn't do a good enough job.

She's lost hope. She'd fully expected him to turn her away. The woman who'd followed Sylvi into his office had kept her eyes down. Her posture had screamed defeat.

And, for a brief moment, that defeat had pleased Burke. Dirty cops were the lowest of the low in his book. But once he'd heard her story—hell, once she'd mentioned Cresswell and Gaffney—that feeling had turned to shame.

She came to me to humbly ask for help. And she shouldn't have needed to tell him that former NOPD Captain Cresswell was involved to elicit his support.

She's brave. Willing to return to prison to protect her son.

She met my eyes. Even though it had cost her to do so. She'd been terrified. But she'd met his eyes and told her truth.

I believe her. Because he knew the cops who'd framed her. Cresswell and Gaffney had tried to frame him, too. He'd just been luckier, apparently.

I respect her. And he'd help her to get her life back.

"I think she's being honest," he finally answered. "Antoine, what have you found out so far?"

"She's thirty-six," Antoine said. "Born and raised in New Orleans. Divorced Jimmy Haywood seven years ago. She has a sixteen-year-old son named Everett."

"The one she wants us to protect," Lucien said.

"Wow," Antoine murmured. "She was sentenced to thirty years for theft and possession with intent to distribute."

Burke remembered the day she'd been sentenced. He'd been glad she would pay for her crimes, that finally a dirty cop was being held accountable.

Except now he didn't believe she'd been dirty.

"How many of those thirty did she serve?" Lucien asked.

"She spent five years in prison and has been out for a year." Antoine frowned at one of his laptop screens. "She spent a month in the hospital and the prison infirmary after she was stabbed in the dining hall, a few days after she arrived. The knife nicked her liver and required the removal of her spleen. She was stabbed six times, including once in the throat. She nearly died."

Remembering the scar on her neck, Burke felt sick. *Six times.*

He cleared his throat roughly. "And after that?"

Antoine gave him a curious look before returning his attention to his computer. "After that, she was put in protective custody."

Solitary confinement. That couldn't have been easy.

"How did she meet Sylvi?" Molly asked, also watching him.

Burke closed his expression, going neutral. But Molly didn't appear fooled. Of all his people, she knew him the best. They'd served together in the Marine Corps, and when he'd decided to start his investigative firm, she'd been the first person he'd called.

She'd been his right hand for six years.

"Sylvi volunteers with the horticulture program at the women's prison," Burke said. "She shows the women how to plant and arrange flowers. The program also teaches them to plant a garden, harvest the vegetables, and cultivate fruit trees. Gives them something productive to do on the inside, plus a skill for when they get out. Naomi Cranston was in Sylvi's class during the final three years of her incarceration."

"I thought she was in PC," Molly said.

"She was for about a year," Antoine said. "After that she was returned to the general population. No other reports of injuries or attacks."

Burke wondered how tough she'd been required to become to escape the remaining years unhurt. Cops were tough, but not prison tough. Especially after being in protective custody. Other inmates would have hated her.

"She became the go-to person if one of the inmates needed help with flower arranging," Burke said. "She also tutored some of the women who were studying for their GEDs. Taught them other skills, too."

"Did Sylvi tell you this, or did Miss Cranston?" Antoine asked.

"Sylvi. Miss Cranston had become emotional by that point." The woman had burst into tears, and Burke had needed to force himself not to round his desk and hold her as she cried. The need to comfort her had been so powerful that it had left him shaken. "She'd excused herself to go to the powder room," he said, "and Sylvi told me that one day, Miss Cranston brought some yarn and a crochet hook into her flower class. One of the younger inmates had mentioned wanting to learn, so Miss Cranston taught her. Before long, they'd started a crochet group. The group continued after she left. They make hats for the homeless and for preemie babies. Stuff like that."

"You sound like you like her, boss," Antoine said, his brows raised.

"I didn't want to at first." He blew out a breath. "At first I told her no."

"I know," Antoine said with a grin. "I could hear Sylvi all the way back in my office. 'Burke Broussard, you come back out here!'"

Burke felt his face heat. "Not my finest moment, I'll admit. I think she got bad legal advice the first time around."

"Who was her attorney?" Lucien asked.

Antoine checked his laptop. "Mason Lord. I don't know anything about him."

Lucien went still, and Burke wondered what he knew about the attorney. But Lucien didn't offer any information, so Burke would wait and ask him in private. A former prosecutor, Lucien would look at Naomi Cranston's case with a different perspective than Burke's own.

"This says that her husband testified against her." Antoine scowled. "What an asshole. Said she was mentally ill and had a drug problem, but there doesn't seem to be any proof beyond his testimony. The report also says that she didn't testify in her own defense, but she also refused a plea bargain."

"There's usually a reason someone refuses to testify in their own defense," Lucien said, and there was something in his tone that got Burke's hackles up.

"Gaffney threatened her with harm to her son if she didn't go along with their plan," Burke said.

"Then why didn't she take a plea?" Lucien asked.

"I don't know," Burke admitted, not liking how defensive Lucien had him feeling. "We should ask her. But she's still protecting her son. She's willing to go back to prison to keep him safe."

"Or so she says," Lucien said mildly, his expression now stony.

"Or so she says." Burke nodded stiffly. "But I believe her."

"And this Gaffney character?" Molly asked.

"He's been in Narcotics for at least fifteen years," Burke said. "He was one of Cresswell's detectives. I wasn't partnered with him, but I did work with him on a few cases. The guy's dirty, but I could never prove it. No one could." He hesitated. "He tried to get me to accept a bag of heroin that he'd skimmed from a bust."

That got a stunned reaction from his people.

"What did you do?" Lucien asked.

"Took the matter to Cresswell, who asked me if I had proof. When I said that I didn't, Cresswell told me it was Gaffney's word against mine and Gaffney had been a detective a lot longer. Then, as I was leaving his office, he said, 'Next time, just say yes.'"

"And you couldn't prove that, either," Molly murmured.

"I hadn't thought about wearing a wire into my captain's office. I didn't think I needed to. I didn't realize until that moment that Cresswell was dirty, too. I considered going to PIB, but that's a big step for any cop." Talking to the Public Integrity Bureau—NOPD's Internal Affairs—could make a cop's life miserable. And dangerous. "But before I could decide if I wanted to go the PIB route, I got attacked by some young punk on the street. My partner was testifying in court, so everyone knew that I'd be alone that day. I called for backup and nobody came. I managed to overpower the little bastard and I hauled his ass in, but he wouldn't say why he'd targeted me. That's when I figured I needed to get out. I tried to transfer to another department, but Cresswell blocked it. I figured that to protect myself I needed something on Cresswell, so I kept my eyes open. I watched him like a damn hawk."

"You once said you had proof that he was hiring male prostitutes," Molly said, "and that was what allowed you to walk away."

Burke winced. "I didn't really have any hard proof. Just rumor, really. If I'd had proof, I would have used it. But Cresswell believed my bluff when I told him I was resigning and that he'd better not interfere. I'd just gotten another visit from Gaffney. He cornered me at the gym, in the shower, actually, so he could be sure I didn't have any recording devices on me. Threatened my family. He had photos of my godsons on his phone. Told me where they went to school and what their after-school schedule was like. Told me he'd send them back to me 'in pieces.'"

"He threatened Naomi Cranston the same way," Molly said.

"He did. That's when I knew she was telling me the truth."

"What did you do?" Lucien asked.

"Told André." Antoine's brother was one of the few cops Burke trusted implicitly. "He was the one who told me about Cresswell and the prostitutes. He'd been watching the man for a long time. But Gaffney is smart. No one can pin anything on him."

"I know," Antoine said quietly. "André had me look at Cresswell, on the down-low, of course. Only time he ever asked me to do something like that for him. And then you quit the very next day. I always wondered if there was a connection."

Burke felt a surge of affection for both Holmes brothers. André was an NOPD captain and one of Burke's closest friends. "Did you find anything on Cresswell back then?"

"Only the prostitution rumor, which I told André about."

"So that was from you. Thank you, Antoine."

Antoine looked embarrassed at the gratitude. "I never found anything concrete on either man. Only a lot of rumor and innuendo. But PIB did look at Gaffney closely after Cresswell went to prison. Unfortunately, nothing came up."

Burke purposely did not look at Antoine's screen. Hacking into the Public Integrity Bureau was a no-no. But Burke wanted the information and was grateful that Antoine could slip in and out of the NOPD's records undetected.

André might not be so grateful, but what he didn't know wouldn't hurt him.

"When did you find the PIB report?" Burke asked.

"This morning. Sylvi asked me if I knew anything about Gaffney and Cresswell. I hadn't checked on them in a while, but I figured you'd want to know."

Molly got up to take notes on the whiteboard. "What specifically did PIB investigate Gaffney for after Cresswell's arrest?"

"Skimming from confiscated drugs and extortion," Antoine said. "But nothing stuck. And, looking at the names of the investigators, I think it was a righteous investigation. André trusts them."

André had been wrong about people a few times in the past, but overall, his intuition was very good.

"Gaffney knows how to cover his tracks," Burke murmured.

"Maybe it made him cocky," Molly said thoughtfully. "It was a risk, coming up to Miss Cranston like that. In public."

"Nobody could hear what they were saying, even if they were captured on a security camera. Antoine, can you—"

"Already on it, boss," Antoine said. "I have access to the security cams around Sylvi's shop. I keep an eye out for her. For Val."

Because they'd all become protective of Val's sister.

"Anything?"

Antoine turned his laptop around so that Burke could see the camera feed from outside Sylvi's shop. Sure enough, John Gaffney was approaching Naomi Cranston, looming over her. She was at least five-ten, but Gaffney was taller. And when the detective backed her against her car, her fear was clear to see. So was the word "no" on her lips, her head shaking vigorously to underscore it.

Burke felt a sting on his palms and realized he was clenching his fists. He relaxed them, but not before catching all three of his people watching him.

"I hate that she's being victimized again," he said. "She got railroaded the first time and now they're coming back for another go."

"Why was she chosen the first time?" Molly asked, noting the question on the whiteboard. "Why frame Naomi Cranston at all? Did she piss someone off? Accuse someone of something? What did she do to place herself in their crosshairs?"

"I asked her the same thing but she said she didn't know. Not six years ago or now. On Friday, when she asked Gaffney why he was coming after her, he said that they'd had a deal and that she'd cheated them when she was released from prison."

"A deal?" Molly frowned. "That sounds like it's personal. When was she arrested?"

"Six years ago last December fourteenth," Antoine said.

"Merry Christmas to her," Molly murmured. "What about the woman she stopped to help?"

"The one who smirked at her when she was being arrested," Burke added. "Naomi thinks the woman was involved."

"Could this woman have planted the drugs?" Lucien asked.

"I think so," Burke said, "and so does Naomi, but all she saw the woman do was put her book bag in her back seat. She couldn't swear to anything else."

"Who was this woman who allegedly put the drugs there?" Lucien still didn't look convinced of Naomi's innocence, but that was okay. He was participating and Burke appreciated that.

"Winnifred Timms. White, age nineteen at the time of the incident. She was initially interviewed by . . ." Antoine sighed. "John Gaffney."

"Surprise, surprise," Burke drawled. "You said initially. Was she interviewed again later?"

"By PIB," Antoine said. "Her story never changed and she was deemed a credible witness."

"She had a book bag," Molly said. "Was she a student? And if so, where?"

Antoine did another search. "University of New Orleans. Majored in finance. It appears that she graduated two years ago and is now getting her MBA at Loyola."

"Dig into her financials," Burke requested. "Find out if she received any suspicious sums in the months after Naomi's arrest."

"Will do." Antoine clicked a few more times. "She lives off-campus. Rents a room in an apartment on Josephine Street."

"We should pay her a visit," Lucien said.

Burke nodded. "Take Molly with you. Try not to let her know why we're asking questions. If Winnifred was involved, she might tell the wrong people that Naomi has hired us."

"What about Naomi's son?" Molly asked.

"I'm going to see his father at work," Burke said. "I can put a detail on Everett without telling the father, but only outside his house, and I want someone closer to the kid. Naomi is afraid her ex will fight her for full custody once he finds out that her son's been threatened, but at this point she thinks that might be safest for the boy."

"Hard call," Antoine said quietly. "Giving up her weekends with the kid like that."

It clearly broke Naomi's heart. "Although it seems he'd rather spend all his time with his father anyway."

But Burke would make sure the kid understood the magnitude of his mother's sacrifice when this was all over.

"And once her ex agrees?" Lucien asked. "*If* he agrees? Who are you going to assign?"

"Probably Harrison." The man had been with them on a part-time basis for three years. "He's retiring from NOPD in a few weeks and has at least that much vacation to use up first. He told me to put him in for full-time."

"Smart—he's good with teenagers," Molly said. "But what if Naomi's ex says no?"

"I'll still have Harrison keep eyes on him, even if Mr. Haywood refuses to cooperate." Because he'd promised Naomi Cranston that her son would not be harmed. "Keep me informed, guys."

Antoine gathered his laptops and waved goodbye. Molly stood, waiting for Lucien, who was frowning.

"Give me a minute, Mol," Lucien said. "I need to talk to Burke."

She silently left the room, closing the door behind her.

"Go ahead," Burke said. "Let's have it."

"You went from telling this woman no to going full throttle for her in a single conversation. How do you know she didn't drop Cresswell's name just to get you on her side?"

"Fair question." Even though the pushback chafed him, Burke was grateful that he didn't employ automatons. "It was what Gaffney said to her. That he'd send her Everett 'in pieces.' I believed her."

"She's pretty," Lucien said mildly.

Burke nodded, refusing to deny it. "She is."

Very pretty.

"But there's more to it than that." Lucien studied him. "She's broken and you want to fix her."

Burke didn't completely agree. "She's a little bit broken, sure. Prison will do that to a person. And then, just when she thought that her life had restarted, Gaffney shows up and pulls the rug out from under her."

Lucien sighed. "I hope we're on the right side here, Burke."

"What do you know?"

"Mason Lord, her first attorney. He was a prosecutor at the same time that I was. He ended up going the defender route. He's a good guy. Honest and upright. Even if he couldn't get her acquitted, I *know* he tried his best."

"She thinks Gaffney got to him."

Lucien shook his head. "I can't see it."

"Tell you what. You and Molly talk to Naomi before you talk to the woman she stopped to help the night of her arrest. Talk to Mason Lord. Then come back and we'll discuss this again."

"Okay." Lucien stood and gripped Burke's shoulder. "You know I'm with you. I just don't want to see you taken in by a pretty face."

"What would be her endgame?" Burke asked. "What can she possibly expect to achieve by lying to us? She's ready to go back to prison to protect her son."

"Or so she says," Lucien said for a second time. "I'll talk to her and I'll let you know."

The Central Business District, New Orleans, Louisiana
MONDAY, FEBRUARY 24, 10:15 A.M.

Detective John Gaffney sat in one of the visitor chairs, a scowl on his face. "You were right. She and her boss went to Broussard's office this morning."

Of course I was right. "We knew this was a possibility. She has a better support network now than she did six years ago."

"Of all the people to give her a job," Gaffney grumbled.

"We've known that Naomi Cranston's boss is the sister of one of Broussard's people for a year now," he said, remaining calm.

Gaffney glared. "Yet you still sent me to threaten the bitch. I'm on camera with Cranston, threatening her. Not you."

"That was your mistake." And it might end up being a costly one.

Gaffney should have confronted her outside her house or in the parking lot of a grocery store. He should have disguised himself better. He was getting cocky, which was what had gotten their former associate into trouble. He hadn't realized how much energy Cresswell had expended managing Gaffney. It was exhausting. "Besides, using her was your idea, Detective."

Not *entirely* true. He'd just let Gaffney think it was his idea.

Gaffney came to his feet, planting his hands on the desk and leaning in, his face tight with anger. "That was before I knew who her new boss was! Afterward I told you that this was a fucking stupid idea."

Gaffney had said exactly that, actually. But it had been worth the risk. It still was. Naomi Cranston needed to go back to prison. It was that simple.

It was also that complicated. He needed the woman back in prison for personal reasons that Gaffney would never be privy to. Not ever.

If Gaffney knew . . .

I'd find myself blackmailed in a heartbeat.

But the man was easily manipulated—useful in a foot soldier, but in a partner? Not so much.

Which was why John Gaffney would never be his partner.

Of course Gaffney thought he *was* a partner—because he *was* easily manipulated.

It was better to let Gaffney think he had an equal say until he no longer needed the detective. He and Gaffney were rebuilding their contacts and connections. Their network had been neglected for the past two and a half years out of necessity.

Cresswell's arrest had shone an unwelcome light on their business, so they'd laid low. That meant their dealers and distributors had gone to work with others. Many had left New Orleans for other cities. They would be rebuilding for at least a year.

More importantly, there was the new business. One he'd put a lot of his own money into financing. He could manage the staffing for the new business on his own while Gaffney ran defense with the NOPD. Making sure the right people looked the other way.

Once they'd solidified the operation, Gaffney would no longer be useful. He'd suffer a heart attack or maybe he'd have a car accident on a rainy evening. Anything that didn't raise red flags within the department.

Gaffney was still leaning into his space, still huffing like a bull. *Daring me to huff back.* But that was never going to happen.

Unlike Gaffney, I maintain my calm.

"Sit down, Detective Gaffney."

Gaffney's nostrils flared and for a moment, he wondered if the man was going to hit him.

Let him try.

But Gaffney's sense of self-preservation must have kicked in, because the detective sat down.

He inclined his head. "Thank you. As I was saying, we knew the involvement of Broussard was a possibility." He hadn't considered it a high likelihood, however, because Naomi Cranston had never sought help in the past. She was supposed to fold in the face of threats to her son, just like she had six years before.

She was supposed to obey.

The woman needed to be brought to heel.

He rested his hands on his desk. "That just means we have to deal with her swiftly. Before Broussard can start digging."

"What does that mean?" Gaffney asked, still belligerent. "Dealing with her? I thought we didn't want to kill her."

"We don't." Not unless it was absolutely necessary. He didn't like murder. It was too messy. Invited too much attention. Murder was what had gotten Cresswell incarcerated, after all. "Clearly she didn't believe you meant business regarding her son. Pick the kid up this afternoon, after school. He's not due to go to his mother's house this week. Where is he likely to go? Will he go home, to his father's house?"

"He doesn't usually go straight home, regardless of which house he's going to. He'll either go to one of his friends' houses or the girl's house."

Because of course there was a girl. Boys Everett Haywood's age always had a girl in the picture.

"Grab the kid and drive him around the block a few times. Blindfold him. Tie his hands. Take his phone. Give him a scare, then let him out only far enough away that he can still walk home. Count on Broussard having someone watching the boy, though. Don't get caught, and don't let him see your face."

Gaffney lifted his chin. "Don't patronize me."

He smiled tightly. "Don't fuck this one up."

Gaffney clenched his teeth. "You're an asshole."

"I am. But I'm the asshole who manages the cash. Speaking of cash, Broussard will find the bank accounts. We need to close them out. Freddie opened them, she'll have to close them."

Gaffney nodded. "I'll take care of it."

"As soon as possible," he stressed.

"*Fine.* I *said* I'll take care of it."

"Thank you. Is there anything else we need to discuss?" Because he was already late for his next meeting, which was clear across town. Unfortunately, he'd have to be even later because there were still several details to attend to.

He was thinking ahead, reorganizing all the plan Bs he'd developed in the event Broussard became involved. He'd been studying Broussard for a while. He knew exactly how to get the PI to back off.

Gaffney scowled at him. "Yeah, what are *you* going to be doing?"

He might not like murder, but he found himself fantasizing about it a lot more often now that he had to manage Gaffney.

That Gaffney hadn't already been arrested by NOPD was merely testament to the strength of the alliances they'd made. *Cresswell and I.*

"One, I'll be reminding Cresswell to remain quiet."

Gaffney scoffed. "He's in solitary. Who's he gonna talk to?"

He just looked at Gaffney, saying nothing. Finally, the man rolled his eyes.

"Fine," Gaffney said. "But his reach is severely limited."

"On that we can agree."

"How are you going to remind him, then? It's not like you can visit him without the entire state knowing about it."

"Did you really think I haven't been monitoring him daily? That I'd just leave him to talk to whoever he wanted? I have people inside."

Gaffney looked reluctantly impressed. "Well, that's good. I wondered why he hadn't caved yet."

"Better hope he doesn't," he said ominously.

If Cresswell talked, they were all toast.

Gaffney shrugged. "He knows his family is forfeit if he does."

"I don't depend on Cresswell's devotion to his wife and kids. So I remind him every now and then."

Daily. Like clockwork.

Because I am organized. Unlike the detective slouched in the chair in front of him.

"And the second thing?" Gaffney asked. "You said Cresswell was 'one.' I assume there's something else."

"I'm going to have that package delivered to Miss Cranston."

"How?"

"Not your concern. You focus on the kid. I'll take care of his mother."

"Okay." Gaffney rose and straightened his suit coat. "I have to get to my desk now or the new captain will nag. Keep me up to speed and I'll do the same."

As if they were partners. "Will do."

He waited until Gaffney was gone, then said quietly, "You can come in now."

Wayne Stanley entered and sat in the chair that Gaffney had vacated and waited, pen poised. His assistant was ruthlessly efficient.

"I assume you heard everything."

Stanley nodded. "I listened, just as you instructed."

"Good. We need to distract Broussard."

"Understood. You'd like me to put plan B into motion."

"I would. I think if you wait outside the Kristiansen woman's flower shop, you'll be able to access the vehicle of at least one of Broussard's people. More, if we're lucky."

"Speaking of luck, you need to get out of here. It's going to take you significantly longer to get to the warehouse, considering the traffic."

He locked up his desk. "At least the Delgados can't start without me. Do you have the files on the new inventory?"

"I've sent them to your phone. I think you'll be pleased with the additions. Freddie and Elaine have really outdone themselves. I do believe we're fully stocked for this weekend."

When the big parades took place. The city would be flooded with more than a million tourists by the weekend. Tourists who'd be looking to party.

He had exactly what they'd be wanting.

"Good to hear." At least something was going right. "Once I've met with Elaine; I'll send her over to you. You'll need another pair of hands to get started on plan B."

Stanley saluted. "Distract Broussard. And if that doesn't work? If he gets too close?"

"Then we'll move along the alphabet."

Plan Z would be their last resort, because he really did dislike murder.

3

Kenner, Louisiana

MONDAY, FEBRUARY 24, 12:05 P.M.

"HEY," SYLVI SAID, sticking her head into the flower shop's workroom, her expression tense. "A car just pulled into the parking lot. This may be the package we're waiting for."

Having been on tenterhooks all morning, Naomi accidentally decapitated the roses she'd been prepping. "Shit," she muttered, then looked to her new bodyguard. "Broussard said to call him when the package was delivered."

Val Sorensen looked up from the camera feed on her phone, her smile calm. "The camera at the front door is showing two of my colleagues—Molly Sutton and Lucien Farrow. Didn't recognize them at first. They're both disguised."

Everett. "Is it about Everett?"

"Burke would have called if it were," Val assured her.

The bell over the front door jingled and Sylvi hurried to the counter, leaving the door open so that Naomi and Val could hear what was happening.

"Ooh, honey, look!" The woman had a twangy drawl. "Can we have roses at our wedding?"

Val snickered. "That's Molly."

"You know my mother is allergic to roses, pet," a man said.

Val's lips twitched. "And that's Lucien. They're pretending to be an engaged couple so no one wonders why they've come in."

"That's why I want roses," the woman said sweetly. "If your mother is sneezing, she can't say awful things to me."

Val chuckled. "Molly isn't normally the dramatic one. That's usually me."

Naomi tried to relax. Val was right. Surely Broussard would have called directly if something was wrong with Everett.

"Welcome," Sylvi said, playing along. "Let me flip the sign to closed and we'll go back to my office and talk about your special day."

Sylvi and the two PIs entered the workroom and Val smirked.

"Wow," Val said to the woman with long black hair hanging halfway down her back and a wide-brimmed hat that hid her face. But her hair wasn't what drew the eye. No, that would be the woman's breasts about to pop right out of her very low-cut dress. "You're bustin' loose, girl."

Molly glanced around the room, then mouthed, "Are we secure?"

Val nodded. "I did a sweep for cameras and listening devices when I got here and I've been running an audio jammer the whole time, just in case anyone's sitting outside with a mic. And no one who might be watching would recognize you, anyway, because no one would be looking at your face."

"That was the point." The woman smiled at Naomi. "Miss Cranston, I'm Molly Sutton. I work for Burke Broussard. This is our colleague, Lucien Farrow. I hope we didn't frighten you."

"Everett," Naomi whispered. "Is he all right?"

"We don't know," Lucien said brusquely, and Naomi's panic took flight, her heart banging against her rib cage.

Oh no. No, no, please no.

"They got him?" Naomi gasped out.

"No, Everett is fine." Molly gave Lucien a puzzled look before returning her attention to Naomi. "What he means is that Everett's not the reason we're here. Burke has assigned our colleague Harrison Banks to watch him. He's parked outside Everett's school. How close he can get to guard your son will depend on Burke's meeting with your ex-husband, which should be happening very soon. Burke's sitting in your husband's lobby, waiting to be called in."

Naomi sank to one of the stools at the worktable, her lungs struggling to take in enough air. Everett was all right. *For now.* "Thank you."

Molly's smile was warm. "You're welcome."

When she could breathe again, Naomi studied the pair. Molly Sutton appeared calm, but the man—Lucien Farrow—was regarding her with subtle hostility.

Naomi couldn't let that stand. These people were supposed to be helping her. They were supposed to be protecting Everett.

"You want me to know that you don't trust me, don't you?" she asked him.

He blinked. "What? No. Of course not."

"Sir, after five years in prison, I can spot hostility when I see it, even if you're trying to hide it. Heck, after one week I was able to spot it."

Too bad that skill had come too late. Her scars were testament to that.

Molly glanced at Lucien before sliding onto a stool at the worktable. "We just wanted to talk with you before we got started on your case."

Naomi believed Molly, at least. "Okay, ask me your questions. I will answer to the best of my ability."

"Why do you think you went to prison?" Lucien asked, still brusque.

"Right to the point," Naomi murmured. She met the man's eyes, refusing to quail at the anger she saw there. "I was framed and then threatened by an NOPD detective, who said if I didn't allow myself to be convicted that they'd hurt my son."

"Detective Gaffney," Molly said.

"Yes, Miss Sutton."

"Call me Molly. What exactly did he say to you and where and when did he say it?"

"He came to my mother's house. I'd been released on bail and I was staying with her. Gaffney showed up with photos of Everett. He knew where he'd be and who he'd be with. His exact words were 'Cooperate and he stays healthy. Fight these charges, and we'll send him to you in pieces.'"

Sylvi shuddered out a breath. "Naomi."

"I'm okay, Sylvi. As long as Mr. Broussard protects him, I'll be okay."

"What did your attorney say when you told him?" Lucien asked, reclaiming her attention. His eyes were cold.

"I didn't tell him."

"Why not?" Lucien asked.

At least his voice was asking. His eyes were demanding.

"I didn't know who to trust at that point. This was my son's life. I wasn't taking chances."

"So your attorney knew nothing about this plot?"

There was something in the way the man said "plot."

"Are you saying I'm lying, Mr. Farrow?"

"Of course not," he said smoothly. "I'm just saying you can't blame your incarceration on your lawyer if he didn't have all the details."

"I almost did tell him," she responded. "But then he said he'd reconsidered my trial strategy. I shouldn't testify in my own defense. There was something in the way that he said it. He just blurted it out and he wouldn't meet my eyes. He was scared. Then so was I. I knew they'd gotten to him."

Lucien's eyes flashed in anger. "You've *assumed* quite a lot, Miss Cranston." He leaned against the worktable, his pose misleadingly unbothered. "Why didn't you take the plea bargain if you were intent on going to prison?"

She glared at him. "Because I was never offered a plea bargain."

Something gleamed in his eyes. "Yes, ma'am, you were." Satisfaction at catching her in a lie? Except he hadn't, because she was telling the truth.

She sat up straighter. "And I'm telling you that I wasn't. If they'd offered me one, I'm not sure I would have taken it, because that meant I was admitting to being guilty and I could never bring myself to do that. But if I had, I probably could have gotten a much shorter sentence. And if I'd taken a plea, Gaffney would have been satisfied that I'd done what he said and Everett would have been safe a lot earlier. But it's moot because there *was no offer*."

Lucien took a piece of paper from his jacket pocket and slid it across the table. Naomi picked it up, frowning at the words on the page, which didn't make any sense. They were printed on the letterhead of the District Attorney's Office of Orleans Parish. A summary of her case. Five words had been highlighted in bright yellow.

Defendant declined a plea deal.

She read the words again and they made no more sense the second time. *Plea deal? What plea deal?*

The deal would have reduced her sentence from thirty years to ten, with time off for good behavior. All she would have needed to do was tell them who she'd planned to sell the cocaine to.

She looked up, bewildered. "I've never seen this document before."

"It has your signature on it," Lucien said, his mouth a flat line.

She shook her head. "That's not my signature. I don't know whose it is." She tossed the page back at him. "Believe me or don't, but I did not know I'd been offered a deal."

He started to take the page back, but Val snapped it up and read it quickly.

"Naomi, this is important," she said quietly. "Did your new attorney know about this?"

"If she did, I never heard about it. I can call and ask her."

"Do that," Lucien said. "I'll wait."

Val scowled at him. "What the fuck, Lucien? She's the client, not a suspect."

"I'm protecting Burke. What if she's lying, Val? What if she wants us to protect her son for another reason? What if she's working for Gaffney?"

"I'd die first," Naomi whispered.

Sylvi blanched. "Naomi." She turned to Lucien. "She was considering it, you asshole. She was thinking of killing herself when I found her on Friday. If you push her into self-harm, there will be nowhere you can hide from me."

"Whoa." Molly lifted her hands. "Everyone calm down. Lucien, you clearly have information the rest of us don't have. What is it?"

"I know Mason Lord. He wouldn't shaft a client like that. He's honest."

Naomi sighed. Mason Lord had seemed honest at first. And

then he'd seemed scared. "Does he have a family, Mr. Farrow? Children?"

Lucien frowned, uncertainty flickering in his eyes for the first time since he'd walked through the door. "Yes."

"Then how do you know that Gaffney didn't threaten them?" she asked. "Like he threatened my son?"

Lucien opened his mouth, clearly ready to defend his attorney friend. Then he frowned. "It's unlikely, but I suppose it's possible."

"A possibility we will check out," Molly said crisply. "Is this why we're here, Lucien? So you could judge our client's veracity?"

"Yes," Lucien said evenly. "That's exactly why. If she's lying, we need to know. Burke's not just looking to protect her, and you know it as well as I do. He wants to clear her name."

Molly nodded slowly. "He does."

Lucien folded his arms across his chest. "So his reputation may depend on this."

"Burke can take care of his own reputation," Val said. "But since you're so worried about it, I think he needs to go with you when you talk to this guy. Just to be sure."

"That makes sense." Lucien drew a breath. "Tell me what your attorney did in the courtroom."

"Not much. Never made a single objection. Only called my mother to the stand, and mothers are not reliable witnesses for the defense. He didn't call any of the cops who would have vouched for my integrity. He didn't object when Gaffney took the stand against me and told so many lies, or when my own husband lied and said I was a drug user. Mason Lord just . . . let it happen. And then the judge said thirty years, and I knew my life was over. But that Everett would be safe. Look, Mr. Farrow, I didn't ask Mr. Broussard to clear my name. I only asked him to protect my son. I need to know that you're at least on board to do that. He's only sixteen."

The man's lips thinned. "I have nothing against your son. We'll keep him safe."

"That's all I've asked for. If I can also be helped, I won't turn that down. But my son is the priority." She was trembling, but she didn't break eye contact with the man. "Are we finished here?"

"For now," Molly said kindly. "I want to try to understand why you were targeted in the first place, but I think we've upset you enough for one afternoon. I'll come back later."

Hopefully without Mr. Farrow. "Thank you."

Carrollton, New Orleans, Louisiana
MONDAY, FEBRUARY 24, 12:25 P.M.

"Mr. Broussard." Jimmy Haywood sat behind his desk, a concerned expression on his face. "You mentioned this is about my son?"

Burke didn't like him on sight, but that could have had something to do with him being Naomi's ex. According to Antoine, they'd been married for ten years before divorcing due to "irreconcilable differences." Naomi had said that Jimmy had cheated with a younger woman.

So yeah, he really disliked Jimmy.

"Your ex-wife came to see me this morning. She hired me to protect your son."

"My ex-wife is mentally ill. I'm so sorry she wasted your time. If that's all, you can stop wasting mine."

Burke didn't believe Naomi was mentally ill, but he thought about Lucien's concerns and knew he had to dig deeper.

He kept his tone confused. "Mentally ill? How so?"

"She's delusional and she's a thief. You know that she was in prison, right?"

"Yes, I'm aware. I'm also aware that her conviction was overturned."

Haywood waved a hand. "On a technicality. Look, she didn't need to steal that cocaine. She didn't need the money. I gave her sufficient alimony." He scowled. "I *still* give her alimony. Way more than she deserves. She steals because it's . . . I don't know. Fun?"

Burke let the alimony comment slide for now. Antoine's cursory check of Naomi's financials showed that, between her salary at the flower shop and the alimony, she was doing all right. The alimony wasn't extravagant, but it was enough to keep her lights on. The mental health claim was more of a concern—mostly because her ex-husband really seemed to think that she had stolen the evidence.

"You think she has kleptomania?"

"That and she's a drug abuser. Why else would she have stolen that bag of coke? If it went missing, she'd have been the first person suspected since handling evidence was her job. She had to have known she'd get caught."

"True enough. Has she stolen anything else?"

"Not that they've caught her doing, but she got cocky."

"I see." Haywood had clearly given this a lot of thought, but he'd ended up in the wrong place. "Did you ever think that she didn't steal the cocaine?"

Haywood laughed, a hollow sound. "No. At the beginning she talked about how she'd been set up by the NOPD and all that nonsense. Then she just folded like a cheap suit. She never even spoke in her own defense. How is that not mentally ill? How can anyone believe her to be not guilty?"

Burke considered his words carefully. Antoine's background check on Jimmy Haywood showed that he was financially solid. He worked for his father's insurance firm, which had an A+ rating.

Jimmy Haywood seemed honest enough from a legal standpoint. Morally, maybe not so much.

"Do you love your son, sir?" Burke asked.

Haywood blinked. "Of course I do. He's my son. I hate the time when he's not in my home. I hate that he's with Naomi. I hate that he's exposed to her mental illness, especially now that she's an ex-con. Who knows how twisted prison left her? But I have to say that now that she's hired you, claiming our son is in danger, I have sufficient leverage to get full custody back. She's delusional."

"What if she's not?" Burke asked quietly.

Haywood shook his head in disbelief. "You *believe* her? Really?"

"I believe certain things she's said," Burke hedged. He actually believed her wholeheartedly, despite Lucien's concern. "Did you know that she was threatened with harm to your son if she fought the charges six years ago?"

Haywood was still shaking his head. "You seem like an intelligent man, Mr. Broussard. I did a quick internet search on your firm before I invited you into my office. You've been very successful since you hung your PI shingle. But as a former cop, surely you see that she's lying. No one threatened her."

"It's because I'm a former cop that I believe her, sir." Burke watched the man's eyes for his reaction and was relieved to see a flicker of hesitation. "Look, I'll be blunt with you, because we're talking about the safety of your son. Naomi Cranston is not the first person to cross my path who was confronted by the NOPD in such a way. And she was confronted again on Friday afternoon. There are recordings of the encounter outside her place of employment."

Haywood frowned. "You're serious."

"I am. And if it makes a difference, she's aware that you'll use this to regain full custody. She thinks it might be safer for Everett not to be with her until this situation is resolved."

Haywood's frown deepened. "That's . . . new."

"She's scared, sir. And, given what I know, she has a right to be."

Haywood drew a breath. "What would your protection look like?"

"A bodyguard attached to your son, preferably twenty-four-seven. At a minimum, he'd sit outside your house, monitoring any risks or threats. Ideally, he'd be stationed inside your home—"

"No," Haywood snapped before Burke had finished speaking. "You will not come into my home. My wife is pregnant and I won't stress her. We have young children and a bodyguard would frighten them."

The presence of a bodyguard might save their lives, Burke wanted to say, but did not. "Then we would station our protection detail outside your house."

Haywood said nothing for a long moment, during which he looked like he might agree to an external presence, at least. Then he shook his head again. "No, thank you, Mr. Broussard. I won't whip my family into a terrified frenzy because my ex-wife is insane. We will be fine. There is no threat."

"She still has custodial rights and she's asked us to watch over Everett. We will do that, with or without your consent." He held up his hand when Haywood opened his mouth, his expression one of rage. "From a distance, of course. It's not ideal, but we'll work with what we have."

"You're as delusional as she is." Haywood's eyes were crackling with fury. "I should call the cops right now and report you."

"That's your right, of course. But, given that the threat is coming from a cop, that will only put your son in more danger."

Haywood lurched to his feet, his fists clenched. "Get out of my office before I call security."

Burke rose, sliding a business card onto the man's desk. "If you see anything odd around your house, feel free to call me."

Haywood ripped Burke's card into confetti. "Get. Out."

Burke got out, exhaling once he was clear of the man's office door.

"He didn't like what you had to say, huh?" the receptionist asked dryly. "Thanks for pushing him into a bad mood. My day's gonna be great from here on out."

"Does he have issues with his temper?" Burke asked.

"I see nothing, I hear nothing." She glanced at a complicated phone, which had just lit up. "He's making a call."

Haywood was probably calling his divorce attorney. Or the cops to report Burke and his wife's "empty" accusations. That had been a possible outcome. But a call to the divorce lawyer was the more likely scenario. "Thanks for the warning."

The woman hesitated. "Is Everett really in danger?"

"You heard that?"

She rolled her eyes. "I may have gotten up to stretch my legs and paused at the door."

"I see. And if Everett is in danger? What would you do?"

"Tell Jimmy's dad." She pointed to the office door to the right of Jimmy's. It bore a gold nameplate that read *James Haywood Sr.* "James Senior loves Everett. If he thought there was real danger . . ."

Burke took the opening. "Would he talk to me?"

"I'll call him right now."

Burke needed to field this with Naomi before discussing her personal business with her ex-father-in-law. "I need to step out and make a quick call. I'll be right back."

He stepped outside and started to dial Val, only to blink when his phone buzzed with an incoming call from Val herself.

"Is everything okay?" he asked.

"Naomi's fine, but you need to have a chat with Lucien," Val said. "He was really rude to Naomi just now."

"Tell me," he said, groaning quietly as Val did. "Yeah, I think I should accompany him when he talks to Mason Lord. Good call, Val. I'll text Lucien to give me the guy's address."

"What happened with Naomi's ex?"

"Is she there with you?"

"Yes."

"Well, it's not settled yet. The ex said no, but her father-in-law might be an ally. Can you put her on the phone?"

"Sure."

A moment later, he heard his client's quiet voice. "Jimmy said no, I take it."

"He did. He thinks you're delusional and a klepto drug abuser and will be suing for full custody."

"I figured as much," she murmured. "Thank you for trying. But the bodyguard will stay on Everett's protection detail, yes?"

"He will. Don't worry. Listen, do you trust your ex's father?"

"James? Yes. Why?"

"Because the receptionist is offering to get me a meeting with him. It seems she listened at the door when I was talking to your ex."

"Rosemary," Naomi said fondly. "She's the real authority in that office. She's nosy as all get-out, but she's got a great big heart. If she thinks that Everett's in danger, she'll make sure James Senior will listen."

"So I have your permission to speak with him?"

"You do. Tell him thank you, by the way. He always sent me a care package with snacks on my birthday. It was supposed to be from Everett, but I know it was from James. Tell him it allowed me to build a lot of goodwill when I shared with the others."

Burke's gut twisted. "Is that how you survived once you left solitary?"

"One of the ways." But the terseness of her answer told him that this was a topic she was uncomfortable discussing.

He could only imagine.

"I'll tell him. Is he trustworthy?"

"Yes. He was like the father I never had. You can tell him that, too."

"Do you not speak to him?"

She sighed softly. "James loves Jimmy, and Jimmy's new wife hates me. If James and I talked and Jimmy found out, it would cause all kinds of friction between them and I don't want that. So no. I don't. I'd like to, but I won't."

"Got it. I'll let you know what happens. Can you give the phone back to Val?"

"Of course. Can you also give my regards to Rosemary? She was always so kind to me."

"I will."

"Hey," Val said a moment later. "Good luck with the father-in-law."

"Thanks. Any package deliveries?"

"Nope, but the day is young."

Burke thought about exactly what Gaffney had said to Naomi on Friday afternoon. He'd wanted her to carry the package in the flower van. "Check the delivery van. Make sure it's not hidden in there."

"I put sensors on it when Naomi and I took it out for deliveries this morning. They'll alarm loudly if someone even touches the van, much less tries to break into it. Antoine walked me through the installation. Pretty simple, overall."

"You done good, kid."

"Aw shucks. Thanks, boss. Anything else?"

Burke thought about the rage he'd seen on Haywood's face. If the man had laid a single finger on Naomi . . . "Make sure her ex didn't abuse her."

"Oh," Val murmured. "Will do."

"Thanks. Talk more soon." He sent a quick text to Lucien. ***Address for Mason Lord? Time you're going to meet with him?***

Lucien's reply came quickly. ***Val told you about my convo w the client?***

Burke sighed. ***Shouldn't she have?***

Dots appeared on his screen. They stopped and started again, indicating that either Lucien was typing a long answer or he was deleting what he'd typed. Finally, the reply came through.

I wanted to tell you myself. But yeah. I was out of line.

At least Lucien was owning up to it. Burke wondered if something else was going on, because Lucien wasn't normally rude. ***Send me address and time and we'll figure this out.***

Then he went back into the insurance company, finding Rosemary the office manager watching for him.

"Mr. James Haywood will see you when he gets back from his lunch meeting. Can you wait an hour?"

"I'll go get lunch and come back. Does that work?"

"Of course."

"Would you like something, Miss Rosemary?"

She smiled. "I've got my lunch, but thank you for asking."

"Naomi says to give you her regards, and that you always had a big heart."

Rosemary's smile dimmed. "I miss her. When she and Jimmy split, I wanted to keep Naomi, but that's not how it works."

"No, ma'am, I guess not."

Hopefully James Senior would side with Naomi in this case. If he didn't, Burke was going to have to get very creative with Everett's protection so that he kept his promise to Naomi Cranston.

Because Burke always kept his promises.

4

Kenner, Louisiana

MONDAY, FEBRUARY 24, 12:40 P.M.

NAOMI WATCHED AS Val set her phone aside, looking troubled. "What's wrong?"

"Not Everett," Val said, then pursed her lips as if she was considering her next words, which made Naomi's panic inch back up.

"We don't have time for niceties, Val. Plus, they're not good for my blood pressure."

"Sorry. Personal question time. Why did you and Jimmy divorce?"

Naomi dropped her gaze to the pile of thorns she'd removed from the rose stems. "Couple of reasons. He wanted me to quit my job. I kept saying no, that it was important to me. He belittled what I did."

"Working in the evidence room?"

"Yeah. It's been my assignment ever since I came back from maternity leave after having Everett."

"Did you want that job?" Val asked carefully.

"Not really. I wanted to go back on patrol, but every time I tried to get a transfer, I got blocked. One of my supervisors told me that it was because they knew I'd be having more babies. To just do my job or quit. So I did the best damn evidence processing in the NOPD."

Val squared her shoulders. "Did Jimmy abuse you?"

Naomi's breath caught in her throat. "Why?"

"Burke wants to know. And now, so do I."

Naomi brushed the pile of thorns into a bucket to be dumped into the composter. "I suppose that depends on your definition of 'abuse.'"

"Naomi. You know you can talk to me. If there's something you don't want the others to know, we can hold it back—unless it's going to put you in danger."

"Why does Mr. Broussard want to know?"

"Why don't you call him Burke?"

Naomi winced. "Old habits, maybe. He's in charge. So are Miss Sutton and Mr. Farrow. I think you're the only one I can call by her first name, and that's only because I knew you through Sylvi before this."

"Prison behavior?"

"Yeah. Lots of 'Miss' and 'Mister.' I didn't call Sylvi by her first name until I'd worked here for six months."

"I get that. I remember coming home from the military. Becoming a civilian again was like . . . being upside down. So, what did Jimmy do?"

Naomi sighed. "I didn't think I'd be able to distract you. It was mostly just emotional abuse, tearing me down."

"There's no 'just.' That's still abuse. Did he hit you?"

"Yeah. Twice. The first time, he was so sorry. He'd had a bad day at work and Everett had colic and had screamed all night long. I let it go, but it was always there, in the back of my mind. I was always waiting for his hand to slap me again."

"Yes, I know," Val said softly.

Naomi shot her a startled look. "You?"

"Not by a partner, but I know what you mean. What happened the second time he hit you?"

Naomi pushed her curiosity aside. Val's pain wasn't her business. Her bodyguard was asking about Naomi's pain so that she could protect her.

"The second time was after we'd gotten into a terrible fight. Everett was eight years old and Jimmy wanted another baby. I didn't. I'd had Everett when I was twenty and—" She shook her head. "I love my son, Val."

"Never doubted it. But you weren't ready for a baby at twenty?"

"I wasn't. When I first started with the NOPD, I figured I'd work for ten years, maybe make detective, before I had a baby. But then . . . boom. I was pregnant."

"You weren't expecting to be expecting?"

"I wasn't. I was stunned. We were using condoms and I was on birth control pills. Which only work when they haven't been tampered with."

Val's eyes widened. "Jimmy messed with your birth control?"

"He did. I didn't know until we had that big fight about a second baby. It wasn't the first time that we'd disagreed, but it was the first time that Jimmy raised his hand to me again. He didn't actually hit me, but I said that him even thinking about slapping me was enough reason not to have a second child. I figured Jimmy would sulk and pout like he always did and then he'd drop it. But three nights later I found him with my birth control packet. He was switching it out for another packet that looked just like mine. I remember just staring at him. Then I grabbed both packets from his hand, and that's when he hit me."

Val closed her eyes. "My God."

"Everything clicked for me then. I remember when I got pregnant with Everett, I was so worried because I was on the pill at the time. My doctor said I was probably okay, but he'd monitor me and the baby for any ill effects. Jimmy wasn't worried at all, and he's a worrier. He told me that we'd been blessed with a baby and that God would make it all okay."

"You realized his calm was unusual."

"Yeah. I was standing there holding two packets of pills and crying because he'd hit me so hard my head slammed into a wall. I straight-out asked him if he'd done this before. He started to deny it but then admitted it. He didn't want to wait ten years for a baby, even though that's what we'd agreed on when we were dating. He admitted to switching my pills and poking holes in the condoms we used." She exhaled. "I moved out that night. Took Everett to my mother's house. Our divorce was finalized a year later."

"Asshole," Val muttered. "How much of that can I tell Burke?"

Naomi massaged her temples, suddenly very tired. "Tell him all of it, if you want. It doesn't really matter now. Did Jimmy threaten him?"

"Burke?" Val laughed. "No. Very few people threaten Burke Broussard."

Naomi thought about the man—all six foot five of him. His shoulders were so broad, his biceps bulging under the polo shirt he'd been wearing that morning. "He *is* physically intimidating."

"But a marshmallow inside. I think Jimmy wanted to threaten Burke but didn't have the guts. Did you tell your father-in-law what Jimmy did to you?"

"My mother did. I got to her house that night and burst into tears. Everett was crying, too. Mom took a photo of my face because my cheek was already bruising. She took a photo of the side of my head the next day because I had a big goose egg. My mother is a rock. I don't know what I would have done without her. Once I'd gotten

Everett to sleep, Mom gave me the third degree and wouldn't take no for an answer, so I told her everything. I didn't want her to tell James. He was an amazing father-in-law. He was always there when I needed him and we couldn't reach Jimmy. Like when Everett had a fever of a hundred and three and I was panicking. James was so calm and took care of us. I really cared about him and didn't want him to know about Jimmy's abuse. I didn't want to hurt him. But my mother told him—at least about the hitting part. I don't think he knows about the birth control part. I don't want Everett to know."

"I understand. I'll be careful with the information."

"Thank you." She turned away when her eyes burned. She was not going to cry. She'd cried enough already. "I'm going to make a fresh pot of coffee. Would you care for some?"

"Sure," Val said kindly. "Is your coffee better than Sylvi's? Hers is like crayon water. So weak it's barely drinkable."

Naomi laughed roughly. "It really is awful. Mine is strong."

"Then you're my hero. Don't tell Sylvi."

"Tell Sylvi what?" Sylvi asked, leaning against the doorframe. From the look on her face, she'd heard most of what Naomi had shared.

Naomi didn't really mind. She had very few secrets from Sylvi. Especially since the woman had found her with a Glock in her hands, contemplating the unthinkable. Few secrets were worse than that.

"That I'm making coffee," Naomi said.

Sylvi groaned. "I'm going to have to water it down by half, at least."

"I'll also make you a pot the way you like it," Naomi promised. "And then I'll do the afternoon deliveries."

"*We'll* do the afternoon deliveries," Val corrected. "I've got Phin coming to keep you company, Sylvi, in case Gaffney comes by. Phin says he'll fix that leaky faucet while he's here. He's Burke's handyman," she explained to Naomi. "But he takes care of all our personal home repairs. He used to work for Burke full-time as his night security, but he got his contractor's license and started his own business. He still does night security for Burke occasionally. If you see him around, don't be alarmed. He's a big marshmallow, too."

"And Mr. Farrow?" Naomi asked. "Is he also a marshmallow?"

Val sighed. "I think something's going on with him, but I don't know what. No excuse for his being rude, though."

"I wanted to smack him," Sylvi said.

"You would have needed a step stool," Val teased.

Sylvi gave her a dirty look, started to say something back, then just shook her head when the front doorbell jingled. "Gotta go."

"I meant that about Lucien," Val said seriously. "He had no excuse to be rude. Burke will find out what's what. He's going with Lucien to talk to your first attorney."

"Thank you. That makes me feel much better."

There had been something about the big, burly Cajun that had made her feel . . . secure.

Seen.

Safe.

Carrollton, New Orleans, Louisiana
MONDAY, FEBRUARY 24, 1:45 P.M.

James Haywood Sr. sat behind his desk, horrified as he listened to Burke describe the threat to his grandson.

When Burke was finished, the older man looked ill. "My son said no?"

"Yes, sir. He didn't believe the threat was real."

"But you do."

"I do."

"I know who you are, Mr. Broussard. You worked for a friend of mine nearly five years ago. He was one of your first clients when you started your firm. I called him after Rosemary called me. He said to believe you."

"Do you?"

"I do. I never thought Naomi was guilty. I should have done more when she was accused. I offered to testify on her behalf, to be a character witness, but her attorney said I wasn't needed. And then he basically sat there and said nothing during the whole trial."

"Were you there?"

"Yes. I sat in the back. I don't think Naomi knew I was there, but Ruthanne did. She's Naomi's mother. I told Ruthanne that I'd offered to testify, too. We were both so frustrated with her attorney."

"We're going to interview him."

"Good. There was something about him that I didn't like. But I'm no lawyer. I'm an insurance agent. I didn't know what else to do. Naomi's silence makes a lot more sense now. Does Ruthanne know why she didn't defend herself?"

"I don't think so."

"Then I won't say anything. Dammit."

"Do you still talk to Naomi's mother?"

James blushed. "Yes. We see each other often. We're really just friends. We mostly talk about Everett. Naomi doesn't know about us, though."

"I won't say anything. Naomi says you were the father she never had, by the way."

James swallowed hard, his eyes bright with unshed tears. "Thank you. That means a lot. I know why she and I don't talk. My new daughter-in-law hates Naomi with the passion of ten thousand suns."

"Why?"

"Because she's jealous and insecure. She doesn't like me, either. I tried to tell her that my son had been physically abusive with Naomi, that that was why she left."

Burke had to shove down his rage. He hated domestic violence. Had lived it for too many years growing up in his own father's house. "I wondered."

"I didn't want to believe it, but Ruthanne had photos. Jimmy hit Naomi hard. I don't know what their fight was about, but Naomi definitely was not the winner."

"What did your new daughter-in-law say when you warned her?"

"That Jimmy had told her Naomi was a lying . . . well, she used a word I won't repeat. McKenzie said if I continued to push the issue, she wouldn't allow me to see Everett. That she'd tell an 'equally despicable lie' about me. I mean, I didn't know what else to do. I'd told her a hard truth and she refused to believe it. But she also doesn't make Jimmy angry. She's a dutiful wife who's already had two children with him—and they have a third on the way. She ignores Everett unless Jimmy is around, then she fusses over Ev."

"Everett doesn't complain about her to Jimmy?"

"No. Everett loves his father. Plus, his world was upended when Naomi went to prison. I think he's clinging to the parent he thinks will stay. He knows Jimmy hit Naomi, though. He was there that night. Saw the bruises. He just doesn't want to think about it or talk about it. When Naomi got arrested, Jimmy said some vile things about her. His witch of a wife continues to do so. I try to intervene, but Ev doesn't want to listen to me."

"Lotta not listening going on," Burke observed.

"Don't I know it. Anyway, if Jimmy went home and told McKenzie that he wanted to bring in a bodyguard for Everett because someone was threatening Naomi . . . well, it wouldn't end well for him. McKenzie was pregnant last year when Naomi was released from prison and wanted visitation with Everett. McKenzie threw a fit. Later she claimed she'd nearly lost the baby. And maybe she did. If there's anything that's important to Jimmy, it's his kids. Him not wanting McKenzie stressed by a bodyguard does make some sense. In his mind, he's choosing the safety of his family."

"But Everett is also his family," Burke said.

"I'll talk to him. Tell him that Everett should stay with me. That way the bodyguard can watch Ev from inside my house. Jimmy doesn't even need to tell McKenzie why Ev is coming to visit. It can just be a visit. If Jimmy's smart, he'll allow it."

"If he's not?"

"I'll petition for temporary custody. It would never get to court, but the filing would be public record and Jimmy would hate that." He sighed. "Jimmy's mother took her own life when he was thirteen. She was sick and in pain and she couldn't take it anymore. Jimmy was the one who found her and he's never been the same. Not an excuse for violence, but . . ."

Burke still disliked Jimmy Haywood. There was never a reason to strike your spouse. *None.* "What would you like me to do, sir?"

"Let me go see Jimmy right now. Can you wait?"

"I can."

James had reached the door when Burke got a call on his cell. It was Harrison. At the same time a text from Harrison appeared on his screen.

911.

Shit. That was their code that meant Burke should drop everything and answer. He abruptly rose, holding up his hand for James to wait. "What's happening, Harrison? Is Everett all right?"

James went a ghastly shade of pale. Burke led the older man back to his chair.

"He is now," Harrison said grimly.

"Hold on. James, Everett's okay. Sit there and try to breathe while I get the details, okay?"

James nodded shakily. "Okay."

"Go ahead, Harrison."

"I watched him come out of the school—early, I might add. He was skipping his last class. He got in his car and I followed him to a house about a mile from where he lives. He got out of the car and an SUV drove up, boxing him in against his car. I'm glad I was there. They nearly dragged the kid into their vehicle."

Shit. "He's okay, though?"

"Yeah. Super shaken up."

"I guess so. Where are you?"

"Texting you the address right now."

Burke's phone pinged and he noted the neighborhood. "Why did he go there?"

"A girl. She was hysterical. She saw the whole thing from her bedroom window. Apparently, she'd called in sick to school so that she and the boy could have a little nookie."

"Okay. I'm with Everett's grandfather now. He's been more receptive to us than Everett's father. I'll find out what he thinks we should do. Any chance the kid will run?"

"I don't think so. He's pale and shaking like a leaf. Um . . . I might have had to get a little physical with one of the guys grabbing him."

"What does 'a little physical' mean?"

"I might have broken his arm. But I was able to pull off the ski mask he was wearing, so I can give a description of his face."

"I'll call André Holmes, give him a heads-up about the abduction attempt. We don't know anything about a broken arm, okay? You grabbed him just hard enough to make him let Everett go. Okay?"

"Exactly what I'd planned to say."

"Good work."

James covered his face with his hands. "Everett's really okay?"

"He's really okay," Burke soothed. "Harrison, give me a minute to sort this out and I'll call you right back. Do you have eyes on him?"

"I do. We're sitting on the girl's front porch. She went back inside to get Everett some water. She says they have security cameras, but she turned them off because she didn't want to get into trouble for having a boy over when she was supposed to be home sick."

Burke sighed. "We'll ask the neighbors. Maybe one of their cameras caught it." He ended the call, then perched on the edge of James's desk to update him. "Harrison won't leave him. What should we do with Jimmy?"

James rose once again, still pale but fiercely determined. "Leave this to me." He started for the door, then turned. "Come on, Mr. Broussard. You need to tell Jimmy the unvarnished truth."

"Okay." Burke was in the lobby, passing Rosemary's desk, when Val called. And simultaneously sent a text.

911.

Fucking hell. "Hold on a moment, sir. This is an emergency." He answered the phone. "What's wrong?"

"The alarms went off on Sylvi's delivery van. You were right, they tried to hide the package versus handing it to Naomi. And when they realized we'd foiled their plan, they shot up the front of Sylvi's shop."

"Oh my God. Is everyone all right?"

"Yeah. Sylvi was up front with Phin. Naomi and I were getting ready to do afternoon deliveries when the alarm went off. Phin saw the SUV driving slowly by her front window. When the first bullet hit the glass, Phin got them both on the floor behind the counter. I've called NOPD. Just letting you know we're okay. Naomi is shaken up and saying she's quitting because Sylvi and Phin could have been killed, but *that's nonsense.*" She spoke those last two words sternly, like she was talking to Naomi. "I figured I'd bring Naomi and Sylvi into the office. We're going to tell the cops it was an attempted robbery."

"Okay. Tell Naomi that . . ." *Shit.* What should he tell her? "Put me on speaker." He waited until he heard someone quietly crying. "Naomi?"

"I'm okay," Naomi said, her words choked. "I'm sorry. I almost got Sylvi and Phin killed."

"No, you didn't," Burke said calmly. "I need you to sit down. Everett is okay, I promise. Are you sitting down?"

"Yes," she whispered.

"Someone tried to grab Everett, but Harrison was there. He stopped it, and Everett is fine. I promise that he is fine. He's safe."

"Oh my God. They said they'd hurt him and they tried."

"Tried," Burke said firmly. *"Failed.* I'm with James now and we're about to see Jimmy. I need you to breathe and do whatever Val says. When we've got Everett in a safe place, I'll come by for you. We'll get all of you to a safe place. I promise. Just let Val and Sylvi take care of you. Val, where's Phin?"

"Up front, waiting for the cops. I'll call you when we know more. Go take care of Everett."

"Okay." Burke ended the call and had to draw in a deep breath himself. "Someone just shot up the flower shop where Naomi works. We need to get Everett settled ASAP so I can help get Naomi moved to a safe place as well."

James's lips thinned as he grabbed the handle on his son's office door. "Let's do this."

Kenner, Louisiana

MONDAY, FEBRUARY 24, 2:50 P.M.

Naomi was not okay. She sat at the workroom table, hugging herself so tightly that her arms ached. She realized she was rocking back and forth and was at least able to stop that behavior.

Everett's fine.

Broussard had given his word. Regardless, her son should have been her biggest worry.

But it wasn't. *Because the cops are here.* At this point, only two uniformed officers were here in the workroom to take their statements and another two up front securing the scene, but that was enough.

The cops knew who she was and looked at her like she'd caused this mess.

And Naomi guessed that she had. In a way, anyway.

As soon as the van alarm had started to blare, Val had tucked her away in the corner of the workroom that was farthest from the door, where she could hide behind the boxes of vases in the event the building was breached.

Which it had been thirty seconds later, with the *rat-a-tat-tat* of semiautomatic rifle fire followed by the crashing of glass.

In her mind, she could still hear Sylvi's scream and Val's anguished cry in the immediate aftermath of the shooting. And then Phin's bellow of rage.

Val had run out to the front, returning almost immediately to tell Naomi that everyone was all right, that Phin had pushed Sylvi down behind the counter. Sylvi and Phin had followed Val back to the workroom, because it was the most secure room in the shop.

Naomi's heart had skipped another beat when she'd seen the dog in Phin's arms—his service dog, a sweet golden retriever named Soda-Pop. The dog's paw had been cut by a shard of glass from the shattered window. It was a small wound, but Phin was shaken.

The service dog aided Phin with the PTSD he'd developed during his service in the army. Of course he'd been shaken at the sound of gunfire. Of course he was furious that his dog was hurt, even if the sweet girl would be okay.

I shouldn't be here. I've caused so much trouble.

But she couldn't leave. She couldn't even move. She was frozen in place, just trying to breathe.

Because the two uniformed officers were staring at Naomi. The man—Ferguson, a rookie cop she'd never met—was studying her with a detached curiosity that made her feel like a bug under a microscope.

The other cop's attention was far worse because Naomi had known her. Had processed evidence for her. Six years ago, Nora Langley had always regarded her with a mixture of disdain and condescending pity that had made Naomi feel . . . *less.* Like she was only a pair of hands. Not a real cop. The same way that Jimmy had treated her. Today Langley's expression was one of open contempt and scorn. And suspicion. As if she was hoping—even expecting—to catch Naomi doing something illegal so that she could send her back to prison.

"Is this everyone?" Ferguson asked.

"It is," Sylvi said, standing at Naomi's side, rubbing her back in slow, soothing circles.

"I need everyone's name, occupation, and relationship to the shop," Langley said, her eyes narrowed, her mouth twisted into a sneer as Sylvi started the introductions.

"I'm Sylvi Kristiansen, shop owner."

"Val Sorensen. I'm Sylvi's sister. I'm here to deliver flowers since it's the busy season."

"Phin Bishop." He gently stroked SodaPop, now curled up comfortably on the worktable. "I'm a friend, here to help load the van with deliveries."

They'd only had time before the police arrived to make sure that they were all okay, to call Broussard, and to agree not to mention the threat Detective Gaffney had made to Naomi on Friday afternoon.

Naomi became aware of the silence in the room, broken when Sylvi, still rubbing Naomi's back, gently called her name.

Naomi cleared her throat. "Naomi Cranston. I work for Miss Kristiansen."

Officer Langley made a scoffing sound. "I hope Miss Kristiansen watches her cashbox."

Sylvi straightened in indignation. "Do you have questions for us, Officer Langley? Because if you don't, I'm going to start sweeping the floor of my shop."

"You have to wait until Forensics is done," Langley said coolly. "So . . . what happened?"

"We have security camera footage," Val said. "I can show you. I'll even get you a copy."

"Why don't you just tell me?" Langley said condescendingly. Then she tilted her head. "Sorensen. Why do I know that name?"

"She works for Broussard Investigations," Officer Ferguson said. "They've brought down some major bad actors in the last few years. I've read the reports. She's a bodyguard. So's he." He nodded at Phin. "The local news did a piece on service dogs a few months back, and he and his dog were mentioned."

"Bodyguards, huh?" Langley asked skeptically. "And you both just happen to be here?"

"I'm a sister, too," Val said. "I come in occasionally to retrieve boxes from the top shelves because my little sister is too short to reach."

Sylvi gave Val a dark look that was purely for show before turning to Langley. "They were here to help us. Normally Naomi and I can handle day-to-day operations, but I have a ton of business this time of year. Lots of people are having Mardi Gras parties, and they hire me to provide the flowers."

All of which were currently stored in the industrial-sized refrigerator that took up one whole wall of the workroom. They needed to get those flowers delivered or Sylvi would lose so much business.

Focus, Naomi.

Because Langley was staring at her again. "How long have you worked here?"

"A year." *Since I got out of prison.* But Naomi wasn't going to give Langley the satisfaction of referring to her own incarceration.

Langley smirked. "Does your parole officer know where you are?"

The question was like a sucker punch. "You know I don't have one of those."

"Because her conviction was overturned," Sylvi added, her displeasure clear. "Do you have any questions about the shooting,

Officer Langley? Or do you intend to continue insulting my employee?"

Naomi had always thought that Sylvi had hung the moon, but right now she swore Sylvi had hung the stars, too.

"You all look so relaxed," Langley noted. "She's practically in the fetal position. I wonder why? Just asking."

Sylvi gave Naomi's back a pat before taking her phone out. She pointed it at the officers and hit record. "For the record, Officer Langley, we were all doing our jobs when someone tried to break into my delivery van. For whatever reason, they got frustrated and drove around to the front of my shop, where Mr. Bishop and I were preparing arrangements to go into the van. I saw an SUV drive past, the passenger-side window went down, and suddenly someone was shooting. I don't know how many bullets, but I'd estimate at least twenty or twenty-five? Mr. Bishop, does that sound right to you?"

"It does," Phin said, still stroking his dog. "I pushed Miss Kristiansen down behind the counter, threw myself over her, and dragged my service dog with me. It was over in a matter of seconds."

If Naomi didn't know better, she'd swear that Phin hadn't a care in the world. But his right hand never left SodaPop's coat and his left clenched the edge of the worktable so tightly that his knuckles were white.

In that moment, Naomi wished she had a dog, too. But she channeled Phin's calm and lifted her chin, returning Langley's stare.

Because I didn't do anything wrong. Not six years ago and not today.

"Please turn off the camera," Langley said briskly. "You're escalating a situation that can be easily handled."

"Then handle it," Sylvi snapped, refusing to stop recording. "We were shot at, Officer. And by the way, we're okay. No, we don't need medical attention, but thank you for offering."

Langley had the decency to look a little ashamed at that. "We have medics coming, just in case."

"That's so nice," Sylvi drawled, still recording. "Do you have any other questions?"

"I do," Ferguson said. "Ma'am," he added respectfully. "Why *your* shop? Why do you think they targeted you?"

"Now, *that's* a good question," Sylvi said. "Thank you for asking it, Officer. I don't know how to answer it, unfortunately. The van is new. New to me, anyway. I bought it used. Had it painted. It still had the temporary plates until just a few weeks ago. Maybe they thought because I had the money to buy a van that I had money to steal."

Sylvi, it seemed, was a master of deflection.

"But why the van?" Ferguson pressed. "Why not hold you up at the register?"

"I don't know," Sylvi said. "I watch crime shows on TV. Sometimes bad guys steal vans to use when they're going to commit more crimes, don't they?"

Sylvi was amazing.

"Can we see the footage?" Ferguson asked. "Please."

"Of course," Val said, producing her own phone. "I have access to the cameras."

"Why?" Langley asked sharply. "Why do you have access to the cameras in a flower shop?"

"Because my sister lives in the apartment upstairs," Val said, annoyance edging her voice. "She lives alone. As Officer Ferguson noted, I work for a private investigator. I see crime every day and I didn't want my sister to be a victim. So I gave her a good security system *with cameras*. I monitor the system. Because I'm a good big sister."

"If you'd asked to see the footage when you first got here," Phin said mildly, "instead of harassing Miss Cranston, you'd probably have the license plate of the SUV that fired the shots. You could have a BOLO out right now."

Of course, that would be pointless, Naomi thought. Val had already run a check on the plates, and they belonged to a stolen car.

Langley flushed angrily and held her hand out for Val's phone, but Val just shook her head and held the phone so that the two officers could see her screen. There was no way Val was voluntarily handing over her phone.

Ferguson leaned in closer. "Okay, so they pull up in the SUV, the guy in the passenger seat gets out, approaches the delivery van, and then . . ." He frowned. "What's in his pocket? It looks like an envelope."

Yes, it had been an envelope, and the guy had been reaching for it with one hand while he tried to open the van with the other. The alarm had gone off, startling him, and he'd hightailed it back to his SUV.

"Another good question, Officer Ferguson," Sylvi said, still recording. "We're hoping your people can zoom in and figure it out."

Antoine at Broussard's office already had a copy of the footage and was working on that very thing.

"The alarm goes off," Val says, "and the guy gets back into the SUV. They drive through the alley to the front of the shop." She tapped her screen. "This is the camera in the front."

Naomi closed her eyes when Val's phone played back the shooting, the sound of the gunfire making her sick all over again.

Naomi opened her eyes when Ferguson made a thoughtful noise. "The shooter aims high," he said. "I wonder if that was intentional."

This young man was going to make a damn good cop. He was

already better than Langley, who'd been on the force for at least fifteen years.

"I wondered the same," Val said. "A message of some kind?"

Ferguson looked at Sylvi and Naomi. "Ladies, have you had someone try to shake you down? Was this an act of intimidation by organized crime?"

Sylvi gave him an approving nod. "No, Officer, no one's tried to shake me down. The business owners in this area have been fortunate in that respect. If anyone tries, I'll report it. I promise."

Naomi noted she'd said "me" and "I." She'd kept the question focused on the shop, managing to protect Naomi without uttering a single lie.

Naomi was grateful for the day she'd been approved to join Sylvi's flower-arranging class in the prison. The woman was a good boss and an even better friend.

"Phin!" a woman called from up front. "Dammit, let me through. My husband's back there."

Phin exhaled, his expression relieved. "Cora's here. My wife." He met a very pregnant woman at the workroom door. She looked like she was ready to deliver any moment. "You shouldn't be back here, Cora Jane. You should have texted me from the car."

"I was scared," Cora said. "I needed to see that you were all right." She lumbered to the worktable, visually assessing the dog without touching her. "Is SodaPop okay?"

"I think so," Phin said. "The bleeding's stopped."

"Good. I was so worried."

"I can't believe those cops let you through," Sylvi said.

Phin smiled down at his wife. "I can believe it. I do everything she says."

Cora huffed, but she smiled back at him before turning to the cops. "I'm going to drive my husband and SodaPop to the veterinarian. Can we leave?"

"Of course," Langley said. She reached out to pet SodaPop, but Ferguson gently grabbed her arm.

"Service dog," he murmured. "She's working."

Langley gave her partner the dirtiest of looks. "Of course." She turned to Phin with a tight smile. "My apologies, Mr. Bishop. I'll need you to sign a statement. Can you come by the police station when you're done at the vet?"

"I will. It may be tomorrow. The flowers still have to be delivered." Phin dropped a kiss on Sylvi's cheek. "I'll be back to do the deliveries and I'll send a few of my construction guys over to cover the window with plywood when the cops are done processing the scene. If you need a place to stay, you're welcome at our house."

"You're the best," Sylvi said. "Call us when the vet's seen SodaPop."

"I will." Phin gathered the dog in his arms. "I want to make sure there's no more glass in her paw." He nodded to the cops. "Officers."

"We'll need access to your camera footage," Langley said once Phin had left the room.

"I'll be happy to download the file and send it to you," Val said easily.

"Thank you, Miss Sorensen," Langley said, both her tone and body stiff. "Is there anything else you can think of? Anything that can help us identify the man in the van?"

"No," Val said. "But I did like your analysis, Officer Ferguson. It didn't appear that the shooter actually wanted to shoot the people in the shop. I think you'll find the bullets embedded in the plaster at the edge of the ceiling."

"You already checked," Ferguson said, unable to disguise the admiration in his tone.

Val nodded. "First thing I did once I made sure everyone was safe."

Langley turned to Naomi. "You've said very little, *Naomi*."

That Langley had referred to everyone else as *Miss* or *Mister* was not lost on Naomi. "Everything's already been said, *Nora*."

Langley's nostrils flared. She opened her mouth, no doubt to chastise Naomi for the familiarity, but glanced at Sylvi, who still held her phone, still recording. "If you think of anything else, please let us know. We'll be going now."

"I'll meet you outside," Ferguson told his partner.

Langley gave him a sharp look but took her leave.

"I know who you are, Miss Cranston," Ferguson said quietly. "I know that you served time and had your conviction overturned."

"Thank you for still being polite," Naomi said, not sure what else she could say.

"Try to have a good evening, ladies. I'm glad no one was hurt." He started to leave, then paused. "Just so you know, I don't buy your story. I don't think this was random, and I don't think they were trying to steal your van. I think they were putting something in it. What that might be, I don't know. But if you figure it out, give me a call."

Naomi didn't say a word. She wished she could believe that this kid was legit, that he'd really work to help her.

But she didn't trust easily anymore. So she dropped her gaze to the worktable, relieved when Ferguson shut the door behind him.

"Well," Sylvi said, putting her phone on the worktable. "That was fun."

"Langley is a real piece of work," Val complained. "I liked the kid, though. Wanted to, anyway. Not sure if he was just playing good cop or not."

"I thought it was just me being jaded," Naomi said.

"We're all jaded," Sylvi said ruefully. "But we've got your back, Naomi. If anyone can get to the bottom of this, it's Val and Burke and their crew."

5

Carrollton, New Orleans, Louisiana
MONDAY, FEBRUARY 24, 2:55 P.M.

EVERETT HAYWOOD WAS a tall, gangly boy with dark hair and brown eyes, just like his mother. But unlike Naomi's, the boy's eyes were filled with rude defiance.

Although his attitude might be residual fear. The kid had been through an ordeal that afternoon.

Jimmy Haywood and his father James had accompanied Burke to the girl's home, where Everett still waited on the front porch with Harrison.

Their location wasn't ideal. Anyone could come by and take a shot at Everett, but Burke understood that that had been the best option. Harrison hadn't been introduced to the boy as his bodyguard, and it wouldn't have been appropriate for Harrison to accompany the boy inside.

Although why Everett himself wasn't in the house was something Burke would ask Harrison later.

"The girl didn't want her parents to know Everett had been in the house," Harrison murmured when Burke got to the front porch.

Harrison was direct, with a no-nonsense demeanor. He'd been an excellent cop, one of the few Burke had fully trusted when he was on the force.

"What's this about, Dad?" Everett blustered. "Who are all these people? Why was this guy"—he gestured to Harrison—"even here to get me away from that . . . whatever he was?"

Jimmy frowned. "It's your mother's fault."

"Oh." Everett folded his arms over his chest. "I should have known."

This kid was a piece of work. Although he didn't know what his mother had sacrificed for his safety. Didn't know what she'd been willing to sacrifice once again.

Burke pursed his lips to keep his words to himself, but the eldest Haywood had no such compunction.

"You watch your attitude, Everett," James snapped. "This is not your mother's fault. She hired these two men to protect you. Someone has threatened her, has tried to use you to force her to do something illegal. They threatened to hurt you if she didn't comply. She's protecting you."

Everett sneered. "No surprise that they asked her to do illegal shit. She's an ex-con."

Burke drew a breath. *Don't yell at the kid.* But he couldn't let Everett's words slide.

Harrison beat him to it. "Your grandfather said to watch your attitude. You don't know what you're talking about."

Everett lifted his chin. "And you do?"

Harrison remained calm. "Yeah. I do. Tell your father and grandfather what happened. And show some respect."

Everett's expression was sulky. "I'd just parked my car at the curb—"

"Why here, son?" Jimmy broke in. "Why are you here?"

Everett looked down. "I came to see Ariana."

"And she is?" Jimmy demanded.

"My girlfriend."

Jimmy clenched his jaw, his hands fisted at his sides. "You skipped school and came to a girl's house without her parents here?"

Everett looked up, his expression going from sulky to mocking. "Yeah, Dad. I have a life. And I don't need your permission."

Jimmy opened his mouth but James Senior gripped his arm. "Just let the boy tell you what happened, Jimmy. We can sort out the rest later."

Jimmy nodded, his anger still evident. "Speak."

"Woof," Everett drawled. "I'm not a damn dog."

Jimmy took a step forward, one of his fists lifting threateningly.

Harrison moved between Jimmy and Everett. "Just let him tell you what happened, sir. Then we can all get off this porch and go somewhere safer."

Jimmy directed his anger at Harrison. "Who the fucking hell are you?"

"My name is Harrison Banks. I'm a bodyguard. I work for that guy." He pointed to Burke. "I think you met him earlier today."

Jimmy glowered at Burke. "I told you I didn't want anyone guarding my kid."

Burke shoved his own anger aside. "If Harrison hadn't been here, Everett might be dead. Everett, can you tell us exactly what happened?"

Harrison moved aside, revealing an uncertain Everett. "You didn't want me to have a bodyguard, Dad? Why?"

"We can get into that," Burke promised. "But later. Tell your father what happened."

Everett suddenly looked very young. "I was getting out of my car. I guess I wasn't paying attention to the other cars because I never saw him following me." He pointed to Harrison. "I didn't see the SUV, either. It came up beside me." He schooled his expression to be stoic and brave, and Burke saw more resemblance to Naomi. "It pulled so close to my car that I was trapped. I didn't even have a chance to panic before this guy jumped out. He was dressed in black, with a ski mask and everything." He laughed nervously. "It was like a really bad movie."

"Did he touch you?" Jimmy asked, his voice not quite a snarl.

"He grabbed my arm and started to pull me into the van. And then this guy came." He thumbed at Harrison. "He grabbed the guy's arm and . . ." He looked at Harrison. "Dude. You have to teach me how to do that."

"Teach you to do *what*?" Jimmy snapped.

"I'm not even sure," Everett said, forgetting to be stoic for a moment. He sounded awestruck. "There was a *crack*, like bone. The guy immediately let me go and made this sound. Like a kicked dog." His eyes widened. "Not that I've ever kicked a dog."

"That's good, at least." Harrison turned to Jimmy. "I shoved Everett out of their path so that he could run, and then I grabbed the guy's ski mask and yanked it off. I saw his face. He was young, about twenty maybe. Latino. Five-ten, one seventy-five. Dark hair, brown eyes, and a tattoo of an eagle on his neck."

"You let them get away?" Jimmy demanded. "What the hell kind of bodyguard are you, anyway?"

The kind who saved your son's ass, Burke wanted to say, but bit the words back. What had Naomi seen in this man to begin with?

Harrison met Burke's gaze, ignoring Jimmy's accusation. "The SUV had to have been here waiting for Everett. I didn't see them on the way here from the high school. The driver was armed. Female. Young, or so she sounded. She had on dark glasses, a big hat, and a surgical mask. So I can't describe her face, but I'd remember her voice if I heard it again. She had a Bersa Thunder .380 with a suppressor. Aimed at my head and told me to let the guy go or she'd shoot me, then the boy. I let the guy go."

"Some fucking bodyguard," Jimmy grumbled again.

"Jimmy!" James's face was pale, but his eyes were livid. "This man saved your son's life. It's evident where Everett is getting his attitude. Thank the man, for God's sake."

Jimmy gave his father a dirty look before baring his teeth in a parody of a smile. "Thank you, Mr. Banks."

"You're welcome, Mr. Haywood. I didn't call the cops yet, Burke. I figured you'd want to do that. Maybe call André first."

"I will." Burke really liked Harrison. *And I really hate Jimmy Haywood.* "Did you get their license plate?"

"Yeah, and I already ran it. Stolen plates, which is what I'd figured."

"When did you do that?" Everett asked, looking intrigued in spite of himself.

"While we were sitting waiting for your father to come. I tossed a tracker in their car before they could shut the door. Antoine tracked the SUV to a few blocks from here, then the signal disappeared. They must have found the tracker and smashed it."

"Good try, though," Burke said. "And quick thinking."

"Why did you have a tracker?" Everett asked. "And where were you keeping it?"

Harrison regarded Everett evenly. "I always carry a few. You never know when you'll have to track a teenager who doesn't want to be guarded."

"Whatever." Everett's interest became a scowl once again. "I wouldn't have run." Then he sighed when Harrison continued to regard him. "Fine. I probably would have. But I don't think I will now."

"Good," Harrison said. "Your mother cared enough to try to save your hide. It would be rude to let the bad guys get you too easily."

At the mention of his mother, Everett rolled his eyes again. "Like she cares."

"She does," Burke said, managing to keep his tone calm when he really wanted to shake the brat. "Look, you should hear this from her, but I don't think you'd listen. Someone approached her on Friday demanding she deliver drugs for them in her employer's van. She said no and they threatened her with harm to you."

"If she does it, she'll go back to jail," Everett said, and Burke couldn't tell what the boy thought of that.

"I think that's the point," Burke said. "So if anyone tries to give you anything, don't take it. If it's contraband of any kind, you could go to jail and that would devastate her. She'd rather go back herself than see you hurt."

Everett said nothing, but he shrugged noncommittally, and Burke figured that was as good as he'd get. He turned to James. "Did you think about my proposal?"

"No," Jimmy snapped. He'd been in the back seat when Burke had suggested they hide Everett in his house in the Quarter and that James accompany them. "My son is not going with you."

"Yes," James said, ignoring his son. "I'll do that."

"I said *no*," Jimmy snarled. "Everett will come home with me."

"Going where?" Everett asked.

"I have a very secure house in the Quarter," Burke said. "You'd be safe there. Your grandfather would stay with you, as would Harrison."

And so would Naomi, but he wasn't going to mention that yet.

Everett frowned. "What about school?"

James put a hand on Everett's shoulder. "We'll tell them that we've had a family emergency and we'll get your assignments. It's almost time for spring break anyway."

"I'll miss the Mardi Gras parties," Everett said, true disappointment on his face. "Dammit."

"No, you won't, because you're coming home with me," Jimmy insisted.

Everett met his father's gaze. "And if they come back? If they get in the house? What about Tina and Joey? And McKenzie? If she gets scared, it could hurt the baby. You remember what happened last time she got agitated, back when Naomi got out. McKenzie was so upset that she nearly lost Tina."

Jimmy's insistence disappeared, but he said nothing.

That Everett called his mother by her first name was not lost on Burke, but the boy seemed to be getting through to his father, so he waited as the boy continued.

"Look, Dad, I get why you're mad. I'm mad, too. Naomi got herself in trouble and now I'm in danger, too. But I'm not so mad that I'm willing to put us all in danger. If I can stay with Grandpa in a house in the Quarter, why not? You can tell McKenzie that I'm staying with my friends so that I don't bother her."

"You don't bother her," Jimmy said.

Everett laughed bitterly. "Whatever. Mr. Broussard, I'll go. I need to pack a suitcase."

"I'll take him to his house to pack," Harrison said. "If your stepmother asks, I'm your friend's dad."

"She won't ask," Everett said with certainty. "She'll be glad to get rid of me."

Jimmy blinked. "Why do you say that?"

"Because McKenzie hates my guts. Maybe pay attention every once in a while."

Burke clapped his hands once, thinking about Naomi, Val, and the others still at the flower shop. They needed to get them to safety, too. "Okay. Let's get moving. James, will you go with Harrison and Everett?"

"Of course," James said. "Thanks, Burke."

"Part of the job," Burke said. "You good, Harrison?"

"As gold. I'll keep you up to date. And I've already arranged with Antoine to sit down with him to create a composite sketch of the guy in the van."

Burke *really* liked Harrison. "All right, then. I need to go take care of Naomi."

Everett's brows pulled down, his bad attitude returning. "Why?"

"Someone shot up the shop where she works," Burke said. "She's fine, but she can't stay there."

"She's coming to your house, too, isn't she?" Everett asked grimly.

Kid's too smart. "Big house. Four floors, including the attic. Lots of room to avoid her. But I won't let her get hurt, Everett. Just like I won't let you get hurt."

Everett looked like he'd protest, but James intervened. "Please, Ev. I can't lose you. Don't fight us on this. Please."

Everett huffed his displeasure. "I'm not talking to her."

"You don't have to," James said. "Thank you. I . . . I almost had a heart attack when I heard you'd been attacked."

So had Naomi, Burke thought.

"It'll be fine, Grandpa." Everett gave Burke a steely-eyed glare. "Go ahead. Go get her."

"Thank you for your approval," Burke said dryly. "Have Harrison text me with anything you want to eat. I'll put in an order for groceries."

Kenner, Louisiana
MONDAY, FEBRUARY 24, 4:05 P.M.

"Have you heard from Phin yet?" Naomi asked Molly Sutton, who'd arrived shortly after Phin had left with his wife and SodaPop. Molly looked completely different than she had before. The black wig was gone, revealing shiny blond hair pulled into a bun, and she was dressed professionally, in a white blouse, slacks, and a blazer that hid the gun at her hip.

Val and Sylvi were up front dealing with the two uniformed officers who remained on the property, waiting for forensics. Luckily Nora Langley and her astute partner Ferguson were long gone.

"Cora texted that SodaPop is fine," Molly said. "I think taking her to the clinic was more for Phin than for SodaPop. Phin just needed to hear it from SodaPop's vet. Cora says that Phin's coming back to help Sylvi with the deliveries. You're leaving soon. Burke will be here any minute to get you."

Naomi glanced at the refrigerator that was still filled with flowers that had to go out, grateful that Phin would make sure that Sylvi met her delivery obligations. "I was afraid the cops would hold our finished inventory while they investigated."

"I was a little surprised that they didn't, actually." Molly went back to watching the camera feed on her phone. "Oh. Well, now that makes sense."

Naomi leaned over to look at Molly's phone and was relieved to see that Burke Broussard had arrived. He was accompanied by a uniformed cop who was every bit as big as he was. The cop was a Black man with a shaved head. He looked familiar.

"Who's that?" Naomi asked.

"Captain André Holmes. He and Burke go way back. He's also Antoine's brother. You met Antoine this morning before you talked to Burke." She glanced at Naomi. "André tends to smooth our way. He's a good guy. You can trust him."

But why is he here? What does he want? Did Broussard ask him for help? She practiced deep breathing, trying to get her rapid pulse under control. "I heard good things about him . . . before."

Before her life turned upside down.

"Burke would never betray you," Molly said, clearly adept at reading the room. "If he asked André here, it's because he thinks André can help."

Naomi hoped that was true. And if it wasn't? If Holmes was here to take her away?

Then he does. You survived prison before. You'll survive again.

But she wasn't sure if that was true.

Nevertheless, she stood as the door opened and the two men entered. Broussard's gaze immediately found Naomi's, his shoulders relaxing a fraction.

Her shoulders relaxed as well and she couldn't deny that the man's sheer presence had a calming effect, despite the cop he'd brought with him.

"I'm okay," she said quietly. And she was. Or she would be.

"I know," Broussard said. "But this has been a day."

She laughed, surprising herself, but his statement was so understatedly true. "That it has. Where is my son?"

"On his way to my house with his grandfather and his bodyguard. I have good security, so you don't need to worry."

Naomi wondered where she'd be going after this, but was almost afraid to ask. She was hoping to go where Everett was, but that might be a big ask. And if Everett didn't want her there, he might run, putting himself in danger again.

She'd do anything to avoid that.

"Thank you. What about my ex?"

"Everett convinced him it would be better for Jimmy's wife and small children if he hides out elsewhere."

She smiled sadly. "My son is smart. I guess he's had to learn to be. Jimmy requires . . . handling."

"I noticed." Broussard gestured to the man beside him. "Do you know Captain Holmes?"

Holmes was watching her with an intensity that was disconcerting. He and Broussard went "way back." What if Holmes didn't believe her? What if he thought she'd somehow set in motion today's chain of events?

"I'm not here to judge you, ma'am," Holmes said, his voice deep and resonant. "I'm here because I heard about the shooting on the scanner and it's not the first time Sylvi's had problems at her shop. I thought I'd stop by and see how she was doing."

"There was another shooting here two years ago," Molly explained. "Poor Sylvi's front window was shot out then, too. Everyone was okay, but it's never easy to process events like this."

"No, it's not," Naomi agreed. *Poor Sylvi.* "I need to go somewhere else, Mr. Broussard. I've put Sylvi through enough."

Holmes frowned. "The way I understand it, this isn't your fault. Or is it?"

Naomi froze, suddenly unable to breathe. "No?" she choked out, but she didn't sound sure.

"André," Molly chided. "You know her history. You know where she's been. Don't scare her."

But Holmes didn't back down. "I'm protecting you all. I need to understand what's happening if I'm to keep you safe." He met Naomi's gaze directly. "That includes you, Miss Cranston."

She closed her eyes, weariness hitting her like a hard wave. "I didn't ask for this, Captain. I never asked for any of this. I didn't steal anything six years ago. I didn't steal anything now. I just want my son kept safe."

"So do I," Holmes said. "I went back and looked at the evidence against you. It was weak. Why didn't you defend yourself?"

She glanced at Broussard, and he gave her a nod of encouragement. Bolstered, she returned her attention to the cop. "I was threatened, sir."

"Please be more explicit. Threatened how?"

The question uttered in his authoritative tone of voice was like a trigger, dragging her back six years to a time when no one believed her except her mother. When every cop turned their back on her. When a judge said thirty years and she'd known that her life was over.

Her heart raced faster and she had to blink away the black dots that were rapidly becoming a dark curtain. Sheer terror overwhelmed her and once again she couldn't breathe.

"Naomi, sit down."

Burke Broussard's rumbly voice cut through her panic. His hand was on her back, gently urging her to sit. His other hand cupped her face, tipping her chin up so that she looked into his dark eyes.

"He's not here to arrest you. He's here to help you. But he's ornery and needs to hear your story from your mouth. Molly, can you get her a glass of water?"

A moment later, the glass of water was pressed into her hand, but she didn't think she could drink it. "I . . . can't," she managed. "I think I'd choke on it."

"Dammit, André," Broussard snapped. "I told you to be gentle."

"And I told you that I need to know what happened six years ago," Holmes snapped back.

"What happened," Broussard said with a fury that somehow made Naomi feel a little braver, a little more in control, "was that this officer right here, whose record was unblemished, who'd never even had a negative report in her file, was accused of stealing evidence. Evidence that Captain Cresswell had been stealing to sell for his own profit."

"Let her tell me that," Holmes said. "Miss Cranston?"

Naomi shuddered, so very cold. But Broussard's hand on her face was warm, his hand on her back steadying. "I don't know if Cresswell was stealing evidence. I only know that I didn't." And then the words were coming in a torrent, and she didn't think she could stop them if she tried. "I did not steal anything, but I couldn't prove it. I was a good cop. An *honest* cop. I gave twelve years of my life to the NOPD, but someone thought I'd make a good scapegoat. I was going to fight. I thought I would win, because"—she drew a deeper breath, feeling her lungs inflate—"because I was a *good cop.* I thought I'd be defended, that my union representative would help me. That someone would step up and say, 'Naomi did not do this.' But that never happened."

"What did happen?" Holmes asked.

"I got a visit from Detective Gaffney. At my home. He got in my face. He grabbed my hair." She'd tried so hard to block out that visit for so long, but now she welcomed the memory. Fury bubbled up and she glared at Captain Holmes. "He grabbed my breasts and told me all the things he'd like to do to me, because he 'owned' me now. He said that I'd be a 'good girl,' that I'd be quiet. That I'd let them convict me." She heard a sob and was startled to realize it had come from her own throat. "He said that he'd kill my son. That he'd send Everett to me in pieces. *In pieces*, Captain. He was going to torture my child. I wanted to believe that someone in the NOPD would help me, but I was on my own. I was a pariah, when I'd been respected before. It wasn't the job I wanted, truthfully, but that's how my career went, so I accepted it. I did my job and I did it fucking well. Until I got betrayed by the men and women who were supposed to have my back. Nobody did. Not the NOPD, not my attorney. Nobody was going to protect my son. Nobody but me."

She sobbed again, leaning into Broussard's hand, still cupping her cheek. His thumb was wiping her tears, but he didn't tell her to stop. Didn't tell her to calm down.

He was letting her speak and she was grateful.

"So I obeyed, Captain Holmes." She spat the words, not caring if she was respectful. Not caring if he sent her back. She was going to be heard. "I said nothing. My mother begged me to defend myself, but I couldn't. All I could see in my mind was my son, my baby, chopped into pieces. So I shut my mouth and hoped the judge would be lenient. Did you know I had a plea deal offered to me?"

"Yes," Holmes said, and, to her relief, he looked shaken.

Not as shaken as she felt, but it was something.

"Well, I didn't. My attorney didn't tell me. So I just hoped. And guess what? The judge was not lenient. He gave me thirty years. I served five. It was only my mother's belief in me—and the fact that you realized that Cresswell was a piece of shit and threw him in prison, too—that saved me. I was lucky, Captain Holmes. I was so damn *lucky*. Because nobody was there for me. Nobody helped me. Just my mother and my second attorney, who believed in checking all the boxes. It was the test she requested that set me free. Not NOPD. Not justice. Just blind, dumb luck." She exhaled, shuddering once again. "And that, Captain Holmes, is what happened."

There was silence in the room for a long, long moment.

Naomi closed her eyes, afraid of what was coming next. "I didn't ask Gaffney to approach me again. I was willing to turn myself in, to go back to prison if my son was kept safe. But these people here convinced me that they could help me, too. So if you're going to send me back, do it now." Her throat closed and she had to get her tears under control. "Because letting me hope for another miracle, for another stroke of blind, dumb luck, is too cruel."

"Okay," Holmes said on a sigh. "That's a lot."

"Yeah," Naomi snapped, opening her eyes to glare at him once more. "It was *a lot* every day for the *five years* I served of a sentence I didn't deserve. Whether you believe me or not."

"I believe you," Holmes said. "Thank you for telling me." He cleared his throat. "Did Detective Gaffney do more than grope you? Was his sexual assault . . . more involved?"

"Oh shit," Naomi breathed. "I didn't mean to say that out loud."

"Well, you did," Broussard said, his tone gruff. "I'm glad you did, even though I want to rip Gaffney's head clean off his neck."

"He didn't," she said quietly. "He would have, but my mother came home. I'd put my house on the market to pay for Mason Lord to defend me, so I was living with my mom. Gaffney ran out the back as she was coming in the front. She knew something had happened, but I wouldn't tell her. I couldn't. I was afraid they'd send her to me in pieces, too."

"Fucking hell," Holmes muttered. "I need to think on how to proceed."

She finally looked at him. "Proceed with what?"

"Gaffney. You're not the first woman who's filed a complaint against him. So far, nothing has stuck."

"I'm not going to file a formal complaint, Captain," she said firmly. No way in hell was she putting herself back in those crosshairs. Not ever again. "I just want to be left alone. I want my son safe. That's all."

"I understand. Thank you for telling me what happened. Burke, I'll see myself out." He paused in the doorway. "Phin's back. He's got plywood for the front window."

"Is SodaPop with him?" Burke asked.

"She is," Holmes confirmed.

"Good," Naomi murmured.

"Miss Cranston," Holmes said, "I understand that you want nothing to do with the NOPD, but I'm offering Burke my help in protecting you and your son. He just has to ask."

Naomi couldn't bring herself to thank the man. So she nodded once.

He left, closing the door quietly behind him.

Which was when Naomi realized she was leaning on Burke Broussard, her head now on his broad chest, his heart pounding hard and fast against her cheek.

Embarrassed, she pulled away. "I'm sorry. I didn't mean to lean like that."

He gently stroked his palm over her hair, and she could feel the tremble in his hand. "It's okay. You were somethin' else."

She slumped. "I'm sorry."

"Don't be. I think you had a lot of anger to let out. I'm . . . proud of you."

She looked up at him, startled. But he was sincere. "Thank you," she managed to say. Then she gathered her thoughts. "Will I be able to see Everett at some point?"

"He's staying in my house. I told him there was a lot of room for him to avoid you if he felt like he had to, but you'll be under the same roof."

"Thank you."

It's a chance, she thought, buoyed just a little.

It was adrenaline, she knew. She'd crash soon. But she'd see her son and that gave her hope.

6

The Central Business District, New Orleans, Louisiana
MONDAY, FEBRUARY 24, 4:15 P.M.

AT LEAST GAFFNEY had the decency to look ashamed when he took one of the visitor chairs in front of the desk.

He hoped the detective had a good explanation, because the afternoon had gone to shit. "Well?"

"We didn't get the kid," Gaffney said.

"You sent Freddie and Pablo to get the kid, even though I told you to handle it yourself."

Luckily Freddie had more sense than Gaffney did. As soon as the op had failed, she'd called him with the news. He was still furious.

Gaffney narrowed his eyes. "Let's get two things clear. First, I'm not your employee. I'm your partner. Just like Cresswell was. Second, I'm not getting caught. That's not negotiable. I figured the kid would have a bodyguard and I didn't want to be seen by him if shit went south—just like it did. The bodyguard pulled Pablo's mask off. We're going to have to reassign him somewhere out of town, because his face was exposed. I told Freddie to keep watch for Broussard's people, but that bodyguard took them by surprise."

First, Gaffney was *not* his partner.

Second, not getting caught was actually a good argument, because if Gaffney ever did get caught, he'd sing like a fucking bird.

So he inclined his head, acknowledging Gaffney's point. "Freddie said that the bodyguard broke Pablo's arm."

Gaffney grimaced. "It's a bad break. He'll be able to return to work, but not until after Mardi Gras."

"That's a shame." Because Pablo wouldn't be going back to work at all. That Broussard's man had seen the kid's face was too damning. So Pablo had already been dealt with. At least Freddie knew how to take direction, unlike Gaffney.

As much as he disliked murder, there were times when it was necessary.

But now they'd have to find someone else to manage the inventory they'd brought into the city for Mardi Gras. Inventory he'd procured with his own money.

He held Gaffney's gaze. "Freddie said that she didn't recognize the bodyguard. Find out who this guy is. Find out about every person Broussard has guarding Naomi Cranston and her son. I don't want to be surprised again."

"What about the flower shop?" Gaffney asked accusingly. "The shooting's all over the police scanners. What the fuck happened there?"

He wanted to rub his temples, because he'd had a pounding headache ever since that op had gone south. "The delivery van was alarmed."

Gaffney frowned. "It wasn't on Friday when I talked to Naomi. I checked this morning, too. And before you ask, no cameras caught my face."

"The alarm must have been installed at some point today. They did a delivery run midmorning." Which he knew because he'd had Wayne Stanley watching the shop all morning. "Broussard must have had it done then."

Gaffney's frown deepened. "Did you tell your men to fire at the window? Because that was a damn mistake."

"No." And he was still furious that they'd done so. "I told them to hide the envelope inside the van where it wouldn't be easily seen. And if, for whatever reason, they were unsuccessful, to make sure that the Cranston woman knew they'd been there. I thought they understood that I meant something subtle, like leaving a damn note. But they got in their mind that a show of force was needed."

Gaffney shook his head. "Now NOPD is involved. This has become a nightmare."

"You're right." On the nightmare, at least. But Gaffney was wrong about NOPD only getting involved because there was a shooting. As soon as Broussard had accepted the case, André Holmes would have been informed. The two were best friends.

"Who did you send to the shop?" Gaffney asked.

"Shep and Blount."

Gaffney winced. "Shep's been using. Swore he stopped, but I don't believe him. He's been twitchy every time I've talked to him recently."

"And you didn't think to tell me this?"

"I figured you knew. He's *your* guy, after all."

"He's not my guy. He's Ortiz's guy."

Gaffney actually rolled his eyes, the prick. "Same thing. It wasn't my idea to include the STs in our operation. That was on you and Cresswell."

That was true. Several years ago, he and Cresswell had decided that they needed the distribution resources of the local gang, so they'd entered into an agreement with Desi Ortiz, the leader of the Saints—or the STs, as they were more widely known. He and Cresswell used the gang's dealers to distribute what they stole from the evidence room in return for police protection by Cresswell's dirty cops. Any dealers who were caught were usually released with a slap on the wrist or never charged at all. That kept the operation running smoothly and allowed them to sell a lot more product than they'd been able to do before the alliance. The gang took their cut, of course, but overall, much more money began rolling in.

Things had normally gone smoothly with Ortiz's people.

Today was a huge exception. But he wasn't going to confront Ortiz. The man was unstable on a good day.

"What are we going to do about Naomi Cranston?"

"We can't use her as our fall guy now," Gaffney said.

Gaffney had believed all along that Naomi Cranston was a simple fall guy. That if they got caught in possession of their newest inventory, Naomi would be exposed as the ringleader. In truth, the woman represented a clear threat.

To me. She needed to go back to prison, but that was looking less likely now.

The only other alternative was removing her permanently.

"No, she's useless as our fall guy now," he agreed, "so stop skimming off the drug busts for now. We don't need any undue attention from the NOPD. We've got enough inventory to supply our customers through Mardi Gras, and if we need more, we can get it elsewhere."

They'd gone through a fair portion of their stash during the recent Super Bowl weekend—the game had been played in New Orleans. But they were on track with sufficient Mardi Gras quantities. They'd be fine.

Gaffney frowned. "Lower profit margins, though."

"Yes." Because the product they'd been stealing from police drug busts was free. Of course that would provide the best profit margin. "But I'd rather lose a little money than leave ourselves open to investigation if anything goes wrong. I'm betting Broussard has already started looking into who was involved in Naomi's arrest six years ago. If we leave any loose ends, Broussard will yank on them."

"He doesn't know anything about the new business, though."

"No, he doesn't. And he'd better not find out."

Gaffney raised his hands. "*My* guys didn't shoot up a flower shop today. *My* guys didn't get the NOPD involved. He's not going to find out through me."

Little shit. But Gaffney would no longer be a problem once Mardi Gras was over. There were plenty of cops like Gaffney, plenty who were willing to play on the dark side in order to make some extra cash. Plenty who'd switch out the drugs they'd confiscated for worthless powder.

Plenty of cops who'd look the other way.

He wasn't worried about replacing Gaffney.

He was, however, worried about his newest enterprise, because he'd sunk a hell of a lot of his own money into acquiring and maintaining the inventory.

People were a lot more trouble to manage than guns and drugs. He had to keep them alive and able to function. Well, the addicts were easy. He just had to withhold their next high for long enough to make them beg to work. With the others, threats and beatings were the tools of choice.

He was fine with threats and beatings. He was fine with using coke as the proverbial carrot on the stick.

He was *not* fine with Burke Broussard getting curious.

"We need to distract Broussard and his people," he said, Wayne

Stanley having put plan B into action earlier that afternoon. "We've already shown we're willing to make good on our threat to take Naomi's son. If we threaten the children belonging to him and his people, they'll be too busy protecting them to come looking for us, at least for the next week." When the city would be filled with revelers looking for drugs and sex, commodities he was only too happy to provide. "Once we get through Mardi Gras, we'll find a new city to house our inventory and Broussard's investigation will no longer matter."

Gaffney grinned. "I like it. Where do we start?"

The Quarter, New Orleans, Louisiana
MONDAY, FEBRUARY 24, 5:05 P.M.

Naomi's eyes widened as Broussard pulled up to a mansion on one of the streets on the edge of the Quarter. "You live *here*?"

It was a perfect example of iconic French Quarter architecture—curving wrought-iron balconies, complete with hanging plants. It was three stories tall with a smaller fourth story that housed the attic.

It was stunningly beautiful.

"I do. It was my uncle's. He left it to me when he passed."

"Oh. It's . . . wow."

He gazed up at his home with affection as he clicked a button on his phone and the gate across the driveway swung open. "That's what I said the first time I saw it."

"How long have you lived here?"

He pulled his pickup truck into one of the three parking spaces between the house and a ten-foot garden wall. "Since I was thirteen. My father had died."

"I'm sorry."

"I wasn't. He was abusive. Big man. Big fists. Beat my mother. And me. A lot." He gave his shoulders a shake as if shrugging off the memories. "Mama hadn't told her brother Larry about my father's abuse because she was ashamed. I finally went to Larry for help when my father knocked her unconscious. I thought he'd killed her, to be honest. Larry took me home in his rusty old truck. Mama was awake but in bad shape. I packed our belongings into Larry's truck while he threatened my father with dire consequences if he followed us."

His asking if Jimmy had hit her made a lot more sense now. He'd grown up with domestic violence and recognized the tendency in her ex. "Dire? Like . . . death?"

"Among other things," Broussard drawled, going heavy on the Cajun. "I think death might have been preferable to some of Larry's threats. He was a very creative man. Made his fortune by painting murals in his best friend's office lobby in exchange for shares of the company. When the company went public, they all became rich. Larry started his own business and became even richer. He always loved the Quarter, and when this house went on the market, he jumped on it. Brought Mama and me here in that rusty old truck and my life was forever changed."

"Um . . ." She hesitated, then blurted it out because it seemed important to know. "How did your father die?"

He chuckled. "The look on your face. No, we didn't kill my father—me or Larry. Although I don't think anyone would have blamed us if we had. After Larry took us away, my father drank himself into a stupor. Stumbled face-first into the bayou and drowned. The gators had themselves a feast that night. We had ironclad alibis, thankfully. His death was ruled an accident."

"Mercy," she breathed, grimacing at the mental picture. It was, however, a fitting end for a man who'd terrorized his family.

Broussard shrugged again. "He was an awful man. Beat my mother nearly every day. She mourned him for a while, but I never did. I was just relieved that he could never hurt us again. Now, enough of my history. Come on in. I'll give you the nickel tour before I go meet your first attorney."

He grabbed a bicycle that had been leaning against an outer wall. It was the bike she'd seen in his office that morning. He brought it inside through a side door into what was a very fancy mudroom.

He opened another door and she found herself in a grand foyer with gleaming hardwood floors and a staircase that curved elegantly.

"The main livin' room," he said, pointing to two sofas, two love seats, several single chairs, what appeared to be an antique settee, and—

She laughed. "Is that your chair?" she asked, pointing to the brown BarcaLounger, which was held together with duct tape. A lot of duct tape.

He grinned down at her. "How'd you know?"

"It's the only thing that doesn't belong. I figured if you'd wanted it gone, it'd be gone."

Someone coughed to hide a laugh. Val Sorensen stood at the front window, watching the street. "She's right, Burke."

"She is, indeed. Miss Cranston, the dining room."

The table looked like it would seat twenty people. "Do you ever use it?"

"Yes, ma'am. For my team and their families. Just about everyone's got a partner now and Val's got two boys, her adopted son and her stepson with her husband Kaj. Molly's sister is married to Lucien and they've got a little girl—Harper."

"And Phin and his wife are expecting."

His cheek dimpled. "They are. I'm going to have another godson."

"What about Antoine?"

Broussard sighed. "If he's got someone, he doesn't say."

She noticed that he hadn't mentioned his own partner and she hoped that meant he didn't have one. It was a silly thought, though. She liked Broussard a lot and he'd held her so tenderly when she'd had the panic attack in the flower shop, but she didn't belong in a place like this. With a man like him.

She refocused on his house. "How many bedrooms?"

"Ten. My uncle was hoping that my mama would remarry and fill this house with more kids."

His tone had abruptly saddened. "She didn't?"

"No. They died. Both my mama and my uncle. Plane crash. I was only eighteen."

There was more to that story, but he looked so sad that she didn't press. And then her mind was wiped blank when she saw the kitchen.

"Oh my goodness. It's gorgeous."

"My mama designed the initial remodel. Phin did an update a few years ago."

"It's incredible. He's talented."

"He is. Molly's husband Gabe comes over to cook every now and again. He's a chef. Says it's a good kitchen, and he'd know."

The kitchen had been fully modernized. "Do you cook?"

"Not really. Do you?" he asked hopefully.

She chuckled. "I make a mean macaroni and cheese from a box."

"Me too," he said. "I have a housekeeper come in once a week. She makes meals and puts them in the freezer. But this is the Quarter, so there's always somethin' delicious to eat."

He led her up the stairs. "My study and a few of the bedrooms are on the second floor. The rest of the bedrooms are up on the third."

She marveled at the sheer space. "How big is this place?"

"Just shy of ten thousand square feet. That's the bedroom for when Joy visits," he said, pointing to a door on his right. "It's ADA accessible and I had a lift installed for her."

Joy, his admin who used a wheelchair. The woman who'd interceded on Naomi's behalf that morning. "She's very kind." And so was he.

"One of my best friends. I'm blessed."

He seemed prouder of his friends than his house, and Naomi thought that said a lot. "No man is a failure who has friends."

He stopped to study her. "Clarence from *It's a Wonderful Life*?"

"Yes," she said, pleased that he got the reference. "My go-to Christmas movie since I was a kid."

"Mine too," he said softly. "Come on."

He led her up another flight of stairs to the third floor, where the bedrooms were smaller but beautifully decorated. "Pick one."

"Where is Everett staying?"

Broussard pointed to the door at the end of the hall, where a man stood sentry. "That one. That's Harrison Banks, Everett's bodyguard."

Naomi approached the man, her hand outstretched. "Thank you for saving my son today."

Harrison gave her a gruff nod. "My job, ma'am. He's a . . . well, a teenager, isn't he?"

"He is." She'd missed a full third of Everett's life. "I'm sorry if he's rude. I'm not in the greatest position to address it."

"I understand. Your mama seems to know how to keep him in line, though."

"My mama? How do—"

"Naomi."

Naomi turned to see her mother standing in one of the bedroom doorways. "Mom? What are you doing here?" James came to stand behind her and Naomi could only blink. "James?"

"We weren't doing anything," James said defensively, sounding like a teenager himself.

Broussard chuckled but said nothing.

"I'm glad you're here, Mom, but . . . how?"

"I asked Harrison to pick her up," James said. "I thought you might need her after the day you've had."

Naomi opened her arms, and for a moment she and Ruthanne held on to each other. Then she took her mother's hand. "Mr. Broussard, this is my mother, Ruthanne Cranston."

"Pleasure, ma'am," he said.

"Thank you, Mr. Broussard. I won't stay long. I just wanted to see my baby girl. You have a beautiful home."

"You're welcome to stay as long as you like. Now, I need to change my clothes. I'm meeting Mason Lord for dinner."

"Thank you so much for everything," Naomi said.

Broussard just dipped his head. "My room is downstairs on the left. If any of y'all need anything, just ask."

Naomi turned back to her mother. "Have you talked to Everett?"

"A little. He's determined to avoid you," she added sadly.

"But he's here. He's safe."

"We'll keep it that way," Harrison said.

Naomi could breathe again. "Then that's enough."

The Quarter, New Orleans, Louisiana

MONDAY, FEBRUARY 24, 5:45 P.M.

Lucien buckled himself into the passenger seat of the firm's SUV, his expression miserable. "I'm sorry, Burke."

"Not me you should be apologizin' to."

Lucien shifted his gaze to Burke's house, which now held five more people, including Harrison Banks. Naomi and her son had been given rooms, as had Everett's grandfather. The presence of Naomi's mother had been a surprise, but a pleasant one. She seemed as kind as her daughter.

Burke didn't believe Ruthanne and James were really "just friends."

Sylvi had decided to stay with Phin and Cora since she and Phin would be out most of the evening delivering flowers.

Val and Harrison were on guard duty, so Burke and Lucien were heading out to interview Naomi's first defense attorney.

"I will apologize to Miss Cranston," Lucien said. "I needed to be sure she was legit. You never accept a story at face value like you did hers. I couldn't figure out what her angle was."

Burke pulled out of his driveway into the busy street. The Quarter was always crowded, but this week and next would be insane with tourists.

"She's the terrified mother of a threatened teenager? You could have kept your distrust to yourself and treated her like any other client, but you didn't do that. You let her know you didn't believe her, and that's not like you, Lucien. What's going on?"

Lucien sighed. "Chelsea hasn't been sleeping and neither have I. Her former in-laws are trying to get custody of Harper. They're saying that Chelsea isn't providing a safe environment because of me and Molly, that our profession puts Harper in danger."

"That's fucking stupid."

Molly's sister Chelsea was a damn good mother. Yes, when Molly had come to work for him, Harper had been a traumatized little girl. Molly, her sister, and her niece had left North Carolina after they'd learned that Chelsea's ex-husband was sexually abusing Harper. He'd attacked Chelsea and Molly, and Molly had killed him.

But after years of therapy, Harper was finally becoming emotionally stable. Burke hoped that the trouble her paternal grandparents were causing wouldn't set her recovery back.

"We all know it's stupid. We've hired a lawyer to help us. But Harper is afraid to leave the house again. She's afraid her grandparents will try to abduct her."

"Not gonna happen," Burke said with a growl.

"Well, yeah. But when I saw that Naomi had fought for custody, I thought that maybe this was some kind of elaborate trick to get full custody of Everett."

"But Naomi was willing to give up custody of her son to keep him safe," Burke said, seeing Lucien's point, but still confused.

"So she said. But what mother willingly gives up custody?"

"The terrified mother of a threatened teenager," Burke said, repeating himself.

Lucien sighed again. "I can't believe Mason Lord was in on a wrongful conviction—any wrongful conviction. We've been friends for years."

"Let's get through this conversation with Lord and see what's what. And once we've sorted out Naomi Cranston, we'll find a way to deal with Chelsea's former in-laws. Nobody's taking Harper away from us."

"Thanks, Burke. And I am sorry. I let my personal situation get in the way of doing my job."

"You did. Just don't let it happen again, okay?"

"I won't."

"Good." And that was all Burke planned to say on the subject. Naomi was safe in his house, as was Everett. Harrison and Val would stay with them until Molly relieved them later tonight.

And of course Burke would be there, too, it being his house and all.

You'd probably volunteer for guard duty even if she was staying somewhere else.

There was something about Naomi Cranston that made his already heightened protective instinct rocket to the damn moon.

She'd been amazing, telling her story to André.

Naomi's story was all too common—both the threat to her son if she didn't comply with Gaffney's orders and the unwanted sexual advances the bastard had made.

Burke really did want to rip the man's head off his neck.

André had been trying to get the goods on Gaffney for a long time. Maybe, once Naomi felt safe again, she'd be willing to press charges.

But he wouldn't push her.

"Why are you grinding your teeth?" Lucien asked warily.

"Not because of you." He told Lucien what Naomi had shared with André.

"Now I feel even worse," Lucien said.

Lucien's guilt wasn't going to help anyone, especially not Naomi. "Tell me about Mason Lord."

"Good guy. Family man. His wife's a schoolteacher and they have three kids. Two girls and a boy. He'd already been with the prosecutor's office for two years when I got hired. He was my mentor. He and Brittney had me over to supper at least once a week in those days. Now we get together once a month or so. His kids call me Uncle Luke."

Burke winced in sympathy. "I can see how you'd be unwilling to believe Naomi's supposition. What will you do if she was right?"

"I don't know. I guess I'm still hoping she's mistaken and that Mason just made a mistake. We both worked long hours when we were with the prosecutor's office. Once he jumped to defense, he had more time. Or so I thought. He's certainly doing better financially since he became a defense attorney."

"Where are we meeting him?"

Lucien cleared his throat. "Broussard's."

Burke laughed. "You're shitting me." The restaurant that shared Burke's surname had nothing to do with his family, but Burke dined there often because why not? Their bread pudding was to die for.

"It's where we meet up for dinner when the wives are off doing their thing. Kind of an inside joke since I started working for you. We had a dinner all set up for tonight already, so I just ran with that."

"Does he know why we're meeting with him?"

"No. I figured I needed to see his face when I asked him. He knows you're coming, though. I told him we needed his help with a case."

"He's going to be angry with you. Either way this flies."

"I know. I'm dreading this."

Burke didn't know what to say, so he drove through the Quarter in silence.

7

The Quarter, New Orleans, Louisiana
MONDAY, FEBRUARY 24, 6:05 P.M.

IT'S NICE TO finally meet you," Mason Lord told Burke when the three of them sat down to dinner.

"Same," Burke said, not even bothering to look at the menu. He knew exactly what he'd order—the grilled pork chop would warm up nicely if this dinner went to shit, as he figured it would. He'd just take the meal to go.

They placed their orders and then Mason folded his hands in front of him. "How can I help you?"

Burke glanced at Lucien, who wore a tortured expression.

Okay, looks like I'm up at bat. "We took on a new client today. Someone you defended six years ago."

Mason frowned. "I can't talk to you about my clients' cases. You know that."

"I'm hoping you'll make an exception," Burke said honestly. "Naomi Cranston."

Mason sat back in his chair, casting an accusing look at Lucien. "Luke? What's this about?"

Lucien drew a breath. "She came to us today for protection. For her son."

"Okay," Mason said warily. "And?"

"You're aware that she was released from prison," Lucien said. "That her conviction was overturned."

Mason's jaw tightened. "I'm aware."

Lucien squared his shoulders and met his friend's gaze. "She didn't get a fair trial the first time around, Mason."

Mason's chin lifted. "I represented her to the best of my ability with the facts in evidence."

Lucien looked sick. "She says she was unaware she'd been offered a plea bargain by the DA."

"She's lying," Mason said flatly. "She lied six years ago. It was only luck that got her out of prison. A goddamn technicality."

Lucien pursed his lips. "You didn't ask to have the drugs tested. The ones she was found with."

Mason leveled Lucien with a furious glare. "I did request it. The test results must have gotten lost."

"Mason, I—"

"You what, Luke?" Mason interrupted loudly, then lowered his voice when other diners turned to look at them. "You believe that liar over me? She stole evidence. She never even testified in her own defense."

Burke's chest hurt, watching Lucien try to talk to his friend. "Look, Mr. Lord, Lucien didn't want to bring you into this. He's done so on my request."

"He could have said no," Mason said acidly.

"You paid off your mortgage on your old house six years ago," Lucien said quietly. "I remember when we had the celebration. It wasn't too long after Miss Cranston was found guilty and sentenced to thirty years in prison."

Mason was clearly struggling to hold his temper. "Are you suggesting I took a bribe, Luke?"

Lucien had gone very still. "Did you?"

"Fuck you," Mason snapped, slapping his napkin onto the table. "I don't have to stay and listen to this."

"You moved your kids from the public school to a private school that same year," Lucien said. "Hefty tuition fees. Brittney said you got a bonus when you joined the firm."

Burke might have missed the fear that flickered in Mason's eyes if he hadn't been watching so closely. But the fear was real.

"When did you talk to Brittney?"

"Today. After I left Miss Cranston's place of employ. Detective Gaffney confronted her on Friday, Mason. Wanted her to run drugs for him. We think this is a way to get her sent back to prison. He said she wasn't supposed to get out. Made it sound personal."

"You talked to Brittney about this?"

"Only about how you got the kids into that school. I told her that we were looking for a more secure school for Harper. And we are. She said you got the bonus."

"Because I did. Because I earned it."

Lucien shook his head sadly. "You'd only been with the firm for a few months at that time. I called your firm. Asked if they gave out bonuses to the new attorneys. They said that their attorneys weren't eligible for bonuses until they'd been there for at least two years."

"That may be the policy now. It wasn't then."

He was lying. Burke could tell. "Sir, did they threaten your family?

If they did, we need to know. We're not going to report you, but we need to know what happened with Naomi Cranston's case."

"No, they did not threaten my family," Mason said, but his discomfort was palpable. He rose, tossing cash onto the table for his meal. "Luke, don't come over anymore. I'll make your excuses to Brittney."

"They tried to kidnap Naomi's son today," Burke said as Mason walked by him. "If they threatened your family, they may do so again."

Mason's eyes flashed with rage. "If my kids get hurt because of you, I will come after you, Broussard. You'll wish you'd never been born."

"Tell them to watch out for a black SUV, tinted windows."

Mason went dangerously pale. "If my kids are sucked into this, I will kill you," he whispered so that only Burke and Lucien could hear.

"Mason," Lucien said, heartbreak in his voice. "How could you?"

"And if they'd threatened Harper? What would *you* have done, *Saint Luke*?"

The venom in Mason's tone made Lucien flinch.

Burke wanted to flinch, too, but he didn't. "What did they threaten to do? Send your children to you in pieces?"

Shock pushed Mason's rage aside. He swayed on his feet before grabbing the back of the chair he'd vacated.

"They did," Burke concluded. "I'm sorry that your children were threatened. They threatened Naomi Cranston with the same thing. That's why she didn't speak in her own defense six years ago. But she hired us to protect him today. His bodyguard was the person who stopped the attempted kidnapping just a few hours ago."

"What are you going to do?" Mason asked, his fingers digging into the chair.

"About your malfeasance in the case of Naomi Cranston?" Burke asked. "Nothing. We only met with you because Lucien was sure Naomi was lying. He didn't think you could have been complicit in her unfair trial. Now, at least, he'll be able to work on her case with an open mind. So thank you for that. Keep watch on your kids."

Mason hesitated. "Luke. Please don't tell Brittney."

Lucien couldn't have looked more devastated. "That's what you're worried about? That Brittney will find out? You don't care that an innocent woman spent five years in prison? Dammit, Mason. I just—" He stopped when his phone began to buzz, his face going as sheet-white as Mason's. "It's Chelsea. She just texted me to pick up. It's an emergency."

Mason Lord stood frozen, watching as Lucien answered.

"Chels? What's wrong?" He listened and his gaze flew to Burke's, terrified. "She says that a black SUV drove up behind Harper when they were coming out of a diner in Mid-City. Someone opened the back door and tried to grab her. A bystander stopped it." He returned to his call. "Where are you now? . . . Okay, that's good. I'll be there as soon as I can." He ended the call. "They ran back inside the diner and called 911."

Burke had already risen and was adding cash for his and Lucien's dinners to the money Mason had left behind. "It might be her former in-laws. It might have nothing to do with this case. Let's go."

But then his phone buzzed, a call from Val, accompanied by a text.

911.

So Burke answered, his stomach roiling. "Val? What's wrong?"

"Jace," she said, choking on her son's name. She sounded frantic. "He almost got grabbed by that fucking black SUV, Burke. They tried to drag him into it, but he fought them off."

"When was this? Where is he now?"

"He was coming out of the grocery store near our house about a half hour ago. He ran back inside the store as soon as he got free and called me. I called 911. I'm almost to him now. He's so scared." Her voice broke on a sob. "Dammit, Burke. I can't have him hurt because of me."

Burke's mind was spinning, his heart racing way too fast. Jace was seventeen now and well over six feet tall. Thank the Lord he'd had enough strength to fight them off. "They tried to grab Harper just now, coming out of a diner in Mid-City."

"Oh my God," Val gasped. "They're going after our kids. I need to tell Kaj to keep Elijah with him."

Kaj was the prosecutor for Orleans Parish. Elijah was his twelve-year-old son.

"Call Kaj now. I'm going with Lucien to get Chelsea and Harper, then I'll be by to get you and Jace. Everyone's coming to my house so we can regroup."

"Okay. I have to go. I just got here and the cops are here."

"Good. I'll be there as soon as I can." Burke ended the call and looked at Mason. "Watch your kids, Mr. Lord. These guys mean business, and if they think you've told us anything, your kids could also be at risk."

"Fuck you all," Mason whispered harshly. "They have no business touching my children. They are innocent."

Lucien rounded the table and grabbed Mason's shirt, lifting him onto his toes and giving him a hard shake. "So is Harper, you selfish prick. So is Jace. So is Elijah. *They're children.*"

"Gentlemen." A man in a black suit approached them. "Please take your argument outside."

Lucien released Mason with a shove. "Yeah. We're leaving. Mason, if you don't tell Brittney about the danger to your kids, I will." Then he walked away without looking back.

Burke pinned Mason with an icy look. "Why didn't you report the threat six years ago, Mr. Lord?"

Mason's shoulders slumped. "Who was I going to report it to? The cops? They *were* the cops."

"Yeah, that's what Naomi said, too. But she was on trial, basically alone. You were a respected former prosecutor. If you'd stood up six years ago, we might not be here right now."

And, Burke thought guiltily, *if I'd gone public six years ago, I might have stopped them, too.*

Burke followed the way Lucien had gone, leaving Mason Lord to deal with his conscience alone, because he had another call to make.

Someone was threatening their children. It was mind-boggling but, in a way, it made a sick sort of sense. Targeting their children was the best way to put Burke's people off their game.

Burke had no kids, but Gaffney had once threatened his godsons. He hated to worry Kaleb and Juliette, but better safe than sorry. They'd want to know about any possible threat to their children.

Dreading the call, he took out his cell phone as he followed Lucien to the truck.

The Quarter, New Orleans, Louisiana
MONDAY, FEBRUARY 24, 6:20 P.M.

"I heard loud voices. What's happening?"

Naomi spun from Burke Broussard's kitchen sink to see Everett hesitating in the doorway.

She'd been talking—more loudly than she'd thought, apparently—with James Haywood and her mother, who were sitting suspiciously close together.

That the two had become fast friends while she was in prison was a topic for a different day, because they'd just received a barrage of calls and texts, tersely telling them to stay in Broussard's house. Harrison was here to guard Everett, and Molly Sutton, who'd come to relieve Val, had just gotten a phone call that had shaken her soundly.

Which was understandable.

"There were attempts to kidnap two more kids," Naomi said, trying not to bend under the guilt that was threatening to crush her. "Val's son and Lucien's daughter. The girl is also Molly's niece."

Molly was in Broussard's living room, still on the phone with her sister. While Harper was physically okay, Naomi knew that Molly really wanted to be with her family.

But Broussard was handling things. Everyone, it seemed, would be coming here.

Everett's hesitation became accusation. "They're coming after the investigators' kids . . . why?"

"I don't know. I only know what they wanted to force me into doing."

Behind her, her mother and James went still. It was like everyone was holding their breath, waiting to see how Everett would respond.

Naomi hadn't expected to see her son. He'd holed himself away in his borrowed bedroom so that he didn't have to talk to her.

But he'd obviously heard them talking. Her voice had pitched higher in panic when she'd realized that other people's children were also being targeted. And then James and her mother had shouted at her to stop being stupid when she'd declared that she should leave, that she was putting everyone in danger with her presence.

At least he'd come down to check. That had to count for something, but she wasn't sure what.

"They don't want Burke's people to haul their drugs," Everett stated flatly. "They couldn't expect they'd cooperate. None of *them* have prison records."

"Everett," James snapped.

Naomi held up a hand. "He's right, James. I have been to prison. There might be an expectation that I'd be willing to break the law again—if they thought I'd broken it in the first place. But *they* don't think that, because *they* set me up six years ago. Everett might not believe me, but that doesn't change the fact that I did not steal anything. Not six years ago. Not ever."

Everett snorted quietly. "I'm going back to my room."

"Wait." Naomi's mother came to her feet. "Everett, I need to tell you something."

"Mom." Naomi switched on the kettle. "You're not going to change his mind."

James hadn't moved from where he sat, but he looked angry as well. "Sit down, son."

Everett smirked, looking so much like Jimmy in that moment. "No."

"Do what your grandfather says, Everett," a deep voice growled. It was Harrison Banks, the man who'd kept her son safe. He lurked behind Everett in the hallway, and that gave Naomi some measure of peace, knowing that the man wasn't letting her son out of his sight. "You're being disrespectful."

"They're going to tell me that Naomi is innocent," Everett said, his tone mocking. "That she went to prison to keep me safe. That I should be grateful. That I should open my arms and give her a big hug. That about right, Grandpa?"

"All but the hug, yes," James said. "I won't ask you to hug anyone you don't want to. But your grandmother says that she wants to talk, so sit your ass down."

Everett rolled his eyes and took a chair at Broussard's kitchen table. "What?"

Ruthanne sank into her seat beside James and folded her hands on the table. "There are a few things you don't know." She cast an anxious glance at Naomi, then James. "Things I haven't told anyone. And I probably should have."

James stared at her. "What?"

"I also got a visit from Detective Gaffney." Ruthanne's gaze dropped to her hands when both Naomi and James gasped aloud.

"What the hell, Mom?" Naomi demanded. "When?"

"When I hired Shavon."

Shavon Campbell, the attorney who'd managed to get Naomi's conviction overturned.

Ruthanne had Everett's attention. "Gaffney was waiting for me at my car when I came off my shift at the hospital. He cautioned me not to proceed with my efforts."

"What did he threaten you with?" James asked, rage bubbling through every word. "'What did he say, exactly?"

"That it wouldn't be healthy for Naomi if I pushed to have her conviction appealed. Or healthy for me." Ruthanne swallowed. "I almost called it off, but I couldn't stand the thought of her being in that awful place for even one more day. I signed Shavon's contract the next day."

"And then what happened?" Everett asked, his tone still suspicious.

"A week later my brakes failed as I drove home."

James sucked in a breath and Naomi's knees wobbled. Carefully she lowered herself into one of Broussard's kitchen chairs.

"Mom." That her mother might have been killed made her chest tight with panic.

Ruthanne took Naomi's hand, squeezing gently. "I was okay. I wasn't going too fast and I was able to get the car to the curb. Scraped my tires up but good and dented my front bumper when I hit a tree, but I was able to stop."

"And you have proof of this?" Everett asked, stony-faced.

James opened his mouth, but Naomi's own fury had already exploded. "You can say what you want about me, but you will *not* question your grandmother's word." She was satisfied when shame flickered in Everett's eyes.

"I apologize, Grandma," the boy said stiffly.

"As you should," James muttered, then turned to Ruthanne. "What did the mechanic say?"

"That my brake line was frayed. He thought it was deliberate, but he couldn't be certain. He took photos of the damage, in case I wanted to file a police report."

"And did you?" James asked.

"No. Because it was then that I realized why my daughter hadn't said a word in her own defense during her trial. I figured she'd been threatened, same as me. So I didn't report it. I was okay, but she couldn't get away if someone tried to hurt her in her cell. Or in the dining hall. Again."

James pushed Ruthanne's hair off her face, a tender gesture. "So you pushed ahead with the new attorney?"

"I did. And if you're about to ask if I was worried they'd try again to hurt me, of course I was. But I worried more about what would happen to Naomi if I allowed her to stay in prison."

"Did they try again?" James asked. "To hurt you?"

Naomi searched her mother's face, because the older woman was hesitating. "Mom? Did they try again?"

"Not to hurt me. But I did notice someone following me home

from work, so I began to carpool with a few of the other nurses. Luckily I'd already put in my papers for retirement, so the work commute became a nonissue."

"Mama," Naomi whispered, feeling like a child again. "I hate that you were in danger."

"I hate that you went to prison for something you did not do."

"We need to tell this to Mr. Broussard," Naomi said. "And to his friend, the police captain. Broussard says we can trust him."

"Did you tell him your story?" Everett asked, still with the smallest of sneers.

"I did, after you were nearly grabbed off the street. I don't care about myself at this point, but that they nearly took you . . . that's what I've been trying to avoid this whole time."

"Everett," James said quietly, "do you still doubt your mother's innocence?"

Everett rose from the table. "I don't know," he said, and he sounded honest. "Even if she didn't do it, I think they had some reason for choosing her—which I don't know yet. But if this was some kind of elaborate setup, they had to have known the accusation would stick. She must have done something that let them know that they could get away with it, that the jury would believe the charges. So maybe she didn't steal those drugs but did something else just as bad."

Naomi was taken aback. "You've clearly thought this through."

Everett met her eyes, his cold and certain. "I've had six years to think things through." He left the kitchen and stomped up the stairs, Harrison on his heels.

Naomi winced when a door slammed on the third floor. "I don't think he'll ever come around."

"Jimmy's been putting lies in his mind," James said sadly. "Maybe give him time."

"Or . . ." Ruthanne bit her lower lip thoughtfully. "Or he could have a point. They had to have some reason to believe that they could get charges to stick. Or at least some reason for choosing you."

Naomi shook her head. "I can't count the hours I spent thinking about this while I lay in my cell, trying to sleep. I had a job that made me vulnerable. I handled evidence, all day, every day."

James sighed. "And you were made more vulnerable because you had a child they could use against you. I didn't realize that Everett had this all figured out in his head. I should have. He's a smart boy. He likes things to make sense."

"So do I." Molly Sutton came into the kitchen, her cell phone clutched in her hand. "I'd hoped to get to *why* you were chosen, Naomi, when Lucien and I came to see you, but we got off on the wrong foot. Once everyone is here and the kids are settled, I'd like to delve into that question again. Understanding why you were chosen, and why Gaffney said you should never have gotten out, might help us figure out how to clear your name."

The Quarter, New Orleans, Louisiana
MONDAY, FEBRUARY 24, 7:15 P.M.

"Thanks, Burke," Jace said, once Burke had pulled up next to his house. "Sorry we had to call you away from your dinner."

Burke turned off the engine and twisted to look at the teenager in the back seat. Val sat beside her son, her arm around his shoulders. Both were pale, nerves shattered, although Jace looked more in control than Val did.

In the passenger seat beside Burke was Val's husband Kaj Cardozo, the prosecutor. Kaj's son Elijah sat on the other side of Jace, holding his hand.

Jace and Elijah had, with Val's marriage to Kaj, become stepbrothers, but they'd been friends first. In that way, their relationship was similar to Burke's bond with Kaleb Marchand.

Who had not called Burke back, even though Burke's voicemail said it was urgent. Juliette hadn't called back, either, and Burke was beginning to worry.

"I will always come to help you, Jace," Burke said firmly.

Val patted his knee. "Let's go inside. You haven't eaten dinner yet. I'll see what's in Burke's fridge."

"I made a grocery order," Burke said. "Lots of snacks, mostly fried, per Everett's request."

"*Yes*," Jace said. "I think I need some comfort food." But then he frowned. "What about Elijah? He shouldn't have that kind of food."

Because Elijah was a type 1 diabetic. Everyone in their circle watched out for the boy, but Jace was his biggest advocate.

"You and I will have something healthier, Elijah. There are veggies and a rotisserie chicken in the fridge, too."

Elijah smiled. "Thanks, Burke."

"Go on in, guys." Kaj waved Val, Jace, and Elijah toward the house. "I'll be right behind you. I need to chat with Burke for a minute."

Val and the boys got out of the truck and Burke watched until they were safely in the house before turning to Kaj. "I'm sorry, Kaj. I hate that the kids got yanked into this."

Kaj shook his head. "Don't apologize. I wanted to tell you that I personally looked over Naomi Cranston's file today. Val asked me what I knew about her."

Burke wasn't sure he was okay with that, but he'd talk to Val later about informational boundaries. Then he scratched the thought. Val was doing her job, using her resources to better keep their client safe. He'd thank her instead.

Somehow, in under a day, Naomi Cranston had upended his thinking. He had loyal people. He needed to trust them to have her best interests at heart, just as he did.

"What did you find out?"

"Hers was on the list of cases that the DA's office started reviewing two and a half years ago," Kaj said.

When Captain Cresswell and several other public servants were found to be guilty of everything from theft to extortion to murder.

"You had to review everything Cresswell touched."

"We did," Kaj agreed. "Miss Cranston was pushed to the front of the line when her attorney—the second one—requested a lab analysis of the drugs she supposedly took."

"They turned out to be ground-up Sheetrock."

"Exactly. The ADA who reviewed her case concluded that they didn't have enough evidence to retry her at the present time, but her case wasn't closed."

"Meaning the option is open to retry her later."

"Yes. I assume you're going to try to clear her."

"That's my plan. She won't be safe until I can prove Detective Gaffney is dirty."

Which I should have done six years ago. Fear for his godsons' safety—and his own—had stayed his hand.

"Well, if you find anything at all, let me know. I'll do what I can to get her case closed for good. Val and Sylvi have kind of adopted her this past year."

"I figured that out," Burke said dryly. "I thought Sylvi was going to smack me this morning."

"She really wanted to. You dodged a bullet."

Burke's phone buzzed in his pocket and he sighed in relief when he saw the caller ID. "It's Kaleb Marchand."

"I'll see you inside."

Burke waited until Kaj was out of the truck before he hit accept. "Kaleb."

"Burke." Kaleb sounded upset. "That you called me minutes before some guy tried to snatch my children can't be a coincidence."

Burke inhaled sharply. "What happened? Is everyone all right?"

"They're okay," Kaleb said tersely. "They were with Juliette, coming out of a restaurant near our house. A black SUV pulled up and tried to grab the boys. Juliette was carrying. She pulled her Sig and threatened to shoot their heads off. They got back in their SUV and drove away."

This entire situation was Burke's worst nightmare. "Did you get a license plate?"

"Trent did. He has that memory, you know? Whatever he sees, he remembers."

"I know." It was what made Trent so successful at school.

"He gave it to Juliette and she gave it to the cops."

"I'm sorry, Kaleb," Burke said, the words getting stuck in his throat.

"I know you are," Kaleb said in the same weary tone, but then the tone hardened. "Why is someone after my children? And do not even consider lying to me, Burke Broussard. Do you know how that feels? Getting a frantic call from your wife while you're sitting in a hotel room, hours away by plane, and hearing that someone tried to kidnap your children?" He made a bitter, scoffing sound. "No, you don't know how that feels because you don't have a wife or kids."

Burke winced, the words as sharp as a blade. Because Kaleb spoke the truth. Burke did not have children of his own. Nor a wife. And Kaleb was the only one still living who knew why.

But Burke didn't lose his temper. Kaleb was a panicking father, his reaction perfectly understandable.

"I can't tell you everything, but it seems like I've pissed off some rogue NOPD detective."

Kaleb was quiet for long moment. "Just like last time. Your job put my children in danger *again*. Dammit, Burke."

Burke felt a wave of shame wash over him. Once again, Kaleb had told the truth. "Yes," he admitted.

"Who threatened my children? I want a name."

Burke nearly told him but hesitated. "What will you do with the information?"

"Juliette's going to give it to the fucking cops that came when she called 911 because someone tried to *grab* our *children*," Kaleb spat. "So *tell me*."

Burke's mind was racing, thinking through all the possible ways things could go wrong—or even more wrong, anyway—should Kaleb tell the NOPD that Gaffney was after his children.

If Kaleb and Juliette reported Gaffney, it would immediately get back to the detective that he'd been named in a possible kidnapping.

But surely Gaffney had to know that they suspected him. He'd come after Everett and then targeted Naomi by shooting up the flower shop. Only after those two failures had the attacks on the other children begun.

And Naomi had told André what Gaffney had done six years ago. And three days ago, as well.

"Burke," Kaleb said ominously. "I asked you a question. I didn't press you for information when this happened before, but I am now."

Before, when Gaffney had been trying to get Burke to join their criminal enterprise. Before, when Burke had barely made it out of NOPD in one piece. Had it not been for Antoine and André and a rumor about Cresswell, he might have been forced to either stay in the NOPD and play Gaffney's game or . . .

Hell. He might have been framed just like Naomi had been.

"You didn't press me before. Why are you pressing now?"

"Because the first time, you said you'd handle it."

"And I did. No one came near your sons." His bluff that Cresswell hired male prostitutes had saved both himself and his godsons. Cresswell had been too afraid that Burke would spill his secret, so the captain had gotten Gaffney to back off.

"Except that it's happened *again*. Tell me. *Now*."

Burke had no argument. "The detective's name is Gaffney. He's already been reported to the NOPD. I'd appreciate it if you didn't tell just anyone in NOPD about this."

The silence on Kaleb's end went on for so long that Burke had to check to make sure they were still connected. "Kaleb?"

"I don't even know what to say to you right now," Kaleb admitted, sounding betrayed and still so very angry. "Someone threatened my children and you just left me a *voicemail*? And then, when they follow through, I'm not allowed to tell the cops who did it? What the actual *fuck*, Burke?"

"I'm trying to protect you, dammit. I don't know which cops I can trust, okay? You know this. You know that's why I left the force. I've told someone I trust that Gaffney is involved. It's being investigated. But if you tell just any cop who shows up . . . what if they're on Gaffney's payroll? I can't promise you that they're not."

"So we're supposed to sit here and take it? Let our kids be grabbed off the fucking street?"

"No. Let me have the boys for a few days. They can stay at my house with a bodyguard. Just a few days, Kaleb."

Kaleb exhaled. "No. I can't trust that they'll be safe with you. I'm going to hire my own security."

Burke flinched like he'd been slapped. "I can keep them safe."

"Maybe you can. But I'm not going to risk my sons' safety in case you can't."

"Kaleb." The single word came out rusty. And hurt.

"Don't 'Kaleb' me. You don't get to sound wounded, Burke. You aren't the wronged party here. Why didn't you go to my house if you knew my kids were in danger? Why didn't you try to find Juliette and tell her in person?"

"Because I didn't get a direct threat," Burke snapped. "And I honestly didn't think they'd go after Braden and Trent."

And because he'd been tending to Harper and Jace. The shame was back, accompanied by guilt. *Which I deserve.* "I can recommend a few security companies in the city. Tell whoever you hire to send me the bill. I'll pay for it."

"Yeah. You will. Text me the names of the companies. I'll discuss it with Juliette. I'm getting on a plane first thing in the morning to come home. And then, when my kids are settled, we need to discuss our working relationship."

"Our working relationship?" Burke echoed, thrown for a loop. "What is that supposed to mean?"

"It means that I can't work with you anymore."

"What are you talking about?"

Kaleb ran the company. Burke signed off on the major hiring decisions and major investments, but Kaleb managed the day-to-day operations, just like Kaleb's father had before him.

"I'm going to assign someone else to give you the quarterly updates. I don't think I can see your face for a while without wanting to smash it."

Burke's heart cracked. "If that's what you need to do."

"I also want you to stay away from Juliette and the kids."

Burke couldn't control his gasp. "What?"

"You attract trouble. People shoot at you. People try to kill you."

"Not recently." But it sounded weak, and Burke knew it.

Kaleb's laugh was full of scorn. "People who are close to you get hurt, Burke. And if you had any decency whatsoever, you'd either quit investigating or you'd cut ties with anyone who might get caught in the crossfire that you draw."

Burke pressed his hand to his heart. Which hurt.

Mostly because Burke could see Kaleb's point.

Association with him was dangerous to the people he loved.

"All right," he said with grim acceptance. "I'll stay back. Will you tell the boys why I'm not coming around anymore? I don't want them to think I don't care."

Kaleb scoffed. "If you *cared*, you wouldn't have *chosen* the careers that you've *chosen*. You go off to war like a goddamn hero, leaving the business to my father and me to run. You come home and then do you join the business? No. You become a cop and my children get threatened. You become a PI so you can save the fucking world while my children—your godsons—pay the price. If you *cared*, you'd make different choices."

Burke thought he might be sick at the torrent of bitter words. "Let me know if you need anything," he finally managed in a strangled whisper. "I'll do anything to keep them safe."

"Just . . . stay away, okay? And send me the names of bodyguards. I'll do the rest. Just like I've always done."

The line went dead.

Burke stared at his phone, unable to believe what had just transpired.

But it had transpired.

And Burke had no one to blame but himself.

Well, and Gaffney.

At least he could focus on taking down that fucker.

And when the next bad guy comes along? When your friends' children are targeted again?

Burke didn't know. He only knew he had a houseful of people who were depending on him to fix this.

Drawing a breath, he texted Kaleb the names of two local companies who could provide protection for his godsons.

Next, he texted one of his part-timers, a guy he'd known since the Marines, and asked him to watch Juliette's house until Kaleb's security arrived.

Then, squaring his shoulders, he went inside.

He had a job to do.

8

The Quarter, New Orleans, Louisiana
MONDAY, FEBRUARY 24, 7:25 P.M.

SOMETHING WAS WRONG with Burke Broussard.

He entered his house, a smile pasted on his face, but Naomi wasn't buying it.

Something terrible had happened.

And it had been in the last few minutes, if the reactions of Val and her husband were any indication. Both did a double take when he approached the large group gathered in his living room.

The couple exchanged a meaningful glance as they took their places on one of Broussard's sofas. At Val's feet was her son Jace. He was a sweet kid. He often treated the flower shop to pastries from the bakery where he worked, never letting Sylvi or Naomi pay him back. He was shy and retiring, his six-foot frame hunched into itself, seeming reticent to take up space.

At Jace's side was Elijah, who Naomi had only met a few times before tonight. He was Val's stepson and was currently holding Jace's hand tightly.

Lucien had returned with his wife Chelsea and their daughter, Harper. Poor little Harper looked shell-shocked. Lucien and Chelsea were sharing looks of worry.

James and Ruthanne sat hand in hand, and Naomi was so happy that her mother now had the kind of support she deserved.

Naomi still couldn't believe that her mother had also been targeted by Detective Gaffney. Ruthanne might have been killed.

Naomi's gaze flitted to Everett, who stood awkwardly alone. He leaned against the fireplace mantel, arms crossed over his chest. He was trying to look bored, but she could see the tension in his shoulders.

She wished she knew what he was thinking, but at least, for this moment, he was safe.

Harrison and Molly stood watch in the corners of the room, but it was clear to see that Molly was focused on her niece.

If Gaffney and his cohorts had done this—and everyone had agreed that was the most likely scenario—they couldn't have picked a better way to distract Broussard's crew.

"Burke?" Molly asked when the man walked into the room and sat in the ancient BarcaLounger.

He gave his people a tight smile. "My godsons were also targeted tonight. Someone tried to grab them when they were out with their mother."

"Oh no," Molly murmured. "They're okay?"

"Shaken," Broussard said. "But unhurt."

"I think that's safe to say about all of us," Lucien said. "I know I'm shaken."

"But Jace isn't unhurt," Elijah declared loudly. "They twisted his arm. It's so bad, it's already red and swelling."

"Jace?" Val said, reaching for his arm. "Let me see."

With a sigh, Jace pulled up his sleeve and Val was immediately on her feet, getting an ice pack.

Kaj leaned forward, gently taking the boy's arm and probing. "It doesn't feel broken."

"It's not," Jace said. "I've had a broken arm before. This is just a bruise. Not even a sprain."

"We need to get you checked out," Val declared, placing the ice pack on Jace's arm. She sat on the floor beside him, a worried frown on her face.

"I'm fine," Jace assured her quietly. "I would tell you if I weren't."

She gave him a tight smile, then put her arm around his shoulders. "Okay."

Naomi wrapped her arms around her middle, trying not to let the panic take over. Because none of this was okay. Not at all. She wondered when these people would decide she and Everett were not worth the trouble.

Broussard looked around the room. "Is anyone else hurt? Even a little? Harper?"

Harper didn't say a word, merely shaking her head.

Broussard sighed. "Okay, let's get all the information on the table. Jace, what happened tonight? Wait." He looked around the room once again. "Where's Antoine?"

"I'm here, Burke." Antoine stuck his head out from the kitchen doorway. "I've made a snack tray for Elijah, but there's enough for everyone."

Naomi looked at the boy sitting on the floor curiously. He saw her looking and smiled. "I have type 1 diabetes. I have to eat regularly."

"Thank you for telling me," she said, feeling even more out of place. This group was a family, and she and her troubles had brought danger to them all.

Antoine brought in a tray of healthy snacks and placed it on the coffee table close to where Elijah and Jace sat, smiling when the boys attacked the food. He then took the last empty seat next to Naomi and offered her some cheese and almonds.

The sight of the food made her want to be sick. She shook her head.

"You need to eat something," Antoine murmured. "You can't do anyone any good if you pass out. One piece of cheese. Please."

"I don't think I can keep it down," she murmured back, and wondered when Everett had last eaten.

"You didn't cause this," Antoine said, so kindly that her eyes burned. "This is not your fault, but we do need your help to figure things out. Your brain will think better if you're not passed out."

She took the cube of cheese he offered and forced herself to nibble on the corner, dabbing at her wet eyes with her fingertips. "I must look pretty awful if you're so worried I'll pass out."

Antoine grimaced. "It's been a rough day for us all, but you all got shot at and your son was nearly taken. Cut yourself some slack. Do you think Everett is hungry?"

Her son hadn't moved, watching as the people in the room helped themselves to the food. "If I try to give him something, he'll say no."

"I won't let him say no." Antoine made a plate for Everett but said nothing to her son, merely placing the small plate on the mantel next to his head. Antoine retook his seat next to Naomi. "I can take notes, Burke."

Broussard inclined his head in thanks. His mouth was set in a determined line, but his eyes seemed devastated. "Okay. Let's get started. Jace? Could you tell us what happened?"

"I was coming out of the grocery store near our house. Nelly's Corner Store."

"When was this, exactly?" Antoine asked, opening his laptop.

"About six. I'd just put the bags in the trunk when this black SUV came up behind me. It stopped real quick. The hatch went up and some guy got out from the very back. He was wearing a black hoodie and a mask. Like doctors wear." The teenager glanced at Antoine. "I couldn't see his face, but he was as tall as me, maybe an inch taller. I'm guessing he weighed two twenty or two twenty-five. He grabbed my arm and twisted it while he dragged me toward the SUV. He was trying to break it."

"Did he say anything?" Broussard asked.

Jace nodded. *"Para mi hermano."*

Broussard's brow furrowed. *"For my brother.* I wonder if his brother was the guy whose arm Harrison broke when they tried to take Everett."

"I don't know," Jace said. "That's all the guy said. I yanked my arm away and ran back to the store. I thought he'd follow me, but he jumped back into the SUV and they drove away. The store owner called 911. I called my mom. And then you came to get us, Burke."

"So," Antoine said, "I have questions."

Jace grinned unexpectedly. "I figured."

Antoine chuckled, but sobered quickly. "I'm looking at the footage from the cameras pointing into the alley. From the moment the SUV stopped to the moment you got away was less than ten seconds."

Jace gaped at him. "That's all?"

"That's all." Antoine picked up a remote control and turned on the large flat-screen on Broussard's wall, having evidently connected his laptop to the TV. "Watch."

Naomi lifted her gaze to the large screen where Jace was approaching his car, carrying three grocery bags. As he'd described, he put the bags in his trunk, then spun around, eyes wide, as the SUV charged toward him.

They all watched as the man jumped out of the SUV and grabbed Jace's arm.

At first, Jace was like a deer in the headlights, not fighting back as the man dragged him toward the back of the SUV. The man's hands twisted Jace's arm as he dragged him, and then he paused at the back of the SUV, grabbing something.

"It's a piece of white cloth," Antoine said.

On-screen, Jace jerked his arm free, giving the man a hard shove before running back to the store.

"Watch the guy's hand," Antoine advised.

The man made an attempt to grab at Jace, but he was already running away. The white fabric he held dropped from his grip and fluttered to the pavement.

"The police picked it up," Val said, her voice trembling. "They found a white powder in it and have sent it to the lab for identification."

Jace shuddered. "That would have sucked."

Elijah shook his head. "But that probably wouldn't have knocked Jace out. That whole thing where you breathe it in and go instantly unconscious, that's just in the movies. That guy was big, but so is Jace. What did they expect would happen?"

Broussard gave the boy a nod. "Very good question. Was anything like that found at the scene of Harper's attempted kidnapping, Chelsea?"

She shook her head. "No. Not that the police found. But Harper's only ten years old. She couldn't fight like Jace did."

Something was bothering Naomi. Something didn't feel right. "Antoine, can you run that clip again? Jace, do you mind?"

"No, ma'am," the teenager said. "I don't mind. I'm kind of interested to see it again, too."

"Why?" Broussard asked, his tone not unkind. Only curious.

"Because something was off about it," she said. "I'm not sure what yet."

From his post next to the fireplace, Everett made a scoffing sound and Naomi winced.

But Broussard did more than wince. He slowly stood and, once again, she was struck by how massive the man really was. He was built like a tank.

A very safe tank.

Broussard turned to Everett. "Got somethin' to say, Everett?"

For a moment, Naomi thought Everett would back down, but instead he lifted his chin. "She's acting like she was a real cop, but she wasn't. Just a glorified UberEats driver."

"What did you say?" Broussard asked quietly in a tone that sent shivers down Naomi's spine. "I could not have heard you right."

Everett rolled his eyes. "She picked up packages from drop boxes and delivered them to the evidence room. Day in and day out."

"You're a fool, boy," Broussard drawled mildly.

Everett didn't seem to have the sense to be wary of that mild drawl, but Naomi sat up straighter. "Mr. Broussard," she started.

"No, Naomi," Everett said, not even looking at her. He leveled a glare at Broussard. "Let the man speak."

James came to his feet. "Everett, that's enough."

Everett rolled his eyes and went back to leaning against the fireplace. "Whatever."

James slowly sat, shaking his head. Naomi had always liked the man, but he'd let his son get away with far too much. Jimmy was bitter and arrogant and now Everett was becoming the same way.

Broussard had not sat, however, continuing to regard Everett with anger. "Where did you hear that, Everett? That your mother wasn't a 'real cop'?"

Naomi cleared her throat, not having expected Broussard to take up for her. "My ex-husband would say that all the time. He never respected my job. That's where Everett's heard it from."

"It's not a lie," Everett said, his handsome face twisted into a sneer.

"No," Naomi allowed, keeping her voice calm in the hopes of defusing a potential argument, "but it's not the truth, either, and I think you know that, Everett. I did gather evidence from the drop boxes, but I also processed narcotics and handguns and other evidence. If you're going to be condescending, at least do it with all the facts."

Everett spared her a glance. "Whatever."

Broussard took a walk around the living room, silent for a full minute. Every eye in the room tracked his progress. Even little Harper, Naomi noticed.

That she was no longer staring straight ahead had to be a good sign.

Finally, Broussard returned to his chair. "My temper is frayed, Everett. This has been a stressful day for us all. I'm going to put this conversation off until I'm not already angry."

Everett shrugged. "Okay. What—"

"Stop." Jace came to his feet, holding the ice pack to his injured arm. "Just stop. I don't know what's between you and your mother, and it's none of my business. But your attitude sucks. This is a serious conversation and, whether you like it or not, it's not all about you. I was nearly grabbed off the street, too, and so was Harper. She's just a little girl and she doesn't deserve this. None of us—including you—deserves this. Look, bro, Burke is a good guy. He will find out who's responsible. But if you can't help him, just shut your mouth, because everyone else here just wants to go home." He turned to Naomi. "Apologies, ma'am. You were saying something seemed off."

Naomi blinked, trying to remember exactly what she had said. "Um, yeah. Antoine, can we watch the footage again?"

Antoine gave Jace an approving nod. "Of course we can." He restarted the clip and Naomi focused on the scene unfolding. When it was finished, she was frowning.

"What is it, Miss Cranston?" Broussard asked.

"The guy dragging Jace is almost . . . polite."

Jace's brows went up. "Polite? Ma'am, he tried to break my arm."

"That wasn't polite," she agreed, "and I didn't mean to insinuate that any of this is okay. Maybe a better word would be 'solicitous.' At one point you stumbled and the guy slowed down and helped you right yourself. When you stumbled, he could have taken advantage of your forward momentum and used it to shove you into the SUV. Instead, he let you get your balance, which allowed you to fight him off."

"Show us again," Broussard instructed, and Antoine played the clip a third time. "I think you're right, Miss Cranston. He could have panicked, of course. Figured that dragging Jace to the SUV would be harder if he fell down. He'd be deadweight and, no offense, Jace, but you're no petite flower. You have to weigh, what, one seventy-five?"

"One ninety-five," Jace murmured, still standing. He stared thoughtfully at the flat-screen. "But this guy had muscles. When I shoved him there at the end, it was like slapping against rock. I think he could have done exactly what Miss Cranston just said—use my stumble to force me into the SUV. All he really needed to do was shove me in and crawl in after me. The driver would have taken us away. Then he could have used whatever was in that cloth to put me out."

Val rubbed a hand over her face. "God, Jace."

The boy smiled down at her. "I'm okay, Mom. And you're the one who taught me to use logic, right? If I let myself dwell on what might have happened, my brain will get all paralyzed and I won't be able to think at all."

She gave his hand a squeeze. "You're right. I'm proud of you. But it's hard for me to see this video."

"Can you make me some hot cocoa?" Jace asked, blinking puppy-dog eyes at her. "It would help my arm."

She snorted a laugh. "Now you're patronizing me. Get your own cocoa."

He laughed. "I didn't want any anyway."

"What are you thinking, Jace?" Broussard asked with a small smile of his own. "Since you're being all logical?"

Jace considered for a moment, then looked at Naomi. "He let me go, didn't he?"

"I think that maybe he did," Naomi said. "Maybe he thought you were more trouble than you were worth. At one point, it looked like he was more interested in hurting your arm than getting you in his vehicle. Maybe he got distracted. At any rate, his message was sent."

That left the room quiet.

"Maybe that was the point," Molly said quietly. She crossed the room and knelt in front of her niece, taking the little girl's hands. "Harper? I need you to hear me. Can you hear me?"

The girl nodded.

"Did the man have a cloth or a hankie? Like he did with Jace?"

"No."

"When he grabbed you, did he hurt you? Like he hurt Jace?"

"No," Harper whispered, pressing her face against her mother's shoulder.

Lucien stroked Harper's hair. "It's okay, honey. You don't have to talk about it if you don't want to."

Molly threw Lucien a mild frown before looking up at her sister. "Tell everyone what you told me, Chels."

"We'd gone to Très Bien, a diner in our neighborhood. I didn't even drive my own car because parking is insane everywhere right now. We were done with dinner and were waiting on the curb outside the diner for our Uber when this SUV stopped right next to us and a man jumped out. He was wearing a dark hoodie and a surgical mask. I didn't see his face at all. I was looking at my phone to see how long before the Uber arrived and I didn't see him until Harper yelped."

"What happened, Harper?" Molly asked. "Harper, honey, it's important. You know I wouldn't ask if it wasn't."

Harper sucked in a deep breath. "He picked me up. Held me against his chest." She paused, wrinkling her nose. "His shirt pocket smelled funny."

"Like how, honey?" Molly pressed, ignoring the scowl on Lucien's face.

"Like . . . sour, but . . . but sweet. Like candy. Made me dizzy."

Naomi exhaled slowly. That had to have been something to knock the child out, just like they'd tried with Jace.

Molly smiled at Harper, brushing trembling fingers over the child's cheek. "That's good, Harper, really good. Did he say anything?"

She swallowed hard, then nodded. "Paramee."

Molly looked at Broussard. "Paramee?"

"Para mi," Naomi whispered, her chest contracting, the man's meaning both clear and vile. "Oh no."

"Yeah," Antoine said. *"Para mi,* Burke. *For me."*

Broussard nodded grimly, having come to the same conclusion. "That's very helpful, Harper. Thank you."

Molly's face had lost some color, but the smile she gave her niece didn't falter. "Uncle Burke's right. You're doing so well. What happened after he picked you up?"

"I got a headache."

Molly nodded, her smile now pained. "I bet you did. What happened then?"

"Mom was there and he let me go."

"I realized she wasn't beside me anymore," Chelsea said, her voice shaky. "I saw her with that man and I ran after them, screaming my head off. A couple on the street saw me and the woman got between the man and the SUV's back door, which he'd left open. He'd been sitting in the back seat, not the cargo hold like he was with Jace."

"Okay," Molly said. "What happened next?"

"More people started looking and the man shoved Harper at the couple, then he got in the SUV, and it drove away. Turned onto a side street. I got the license plate."

"Stolen," Molly said. "I ran the plate."

"I knew you would," Chelsea said, then started to quietly cry. "I couldn't thank that couple enough. They saved Harper." She clutched her daughter close.

"Did you get their names?" Antoine asked. "We should talk to them again. See if they remember anything about the driver, the man, or the SUV itself."

Chelsea leaned into Lucien. "I did. Bill and Donna Burrell. Visiting from Galveston."

"I'll check into them ASAP," Antoine promised. "What next, Burke?"

Broussard studied all the faces watching him, waiting for their marching orders. "Naomi and Everett stay here, along with her mother and James. The rest is up to you all. We can defend ourselves better if we're all in one place, so I'd prefer if you all stay here—at least until we get an idea of who's behind this. I don't have enough full-time staff to assign each of you bodyguards, but I can call up some part-timers if you want to go home. I'll support your decision either way."

Elijah looked up at his father. "I'm staying wherever Jace is staying."

"I'll watch him, Kaj," Jace said soberly.

"Val?" Kaj asked. "What do you want to do?"

"Grab our boys and run for the hills," she said weakly, "but that won't work, either. I'll stay here with Elijah and Jace. I'll bring the dogs over, if Burke is okay with that."

"Absolutely," Broussard said. "I'll feel safer with Czar around."

Naomi had met Val's Black Russian Terrier, one hundred thirty-five pounds of protection dog who took his job very seriously.

"And Delilah?" Elijah asked. "You'll feel safer with her, too, won't you?"

"Delilah is Elijah's retriever mix," Antoine whispered, filling Naomi in. "Adopted from the pound. She's a fur ball who loves everyone."

Broussard chuckled and the sound was soothing. Naomi thought she could listen to that sound all day long. "Delilah would be more likely to lick them to death."

"Well, that's true," Elijah conceded, "but it's still to death."

Broussard grinned at the boy. "Then, yes, she can come, too."

"We'll stay, too, Burke," Lucien said. "I don't want Chelsea and Harper alone. Consolidating our bodyguard resources seems like a smart decision."

James waved to get Broussard's attention. "When there's time, Ruthanne needs to tell you what she told Naomi and me earlier. Detective Gaffney tried to kill her."

Naomi shuddered while the others in the room gaped. She'd almost managed to pack that little fact away, but it came screaming back. *Gaffney tried to kill my mother.*

Broussard's brows shot up. "Can you tell us now?"

Ruthanne nodded, retelling her story.

When she was finished, Broussard nodded soberly. "You're welcome here for as long as you want to stay." He clapped his hands once. "Let's eat, regroup, and then we will make ourselves a plan."

9

The Quarter, New Orleans, Louisiana
MONDAY, FEBRUARY 24, 9:00 P.M.

CELL PHONE CLUTCHED in his hand, Burke stepped out into the courtyard behind his house, closing the door behind him. The crowd in his house was just finishing dinner. The instant quiet outside was a balm to his senses.

It wasn't silence, of course. Strains of music from the bars a few blocks over wafted through the night, and there was always a low hum of voices from the people crowding the streets. Especially this time of year.

The city was his home and, to him, had always been safe. Sure, there had been individuals who'd meant him harm—Cresswell and Gaffney, primarily—but overall he'd never feared his hometown.

Until now.

Someone had put hands on their children. Jace and Harper. Everett.

Braden and Trent. His godsons.

Burke wondered how long Kaleb would stay mad at him.

He wondered how long Kaleb had *been* mad at him. Because there had been so much bitterness in his old friend's words. He'd clearly been angry for a long time—at Burke for running off to join the Marines and then for coming back and not working with Kaleb in the business.

He sat on the bench under his favorite magnolia tree and stared at his phone, debating calling Juliette. Kaleb had told him to stay away, but he couldn't.

He couldn't lose this connection.

They were his family. The only family he had left. Even if they weren't blood.

Someone had tried to hurt his godsons. The thought would not go away, circling his mind, taking up space he needed for thinking.

I need to know they're okay. Really okay.

Kaleb was already mad, he reasoned. And Juliette could tell him to go to hell if she wanted to. Burke would comply with her wishes.

He called her number before he could change his mind.

"Burke! I'm so glad you called."

He let out the breath he'd been holding. "Juliette. I wasn't sure if you'd take my call."

"What? Why wouldn't I?"

"Kaleb is really mad at me."

She sighed. "He's scared. Which he should be, but I told him not to take it out on you. I guess he did that anyway."

"It's my fault."

"No, it's not. It was terrifying, I'm not gonna lie. But the boys and I are safe at home."

They're safe. All their children were safe. "Can you tell me what happened?"

"We'd gone out for ice cream. I had to park down the street, so we were walking to the car when this black SUV stopped in the middle of traffic and the hatch went up. A man jumped out and grabbed Trent under one arm like a football and grabbed Braden by the arm and started taking them to the SUV. I froze for a second, but then I took out my gun and threatened to shoot the man's head off if he didn't let my sons go. The guy hesitated and kind of . . . stared at me. He had on a hoodie and a mask, so his eyes were all I could see. But he looked scared of my gun."

"And he dropped the kids? Let them go?" Just like with Jace and Harper, this was a brazen thing to do, to try to grab children on a busy street.

"Yes, he did. The guy jumped back into the SUV and it drove away. Trent remembered the license plate and I gave it to the cop who responded when several onlookers called 911."

"The boys weren't the only ones to get grabbed today. Three other kids were almost kidnapped and the situation was exactly the same. Except you were the only one to pull a gun on the guy."

Part of Burke wished she'd fired so that they'd have the kidnapper in their hands, but so many things might have gone wrong had she pulled the trigger. Someone—the boys or innocent bystanders—could have been hurt.

But, thank God, it had been enough to scare the kidnapper away.

Juliette gasped. "I didn't know that."

Burke frowned. "Kaleb didn't call you?"

"No, he said he was in meetings and would call me after. He's getting his meetings finished tonight so that he can get on a plane and come home first thing in the morning."

"Then you should know that I recommended two security companies that can provide protection services."

"Bodyguards?"

"Yes."

"Oh. Why . . . didn't you offer to do it yourself?"

Burke's heart lightened, just a fraction. At least Juliette hadn't cast him aside. "I did, but Kaleb said it was better if I stayed away."

"Oh, Burke. He was just angry. He'll change his mind by morning."

"Maybe, but until I get this case resolved, he could be right. It might be better that I stay away. Just to keep you all safe. But if you don't like the people those two companies provide, know that I will find protection for you. Okay?"

"Okay." She sounded frustrated. "I knew Kaleb was shaken up, but I didn't expect he'd tell you to stay away. The boys are going to be heartbroken. Trent was counting on you coming to his award ceremony the week after Mardi Gras."

"Then I'd best get busy solving this case. Are you all right staying by yourself tonight? I have a house full of people. If you want, you're welcome to bring the boys over here. Or I can send someone to watch your house."

Which he'd already done, but he didn't want Kaleb to know that.

"Um . . . I think it would be better if you could send someone over here, just until Kaleb hires someone."

He hadn't realized how much he hoped she'd choose him until she didn't. But this wasn't about him. "I'll take care of it."

"Okay. Until then, I'll keep my gun loaded."

Juliette was an excellent shot. Burke had taught her himself. "If you hear a bump in the night, you call me, y'hear? I don't care what time it is."

"Thank you, Burke. Love you."

"Love you, too." He ended the call and pocketed his phone.

He was so damn tired. He just needed a minute of quiet. A minute to think. But the shutting of the door behind him told him that wasn't going to happen.

He turned to find Naomi Cranston standing uncertainly, her back to the door.

"I wasn't listening," she said. "I waited until you put your phone away to come out. Is this a bad time?"

He barked a laugh. "This whole day has been a bad time, Miss Cranston. But come, have a seat." He patted the back of the bench. "It's a nice night."

"It is," she agreed, sitting next to him.

This close he could smell her perfume. Or maybe shampoo. Honeysuckle.

He'd always liked that scent. But there was something else. Something . . . *Bacon?* He tried to sniff the air discreetly, but she must have noticed because she leaned away from him.

He winced. "Sorry. I thought I smelled bacon."

A blush lit her pale cheeks. "You do. It's me. I'm the one who should be sorry." She started to stand, but he gently gripped her arm and pulled her back down.

"Don't be sorry. I mean, bacon is one of the best smells ever, so I'm good."

She smiled uncertainly. "It's just that . . . well, I'd almost broken the habit, but today's been stressful."

"You have a bacon habit? Because there are a whole lot worse habits to have."

She sighed. "Well, not bacon specifically. It's a habit left over from . . . you know. Prison. We'd always try to take something from the dining hall back to our cell for later. Tonight, I took an extra biscuit with bacon."

"Ah. I understand. Food insecurity?"

"Yeah." She looked away, embarrassed. "It's a stupid habit. I won't do it again."

Burke hated to see her feeling embarrassed. After surviving what she had, she shouldn't feel anything but pride. "I think we all develop weird habits along the way." He stuck out his boot. "I always replace the laces that come with any of my shoes with Kevlar string. I started doing it after I went through SERE."

"The military survival training?"

"Exactly. Kevlar string can be used for all kinds of things, from fishing to stringing a bow to creating a snare to catch a rabbit. All kinds of things. I came home from the Corps fifteen years ago and I still do it. It's . . . soothing."

She smiled again, this time with gratitude. "Thank you, Mr. Broussard. You're very kind to try to make me feel better."

Try. So he hadn't succeeded. *Damn.* "What can I do for you?"

She folded her hands in her lap, gripping her fingers tightly. "How did they know where Everett would be? He didn't tell anyone he was going to see his girlfriend, not even his best friends. How did they know that Chelsea and Harper would be having dinner at that diner? Or that Jace would be stopping at that grocery store? Or where to grab your godsons?"

The haze of exhaustion began to lift. "Very good questions, Miss Cranston."

"Can you call me Naomi?"

"If you'll call me Burke. We're pretty informal around here."

"I got that." She tucked her hair behind her ear before flinching slightly and brushing the hair forward.

To hide the scar on her neck. Where she'd been stabbed. When she'd nearly died. Because Cresswell and Gaffney had framed her.

"Why you?" he murmured. "Another good question, I think."

"I'm still thinking I was a random choice, or I was picked because they knew they could manipulate me by using Everett."

But that didn't feel right.

None of this feels right.

Except . . . having Naomi sitting beside him. Despite what she'd been through, she had a calmness, a serenity that soothed his heart. That felt right.

Which was a surprise. Maybe even a good surprise.

She was strong, this woman sitting beside him. She'd survived, retaining her empathy and compassion.

And she was ridiculously patient with her son.

Burke had hated the way her expression had grown pinched when Everett said she was only a glorified UberEats driver. Like she'd heard it too many times. Turned out that she had, from her ex.

Concentrate. Stop thinking about her, about her honeysuckle hair and her strength. About her big brown eyes that hid nothing.

Concentrate on fixing this mess.

"Maybe it was because they thought you'd be easy to manipulate, but that doesn't answer the question of why they hid drugs in *anyone's* car. And why wait until you'd been out of prison for a year before trying to manipulate you again?"

"I assumed it was to take advantage of all the deliveries I've been making the past few weeks."

"Maybe." But it still didn't feel right. "But Gaffney wanted you to stay in prison, and he was willing to harm your mother to keep you there over a year ago. There's something about you specifically, Naomi."

She exhaled, a weary sound. "Maybe. But I can't think of what that could be."

"We'll figure it out," he said with more confidence than he felt. "But back to what brought you out here tonight. We'll find out how they knew where all our kids were going to be, including Everett."

She hesitated. "I know this sounds paranoid, but could they have a tracker on his car? They *have* been watching him. Gaffney knew Everett's routine. He knew which friends he hangs out with."

"A tracker is a possibility," he allowed. "We'll check for one. But Harrison thought they were already at the girlfriend's house, waiting for Everett to arrive."

"They communicate using cell phones—Everett and his friends, I mean. Probably throwaways."

Burke lifted his brows. "Everett has a throwaway phone?"

"I've suspected for a long time. Once I got a text from a different number, but it sounded like it came from Everett. When I asked him, he got squirrelly and said it must have been a spam text from a stranger. He's not a good liar."

"You think someone's bugged his phone?"

"If they want to get to me—for whatever reason—going through Everett worked before."

"I'll find out if his phone is bugged."

She tilted her head. "How?"

"Antoine will know how."

"He's a kind man. Seems smart."

"Smarter than me." Burke studied her while her questions bounced around in his head. She was so very pretty. She looked like Snow White with her shiny dark hair and pale complexion. "What else have you noticed?"

She looked away. "You don't have to humor me."

He tapped her shoulder, waiting until she met his eyes. "You'll find that I rarely humor people. I'm kind of a crusty bastard."

She laughed, the sound making him smile. "I don't think so. Your people care about you and seem to be incredibly loyal. I'd say you're more like a toasted marshmallow."

"Because I'm tanned or because I'm crusty?"

"Both," she said dryly, then sobered. "I want to talk to Cresswell."

"So do I. I made some calls today to the warden at the prison where he's being held. Cresswell's in the isolation unit for his own protection."

She grimaced. "I know about that. So was I."

"I know. We checked."

"Figured you would. What did the warden say about Cresswell?"

"That he hasn't said a word to anyone in the two and a half years that he's been incarcerated. Not to his lawyer, or his guards, or reporters, and definitely not to the warden. Whenever he's brought out of his cell, he sits silently and just waits to be taken back."

"I'd be surprised if he's still sane." She looked genuinely distressed on Cresswell's behalf. "That's a long time to be no-contact."

Burke was surprised she could find it in herself to care about the former NOPD captain. Cresswell had been officially charged and convicted of the murder of a suspect. He'd chosen prison over allowing that suspect to spill everything he knew.

The "everything" the suspect had known likely included crimes like the framing of Naomi.

That she seemed to have compassion for the man who'd ruined her career and damaged her life said a great deal about her.

"I don't think we'll get anything out of Cresswell, unfortunately," Burke told her.

She sighed. "He has children, too."

That made Burke remember his and Lucien's conversation with Naomi's first defense attorney. "You were right about Mason Lord.

Gaffney threatened his children to ensure his silence and his cooperation in getting you convicted."

"I can understand his motivation, even though I don't forgive him. Poor Lucien. He must be devastated. He was so certain that Mason Lord wouldn't have thrown me under the bus."

"You're remarkably accepting of people's failings."

"Loyalty to a friend isn't really a failing."

"Teenagers being rude is."

She studied him for a long moment. "You mean Everett."

"Yeah. If I'd talked to my mama that way . . ."

"Don't be too hard on Everett. His father's had years to fill his mind with lies. James is a steadying influence, but Jimmy's really controlling about how much access James has to any of the grandchildren—Everett or Jimmy's kids with McKenzie. I'm not saying that Everett's not rude, because he is. And I'm not saying it doesn't break my heart in two every time he makes snide comments about me, because it does. But I lost five years with my son. I'm not getting those years back. I'm hoping to forge a new relationship with him, but so far, that hasn't worked so well."

"What was he like before you went to prison?"

"Happy, mostly. Active. Had a lot of friends and a natural curiosity. We did a lot of science experiments at home because Jimmy worked late. Took a lot of nature walks." She made a face. "So did Jimmy, with McKenzie. Everett and I were in the park one night and who should we see canoodling on a park bench but Jimmy and the other woman."

"Ouch."

"Yeah. I think that broke something in Everett. He started putting up walls, and when my divorce was final, Everett was angry at me. Said I should have forgiven his father, that I was selfish. Maybe in his mind I was. I'd appreciate patience with him, Mr. Broussard—I mean Burke. You don't have to like him. Just, please, keep him alive."

It was the first time she'd called him by his name and he couldn't ignore the rush of pleasure. "Alive I can do." He rose and held out his hand. "Come on. Let's find out how the folks in the black SUV knew our children's movements today."

After a moment of hesitation, she allowed him to pull her to her feet. He dropped her hand immediately, as was proper, but he hated to do it. He wanted to take care of her.

I take care of everyone. It's not just her.

But he wasn't fooling himself. What he'd felt for Naomi Cranston from the moment she'd come into his office with her gaze averted and her shoulders slumped . . . It wasn't like anything he'd felt for a very long time.

That should scare him. On some level it did. For now, he'd keep both her and her son alive.

The Quarter, New Orleans, Louisiana

MONDAY, FEBRUARY 24, 10:20 P.M.

"Hacked," Antoine said grimly.

Everyone was back in Burke's living room, except this time she and Burke sat on the settee and Antoine stood in the middle of the room, holding a Faraday bag.

Naomi had seen the bags come through the evidence room. They blocked electronics from connecting with the outside world. Antoine's Faraday bag contained both of Everett's phones—his personal phone that Jimmy paid for and the simple throwaway flip phone that Everett had purchased himself.

Everett had been loath to admit that he had a throwaway. It had finally taken Antoine telling him that the phone could be listening to their conversation at that very moment, and did he want to feel responsible for putting all these nice people in danger? Did he want to put *himself* in danger?

Everett had grudgingly given in, handing over the throwaway, muttering under his breath. Now her son was back in his place against the wall by the fireplace, but his stony-faced facade was shaken. "Which one?" he asked.

"Both," Antoine said. "There are keystroke counters on both phones. Anything you typed was being monitored."

"How did they hack my phones?" Everett asked, his voice hitching up a panicked octave.

"Probably through your girlfriend's phone," Antoine said, "or through one of your friends at school. If they used their phone number when they signed up for any social media app, a hacker can get their number. Typically they'll hack a friend's non-burner phone, then use that information to get your cell numbers. They'll go through the friend's call log and start dialing numbers until they recognize your voice or get you to tell them your name. Have you gotten any calls that were claiming to be wrong numbers?"

Everett nodded tightly. "Got a bunch of them back in September."

"That could be when your surveillance began," Burke said.

"September," Naomi whispered. "They've been watching my son since September." Naomi had to slow her breathing because she felt light-headed.

Beside her, Burke quickly squeezed her forearm. "He's safe, Naomi. Antoine, are any of the rest of our phones compromised?"

Antoine shook his head. "I checked. I keep our phones closely monitored for spyware and hacking." He looked at Jace and Elijah. "All of our phones."

Jace shrugged. "I just play Candy Crush and watch movies."

"And I read about politics," Elijah added.

Antoine winced. "I know."

Kaj chuckled, mussing Elijah's blond hair. "We all know."

Elijah jerked away, fixing his hair. "Dad."

Naomi was suddenly conscious of the fact that she'd missed the moments of Everett becoming a teenager, worrying about his appearance.

Cresswell and Gaffney had stolen that from her, she thought, more determined than ever to see them punished. Keeping Everett and the other children safe was paramount, but exposing Gaffney for the dirty cop he was would be the icing on the cake.

"So," James said, "when Ev texted with this girl that he'd be by today, that's how whoever was trying to kidnap him knew where he was going to be."

"That's what I think," Antoine confirmed. "Nobody else knew where Everett was going—did they?"

Everett shook his head mutely.

"I'll wipe your phones, Everett, and make them secure."

"But how did they know where the other kids would be?" Naomi asked. "They would have had to have been watching Harper, Jace, and your godsons for their routines, and that doesn't make sense. I only showed up on your doorstep this morning."

The adults in the room went quiet, looking at each other for answers.

"You're sure that our phones are secure, Antoine?" Val asked.

"Very sure," Antoine said. "Why?"

"Because I called Jace this afternoon to tell him I'd be working late and to ask him to stop by Nelly's Corner Store for groceries."

Burke's brow creased in thought. "Was this before or after the shooting at the flower shop, Val?"

"After. I called him from my car on my way here." Val briefly closed her eyes. "My car, which was parked outside Sylvi's all day. I'll go check it."

Antoine shook his head. "I'll go check. Don't discuss any sensitive information while I'm gone."

Molly raised her hand, then pointed to herself and Chelsea while miming talking on the phone.

"I'll check your car, too, Mol." Antoine held out his hand for Val's keys, then turned to Molly for hers. Burke tossed his and Antoine caught them. "You didn't drive your car today, did you, Lucien?"

Lucien shook his head.

"Okay. Be right back." Antoine left and silence descended for two excruciating minutes.

Until Elijah cleared his throat. "Is this a bad time for me to practice my comedy routine? I'm doing it for the school talent show."

Jace moaned. "Don't make me hear it again."

Elijah smirked. "It's not that bad."

"It's not that good, either," Jace countered.

Elijah laughed. "I'm only doing it so that the teacher will be appalled and not make me do an act in the future."

"Sneaky," Jace said. "I like it. Do you do talent shows at your school, Everett?"

Naomi wanted to hug Jace. Everett had been watching the two boys laughing, loneliness clear on his face. Jace must have noticed, trying to draw her son into the conversation.

Everett startled, then cleared his throat. "No. I don't think we've ever had a talent show. After hearing you talk, I'm glad we don't."

"Be very glad," Jace said glumly. "I'm doing a dance with some of the kids in my class. It's going to be so embarrassing."

"I'm going to record it on my phone," Elijah said, giggling when Jace gave him a playful shove.

Harper slid off her mother's lap to join in the fun, snuggling into Jace's chest when he wrapped an arm around her. The teenager dropped a kiss on Harper's head.

"You okay, little bit?" he asked.

"No," she said honestly. "You?"

"No," he replied. "But we will be."

Naomi had to look away, her eyes stinging. It was so sweet. She wanted Everett to have that kind of acceptance. He might, with his friends from school. She just didn't know.

The front door opened and Antoine came in, looking even grimmer than he had before. He held up two fingers, then pointed to Val and Molly in turn. "Give me a few minutes."

He started passing a small metal wand over lamps and tables, under chairs, and along the fireplace.

He then set up a device similar to the one Naomi had seen Val using that morning. "Okay, jammer's in place, just in case. I think the house is clean, Burke, but we can't take chances."

"Our vehicles were bugged?" Molly asked. "How did they break into our cars?"

"Only yours and Val's. Burke's is clean. They probably used a range extender. One person uses the device to boost the signal from your key fob to his partner's device, which unlocks the doors because it thinks it's your fob. But they'd need to get close to your keys."

"My keys were in my pocket," Val said.

"Mine too," Molly said.

"You were both in the flower shop this afternoon. I'll check the cameras again to see if anyone got close enough to redirect your signal. At least we know how they knew where Jace, Harper, and Everett would be and when."

"But not your godsons," Naomi said to Burke.

He frowned. "True. We need to find out who knew where they'd be. I'll call Juliette when we're done here." He sat back, arms crossed over his powerful chest. "Okay. Now what?"

"I still want to know why they picked Naomi," Molly said. "That was on our next steps this morning."

Naomi nodded. "Please and thank you."

Burke pinched the bridge of his nose. "We didn't do most of the things we planned this morning. We still need to interview Winnifred Timms, the woman Naomi stopped to help five years ago."

"We went to her apartment near the university campus after we saw Naomi at the shop," Lucien said, "but they said she didn't live there. We were going to search for her actual address, but things got crazy."

Burke frowned. "We got distracted with the kids being grabbed."

"Which may have been the point," Molly said. "If they'd actually managed to take even one of our kids, we'd be tearing the city apart to find them. And not working on this case."

"That's so evil," Ruthanne whispered. "It was bad enough to frame my daughter, but this? Taking children?"

"Beyond comprehension," James said.

"It is," Burke agreed. "Antoine, did you get a sketch on the guy whose arm Harrison broke?"

Antoine nodded. "I did. I sent it to André and I'm running it through facial recognition on my own." He pointed to his laptop. "So far I haven't gotten a match against the DMV database or the mug shots. I'm hoping someone in NOPD recognizes him."

"Whoever this is," Val said, "they're playing the long game. If those wrong numbers Everett got back in September were part of this, they've been planning this for a long time. What is Gaffney up to?"

Burke scowled. "Gaffney's always been dirty. He tried to get me to skim drugs from what we'd confiscated in busts."

Naomi stared at him. "Really?"

He nodded. "Yeah. That's when I quit."

From his spot next to the fireplace, Everett straightened to his full height. "He did?"

"Yeah," Burke repeated. "I left the NOPD over it."

"Why didn't you report him?" Everett demanded, eyes snapping with anger. "You could have kept Naomi out of jail."

"I did. His boss was in on it, too. But I had no proof."

"And then he got stranded on a bust," Antoine added. "Nobody in NOPD backed him up. He was lucky he got out with his life."

"Oh," Everett said, going back to leaning on the fireplace. But his expression was now thoughtful instead of surly.

It would have been nice if he'd believed me on his own, Naomi thought. *But I'll take what I can get.* "Once you ID the brother with the broken arm, that should lead you to whoever was busy grabbing kids tonight. If they're real brothers and not just fellow gang members or friends."

Molly nodded, taking notes. "We also need to track down the couple who helped Harper. What were their names again, Chelsea?"

"Donna and Bill Burrell," Chelsea said.

"From Galveston." Antoine sat on the floor and pulled one of his laptops close. "I checked during dinner and I couldn't find a couple by that name in Galveston. Are you sure that's where they were from?"

"Yes," Chelsea said.

"Let's put together a composite," Antoine said, "like I did with Harrison and the broken-arm guy. They may have said Galveston when it's really a much smaller town nearby. People do that when no one's heard of their town."

Chelsea bobbed her head. "Okay. Sure. Whatever you need."

It seemed as though their conversation was winding down, but nothing felt resolved. Nothing felt finished.

They still had no idea what Gaffney and his people were planning or why they'd dragged Naomi back into their web.

Why me? Why now?

Drugs were definitely part of Gaffney's plan. Naomi had no doubt that the envelope that had failed to make its way into Sylvi's delivery van had contained drugs that would have been her downfall when inevitably discovered through an "anonymous tip" to the NOPD.

The *why now* was also not a huge mystery. Mardi Gras was coming up and the city would be inundated with more tourists than at any other time of the year. Hundreds of thousands of people would flood the city, looking to party.

Every cop knew that drug sales went through the roof during Mardi Gras. Even "glorified UberEats driver" cops relegated to the evidence division.

Naomi closed her eyes and considered everything they'd heard that evening and then she remembered Harper's whispered words. *Para mi. For me.*

The man had wanted Harper for himself, and there was really only one reason he'd want a ten-year-old child. It was a sickening reason and one she didn't want to discuss in front of the kids, who'd already been traumatized that day.

But . . . *for me* as opposed to whom?

It was possible Gaffney and his thugs had only wanted to scare them—at least with Jace and Harper—but what if they'd been serious?

What if they'd been successful? What would the kidnappers have done with their kids once they'd stolen them?

A chill spread across her skin, freezing her heart for a beat.

Drug sales weren't the only illegal vice that skyrocketed during Mardi Gras.

"Burke," she murmured. "Can the adults talk? Maybe send the kids upstairs to play video games?"

Burke nodded. "Sure, but why? What are you thinking about?"

She leaned in to whisper, "What were they planning to do with our kids if they'd been successful in abducting them? Would they have killed them? Or something else?" She looked meaningfully at Harper. "Would they have sold them?" she whispered into Burke's ear. "It's Mardi Gras, after all."

"Oh my God." He looked stricken. "I hope you're wrong."

"I do, too."

"What's going on?" Elijah asked suspiciously. "Are you guys flirting?"

A glance at Everett from the corner of Naomi's eye told her exactly what her son thought of that. The word "flirting" had set off butterflies in her own stomach, but her son looked at her with revulsion. And maybe a little hatred.

Burke laughed self-consciously. "Um, no. But I do need you four to go upstairs. The spare bedroom on the second floor has a TV and a video game console."

"I don't want to play a stupid game," Everett said.

"You don't have to play," Naomi told him, not wanting him to experience any more ugliness than he already had that day. "But . . . you don't want to be down here. Please, Everett."

Everett stared at her, and then something flickered in his eyes. Acceptance? Understanding? He shrugged, like he didn't care at all. "Fine. Whatever." He headed up the stairs, followed by Harrison.

Burke took Jace aside. "Make sure the volume's turned up on whatever movie you watch or whatever game you play."

Jace was instantly sober and in control. "Yes, sir." He shepherded the two younger children up the stairs, tickling Harper and making her smile.

"Jace is a good kid," Naomi said, hoping some of that steady goodness would rub off on Everett.

Val smiled proudly. "He is." Then she sobered, waiting until they heard the television blaring upstairs. "What's going on?"

10

The Quarter, New Orleans, Louisiana
MONDAY, FEBRUARY 24, 10:45 P.M.

IT'S ALL YOURS," Burke said, gesturing to the room where every eye now rested on Naomi.

She looked uncomfortable with the attention. "We've asked why they chose me. I still don't know. What we really haven't asked is what they're planning and why now. We now know that whatever they've been planning, it's been in the works since September, at least. But whatever it is, I think it has something to do with Mardi Gras."

"Drug sales," Val said. "That's why they said they wanted you to deliver for them."

"Yes," Naomi said. "But not only drug sales." She glanced at Chelsea, concern in her dark brown eyes. "This might be difficult for you. Do you want to join the kids upstairs?"

Burke once again was struck by the empathy in this woman's heart. Naomi had been through hell and back, yet she'd retained her humanity.

He respected her. He *liked* her.

Which was probably unwise, considering she was his client, but that didn't change the reality of his feelings.

Chelsea shook her head. "I think I've already thought of what you're going to say."

Naomi's smile was gentle and sad all at once. "I wondered what the kidnapper meant by '*para mi*.' I mean, *for him* as opposed to whom? Who else might have wanted our children? It's very possible they were only trying to scare us, but what if they were serious? What were they planning to do with our children once they'd taken them? Now, we all know that sporting events and major influxes of people into a city for festivals like Mardi Gras mean increased drug trafficking. People are coming here to party. The correlation to sex trafficking is less direct, but the possibility exists. I don't think we can ignore it at this stage."

Molly's obvious shock eased into respect for Naomi. "I hadn't considered that this could be part of a bigger criminal enterprise."

"It might not be," Naomi hastily allowed. "It might only be a way to get back at your firm for agreeing to help me and for that, I'm sorry. Either way, your involvement in my case has clearly struck a chord."

"Don't apologize," Val said firmly. "Clearly they wanted to deter us from investigating this case, but trying to take our children is extreme. They wanted us to stop investigating immediately."

"And they did it quickly," Kaj added. "All I've been able to think about is that you just met Burke this morning, Naomi. And only a few hours later, these people have bugged our vehicles and know where our kids are. Someone had to have known you were in Burke's office this morning. That's the only thing that makes sense."

"Did you see anyone following you?" Molly asked.

"I didn't see anyone, but I wasn't watching. I should have been, but I was so worried that Burke was going to turn me away that I don't remember much of the drive to his office."

Once again, Burke felt ashamed of his initial reaction on seeing Naomi that morning. Once again, he determined he would make things right.

"What surprises me," Ruthanne said from the love seat where she sat beside James, "is how they were bold enough to try and grab Jace and Harper in places with heavy traffic. Mid-City is crazy right now. And, Burke, your godsons were coming out of where?"

"The Creamery in Uptown," Burke said, having had the same thought when Kaleb had first told him what happened, but he'd been so distracted with all the other details that the concern had slipped away. "They had to park down the block because it was so crowded."

"So why would they risk it?" Ruthanne asked. "Their attempt to take Everett makes sense. They waited for him on a street in a quiet neighborhood where no one would try to stop them. Luckily Harrison was there. But how did they think they'd get away on a crowded street during the dinner hour? How *did* they get away?"

"Damn good questions, ma'am," Lucien said. "Chels, which way did they go when they drove away from the diner?"

"I don't know," Chelsea said. "I was so busy making sure Harper was okay that I didn't notice. Can you look at the traffic cams?"

"I just did," Antoine said. He'd had access to the city's traffic cams for years. Burke didn't want to know how and didn't ask. But it frequently came in handy. "You were at Très Bien, right, Chelsea? This is odd. I can see the black SUV stop in front of the diner, then the guy grabs Harper, and I can vaguely see the couple stepping in. And that's when it gets odd. The SUV goes to the end of the block and turns onto the next side street. A group of people who'd been congregating on that street corner moved into the street and were dancing, drunk as skunks. They're blocking all the traffic in that intersection. The SUV moves like it's going to run them down and they all move out of its way, like water flowing. Really smooth. Then they move back into the street and start dancing again. No one could have followed that SUV if they'd tried."

"Really smooth," Burke said. "Like too smooth?"

Antoine shrugged. "Quite possibly."

Kaj raised a hand. "So, let me get this straight. They not only know Naomi has sought help from Burke, they're able to bug our cars and arrange for a flash mob to aid their getaway after trying to abduct Harper? Really?"

Val pointed to the flat-screen. "Show us the footage, Antoine, if you would."

Antoine did and yes, it did appear that the group of drunken revelers in the street had purposely aided the SUV's getaway.

"That's freaky," Lucien said flatly.

Burke had to agree. "We're looking at a highly organized group with significant resources."

"Damn," Molly muttered. "Every question generates more questions. We need a few actual answers."

"I do have at least one answer," Antoine said. "I know who got close enough to your car keys to break into your cars and bug your vehicles." Antoine tapped a few keys on his laptop and the image on the flat-screen changed to a woman standing at the counter in Sylvi's flower shop. "See her hand, the one she keeps at her side? That black box she's holding is the signal amplifier."

She was about thirty-five, of average height, with short blond hair and a big smile. She looked at the flowers in the small refrigerator that Sylvi kept up front, then bought a bouquet of roses, paying with cash. For just a second, she looked straight into the camera.

And Chelsea gasped. "Oh my God."

"What is it?" Lucien demanded. "What's wrong?"

Chelsea pointed a trembling finger at the screen. "That's the woman from Très Bien, the one who helped Harper. Donna Burrell."

Antoine sighed. "Who, I'll bet, is not from Galveston."

Burke pinched the bridge of his nose as everyone started talking, his living room descending into chaos.

Fuck.

The Central Business District, New Orleans, Louisiana
MONDAY, FEBRUARY 24, 11:00 P.M.

"Say that again," he said evenly, folding his hands on his desk. "I'm sure that I didn't hear you right."

Elaine Billings looked nervous. "I didn't know Ernesto was going to try to keep the girl."

"He was supposed to take Jace. He was only supposed to *pretend* to take the little one. I made that perfectly clear."

It was one of his hard limits. No kids. Teenagers were the goal. Twelve was borderline possible, but ten was not permissible. "Did he believe I'd be okay with adding a ten-year-old to our inventory? Did I not make myself clear?"

Elaine fidgeted in her chair. "I don't think he intended to surrender the child to you. I think he was planning to . . . keep her. For himself."

He drew in a breath. Ernesto and Pablo were not his people. They were Ortiz's, members of his gang. They'd been reliable up until today. Trustworthy, even. Which was why he'd elevated them to the positions they held. Up until today.

"Did Ernesto know about his brother?" he asked.

"Only that Broussard's bodyguard broke his arm. I don't think he knows that his brother is dead."

He blew out a breath. He was going to have to explain to Ortiz why two of his men were dead, but he'd deal with that later. Ernesto had to go, too.

This was why he disliked murder. It complicated things.

"Why do you believe he planned to keep the child?" he asked.

"Because when I got in his way, he said, *'Para mi.'*"

"Idiot."

Elaine nodded uncomfortably and said nothing, because she'd fucked up, too. Fear filled her eyes. *Good. She should be afraid.* She'd gotten involved and called attention to herself. *A pity, because she's far more valuable than both Delgado brothers put together.*

"The mother of the girl saw your face."

Elaine nodded again, miserably this time.

"Why did you step in?" he asked.

"It was instinct. She's ten and small for her age. I knew you wouldn't want her."

Others would use children, but he wasn't a monster. Kids were off-limits. Period. So he understood Elaine's knee-jerk reaction, but she'd be on Broussard's radar from here on out.

"Where is Ernesto right now?"

Relief replaced the fear. She thought she was out of the woods and, for now, she was.

"I don't know. He got out of the SUV while Wayne and I were enabling Freddie to get away."

"That was smart thinking, getting the tourists to dance in the street so that Freddie could get away."

"Thank you."

He waited a moment, but she didn't give Wayne Stanley credit for the plan he'd crafted. Stanley always planned a getaway strategy. It was one of the things that made him so ruthlessly efficient. He'd recruited the tourists, who thought they were doing a good deed for a man proposing to his lover.

It would have worked like a charm had Elaine not shown her face to the mother of that child.

Elaine would have to go, too, but not yet. He needed someone to manage the inventory now that Pablo was dead.

"You've used the scheduling program?"

"Yes. I know how it works. We're booked to capacity for the next two weeks."

"Good." They just needed to get through Mardi Gras and then he and Stanley would regroup. They could deal with Elaine then. "Lay low for the time being."

"What about the girl in the hospital?"

The girl was one of their inventory who'd been beaten nearly to death in a motel room by a john hyped up on coke during Super Bowl weekend. They'd thought her actually dead, but she'd been—unfortunately—resuscitated. "Is she still unconscious?"

"According to my source in the hospital, yes. But they've been bringing her out of the induced coma, so that could change at any time."

They needed to eliminate her before she could speak.

"Who's on guard duty?" NOPD had posted an armed officer outside the girl's room, impeding his ability to take care of the problem.

"None of ours. Not until Wednesday."

"Okay. Then lay low until then. You'll need to get in there and take care of her once our cop is at the door. You may go."

She rose and left quickly, likely before he could change his mind.

Elaine wasn't a stupid woman. Stanley had met her online while researching their competition. She had a network of people—usually men—who liked teenagers, and she knew where to find the ones that no one would miss.

He dialed Stanley as soon as she'd closed his office door. "Is Ernesto home yet?"

"Not yet. He'll probably stay out for a while, licking his wounds. Freddie gave him hell for trying to take the kid. I don't think he expected everyone to enforce your rule."

"Idiot."

"He is that. I'm at his house with his grandmother. If he doesn't come home in the next few hours, I'll have her call him. She always does what I say and he always comes home when she calls."

Because the Delgado matron was not stupid. Unlike her grandsons, she knew who held the power.

"Good. When he does come home, kill him."

"Understood. There are two girls here. The ones who needed medical attention. What about them?"

That was Elaine's other purview. She'd once been a nursing assistant and could take care of basic injuries. Anything more serious required that they put the pieces of inventory out of their misery.

"Are they fixable?"

"Eventually. I think it'll be at least three weeks before we can put them back into rotation."

"Then kill them, too."

He really hated murder, but sometimes it was unavoidable.

"Understood. And Broussard?" Stanley asked.

"He's gathered up his people." He'd sent Gaffney to watch Broussard's street. "They're all in his house. They'll hunker down for at least a day or two, protecting their kids."

"So it worked."

"It did. For now."

"And when they get back to investigating?"

"We move on to plan C."

Stanley frowned. "We could go straight to plan Z."

Which was killing Broussard. "We'll get there. I promise."

"And you'll let me be the one?"

"Yes. You've earned the right." Stanley enjoyed killing and was very good at it. He also hated Broussard.

"Thank you," Stanley said. "I'll let you know when the Ernesto issue is resolved."

The Quarter, New Orleans, Louisiana
MONDAY, FEBRUARY 24, 11:55 P.M.

The house was finally quiet. Burke crept down the stairs to his darkened living room, exhausted.

Everyone was in their rooms. He had a full house.

His mother would be so pleased. God, he missed her. He didn't think of her every day anymore, but sometimes there'd be something he wanted to share with her.

Like, look, Mom. The house is teeming with life.

Not necessarily the best reason to have a full house, of course, but they were making do. Molly was standing guard on the upper floor, Lucien on the second floor. He'd pulled in two of his part-timers to sit outside his house and Antoine had beefed up the alarm system.

For now, they were locked up tight.

Come dawn, he'd figure out what to do next. For the next few hours, he just wanted to sleep.

But he hadn't been able to, all kinds of nightmare scenarios going through his mind. So he'd finally given up. He'd try to doze in his chair. It wouldn't be the first time he'd slept there.

He was lowering himself into his BarcaLounger when he saw Naomi, her presence nearly surprising him into a shout.

She was sitting on the settee she'd shared with him earlier, the low glow of a lamp illuminating the knitting in her hands. She gave him a rueful look as she began to put her project away.

"I'll go back to my room," she said quietly. "I didn't mean to bother you."

"No bother at all." He walked to the settee. "May I?"

"Of course. Are you all right? You look tired."

There it was again. Her empathy.

He settled in the corner of the settee, once again thinking of his mother. She'd always had a ball of yarn in her huge pocketbook.

"I am tired, but I couldn't sleep. You?"

"Same. It's always the wee hours when I wake up."

"Nightmares?" he asked.

"Yes." She folded her hands atop a small project bag covered with butterflies. "You have a beautiful home, Burke. Thank you for inviting us to stay here. Especially Everett and my mom."

His mouth quirked. "And James."

She laughed softly. "And James. I don't know how I didn't know they were together."

"He told me they were just friends."

"Sometimes that's more than enough. Or at least the best place to begin."

They sat in silence for a long moment that felt . . . comfortable. He finally pointed to her bag. "What are you making?"

"Knockers."

He blinked. "Excuse me?"

She grinned and it lit up her pretty face. "Knockers. They're prosthetics for women who've had mastectomies or lumpectomies and who are either waiting for reconstructive surgery or who've decided against it for whatever reason. They're soft and breathable compared to the silicone bra inserts. Plus, they can be worn a lot sooner after surgery. They're distributed by a nonprofit organization for free to women all over the world. Volunteers like me make them."

A warm feeling filled his chest. "That's really nice."

She pulled the project she'd been working on from the butterfly bag. "I started making them when I was inside. One of the women in my cellblock had had a double mastectomy and it was going to be a long time before she could have reconstructive surgery—if she got it at all. And wearing silicone inserts—even if she could have gotten them—would have been so uncomfortable in the heat."

"No air-conditioning."

"Not for us. They were putting it in some of the areas, but we hadn't gotten any yet. So I made her several pairs. Those were crocheted since I wasn't allowed knitting needles, but they did the job. My mom would send me yarn. Kept me sane."

"Has the woman gotten reconstructive surgery now?" Burke asked.

Naomi swallowed hard. "No. Her treatment was so delayed by the prison system that the mastectomy didn't get it all. It had spread and . . . she died. Now I make these for other people in her name. Some people think that she deserved to die, but she was in for possession of heroin. It was her personal stash. She wasn't a dealer. She should have paid for her crime, but not with her life."

"I believe in punishing criminals, but you're right. She shouldn't have died." He exhaled slowly, using his thumbs to wipe the moisture from his eyes. He wasn't a crier, but today had been a shitty day.

"Burke?"

He forced a smile. "Long day," he said.

"It has been. You're going to figure this out. You and your people will, anyway. You aren't doing this alone."

"We're normally so on top of our cases. We have to-do lists and whiteboards filled with leads and suspects. But this one kind of cut us off at the knees."

"They tried to take our children."

"They did." He motioned to her knitting. "You can continue. I won't bother you."

"You're not bothering me. I figured you'd want a moment alone."

"I did, but I'm happy to share my alone time with you."

She laughed. "That was cheesy."

He found himself grinning. "It was, wasn't it?" He watched as her hands began to move again, her stitches small and even. "My mother knitted. You made me think of her just now."

"What did she knit?"

"Baby things. She donated them to the hospital or to shelters."

"I do, too. We did a lot of that inside. It gives a sense of purpose, that what you're doing will help people. Or at least allow them to know someone cared enough to make them something. I'm sorry about your mother. You must miss her."

"I do. She gardened and cooked and baked. All the mom things."

"She raised you, too," she said lightly. "So that's a check in her plus column."

His mother would approve. "Thank you. That's kind of you to say, but you don't have to."

"Like you, I rarely humor people. I try to call it like I see it."

Except with her son, but he supposed he understood that. Coming back from prison to find your son hated you couldn't have been easy.

He wanted to fix their relationship, to get Everett to see how special his mother really was. He wanted to clear her name. He wanted to keep his people safe. He wanted to get rid of Gaffney once and for all.

"Burke?" She was leaning toward him, her face concerned. "You spaced out."

"My mind is spinning," he confessed. "I don't know what to do next."

"I know the feeling." Her gaze fell to her hands and she started knitting again. "I asked ADA Cardozo if we could talk to Cresswell. I figured if anyone could get me in, it would be the assistant district attorney."

"You did?" Burke was surprised. "When?"

"When he came back after fetching Czar. Cardozo said he'd talk to his boss about it."

"Kaj will do whatever he can. He's a good guy."

"Val thinks he hung the moon, and he's so good to Sylvi. I hadn't talked to him before tonight. I think he was avoiding me because of conflict of interest maybe. Since I could be prosecuted again at any time."

"Let's make sure that doesn't happen."

"I hope you can. I really don't want to go back."

He could hear the fear and the hopelessness seep into her voice and he hated it. He'd steer her back to a topic that gave her strength—investigating her own case. "Of course you don't. What will you ask Cresswell, if you're able to see him?"

"Of course I'd ask why they picked me for their frame. I'd ask why they needed to frame anyone. What were they trying to cover up? Or if I was a distraction, then from what? I'd ask who took over when he went to prison, because I don't know that Gaffney is capable of heading a large, organized operation like we were talking about tonight. He seems like more of a hired thug."

"Agreed. Those are all good questions. Have you written them down?"

She patted her pocket. "I'm keeping a list on my phone. I'd also ask him about the scope of the operation he had with Gaffney. They tried to get you to help them skim drugs from busts, but what else did they do? What kind of drugs did they distribute? Only what they stole from evidence, or did they buy and sell other substances?"

Burke was impressed. "If knitting helps you think like that, maybe I should give it a try."

She chuckled. "I'll teach you if you want." Then she sighed. "I'd ask him if they trafficked human beings, too. I hope I'm completely wrong about that."

"For what it's worth, I think you might be right."

"Whatever they have planned, I think it's going to be big for Mardi Gras, but we just had the Super Bowl here a few weeks ago. Surely they wouldn't have let that opportunity pass by untapped. I wouldn't ask Cresswell this, but I would ask your friend André if they saw any evidence of organized drug distribution or sex trafficking operations during Super Bowl weekend."

Burke hadn't thought that far yet. That she had, given the upheaval of the day, was impressive. "Very good thinking."

She threw him a self-effacing smile. "I was a cop. Not like you were, I know. Not a detective. But I was good at processing evidence and I'd follow the interesting arrests as they went to court. Played my own version of Clue as the investigation and the prosecution unfolded. Never thought I'd be a felon, though."

"You aren't anymore."

"No, but if they ever decide to retry my case, I might be. And I'm not going to think about that tonight. Can you ask your friend André about the Super Bowl?"

"I will. We're going to investigate Winnifred Timms, too. Antoine's looking into her financials."

"Good. To think that I felt sorry for her that night, her car wrecked on the side of the road. Until I saw her smirk when the responding cop cuffed me. 'Oh my,'" she mimicked in a falsetto, her accent growing mockingly heavy. "'I'm just going for my book bag and oh, my goodness, what is *that* on the floor?' Bitch." Then she grimaced and peeked up at him. "Sorry."

He laughed. "Don't be. I'm surprised you haven't sought her out."

She bit her lip and said nothing.

Huh. He leaned forward, just as she'd done. "Naomi? Did you seek her out?"

"I did. I got her address from the internet but she didn't live there."

"That's what Molly and Lucien said. They tried to interview her after they saw you at Sylvi's shop. Did you ever find her?"

"I did. The person who did live there suggested I check the building where she takes some classes, so I waited outside the building for her to come out."

"That was lucky."

She winced. "I might have tried every day for three weeks until I spotted her."

His lip twitched. "And then?"

"And then I followed her home. She went to an expensive high-rise on Poydras. I know, it was stupid and I shouldn't have done it."

She shouldn't have done it, but this was information they didn't yet have. "Do you remember the address?"

"Oh yes." She looked pleased. "Did I get info that Molly didn't?"

"You did."

She grinned. "Good for me."

He smiled at her. "So what did you see when you followed her home?"

"She met up with a man. Tall, dark, and handsome. Older than she was, by at least fifteen or twenty years. They were lovers or at least dating. I followed them to the Quarter one of the nights—"

"Wait. How many times did you follow her?"

Another wince. "Too many?"

"Okay. What happened when you followed them to the Quarter?"

"They went to a fancy restaurant and he kissed her very thoroughly before they went in. I didn't follow them inside, but I did follow them when they went back to her place. He went up with her. After that, I went home. I guess she wasn't a poor college kid after all, or maybe she was until someone paid her to set me up. Made me wonder what else she was into to be able to afford that lifestyle."

"Can you describe the man to Antoine? He's pretty good at creating sketches with software."

"I'd be happy to. I got a clear look at his face and it wasn't so long ago that I've forgotten what he looked like. I honestly thought she'd be meeting up with Gaffney himself, but she didn't. I might also ask Cresswell if he was involved with her. They needed someone they could trust to set me up."

"Is that on your list of questions?"

She pulled her phone from her pocket and typed. "It is now. I also just texted you the address on Poydras so you can track her down yourself."

He yawned. "My mind is settling down." He regarded her for a long moment, watching her knit. She was smart and observant. Maybe he could clear her name, get Gaffney, and make her happy. "You want to help? To come with me to investigate?"

It was ill-advised, spending more time with her. He liked her way too much already. But he was going to do it anyway.

She stared at him, her hands freezing mid-stitch. "Seriously?"

He wondered if she would have been so stunned at the request before prison or if her ex-husband's emotional abuse had already whittled down her self-esteem at that point.

"Seriously. I'd like to get your opinions. If it becomes in any way dangerous, I'll bring you back here."

"Molly is usually your investigator. But she's going to be guarding the children."

He nodded. "She'll say that she can still work the case, but her attention is splintered, and rightfully so. It's not the first time that her niece has been in danger because of a case she was working." Which Harper's paternal grandparents were trying to use against them, trying to get custody of Harper. "I won't ask her to leave her niece right now."

Because I'm not a total asshole, despite what Kaleb thinks.

"Can I ask you a question first?"

He stiffened at her careful tone. "You can ask."

"What happened tonight that made you so sad? Between arriving with Val and Kaj and the boys and when you came back in the house? I know your godsons were attacked, but you didn't look like you were afraid. Only sad. Like you'd lost your best friend."

He sighed. Somehow, she'd hit the nail on the head. "My family is all gone, all but one brother who really isn't my brother. We share no blood."

"Blood doesn't make a family."

"It doesn't. Kaleb and I met when we were kids. I was thirteen and he was twelve. My uncle and his dad were business partners and Kaleb's mom had already passed. Kaleb and I were inseparable. When Mom and I came to live here, with my uncle, we saw Kaleb and his sister nigh on every day. Then my mom and my uncle died. Kaleb and I only had each other and his father. I was devastated after the plane crash, and I just couldn't stay here. So I put aside my college plans and joined the Marine Corps, even though my uncle had left this house and the business to me. But I didn't stick around."

"Kaleb did."

"Yeah. And when I came back from the Corps, I became a cop. Made detective and met a guy named Gaffney."

"This story doesn't have a happy ending," she murmured.

"No, it doesn't. Gaffney threatened my godsons—Kaleb's boys—to get me to work with him in the drug-skimming op. I said no and managed to get away from the NOPD with my hide intact."

"Someday you'll have to share how you did that with me."

"I will." *But not tonight.* He had to work through his guilt first. He should have exposed Gaffney back then. "I started my PI firm and thought that my godsons would be safe."

"And then they were threatened again tonight. Did Kaleb blame you?"

"He did. I've never heard him so angry. He told me that I was selfish to do a job that put others in danger. He told me to stay out of the boys' lives."

Her hands stilled, the needles pausing. “Oh, Burke,” she said sympathetically. “I hope he’ll cool down and change his mind.”

“His wife thinks he will. She didn’t blame me. But . . .”

“You feel guilty anyway.”

“Yeah.”

“And Kaleb’s sister?” she asked.

Burke flinched. “What?”

“You mentioned that Kaleb had a sister, but after the plane crash it was just you, Kaleb, and his father.” Her gaze sharpened. “She was on the plane, too?”

This woman was too smart. He’d have to watch what he said. “She was checking out a university up north and my mother went with her. My uncle had a meeting with a vendor in the same city, so he took them with him on the company plane. She didn’t even want to see that college, because we’d both gotten into Tulane, but my mother insisted she at least look at the place. So they went. The plane had engine trouble on the way back. Everyone on board died.”

“She was special to you,” she said softly.

“We were engaged,” he said, unable to believe he was sharing this. Not even Molly knew about Kyra. “We were young, I know, but we knew what we wanted. We were going to wait until we’d graduated from college to get married, but for me, she was it.”

“I’m sorry. That you lost her and that it still hurts you to talk about her.”

“It’s okay. I’m okay.” He wasn’t, but he never was when he remembered Kyra.

“So this investigation will help you save my son, all the other kids, your godsons, and maybe your relationship with your brother?”

“And maybe clear your name completely.”

"Then I'm in. We'll ask Captain Holmes about any drug or sex trafficking arrests during Super Bowl weekend, maybe talk to Cresswell, and hopefully track down that bitch Winnifred Timms. When do we leave tomorrow?"

"After breakfast."

"Then I'll be ready."

11

The Quarter, New Orleans, Louisiana
TUESDAY, FEBRUARY 25, 9:30 A.M.

NAOMI HAD HOPED that seeing Captain Holmes would be easier after spilling her guts to him the day before, but not so much. She was still wary of the captain, who'd arrived at Burke's house in the Quarter in time for breakfast.

Everett sat at one end of the table. He'd been alone for a few minutes before everyone began to shuffle downstairs and take their places. But it seemed Jace had taken her son under his wing, because he'd sat next to Everett and had drawn him into a debate with Elijah on their newest video game. Everett seemed to be in good hands, so she turned in her seat when André Holmes wished her a good morning.

"Good morning, Captain," she replied, her back going ramrod straight.

She would have done the same while a cop, but the rigidity of her spine—and the resulting pain from that rigidity—was one hundred percent due to prison. When a guard had said her name, she'd been on instant panicked alert.

Captain Holmes must have detected her flare of panic, because his expression saddened. "I'm not here to hurt you, Miss Cranston."

"I know. Here." She tapped her temple. "But it's okay. I'm dealing."

"Burke says you have questions for me."

She glanced at Burke before checking to make sure the boys and Harper were occupied. "Maybe we could discuss this somewhere else?"

Burke nodded. "Little pitchers seem to be chatting among themselves, but their big ears are always listening."

The little pout on Elijah's face proved Burke to be correct. "Gee, thanks, Burke," the boy said, rolling his eyes.

"I have a lot to learn before our baby arrives," Holmes said. "Or so my wife tells me."

"She's right," Antoine said, needling his brother. "Kids hear everything."

"Like how to hack into—" Elijah started, but Jace covered his mouth with his hand.

"Not okay, dude," Jace said, then grimaced. "Neither is licking my palm."

Elijah cackled while Val shook her head fondly. "Go somewhere else, Burke, before these boys get too riled up. Lucien and I will take care of things here. Molly and Harrison are asleep. We'll do guard duty while you go out and do the investigating for a change."

Burke raised his brows. "For a change?"

"You spend too much time behind a desk," Lucien said, Harper sitting beside him. He hadn't let the child out of his sight. "Time to mix things up a little."

Harper turned serious eyes on them. "Please find them, Uncle Burke. I want to go home."

Burke's face fell and Naomi could see the guilt that hovered over him like a dark rain cloud. "I know, honey. I'm gonna fix this."

Naomi rose, giving Burke's shoulder a quick squeeze. "Is your office safe? I mean, has Antoine checked it for bugs?"

Holmes's eyes went wide. "Bugs? What have I missed?"

"So damn much," Burke muttered. "You know about the attempts on the kids, but now we know more."

"And I want to hear it," André said.

"The study's clean, Naomi," Antoine said. "The whole house is. I checked and then double- and triple-checked. You don't have to worry."

She thanked him before following Burke and Captain Holmes up the stairs and into a study. Burke sat on a love seat, patting the cushion beside him while Holmes took a recliner that was in only slightly better condition than the BarcaLounger downstairs.

"What's this about bugs?" Holmes asked.

Burke told him everything, from the bugged cars to the couple who'd stepped in to "save" Harper the night before but who'd been the ones to break into their cars and plant the bugs.

Holmes was rubbing his temples by the time Burke was finished. "You never do things the easy way, do you?"

"I think I did something the easy way," Burke said. "I should have exposed Gaffney five years ago."

"With what?" Holmes said. "With rumors like you had on Cresswell? A claim with no evidence like you had on Gaffney? If PIB couldn't get Gaffney, you turning him in would only have ended poorly."

"But it might have kept Naomi out of prison. Or at least made everyone look at Gaffney's testimony more closely."

"He'd threatened your godsons," Naomi said. "I let myself go to prison because he threatened my son, Burke. If I'd stood up, maybe he wouldn't have tried to kill my mother."

"Whoa!" Holmes lifted both hands. "What?"

Naomi recounted her mother's story with a sigh.

Holmes shook his head. "Why can't we find anything on John Gaffney? We've tried several times, but there's never any evidence."

"There has to be some," Naomi said. "Even if it's not been identified yet. I think better questions are: Who is smoothing Gaffney's way and why? More threats, or is it old-fashioned bribery?"

Holmes closed his eyes. "I know. I've asked those questions myself." He gave himself a shake. "What is it you'd like to ask me, Miss Cranston?"

"Have you seen an uptick in human trafficking in the city? Like, during the Super Bowl?"

Holmes considered her for a long moment. "Why do you ask?"

Burke rolled his eyes. "Can you answer the question, André?"

"Oh, I will. I just want to know what prompts Miss Cranston to ask."

She feared that he wouldn't take her seriously, but a nod from Burke gave her confidence. "I was wondering what Gaffney's game is. Whatever it is, it's big enough and urgent enough for them to try to take our kids."

"True," Holmes allowed. "We don't have any real leads on that black SUV, by the way. They changed their license plates. We found the stolen ones in a dumpster."

"Did you get them changing the plates on any city cams?" Burke asked.

"Nope. It's like they know the dead zones."

"So they're organized and they know the area," Burke grumbled. "Terrific."

Holmes turned back to Naomi. "Keep going."

"They don't want Burke and his team operating efficiently, so the best way to shut down their investigation immediately is to threaten the children. I figure whatever they're planning, it has to do with Mardi Gras. Which made me wonder if they hadn't also operated two weeks ago during the Super Bowl. It would have been a difficult opportunity to pass up."

"That makes sense. But why ask me about sex trafficking in particular?"

"The man who grabbed Harper said 'for me.' That made me wonder what they'd planned to do with our kids once they'd taken them. It's Mardi Gras. We'll have a million extra people in the city and some of those people will be here for more than the floats. I met several women in prison who had started on their path by being forced to do sex work. That led them to drugs and then other crimes, which landed them in prison. It's where my mind went when I thought of what Gaffney might have done with our kids if he'd gotten them."

"So?" Burke asked. "Is she right, André?"

"Yeah, she is. We took two young women into protective custody during Super Bowl weekend. One was fourteen and the other sixteen. The fourteen-year-old stabbed her client and got away. The sixteen-year-old was found bleeding out in a hotel room, left for dead by a john, but the doctors saved her. The fourteen-year-old knew the older girl, but only by sight. They were being held in the same place, but she couldn't tell us where it was."

"They blindfolded them going to and from their johns," Naomi said.

André nodded. "It's common. The doctors had to put the sixteen-year-old into an induced coma so that she could heal. She's still intubated, but she's coming around. The fourteen-year-old was kidnapped from a Halloween party in Baton Rouge and forced into prostitution. She sharpened a metal shower hook into a shiv and sliced the face of the next john."

"Did she hurt him?" Naomi asked, feeling ill.

"She did. The john ran from the motel room, screaming. The girl got lucky after that. Some college kids who were partying in the room next door gave her cab fare. They didn't want to get involved with NOPD, but they gave her one of their burner phones and she used it to call 911."

"Did the girl give a description of her pimp?" Naomi asked.

"Not a good one. She was very traumatized and was returned to the foster family in Baton Rouge who'd reported her missing after that party. But we were still looking for the pimp."

Naomi heard his use of the past tense. "*Were?*"

"He's dead?" Burke guessed.

Holmes nodded. "Found him last night. Bullet right between the eyes."

Naomi considered the possibilities and chose the one that made the most sense. "He's the guy with a broken arm, isn't he? The one who tried to kidnap my son."

Holmes stared at her, stunned. "How . . . ?" He glared at Burke. "How the hell did you know?"

Good, Naomi thought. *He can never hurt Everett again.* There were others, of course, but at least one of the monsters was dead.

Burke shook his head. "I didn't. She's smart, André."

Holmes slowly turned his gaze on Naomi. "How did you know, Miss Cranston?" he asked, his tone low and ominous.

Bristling at the accusation in his voice, she lifted her chin. "Because you were looking for him, but you didn't have a good description. Yet you found him. Your brother did a mockup based on

Harrison Banks's description. Either his body turned up randomly and you said, *Hell yeah,* or you recognized him from your brother's sketch, knew where to look for him, and found him dead. And you said, *Hell yeah*. Am I right?"

Holmes's mouth quirked up on one side. "Hell yeah, ma'am."

"Which one?" she asked.

"Which do you think?" Holmes countered.

"The first one. Someone discovered a body and it turned out to be him."

"Because you don't think we could have ID'd and found him on our own?" Holmes asked, sounding defensive.

"*Did* you ID and find him on your own?"

He frowned. "No. Anything else you want to add?"

Being right felt good. "The second girl, the sixteen-year-old who's 'coming around' from the induced coma. I'm thinking that, despite being intubated, she was at least able to identify the pimp from the sketch or from whatever photo you took of his dead body, which is why you're certain you have the right man."

Holmes shook his head in mild bewilderment.

"Did she ID him, André?" Burke asked.

"She did. She'll stay in protective custody until she's fully recovered, and then we'll figure out what to do with her. She has no family. She was another foster kid, also grew up in Baton Rouge."

"Does the dead man have a name?" Burke asked.

Holmes hesitated, then shook his head. "Not gonna give you that."

"Did the dead guy have a brother?" Naomi asked quietly.

Holmes sighed. "I'm not telling you that information. I will only tell you that the man who attempted to kidnap Harper and Jace is being searched for. I promise you that."

"Jace and Harper didn't see his face, Captain," Naomi said, suddenly furious. "If they come upon him again, they'll be unaware. Lambs to slaughter, and that is not hyperbole. These people were selling children for sex. My son is sixteen. Jace is seventeen. Harper is only ten." She was building up steam and she let the angry words flow. "You owe it to Burke and his people to give them not only the man's name but his description, because I'm sure that you have it now. What is his name?"

Burke leaned back, folding his hands over his stomach, his expression one of approval. "You go, girl. Let him have it."

"Burke!" Holmes snapped.

"She's right, André."

Naomi stood, her body shaking with rage. "You let me be thrown in prison. Not you personally, Captain Holmes, but NOPD failed me. Your dirty cops stole five years of my life. They terrorized me through my son. But I didn't fight because Everett was safe. Until he wasn't. That dead man who you will not name *put his hands* on my son. If it hadn't been for Harrison Banks, Everett would be taken and God only knows what would be happening to him. It was not okay when you hung me out to dry, but it is *inexcusable* when our children are targeted. I don't want empty promises that you'll 'investigate Gaffney.' I don't want promises that you're looking for the man who put his hands on Jace and Harper because, quite frankly, I do not trust the NOPD to do their job. Gaffney is in this up to his eyeballs and he is one of yours."

"Not mine," Holmes said quietly.

It was like his words lit her on fire, and she leaned into him, getting in his space.

"I don't care!" she shouted. "He is NOPD and he has been allowed to terrorize innocent people without consequences for years. NOPD obviously won't take care of this, so give his name to Burke and let him take care of it." She slowly straightened, aware that she'd been screaming into the face of an NOPD captain. But she didn't regret a single word. "You don't have to tell me his name. I'll leave the room. But if you want to make things better, just give Burke his name and let him do your job." She looked at Burke, who was staring at her. "I'm sorry I shouted. But not for what I said."

Burke barked out a laugh. "Darlin', you can shout anytime you please. Because you are one hundred percent right. You've done your part. Go and get some coffee."

"She doesn't need any more caffeine," Holmes grumbled.

Burke laughed again. "Relax, Naomi. Put your feet up, let your heart rate come back down. Maybe knit some knockers. I won't let you down."

She nodded. "Okay. Thank you."

She was halfway out the door when she heard Holmes ask, "Knit some knockers? What the hell, Burke?"

She closed the door and ran right into Antoine, who'd been unashamedly listening at the study door. He was grinning ear to ear. "Oh my God. That was epic."

Now that it was over, her adrenaline crashed, and she sagged against the door. "He made me angry."

"He makes me angry every day, but he really is a good man. He'll do the right thing. Especially after you pointed it out so very clearly." He took her arm gently. "Come on. Let me help you downstairs. You look shaky."

"I am shaky. Will he give Burke the man's name?"

"Probably, but it doesn't matter if he doesn't."

"Why?" Then she understood. "You've figured it out on your own."

Antoine nodded with satisfaction. "I was coming to tell Burke that my facial recognition software finally pulled a name on the guy, who we now know is dead. From there I got his brother's name. Two-bit punks who were part of the STs—one of the local gangs—before they were apparently recruited by Gaffney. But just as I was about to knock on the door, what should I hear? The dulcet tones of Miss Naomi Cranston dragging my brother to a come-to-Jesus meeting. It was awesome."

Val was standing guard near the front door. "What's this about Naomi dragging André somewhere?"

They had the attention of the whole room. Antoine led her to the settee and lowered her into it. "Get her a glass of something sweet. Orange juice if we have it."

"On it," Jace called, and a moment later the teenager was pressing a cold glass of juice in her hand. "Drink it, Miss Naomi. You look pale."

She obeyed. "Thank you, Jace."

"What happened?" Everett demanded. "Why do you look like that?"

Antoine chortled. "Sit down, boys and girls. I have a story to tell you."

Naomi's gaze flew to his. "Not all of it."

Antoine nodded at her kindly. "I'll keep it PG."

And he did, skipping the part about the sex trafficking victims, focusing instead on the dead kidnapper and the demand for the brother's name. When he was finished, her mother and James wore huge smiles of approval, and Val came over to give her a hard hug.

Kaj, who'd arrived at some point while she'd been upstairs, held his fist out for her to bump. "Nicely done, Naomi. Burke should add you to his payroll."

"Um, no," Val said. "Not that you wouldn't be welcome, Naomi. You'd be amazing here, but Sylvi will cut you, Kaj, if you make her lose her employee."

Naomi shook her head. "You're all ridiculous."

Antoine sat beside her. "Now, I have to know. Why *did* Burke tell you to knit some knockers?"

She chuckled and told them about her project. Elijah looked at her with tears in his eyes.

"My mom died of cancer," Elijah said. "Not breast cancer, but still. Is that something a kid could do? Like me?"

"Absolutely," she said. "I'll teach you how."

Kaj squeezed her shoulder. "Thank you," he murmured.

And then she looked up at Everett, who looked . . . unsettled. Of course he was. The man who'd nearly kidnapped him had been shot in the head. Everett had never been exposed to death. This had to be difficult for him. "Are you all right?" she asked her son.

"Yeah," he said shortly. "I'm going to my room for a while."

He went up the stairs, Lucien trailing him because Harrison was sleeping.

At least he hadn't yelled at her or ridiculed her. *Progress.*

"He'll come around," Jace said. "I don't think he's a bad guy. Just mixed up."

Naomi's eyes burned. "Thank you, honey."

"Can I get you anything else? More juice?"

"Coffee?" she asked hopefully.

Antoine laughed. "I'll get it," he said, getting up from the settee. "I think Kaj wants to talk to you."

Kaj Cardozo took Antoine's seat. "My boss is going to talk to Cresswell today. He doesn't anticipate getting any answers. He says you can join him, if you wish."

Naomi's eyes widened. "Really?"

He nodded. "He's hoping seeing you will make Cresswell surprised enough to say something. The chance is very small. Almost infinitesimal, but if you're willing to go back to prison as a visitor, you may attend."

She sucked in a breath. "Oh. When will this be?"

"This afternoon. He's setting it up now and will let you know the time. If you decide not to join him, you can email me your questions and I'll make sure he gets them."

Once again, Naomi's eyes burned. "You convinced him to include me."

Kaj lifted a shoulder. "I advocated for you."

"Thank you," she whispered.

"It's about time the system worked for you."

She blinked and let the tears fall. "Yesterday morning, I had no hope. But today . . ." She wiped at her eyes. "I have Sylvi to thank."

"I think she's your strongest advocate. We'll do our best for you, Naomi."

She closed her eyes, overcome. "Thank you."

The Quarter, New Orleans, Louisiana
TUESDAY, FEBRUARY 25, 9:55 A.M.

Burke waited until Naomi had closed the door before turning to André. "Well?"

She had been amazing. Absolutely stunning. Watching her get all up in André's face like that had lit something within him.

He hadn't realized that strong women were such a turn-on, but she was.

And she'd been right. About nearly everything. Especially about trusting the NOPD to do their job. As good a man as André was, he couldn't force the entire police department to behave with the same honor that he did.

"Tell me his name, André."

"Dammit, Burke."

"She's right. Somebody is shielding Gaffney. No way he's so clean that nothing sticks to him."

"I know," André said quietly. "If I give you the kidnapper's name, what will you do with it?"

"Track him."

"And when you find him?"

"We'll hold him and call you."

"How hard will you hold him?"

"As hard as we need to. And if we shoot, it'll be to wound. Unless he's shooting back."

André closed his eyes. "You suck."

Burke chuckled. "Just tell me. You know you're gonna."

André opened one eye. "You like her."

Burke flinched. "Of course I do. She's my client."

André slowly grinned, both eyes going wide and sparkling with unholy glee. "You're normally a better liar."

André was right about that. About Naomi, too, but Burke wasn't going there. "Don't be trying to distract me. Tell me the bastard's name."

André sighed. "Ernesto Delgado. His dead brother is Pablo."

"What do you have on the dead brother?" Burke asked. "I'm thinking he doesn't have a record."

André gave him a pointed look. "Because Antoine hasn't yet found him with his facial recognition software, and I'm sure he already checked the mug shot database."

Burke just shrugged, unwilling to admit to the hacking that everyone knew Antoine did routinely. "Do you have any forensics?"

"The bullet was a .380, still in the punk's skull. He was found in the river. His body had gotten tangled up in some fishing line. A fisherman found him when he went to get into his boat."

"Tangled up on purpose?"

"I don't think so. His feet were the only things sticking up out of the water. He had a cement block tied to his body. He was supposed to have sunk. I think he was tossed off that particular dock where he was found."

"Gators?"

"Only a little. His face was still identifiable. He'd only been in the water for a few hours at most. He was found at ten last night. Your man Banks has an alibi, yes?"

"Oh yes. He's been here with Naomi's son, her mother, and her ex-father-in-law since five yesterday. I put Harrison on the kid's six even though the father said no, because the mother said yes and she still has shared custody."

"Still? You expect that to change?"

"Asshole ex came right out and said he would petition for full custody because Naomi put his kid in danger and that she was delusional."

"Does Miss Cranston know he's going for full custody?"

"She does. She knew that was a near certainty when she asked for my help yesterday morning. She was willing to accept the risk, thinking it might even be safer for Everett if she did lose custody."

"Why do you think Gaffney went after Everett and shot up Sylvi's shop? That was a rapid escalation."

"We think they followed Naomi to my office yesterday. Once they knew she'd involved us, they knew they'd lost control over her. I guess grabbing Everett and shooting up Sylvi's shop were last-ditch efforts to bend her to their will."

"Somehow I think there's no danger of her doing that now."

"You're right." Burke felt pride for her courage. "Anything else on Pablo? Camera footage from the dock?"

"None. Everyone we talked to knew the cameras were out and had been for at least a month."

"So, once again, they know the area."

"Fair to assume. Or at least one person in their organization does. Can I get the footage of the woman who bought the flowers from Sylvi?"

"Of course. I would have called you last night, but everything was . . . insane. I couldn't think straight."

"That was their goal."

"I know," Burke said grimly. "We all know. And I'm shorthanded now, with all my main people guarding the children, but I'll figure it out."

"What about Kaleb's kids?"

"The bodyguards he hired showed up this morning, so my guy took off. Juliette didn't seem inclined to tell Kaleb I'd put someone in front of their house last night. I don't think she wants to fan the flames."

"That's a mess, B."

"I know." Burke shook his head. "He said I was selfish. That I didn't care about him or his kids because I chose to be a cop and a PI. That my job had nearly gotten his kids hurt once before. And I couldn't deny it."

"Burke." André's tone was gentle. "You are not selfish. And that Gaffney threatened Kaleb's kids six years ago and last night is on Gaffney."

"Easy to say until someone nearly grabs them off a busy street."

"Did you blame Kaj Cardozo for being a prosecutor? That nearly got Elijah kidnapped."

Burke shook his head. "No, of course not."

"And Molly? Did you blame her when assholes tried to take Chelsea and Harper when you were investigating the murder of Gabe's father?"

Burke shook his head again. "No."

"Then hold yourself to that same standard."

Burke finally nodded, exhausted. "I didn't sleep much last night." Not even after talking to Naomi. He'd lain in his bed, his thoughts no longer a maelstrom. They were focused like a laser on Braden and Trent, seeing them being taken away in a black SUV. He knew that disaster had been avoided, but his mind kept playing the what-if game.

When he'd finally fallen asleep after dawn, he'd dreamed of Snow White, with her dark hair and pale skin. She was knitting.

That made him smile. Naomi had been incredible just now. He had the feeling that was the real Naomi Cranston, the firebrand who fought for the safety of their children.

"What?" André asked. "Why does a sleepless night make you smile like that? Or is it a certain woman with a tongue that could cut through titanium?"

Burke chuckled. "She put you in your place."

"She did. Makes me wish I'd known about her issue when she was accused. It wasn't my department, so I only paid a passing bit of attention."

"She was wronged."

"I'm beginning to see that. What are you going to do next?"

"About Naomi or the case?"

"Both."

"I'm going to clear her name."

"I figured that. I meant specifics."

"She's trying to get in to see Cresswell."

André's brows shot up. "She's got even more guts than I thought."

"I don't think it'll happen, and if by some miracle it does, then I don't think we'll get anything out of Cresswell. He's been threatened. No other explanation for why he's clammed up. I bet he's got enough dirt on NOPD folks to get himself a reduced sentence, but he hasn't even tried. He'll serve his entire sentence for his crimes."

"I know. I've talked to him myself. He said not one word."

Burke sighed. "It's less than a week till Mardi Gras."

"Which means we need to work fast to stop whatever they're planning."

"That's the idea."

André rose, then pulled Burke to his feet, giving him a one-armed hug and a back slap. "You never did tell me why she's knitting knockers."

Burke chuckled. "Come on, let's get some coffee. I'll have her show you."

André gave him serious side-eye. "Will my wife be angry with me?"

"That's a guaranteed no. But you might have to dodge Naomi's knitting needles if she's still mad at you."

12

The Quarter, New Orleans, Louisiana
TUESDAY, FEBRUARY 25, 10:30 A.M.

FROM THE PASSENGER seat of Burke's company SUV, Naomi watched Captain Holmes drive away. They were right behind the cop, Holmes heading back to his office, only a few blocks from the condo Naomi had seen Winnifred Timms entering. Which was where she and Burke were headed.

"Should I have apologized to Holmes?" she asked when indecision got the better of her.

"No," Burke said, his drawl a deep rumble that sent butterflies fluttering in her belly. "He knows you were wronged."

"But not by him."

"No, but he understands. He went through that with me, too. And with others who've left the force. You're not the only one."

She frowned when he turned away from where she thought they were headed. "Burke? Where are you going?"

He held up his phone. "Antoine texted me the names and address of the kidnapping brothers. He couldn't tell me in person while André was there."

Pablo Delgado was the one whose arm was broken when he'd tried to take Everett. His brother, Ernesto, had tried to grab the other kids.

"Are we going to their house?" she asked.

"We are. I don't expect to find Ernesto there, especially if he knows his brother is dead. But we can scope out the place, talk to the neighbors."

"Investigate," she said, satisfaction welling up within her. "Antoine said the brothers were part of the STs gang, but that they left to work for Gaffney. I didn't think that walking away from a gang was so easy."

Burke glanced over at her. "It's not. What are you wondering now?"

"If they actually left the gang at all. Gaffney wanted me to transport drugs for him. What if the Delgados are running Gaffney's drugs using their gang members?"

"It's certainly possible. Probable even. I'll have Val start researching gang members, see if any of them are in prison. Maybe we can ask to talk to them when we go to see Cresswell."

"Kaj talked to you, then?" she asked.

"He did. They might not let me go with you, but Kaj's boss is a good guy. You'll be safe."

"I'll feel safer if you go with me."

He looked pleased. "Kaj said he'd try. Can you text Val? Ask her to start researching ST members."

"She'll appreciate having something to do. She and Lucien were questioning if all of them need to be there to guard the kids. I think now that it's daytime, things are looking less apocalyptic. But that's when they get you." She winced. "That sounds so paranoid."

"Except that it's not."

She texted Val and, as she'd expected, Val was enthusiastic. "Val's off and running. She says Antoine is still trying to determine the identity of that couple who pretended to help Harper last night. Which has also been bothering me. The couple, I mean. If they were involved in the plot to take Harper, why get in Delgado's way? Why let her go?" She bit her lip, hesitant to share her thoughts. But Burke seemed open to them, so she plowed ahead. "They could have had a change of heart. Like maybe bugging your people's cars was okay, but stealing a child was not. Except that they were *there*, where an attempted kidnapping was about to happen."

"And?"

"And . . . their involvement just doesn't make sense, whether they were only pretending to take Harper or if they were serious. I feel like there's an important piece that we're missing."

He gave her another sharp glance. "I've been thinking that, too. I even wondered if we should keep the children on lockdown, but there are too many unanswered questions—like why that couple saved Harper. I'm hesitant to remove the protection detail just in case I'm wrong. It's not worth the risk."

"Except now your people are guarding their children and you're stuck with me," she said with a shrug.

"Hey." He snapped the word, making her eyes widen in surprise. "You don't talk like that. I'm not *stuck* with you. I asked you to accompany me because you notice things and you're smart."

She was torn between shrinking away from his harsh tone and lifting her chin in pride. She went with the latter, because she knew this man wouldn't hurt her.

That was a good feeling. It had been a long time since she'd experienced it.

Security.

Burke Broussard was *safe.*

And handsome, too. But a pretty face could fool. One had to only look at Burke's friends to know that he'd proven his loyalty and good heart.

Her phone buzzed. "Val texted. She says that Antoine's done a quick-and-dirty search on the Delgados and sent it to both of us." That was another good feeling.

Inclusion. Respect.

She opened the file. "The Delgados live with their mother and grandmother. Well, I guess just Ernesto does now. Pablo's living in hell."

Burke chuckled. "And the claws come out."

"I'm not sorry Pablo is dead. I might be questioning Ernesto's motive for Harper's attempted abduction and maybe even Jace's, but Pablo wanted to hurt Everett. Okay, so the mother works in the local elementary school cafeteria and the grandmother is retired. They had a good relationship with their neighbors until the brothers moved home."

"When was that?"

"In September. When Everett's phone was probably hacked."

"Is September when the Delgado brothers supposedly left the gang?"

"That's less clear." She read further, skimming the police reports Antoine had sent for the most relevant information. They wanted to talk to the neighbors, so she focused on them. "Looks like the neighbors did not want the brothers living there. They called 911 on the Delgados several times. The neighborhood started getting 'gang punks' driving through. Cars would rev their engines in the middle of the night, blow horns, knock down mailboxes. Nuisance stuff. But then there was a drive-by shooting at the house that the mother and grandmother live in."

"Like Sylvi's shop today?"

"More than that. At Sylvi's shop, it was just broken glass and some bullet holes high on one wall. In this shooting, the bullets hit high in the Delgado house, just like Sylvi's, but stray bullets hit the neighbor's house, too. A six-year-old boy who was sleeping upstairs was hit by one of the bullets. He didn't die, but it was close."

"Damn," Burke breathed.

"Yeah. After that, the neighborhood took legal action to make the brothers leave. They wanted the Delgado women's lease revoked."

"It didn't work, I take it, because they still live here."

She sighed as she read on. "No, because the house belonging to the woman organizing the legal challenge burned down. The woman died of smoke inhalation. The arson investigator found the fire was deliberately set. After that, the neighbors withdrew their legal action. I don't think the neighbors are going to talk to us, Burke. At least not openly."

"You could be right, but we can try. When was the fire? And did the NOPD think it was the gang who set it or the Delgado brothers?"

"The fire was this past November and the police report doesn't say who they suspected of arson. It does say that not a single neighbor would talk to the investigators."

"Getting any information is looking kind of bleak, but we'll still try."

"Good." She read to the end of Antoine's report. "Oh, this is interesting. The house the Delgado women were renting was recently sold. Guess to whom?"

"The Delgados?"

"Yep. The women—the mother and grandmother—are listed on the deed. And the house was paid for in cash."

"And that's not suspicious at all," Burke said sarcastically. "Two women, barely scraping by, suddenly buy a house with cash. It had to have been the brothers' money."

"Clearly. It's harder to get rid of the Delgado brothers if the women own the home. Well, if we don't get anything from the neighbors, we still have Winnifred Timms." Her lip curled at the very thought of the woman who'd sandbagged her. "We can go to her condo after we're done at the Delgados'."

"Except she's not home right now."

Naomi lifted her brows. "You've got eyes on her?"

"Yep. I texted one of my part-timers last night after you gave me the condo's address. Sent him over to keep watch."

"You keep a lot of part-timers?" Because he'd mentioned that he'd put a part-timer on his godsons' protection detail the night before.

"I do. Cops who I trust or old military buddies who don't want to work full-time or those who have other jobs. Harrison Banks was a part-timer, but he's retiring from NOPD and asked to be bumped up to full-time."

"I'm so glad he did." Because Everett was safe. "So do you know where Winnifred is? Or just that she's not home?"

"Devonte followed her to Loyola. She's in class at the moment."

"Must be nice," Naomi muttered. "She gets to go to college and I got to go to prison."

He reached across the console, took her hand, and gave it a brief squeeze before releasing her. A shiver tickled her skin from the contact, and she missed the warmth of his hand once it was gone.

"We're looking at her closely," he promised. "We'll find out if she was involved."

"She was." Naomi was sure of it.

"I think so, too. In her case, we're following the money."

"Thank you. That condo of hers isn't cheap. Average rent for the building is three grand a month."

His lips tipped up. "Looked it up, did you?"

"I did." She hesitated, then shrugged. "I also tried to follow the money, but I didn't get far. Not so easy when you don't have police credentials. I don't think that stops Antoine, though."

He chuckled. "Antoine's never met a firewall he couldn't break through. Did you find out anything about Winnifred?"

"That she continued seeing that older guy she met that night for dinner."

He glanced over at her before returning his eyes to traffic, which was stop-and-go. They'd left the Quarter behind and were heading east. The area wasn't plagued with tourists flooding the streets like it was in the Quarter, but there were many more cars on the road than normal.

The city welcomed over a million people during Mardi Gras season, and this season had been longer than most. Fat Tuesday was in a week, but it was late this year. Early March instead of mid-February like it had been the year before.

People kept pouring in, looking to party, and a few of them had "partied" with teenagers against their will. It made her ill to think about. She wondered where the teens were being held. She wondered if they had anyone searching for them. She wondered if any of them were being sold for sex at that very moment.

"How many times did you follow her?" Burke asked. "You didn't answer me last night."

She jerked out of her grim thoughts, grateful for the interruption. It took her a moment to remember what she'd been saying. *Winnifred Timms.* "For several weeks." She waited for him to shake his head at her folly, because what she'd done had been foolish. If she'd been caught, Winnifred could have pressed charges against Naomi for stalking.

"What else did you see?" he asked.

No recriminations would be coming, she realized, because he would have done the same thing. "Sometimes nothing. She'd go to the grocery store or to the park to run. She's pretty damn fast."

"You followed her on foot?"

"I did. I'm fast, too. In even better shape now than I was before prison."

"Lots of time to work out, huh?"

"Yes. And one of the friends I made there had been a personal trainer. She gave us sessions on the barter system."

"What did you trade?"

"A blanket that I'd crocheted. She liked cozy things."

"What was she in for?"

"She killed her husband."

Burke flinched. "Oh. Why?"

"He slept with her sister. She allowed that her reaction may have been extreme."

He choked on a laugh. "May have been?"

"May have been," she repeated. "Now, she deserved to be in

prison. She even said so. But it's a shock, when you first find out that your husband's been cheating. She just . . . reacted. And she's paying for that. As she should."

"What did you do? When you found out?"

"Got a lawyer and took Jimmy to the cleaners. We sold the house and I bought a much smaller one."

"Which you sold to pay for Mason Lord to defend you after your arrest."

She sighed, because that hadn't ended well. "Yeah. There wasn't much left over, but I don't need much these days. I learned to be a minimalist after five years in a cell."

He stopped for a traffic light and turned to look at her. "So what did you find out about Winnifred other than she's not as fast a runner as you are?"

"The older guy she was seeing is married."

The light turned green and he started driving again. "How do you know that?"

"Winnifred went to a fancy restaurant one day, all dolled up. Unfortunately, he showed up with another woman on his arm. Winnifred looked like she'd been slapped in the face when she saw them."

"She didn't know he was married?"

"Oh, she knew. I overheard that much when he came back out of the restaurant a few minutes after going in. He'd seen her waiting outside and was not happy that she'd invaded his space. He demanded to know how she'd known he'd be there and she said she'd heard his secretary making the lunch reservation. She'd assumed it was for her and him, not him and his wife. I think Winnifred worked for him, at least then. I don't know if she quit or was transferred, but that didn't stop them from continuing to see each other. He'd always go up to her apartment, but they didn't go out together to any more restaurants. Not that I saw."

"And they never saw you?"

"I'm pretty sure they didn't. I'm good at fading into the woodwork." She hadn't always been, but she'd honed the talent in prison. It had kept her safe and out of trouble more times than she could count.

Burke was quiet for a long, long moment, appearing to be deep in thought. Then he blurted out, "Are you happy at the flower shop, Naomi?"

She blinked at the topic change. "Very much so. Why?"

"Because I'm always looking for good investigators. I think you'd fit right in."

Once again, he'd validated her skills. "As one of your part-timers?"

"I was hoping for a full-time commitment, but I'll take what I can get."

"Can I think about it?" Because the idea appealed for more than just the thrill of investigating. She liked Burke Broussard. He was a good man who'd earned the loyalty and affection of his people. He made a difference in people's lives.

He'd already made a difference in hers.

That he was sexy and made her stomach flutter was an added bonus.

"Please do. We're getting close to the Delgados' neighborhood. Can you navigate us there?"

"Of course. We're only five minutes out."

But they saw the smoke three minutes later. Heard the sirens a minute after that.

"Shit," Burke muttered, pulling over for a fire truck. "How much do you want to bet that it's the Delgados' house?"

"Sucker bet, Burke."

Because the fire truck stopped in front of the address she'd put into her map app, the firefighters jumping out to fight the fire that blazed high into the sky.

Burke turned the SUV around, using his handsfree to make a call.

"Hey," a deep voice said.

"André," Burke said. "I have you on speaker. Naomi's with me. You need to send one of your people to the home of Ernesto Delgado. It's on fire."

Holmes made a growling sound. "Fucking hell."

"Yep. I figured one of your people needs to be on-site when they go in, after the fire's out. I'm betting you'll find Ernesto's body inside."

"Goddammit," Holmes snarled. "He was our link to the traffickers. But I already have one of my detectives en route. He was to bring Ernesto in for questioning."

"Why didn't you do that last night?" Naomi asked, unable to keep the censure from her voice.

"We tried," Holmes replied with an edge of his own. "We went to the Delgado house with a warrant for Ernesto's arrest. And to notify the family of Pablo's murder, of course. The mother and grandmother claimed they hadn't seen either of them in days."

"And the neighbors?" Burke asked. "What did they say?"

"It was midnight by the time we got there," Holmes said. "We knocked on doors then and again this morning, but no one answered."

"Not a shock," Naomi said. "Nobody's going to talk to the cops after the previous fire in this neighborhood."

"True enough. I have to go. Thanks, Burke."

The line went dead.

"Maybe the neighbors will talk to us," Naomi said quietly. "Because we're not cops."

"I was thinking the same thing. We'll park up the street, out of the way of the emergency vehicles. You stay by my side."

"I never considered anything else. I've no desire to become a target."

"There's a Kevlar vest in the back. It's Val's, so it should fit you. Put it on under your coat."

Kevlar? She hadn't worn a vest since her first year on the force, when she'd been on patrol. But it made sense. "Yes, sir."

Chalmette, Louisiana

TUESDAY, FEBRUARY 25, 11:15 A.M.

Yes, sir.

Naomi had said it somewhat dryly, but Burke felt a shiver go down his spine nonetheless.

Damn. He really liked this woman.

Too much? He supposed time would tell. But for now he set his personal feelings aside, because he was here to keep her safe.

And to find out who'd been seen around the Delgado house the night before. André would be angry that they'd poked their noses into the investigation, but that would have to be André's problem.

He parked the SUV, then helped her with her vest before suiting up himself. He didn't anticipate the arsonists were waiting around with a sniper rifle, but he was playing it safe.

"Did Antoine include which neighbors had been involved with the suit to get the Delgados evicted?" he asked.

"He didn't originally, but I emailed him once I saw the smoke. I figured we'd be talking to the neighbors, so I asked him for names and addresses of the ones involved." She held up her phone. "I have it here."

So smart. "Excellent. Molly couldn't have done it better."

His heart squeezed at the pleased look on her face. She held herself so much taller than she had the morning before. It was like watching a flower blossom and turn its face to the sun. "Then let's go."

The first five houses were a bust. Either no one was home or no one wanted to answer the door, so they were surprised when a knock on the sixth door got a response.

An elderly Black woman glared up at them. According to Antoine, this would be Mrs. Eleanor Jackson, age eighty-two. She was a widow and a retired clerk for the court of Orleans Parish. "I don't want whatever it is that you're selling. Go away."

Burke found himself taking a step back, intimidated despite the fact that the woman was, at the most, five feet tall.

"We aren't selling anything, Mrs. Jackson," Naomi said warmly. "And we're not cops. We're just trying to get information about the Delgado brothers."

Eleanor's glare intensified. "You have a death wish, girl?" She pointed to the burning home, six houses away. "Don't you see that fire?"

Naomi nodded. "Yes, ma'am, I do. But . . ." She hesitated and the woman's eyes narrowed.

"But what?"

"But one of the Delgados tried to abduct my sixteen-year-old son yesterday."

"Thugs. Your son's okay?"

"He is, thank you. Someone intervened and helped him. But the man who tried to take him is dead. Pablo Delgado."

The woman sighed heavily. "What's your name?"

"Naomi Cranston."

"And him?"

Burke cleared his throat. "Burke Broussard, ma'am."

"Wait here." The woman closed her door with a soft *click*, leaving Naomi and Burke standing on her front porch.

"I'm so rusty," Naomi murmured. "I haven't done this kind of work since I was on patrol. You know, dealing with the public."

"Wouldn't know it to watch you."

Her slow smile was more confident, and he knew he'd said the right thing. "Thank you, Burke."

The front door opened and the small woman reappeared, still glaring up at them. "You a dirty cop?" she asked Naomi bluntly.

"No, ma'am. I was framed. My sentence was overturned."

"On a technicality," the woman said archly.

Naomi winced. "Yes, ma'am. But I am innocent. More importantly, my sixteen-year-old son is innocent. I want to keep him safe."

She gave Burke a critical appraisal. "You're a PI? Broussard Investigations. Private investigator and protection personnel."

"You're a fast googler," Burke said.

Eleanor sniffed. "You young people think you're the only ones who can do a damn search. Well, you might as well come in. You've already painted a target on my ass by standing on my front porch."

Naomi hesitated. "We don't want to cause you trouble."

"You aren't. Not new trouble, anyway. Get yourselves in here."

"Don't make her annoyed with us," Burke whispered loudly and thought he saw the older woman's lips twitch.

They followed her into an immaculate living room. Framed photos covered every single surface. Eleanor gestured toward a sofa as she lowered herself into a chair.

"What do you want to know?" she asked when they were seated. "I'm eighty-two years old. I don't have time for any foolishness."

Naomi smiled, despite looking more nervous than she should have been. She had this. Burke was certain.

"We'll try not to be foolish," she said. "Do you know if anyone was in the Delgados' house when the fire started?"

Eleanor closed her eyes. "Probably both Rosanna and Carmen were in there. Rosanna normally would have left for work but her car was still in the driveway this morning."

"The police came by last night to tell her that Pablo's body had been found," Burke said.

Eleanor sighed. "Then it makes sense that she'd have called in to work. Carmen—she's Rosanna's mama—rarely leaves the house. She's retired. If she and Rosanna were in the house, they're probably dead."

Burke pointed to the front window. "Do you mind if I take a look?"

"Have at it."

Burke pulled the curtains back enough to peek onto the street, but the angle was wrong. He opened the front door and stood on the front porch so that he could see the still-burning house. The structure was fully engulfed in flames, the firefighters now just trying to keep it from spreading to the other houses.

The medics were also there, having arrived shortly after Burke and Naomi had knocked on the first door. He'd seen them bring out one person, but now three stretchers were occupied.

All three had sheets pulled over the victims' faces. Burke watched as the medics loaded the first victim into the ambulance. The Delgado family would be going straight to the morgue.

He returned to the sofa. "It appears there are three bodies in the Delgados' front yard."

Eleanor's thin shoulders sagged. "Dammit. I'd be a liar if I said I was surprised. We all knew Rosanna and Carmen wouldn't survive the trouble those boys brought to their doorstep. But just . . . dammit."

They were quiet for a long moment, allowing the woman to regain her composure. Finally, she gestured to Naomi. "Start at the beginning."

Naomi exhaled quietly. "Pablo Delgado tried to kidnap my son yesterday. Another man—Ernesto, we believe—tried to take four more children in three separate attempts. None were successful."

Eleanor lifted her brows. "That doesn't sound like the Delgados. They don't usually fail to accomplish what they set out to do."

"I'd hired a bodyguard for my son," Naomi told her.

"One of Mr. Broussard's people," Eleanor said.

Naomi nodded. "Yes. The bodyguard managed to break Pablo's arm before the getaway driver pulled a gun. The bodyguard was forced to let them go."

"It wasn't his job to catch them," Eleanor said tartly. "It was his job to keep your son safe."

Naomi smiled. "Yes, ma'am, and I am so very grateful to him."

The older woman's gaze became shrewd. "You'd already been threatened. Or your son was. That's why you hired a bodyguard."

"Yes, ma'am. Someone wanted me to distribute drugs for them. When I refused, they threatened my son."

"Now *that* sounds like the Delgados. Turned their mama's house into a distribution center. Ne'er-do-wells traipsin' about at all hours of the night. Horns blowin', tires squealin'. Gunshots, too."

"Did you ever see anyone who might have been in charge?" Burke asked. "Someone who the brothers deferred to?"

"Not a person, just a vehicle. A black SUV would pull into the driveway, usually between midnight and one a.m. One brother—or sometimes both—would come out of the house and get into the

SUV. They'd be carrying a paper bag to the SUV. Left the same way, carrying into the house whatever bag they'd brought outside with them. The bags were always filled with something. We all figured that's when they were doing the money drop and new drug pickup. But none of us ever saw the driver's face. He was real careful that way."

"He?" Burke asked, disappointed that Eleanor couldn't identify the driver. "Or could it have been a she?"

Because whoever had been driving the SUV with Pablo Delgado yesterday had been a woman.

"I don't know," Eleanor admitted. "I guess it coulda been a woman just as well as a man."

"Did you ever see them bringing teenagers into the house? Male or female?" Naomi paused before adding, "They might have been barefoot, even if it was cold. Maybe forced at gunpoint."

Burke wondered at the details Naomi provided, then figured they'd come from women she'd known in prison, women who'd also been forced at one time in their lives.

"We think they were into human trafficking," Burke said quietly when Eleanor shook her head. "Did you see anyone like that?"

"No. I'd have called 911 if I had. Not that they've done us a lot of good. To be honest, if you'd been cops, I'd have slammed the door in your faces."

"Why did you open the door?" Naomi asked.

Burke had wondered the same thing.

"Curiosity, mainly. The cops were out this morning, banging on doors before a decent hour. But now that I know that human trafficking's involved, I guess I understand the urgency. But my last encounter with the NOPD didn't end well."

Naomi leaned forward. "What happened?"

"I called the cops because it was two in the goddamn morning and those brothers were playing loud music and shooting guns into the air. Or so I assumed. I hope they weren't actually shooting at people. That night I was so angry," Eleanor said. "Our neighborhood was being violated all the damn time. It was after the little boy was shot by a stray bullet and still the cops did nothing. I don't even think they hauled the brothers' asses in for an interview. I got in one of the cops' faces and let him have it. Called him a lazy-assed coward. Shook my finger in his face. He cuffed me." She thumped her chest. "Me! A law-abiding, churchgoing woman."

"I'm familiar with that outrage," Naomi said.

"I guess you are. Anyway, his partner intervened. I was yelling that I was a retired court clerk and I knew my rights. That they had no business putting me in handcuffs." She shrugged. "I *might* have even acted like I was having a heart attack."

"No charges were filed?" Burke asked.

"Not a one. But that left a bad taste in my mouth. I shouldn't have yelled at the man, but I was so angry that they did nothing."

"Do you remember the names of the officers who came out?" Naomi asked.

"I have their names and badge numbers." Eleanor shoved herself out of her chair and wobbled a little before righting herself, shooting them a look that said they'd better not offer to help her. She retrieved an envelope from her desk and gave it to Naomi. Two names and badge numbers were scrawled on the back of the envelope in spidery handwriting. "You can't keep that, but you can copy it down."

Naomi took a photo with her phone. "Thank you, Mrs. Jackson."

The old woman sank back into her chair. "You're welcome."

Naomi bit at her lip, glancing at Burke from the corner of her eye. It was a hopeful look that warned him of what was coming. "I'm worried about you, ma'am. Because of the target we painted on your back."

"I think I said it was my ass," Eleanor said dryly. "I'll be fine."

"And if the arsonist returns?" Naomi asked. "I don't want you hurt because you talked to us. These men are not to be underestimated."

Eleanor just shook her head. "I've got nowhere to go. Nowhere that I'd want my trouble dragged to, anyway."

Burke knew what needed to be done. He might not have thought to offer had it not been for Naomi's hopeful little glance, but she was right. They'd endangered this woman and it was their job to protect her. "And if I found you somewhere to go? Would you evacuate for a little while?"

Eleanor's eyes narrowed. "Where?"

"My house. It's a little full at the moment, but I've got one empty bedroom."

"Are there stairs?" Eleanor asked.

"Yes, but I also had a lift installed, so you don't have to worry about stairs."

Naomi smiled at him and he felt like a superman. "You put the lift in for Joy. Because of her wheelchair."

"I did." He turned to the woman, who watched them intently. "What do you say, ma'am?"

"I say thank you," she said.

Naomi stood up. "I'll help you pack a bag. Burke, why don't you get the SUV?"

"I will, but I have a question for Mrs. Jackson first."

Eleanor's expression became wary. "What?"

"Was the decision to withdraw your legal action against the Delgados unanimous?"

"Far from it. Several of us—me included—wanted to keep going, but after the fire killed Maisie Richardson—she was our organizer—the younger families on the street were afraid for their children. Ultimately, that's what convinced us seniors to withdraw. I would have kept going until that scourge was gone from the neighborhood, but I understood the other families' fear. Why do you ask?"

"I wondered who on the block might be open to talking to us. Someone might have seen something that we can use." He thought of the two young women who'd escaped the Delgados' clutches two weeks ago and the teenagers who were probably still being held somewhere in the city. "If it weren't important, I wouldn't risk the safety of others, but I won't knock on doors and implicate them like we just did to you. I hate that we put you in danger, but our children are at risk. And not just ours. Maybe your neighbors will meet us in a neutral location."

"That's possible. I can make the calls, if you like."

Burke smiled at her. "Thank you."

"Teenagers being kidnapped," Eleanor said heavily. "I understand why you're pushing and so will they. Now, this old woman is going to pack."

Burke looked at all the framed photos. "Do you want me to put your photos in my vehicle? We can keep them safe for you."

"Because they might set fire to my house, too." She pushed herself out of the chair and looked around her home, her eyes incredibly sad. "Yes, please, Mr. Broussard."

"You're going to be my houseguest. You should call me Burke."

Eleanor nodded once. "Thank you, Burke. You may call me Eleanor."

Naomi offered her arm. "And I'm Naomi. Will you let an ex-con escort you?"

Eleanor took Naomi's arm, leaning against her, visibly fatigued. "Your sentence was overturned."

"On a technicality," Naomi responded lightly.

Eleanor cackled, and Burke's heart squeezed hard. *Affection,* he realized. Damn, but he really liked her.

"I like you, Naomi," Eleanor said, echoing his thoughts.

"I like you, too," Naomi said.

Burke shot a text to Val, asking her to prepare the remaining bedroom, then began gathering Eleanor Jackson's photos.

13

St. Gabriel, Louisiana
TUESDAY, FEBRUARY 25, 1:20 P.M.

NAOMI FELT SICK. Her skin was clammy and her throat burned from the bile rising from her churning stomach. She shook like she was coming down with the flu.

But it wasn't the flu.

She was back.

Back in the place that tormented her dreams. In the place where she'd nearly been killed.

Back in the place she'd vowed never to see again.

But here she was, of her own volition.

"Naomi." The word rumbled deep and soothing and she could almost feel Burke's voice on her skin. His hand rubbed circles on her back, the contact the only thing keeping her from flying apart. "We don't have to do this, darlin'. *You* don't have to do this."

Darlin'. He'd called her that once before. That morning when she'd yelled at Captain Holmes.

He's just being nice. He probably calls everyone darlin'.

You're not special.

You're an ex-con who can't control her fear of this place.

"We can't do this," Burke told the district attorney, a man with a kind face. Reuben Hogan was his name. "Not today, at least."

"I understand," Hogan said. "It's all right, Miss Cranston. I can take your questions to Cresswell myself."

No. No. "No," she blurted out, clenching her fists so hard that her nails dug into her palms.

She would not let this fear control her. They couldn't keep her here.

Can they?

No. They cannot.

"You're going to walk out of here the way you walked in," Burke murmured. "A free woman. Whether you walk out now or after you see Cresswell is entirely up to you. It's your choice."

She could feel both men watching her. Probably assessing her for a nervous breakdown. No way were they letting a crazy woman into the prison. Or if they did, they might not let her out.

Stop it. You're losing control and this is not okay. You can do this.

I can. I can. I can.

Eyes closed tight, she kept repeating the words in her mind and drew a deep breath, smelling Burke's aftershave. They'd both showered upon returning to his house in the Quarter, Eleanor Jackson in tow. They'd smelled like smoke from the fire.

The scent of his aftershave helped. Burke was safety. Security. He could protect her. He'd promised to.

She kept breathing until her heart was no longer beating in her sore throat. She'd played this game before, calming the panic that rose every time her cell door had slid closed.

What do you hear?

Burke's deep, even breaths.

What can you smell?

Burke's aftershave. Clean laundry, also Burke's.

What can you feel?

Soft fabric on my cheek.

That ground her thoughts to a halt and she opened her eyes. And saw Burke's white shirt, because she was clinging to him, her arms wrapped tightly around his waist.

His arms had wrapped around her, too, and he held her close. One hand stroked her hair and he was murmuring kind words in that Cajun rumble.

She should be embarrassed to be clinging to him like a koala. But she wasn't.

This was hard. It would be hard for anyone, she thought. And if he was willing to give her comfort, she was going to take it with gratitude.

"I'm okay," she whispered.

"I know," he said with a confidence that rang true. "But even if you want to leave right now, you're still okay. You're still strong."

But she'd regret it. Now that she could breathe, she could also think.

"I'll be sorry till the day I die if I turn around now," she mumbled into his muscled chest.

The man had a very, very nice chest.

"Would you like a bottle of water?" DA Hogan asked.

She forced herself to pull away from the safety of Burke's arms and to face the DA. "Please. Thank you."

Hogan disappeared into an office and Burke lifted her chin with his finger. His eyes were serious.

"You do not have to do this, Naomi. No one will think badly of you if we leave right now."

"I'll think badly of me. This is my chance to face the man who sent me here. One of the men, anyway. This is my chance to get to the truth, so that Everett will be safe. I can't walk away."

"Okay," he said simply. "Hogan says I can come, too, so you won't be alone."

She stared up at him, sure that every one of her emotions was painted across her face with neon. "Thank you."

He stroked her cheek with his thumb. "You're welcome. Here comes Hogan."

Naomi straightened her spine and thought she at least looked composed when the DA came back with a bottle of water.

"Unopened," he said.

She appreciated that. "Thank you."

"Shall we go?" Hogan asked. "Cresswell and his attorney are waiting for us in one of the interview rooms."

They had to go through several sets of doors before reaching the interview room. She'd been in a similar room when her second attorney had come to speak to her. The women were housed in a different section of the facility, but the layout was similar.

Similar enough to send another wave of nausea through her.

She gripped Burke's hand hard. "Sorry," she whispered. "Am I hurting you?"

"No. Hold on as tight as you need to."

Thank you, Sylvi. Thank you for bringing me to this man.

So it was with a thankful heart that she walked into the interview room, getting her first glance at Arthur Cresswell in more than six years.

She couldn't control her gasp. Two and a half years in prison had aged him twenty. He looked old and frail.

And vacant. His eyes were empty.

She knew that look. She'd seen it in her own reflection when she'd been in protective custody. It was despair and hopelessness.

And maybe a touch of madness.

But she wasn't going to feel pity for him. He'd ruined so many lives.

He tried to ruin mine.

But her life was not ruined. She would leave here a free woman. She would leave here to go back to her mother and James and her new friends.

She had a job she loved with Sylvi and the offer of an investigator position with Burke.

Her life was far from ruined. It felt like she was beginning again.

Her trembles were abating. Silently, she sat in the chair that Hogan pulled out for her. Burke sat on her left, Hogan on her right.

Cresswell was directly across from her, his attorney on his left. Behind them, a guard stood at attention.

Cresswell was staring down at the table. His shoulders were slumped, his demeanor defeated.

"Mr. Cresswell," she said quietly. Steadily. "Do you know who I am?"

No answer.

"I know you've been in isolation for two and a half years. I know what that does to a person. I was in isolation for a year." She drew a breath and released it. Let Burke's aftershave soothe her once more. "Do you know why I was in isolation?"

No answer.

"Because I was stabbed in the prison cafeteria my first week here." She pulled her hair back, exposing her scar, but Cresswell's gaze was still fixed on the table. "Look at me, Cresswell," she snapped. "You owe me that much."

He startled and glanced up, meeting her eyes for the briefest of moments. But he saw her scar, so she let her hair fall back into place. "I nearly died. After that, I went into isolation. It was . . . well, you know what it's like. Except *I* didn't belong there. I was—and am—innocent."

Still not a word. She hadn't expected one.

"Why?" she asked. "Why did you pick me to frame?"

He simply shook his head and kept staring at the table.

He wasn't going to speak to her, not yet.

So she leaned forward, lowering her head so that she could see part of his face. "Did they threaten your children like you threatened my son?"

His body jerked like he'd touched a live wire.

"I'll take that as a yes. You can't tell anyone at NOPD because they're involved, isn't that right?" No response. "You can't ask for help because you've burned every single bridge you ever crossed."

A shallow exhale was the only reply she received, but it was enough.

"What if we protect your children? They're in high school now, but still vulnerable. Just like my sixteen-year-old son was yesterday when one of Gaffney's thugs tried to grab him off the street."

Cresswell glanced up and some of the vacantness was gone, replaced by a raw hope that she also understood.

"We can protect them. Not for you, but because they're innocent and don't deserve to pay for your crimes. Burke Broussard is a good man. He'll guard your children." She hoped she wasn't making an offer that Burke would deny.

"Yes," Burke said quietly. "If it were only you, I'd let you rot in here. But your kids are innocent. If you want them to be able to live their lives free from fear, all you need to do is give us the information we're asking for. Why Naomi? Why frame anyone at all? Who is Gaffney working with now? Because he's resurrected your business."

"And he may have even expanded it," Naomi added. "Unless you stole children and trafficked them for sex."

Cresswell's attorney shook his head. "He's not answering that."

"He doesn't have to," Naomi said.

Because Cresswell had fully lifted his head, and there was horror in his eyes. He still said nothing, but his expression was one of unfettered revulsion.

So it appeared there was a line the bastard hadn't crossed.

"Will you cooperate with us?" Naomi said. "In exchange, your children will be protected. Your wife, too, assuming she's also innocent."

His eyes shone with unshed tears. Still he said nothing.

"Do you know who Gaffney is working with?" Naomi asked. "We will protect your children. Mr. Broussard keeps his word. As do I."

Cresswell glanced at Burke before returning his gaze to hers.

Oh, he knows. Naomi was certain of it.

"Who is it?" she pressed.

Cresswell opened his mouth, then shut it quickly. He dropped his gaze to the table once again.

"Are we done?" the attorney asked placidly.

"They threatened my first attorney's children, too," Naomi said to the lawyer. "Do you have children, sir?"

"That is none of your affair," the attorney snapped. "Guard, please take my client back to his cell."

The guard gripped Cresswell's shoulder, hauling him to his feet.

The frail man stumbled before straightening his body and locking his knees so they didn't buckle.

She watched as Cresswell was escorted from the room. His attorney exited the room as well, heading toward the entrance.

When she, Burke, and Hogan were alone, she sighed. "He knows who Gaffney's working with."

"He does," Hogan confirmed. "I didn't expect him to speak, because he hasn't for two and a half years. But I really thought you had him, Miss Cranston."

"I let myself hope for a second or two," she admitted, then stood, completely exhausted. "Thank you for giving me the opportunity, sir."

"You're welcome. Let me know how I can help you going forward."

"You can clear her name," Burke said brusquely.

Naomi wanted to smile at him, but she was too tired.

"And when we get evidence to support that, I will," Hogan replied evenly, but there was regret in his eyes.

Naomi mostly understood. The man wanted to help, but he had to work within the system. He *was* the system.

"I'm ready to leave now," she told Burke. "Thank you for staying with me."

He pushed a lock of hair from her cheek so that it hung properly. She hadn't even realized until that moment that she'd shown him her scar when she showed it to Cresswell.

But he didn't look repulsed. He looked proud.

Of me.

I'm proud of me, too.

St. Gabriel, Louisiana

TUESDAY, FEBRUARY 25, 1:40 P.M.

Arthur Cresswell shuffled back to his cell, his hands and ankles shackled.

I did it.

Every time he was called to the interview room, he felt like he'd be ill. Every time, he had to steel himself not to speak.

Not to beg. Because he would beg—for his family.

Should've thought of that before you stole the first kilo. That had been more than fifteen years before, and he'd confiscated the kilo in a drug bust he'd made as a Narcotics detective.

His son had been only two years old, and had needed so many things. Cribs and car seats and fancy food that his wife swore was healthy. So he'd succumbed to temptation.

He'd sat on that kilo for weeks, terrified the NOPD knew he'd taken it and that they were just waiting for him to sell it to grab him and throw him in a jail cell. But that never happened, not even when he finally got the courage to approach the dealer he'd arrested four times.

The dealer had taken him to his boss and he and Cresswell had made a deal.

Then Cresswell had more cash than he'd ever seen in one place at one time.

It was just going to be the one time. But then the bills piled up. They'd been living beyond their means, but he hadn't had the heart to tell his wife to stop spending. It made her so happy and she was so lonely when he was out doing undercover work.

Excuses.

He'd done so many crimes over the years and had only been punished for a small fraction of them. He guessed that it was his turn now, and it would be for the rest of his life because he was never getting out of this place.

The DA had offered him a deal. The WITSEC people were willing to hide them all. But his partner had been perfectly clear.

Say one single word and they die.

His wife. His son. His daughter.

And to bring the promise home, his partner had sent him a gift, via his attorney. A finger in a box.

A finger wearing a very familiar ring.

He'd slipped that ring on his wife's hand the day he'd promised to love, honor, and cherish her till death did they part.

Someone in security had to have been paid off or his attorney never would have been allowed to bring such a thing into the prison. That had been a wake-up call, early on.

Nowhere is safe. No one is safe.

And his partner had meant every word he'd said.

His wife had been devastated and beyond furious when she'd come to see him—the first and only time she did so. Her hand was swollen, still bandaged.

She would never forgive him and he could not blame her.

But he could continue to protect her by saying nothing.

Just as he had today.

He'd been tempted. So very tempted.

Not by Naomi Cranston. He didn't give two shits about the woman. Framing her had been a simple necessity. It wasn't personal.

Not to Cresswell, anyway.

His partner, however, was another story. For him, framing Cranston had been very personal.

Cresswell had been tempted by her offer, though. Burke Broussard was the last person he would have gone to for help, but there wasn't anyone he trusted more to keep his family safe.

Broussard wasn't infallible, though. And his people wouldn't protect his family forever. So Cresswell had held his tongue.

He arrived at his cell and didn't wince when the door shut in his face. He was beyond that now.

He stuck his hands through the opening in the door, patiently waiting as his shackles were unlocked and removed. The same happened with the shackles on his ankles.

Throat parched, he went to the sink, bent over and filled his palm, using it as a cup. But his hands shook and he couldn't get the water to his mouth.

It took two tries, but he managed to grip the metal travel mug he kept next to the coffee maker he was allowed to keep.

No ceramic mugs. Could be used as a weapon if broken. He filled the metal mug and drank it all down.

And then realized his mistake.

The water didn't taste the same. It didn't taste like metal and rust. It tasted bitter.

The bottom of his cup smelled like . . .

Oh no. Bitter almonds.

He dropped the cup and it fell to the cell floor with a clang. Stunned, he turned to the door, where a guard watched him through the window.

"I didn't say anything," Cresswell rasped, speaking for the first time in two and a half years, knowing and fearing what was coming.

"You wanted to," the guard said quietly.

"You're on his . . ." Cresswell sank to the floor, the dizziness overwhelming.

They hadn't even waited until dinnertime so that they could hide it in his food. Or maybe they would have if he hadn't chosen that mug.

He cast a glance at the coffee maker and wondered if the carafe had been poisoned as well.

". . . payroll," he gasped out as the guard said nothing. Merely watched him.

Waiting for me to die.

Cresswell clutched at his chest, his breathing becoming labored. His head pounded with a blinding pain. Confusion made him shake his aching head, trying to clear it. But it didn't clear.

It wouldn't clear. It would just get worse.

"Autopsy." He forced out the word, then another. "You."

"You think they'll suspect me?" The guard didn't look worried. "You kept cyanide pills in your cell in case you were pressured to speak, like what happened today. The cops will find the pills when they search your cell. Your death will be ruled a suicide."

They'd thought of everything, then. He'd never stood a chance.

I should have asked Broussard for help.

14

The Quarter, New Orleans, Louisiana
TUESDAY, FEBRUARY 25, 3:30 P.M.

NAOMI HAD FALLEN asleep on the way back home, and Burke hated to wake her. He got the feeling that she hadn't slept well, either, maybe not in days, but she hadn't complained.

Instead, she'd been amazing. A couple of times he'd thought she'd actually get Cresswell talking, but whoever owned him had truly scared him into silence.

Burke would watch over Cresswell's kids anyway. No child should be held accountable for their father's misdeeds. He'd pay a visit to Cresswell's wife before the day was out. After he'd gotten Naomi back to his house where she could rest. The visit to the prison had been both emotionally traumatic and physically draining for her.

And for me, on her behalf. He might even take a nap himself.

But not with Naomi. Because his mind had already gone there. Holding her back in the prison when she'd had that panic attack . . . it had felt right.

He gently shook her shoulder. "Naomi, we're here. Wake up."

She jerked a little, then relaxed when she realized it was him, a smile tipping her lips. Which made him feel ten feet tall.

"Sorry," she said. "I guess I was more tired than I thought."

"You worked hard today."

"Well, at least Eleanor Jackson talked to me."

"Cresswell wanted to. We might try again later."

She released her seat belt. "I'm surprised he's still alive, to be honest. Why would his former associates risk his talking someday? How do they know that he hasn't? Just because he hasn't talked to the DA doesn't mean he hasn't talked to anyone."

The thought had crossed Burke's mind many times. "I think he hasn't. He was too afraid for his kids."

"You're going to offer them protection anyway, aren't you?"

He frowned. "Should I be alarmed that you find me so easy to read?"

She shrugged, an elegant movement. "You're not that difficult. You're a protector. Just ask anyone currently staying in your house."

Kaleb's words came back, hitting him hard. Their children were in danger because of choices Burke had made. At least partially. "I'm no knight in shining armor."

"That's where you're wrong. You rode in to save me."

Her words left him stunned, but in a good way. He was a protector. He'd always known that about himself. But to have her say so was . . . nice.

He followed her to the door, opening it to the amazing aroma of garlic and onions. He sniffed. And sausage.

"Oh my God," Naomi groaned quietly. "We forgot to eat lunch."

He had to clear his throat because the sound of that groan made him want things that were best left alone. "Let's see who's cooking."

They followed their noses to the kitchen, where Eleanor was holding court. Naomi's mother and Jace were cutting vegetables and Elijah was at the sink with Everett, washing pots and pans.

Ruthanne looked up when they entered the kitchen. "Oh, good. You're back. Eleanor and I are giving the boys a cooking lesson."

Eleanor sniffed. "Boys need to cook, too. Shouldn't be only a woman's job. Right, boys?"

Jace bobbed his head. "Yes, ma'am."

"Yes, ma'am," Elijah echoed. He gave Everett a slight nudge with his elbow. "Right, Ev?"

Everett looked uncomfortable. "Right. Of course."

Eleanor glanced at Naomi. "This one's yours?"

"He is." Naomi smiled at Everett. It was a sad little smile as she clearly didn't expect anything back. But he gave her a measured nod and her smile became radiant.

Burke thought that she settled for too little. *She deserves so much more.*

But it was a step in the right direction, so he gave Everett a nod of his own.

Eleanor's eyes narrowed at the exchange, but she said nothing. Crafty old woman probably had it all figured out.

"You have a nice kitchen, Burke Broussard," she said. "It is a real pleasure cooking in it."

"Thank you. My mother designed this space. She was an amazing cook."

"We found some of her cookbooks," Jace said, then winced. "Was it okay that we looked? They were on the shelf in the living room."

"It's fine, Jace." The boy still needed reassurance. Being Val's adopted son had made him so much more confident, but a lifetime of abuse wasn't resolved so quickly. Burke knew that from experience.

"My mother would have been so pleased that someone was using them."

He led Naomi to the kitchen table, gently pushed her into a chair, then set about making her a cup of tea. He'd watched her at breakfast, so he knew what she liked.

"Well?" Molly stood in the kitchen doorway. "Did he tell you anything?"

Naomi shook her head wearily. "Almost, but he stopped himself. Never said a word."

"He never said anything out loud," Burke said, "but he confirmed—wordlessly—that he'd also been threatened with harm to his family. He also knows who Gaffney is working with, but he wouldn't tell us who."

"Maybe if you protected his kids, too . . ." Jace ventured cautiously, then shook his head. "Sorry."

Burke squeezed the boy's shoulder. "It's a good suggestion, Jace. And we offered, but he said no." He'd call on Mrs. Cresswell later tonight. Or maybe tomorrow morning. He'd ask Naomi if she wanted to go with him, because Mrs. Cresswell might be more inclined to talk to another woman. He was pretty sure Naomi would say yes. "We'll keep digging for answers. Don't worry."

Molly took the chair beside Naomi. "How are you?" she asked. "I should have gone with Burke and not made you face the prison again. I wasn't thinking. This case has short-circuited my brain."

"I needed to go," Naomi said. "It wasn't easy, I'm not gonna lie. But I wasn't alone, so that made it easier."

Ruthanne gave Burke a look of intense gratitude that squeezed his heart. "Thank you," she mouthed.

He gave her a wink and poured hot water into Naomi's teacup, sliding it in front of her, then leaned against the refrigerator, basking in the activity. His house had been too quiet with just him all these years. This was the way it should always be.

Except not because an asshole was trying to take their children.

He wondered how Braden and Trent were doing. He'd sent a message to Juliette when he'd woken that morning, asking if they were okay. It had taken her over an hour to reply. She'd been picking up Kaleb from the airport, she'd said when she finally replied. They were fine, and the bodyguard Kaleb had hired was camped out in her living room watching over the boys.

He and Kaleb needed to talk. There had been such animosity in Kaleb's voice the day before. Most of it was well-earned, Burke thought, but the bit about not working in the business had surprised him. He hadn't realized that Kaleb was so angry with him.

He needed to fix this. So he drew up his courage and typed a text to Kaleb. ***Can we talk?***

Kaleb might not answer, and Burke wasn't going to watch his phone for an hour like he'd done that morning with Juliette. He put his phone away and looked up, catching Molly watching him.

Her eyes were as calm as usual, but something was off.

"What?" he asked quietly.

"We need a meeting. Naomi, too."

Naomi's eyes went wide, her cup of tea halfway to her lips. "Okay?"

Molly smiled at Naomi. "It's nothing we can't fix. Bring your tea and come with me. Miss Eleanor, when should we be back down for whatever smells so darn good?"

"It needs a few hours to stew."

"A few hours?" Jace whined. "But I'm hungry now."

Elijah snickered. "I'll make us an omelet. That'll tide you over."

"Can you make one for Naomi and me, too?" Burke asked. "We didn't eat lunch."

Jace was already fetching the eggs from the refrigerator. "Yes, sir."

Burke got up to follow Molly and Naomi, nodding to Lucien, who stood guard by the front door, then picked Harper up from the sofa, where she sat watching a movie with Chelsea. He blew a raspberry on Harper's cheek, making her giggle.

It was a precious sound.

"How's my girl?" he asked, once he'd settled her back on the sofa.

"Okay." Then she shook her head. "Nightmares last night."

He hated that. Hated that someone else had tried to hurt this child when she'd finally gotten to the place where she could sleep.

Then she shrugged. "But at least it wasn't Gramma and Grampa. I was afraid they'd take me from my mom, but they can't get to me in here."

He'd almost forgotten about Harper's grandparents fighting for custody. When the couple got word about last night—and they would—it would give them even more ammunition with the courts.

Yet another reason to bring down Gaffney and whoever was working with him. He made himself smile at the child. "Silver lining, huh?"

"Yeah. And your TV is bigger than ours."

"Priorities. Try to be good. I'll see you in a bit." He headed up the stairs to his study, finding it already packed with people.

Val was awake, as was Harrison. Both were up and moving, pacing the floor. Antoine was sitting at Burke's desk, his laptops set up in a semicircle before him. Molly still appeared calm—unless you really knew her.

He sat next to Naomi on the small sofa. "What's going on?"

"I've been checking financials all morning," Antoine said. "Winifred Timms, John Gaffney, Jimmy Haywood."

Startled, Naomi stared at Antoine. "Jimmy's financials? Why?"

"Because I'm not as kind as you are," Antoine said dryly. "I was irked that your ex testified against you and I wondered why he'd say the things he said."

"I was stunned when he said that he'd witnessed me using drugs. I've never done illegal drugs. I don't even like to take over-the-counter painkillers."

"Didn't that make you angry?" Molly asked, because she looked angry.

"Of course it did. But Jimmy lied about so many things. I mean, at first, I reeled at his lies in court, but later, when I could think again, it made sense. I figured he was laying it on thick to make sure I went to prison so he could get full custody of Everett." She looked at Antoine. "What did you find in his financials?"

"His mortgage was miraculously paid off a few weeks after your trial," Antoine said. "I was wondering if you knew where that money came from. Did he have any investments he could have sold off? Or maybe an inheritance?"

"Not that I know of. But if someone gave him money, they sure wasted it. He would have testified against me for free." She eyed Molly warily. "What's really going on? I'm not that shocked that Jimmy would take a bribe. Why are you all so upset about this?"

Val sighed. "I drew the short straw, so I'll just say it. Antoine ran your financials, too."

Naomi's eyes widened, flashing with hurt before her shoulders slumped. "I guess that makes sense. You want to make sure I'm not hiding ill-gotten gains from stealing drugs from the NOPD. It's okay, Antoine."

No, Burke wanted to snarl. It was not okay. He wanted to rip into Antoine, but the look on his hacker's face silenced any angry words Burke might have uttered.

"That's not why I ran them," Antoine said firmly. "Molly kept coming back to 'Why Naomi?' Why frame *you*?"

Burke's stomach gave a nasty lurch. He didn't like the direction this was going. "What did you find, Antoine?" he asked, taking Naomi's hand in his.

"Three bank accounts," Antoine said. "Each in a different bank. They total over five hundred thousand dollars."

Naomi gasped, the color draining from her face. "No. That's not mine."

"We believe you," Val said. "I promise we do. But when Antoine found the accounts, he brought us all in so that we could help him follow the money. It doesn't look good, Naomi. Lots of deposits on a regular basis, most in cash. It ghosts under the ten-thousand-dollar reporting limits for deposits and withdrawals every week, but banks watch for this. If the small deposits add up to more than the reporting limit, that's a federal crime. It was just a matter of time before the banks caught on and reported you."

"And then they'd investigate me again," Naomi said, her voice faint. "My previous record would make me look even guiltier. And then, if I was caught with drugs in Sylvi's delivery van, they could have said I really was a drug dealer, that I got off on a technicality, but that I really was guilty then, too."

Burke had to breathe through his fury. Gaffney and whoever the fuck he was working with had planned this. "When were the accounts opened?"

"September," Molly said.

When Everett's phone had probably been hacked. *Not a coincidence.*

"How did they open three bank accounts in my name?" Naomi demanded. "Did no one ask for ID?"

"That's what we have to find out," Molly said. "We *will* investigate this on our own, don't you worry. Banks tend to give security footage only to the cops, but we can find ways around that. Importantly, we need to decide if it's best to come clean with the NOPD about this or chance them finding out on their own."

Burke gently gripped Naomi's chin and turned her to look at him. Her eyes were glassy with unshed tears. "Ultimately this should be your decision, but my vote is that we find out who's behind this before we report it."

She blinked, sending tears down her cheeks. He wiped them away with his thumbs.

"And if Gaffney decides to report me himself?" Then she stilled. "Five hundred thousand dollars is a lot of money for someone to deposit just to frame me."

Molly gave her an approving nod. "It is indeed. We were wondering if it's Gaffney's money, from whatever scam he's running. We think he would have reported you—anonymously, of course."

"Of course," Naomi murmured faintly. "But surely he wouldn't just abandon half a million dollars in fake bank accounts."

"The bank accounts aren't fake," Antoine said. "They're very real and in your name, but you're right. We figure he'd withdraw all the cash, leaving a trail that points to you. Then he'd report you. The bank would report you, too, for withdrawing that much money at one time. You'd be screwed."

Naomi nodded slowly. "How do we find out who really opened the accounts?"

"Good question," Burke said. "We're going to figure this out, Naomi."

"I know. But Gaffney and whoever's in this with him might decide to report me before you get a chance. If for no other reason than to create a . . ."

She trailed off, her mouth forming an O.

Oh. Burke got it now, too.

"What?" Molly asked.

"I'm a smoke screen," Naomi said. "Or a fall guy. Either works for them. They have to be anticipating trouble. Captain Holmes said that two young women escaped human traffickers during Super Bowl weekend and they identified Pablo Delgado as their pimp. Pablo's attempt to abduct Everett connects the traffickers to Gaffney. NOPD is going to investigate Gaffney for this, so he needs a diversion. I'm the diversion."

"But that's now," Molly said. "These accounts were opened in September. Why *you*, Naomi? Why September?"

"I don't know, but I'm betting that I was always going to be the diversion for something. Cresswell seemed horrified at the idea of trafficking teenagers for sex, so I'm assuming that this is a new operation. If they ever had a glitch or a snafu, they'd need that diversion. I think they planned for a long time to set me up with these bogus accounts, in case things went south for them."

"That makes some sense," Val said. "But knowing it doesn't eliminate the bogus accounts."

Molly frowned. "Nor does it answer 'Why you?' But the immediate need is to deal with these accounts. We've been discussing how to extract you from this situation in a way that protects you."

Naomi was quiet for a long moment, her teeth sinking into her lower lip. Burke pulled her lip free, not liking that she was hurting herself.

She gave him an amused glance, and that, more than anything, let him know she was going to be okay.

"Can you get into the actual accounts, Antoine?" she asked. "Or only see the overall balances?"

"So far only the balances. Why?"

Naomi glanced at the time on her phone. "Because I know what I want to do. The banks don't close until five. If we play our cards right, I can visit all three."

Burke shook his head. "Naomi, I don't think that's a good idea. They won't tell you anything."

"Probably not," she agreed. "But I can, as the account owner, put a freeze on all three accounts. That way Gaffney and his friends can't get their money back. I have my ID. The bank rep will check it against the ID that opened the account. It won't be me, and I'll be able to make a fraud claim."

It wasn't, Burke thought, a horrible idea. "How will you explain how you knew about the accounts?"

She tilted her head, thinking. "I was going to borrow money from you to pay for Everett's bodyguard. You ran a credit check and found three accounts that I knew nothing about. Anyone would be alarmed. *I* will be alarmed. And then they'll have to tell me that there's an issue with the accounts—specifically, they were opened without my knowledge. The bank will be the one dealing with the cops, not me. And any consequences will be on their heads, not mine, because they allowed someone using a fraudulent ID to open an account."

It really wasn't a horrible idea.

It might even be a very smart one.

"Not bad, grasshopper," Val said with a smile. "We'll make a sneaky PI out of you yet."

Naomi smiled, the praise making her shine brightly once again. "Thank you. Antoine, what are the options for spying on someone's computer monitor when it's facing away from you?"

Antoine grinned. "I have a few ideas."

"Good. Because the ID of the person who opened the account will pop up on the banker's screen. The name will be mine, but the photo won't match, I'm sure. I want to know whose photo that is."

"As do we." Burke stood, took Naomi's hand, and pulled her to her feet. "Let's go. Time's a'wastin'."

Metairie, New Orleans, Louisiana
TUESDAY, FEBRUARY 25, 4:30 P.M.

Traffic had stymied Naomi's plan and they'd made it to the first bank only forty-five minutes before it closed. They were still there—she, Burke, and Antoine. She was playing the part of the alarmed client pretty convincingly, if she said so herself. Burke stood behind her chair, his hands on her shoulders.

Anchoring her. And protecting her.

Antoine was still monitoring the banker's computer screen with a small camera he'd placed discreetly on a wall behind her station.

They'd lucked out with this banker. Her station was in the middle of the bank's open area, rather than being in an enclosed office.

It was about time they got a lucky break, so Naomi wasn't going to worry that it was too good to be true.

"Tell me again why you're here," the bank manager said, with a hint of a threat in his tone. The woman at the desk had called him over as soon as she'd pulled up Naomi's account.

Naomi stared the manager down. "I've told you three times already, sir. I was hoping to secure a private loan to pay for a bodyguard because I was shot at yesterday. Maybe you saw that in the news? The flower shop that got shot up?"

"I did," the manager said. "Who found the discrepancy in your account?"

"The personal protection company. While running my financials, they turned up this bank account, which came as a complete shock."

"What do you want to do with this account?" the manager asked.

"I want to have the account frozen pending an investigation."

The manager looked surprised at that. "You don't want to cash it out?"

Naomi lifted her chin, channeling the haughty inmate who'd ruled her cellblock. "I'm no criminal, sir. I want your bank to make this right. I want you to find out who opened an account in my name."

The manager gave her an up-and-down appraisal that felt nasty. "I only ask because of your . . . past."

She stiffened, Burke's hands lightly squeezing her shoulders. "Because I was unjustly imprisoned?" she demanded, raising her voice enough that the other patrons could hear. "Because I was framed for something I did not do? I'm sure you'll understand why I'm so concerned about protecting my reputation after a negative experience like that. Surely your bank doesn't want to be complicit in another frame. Do you?"

"Of course not," the bank manager blustered. "We're a reputable financial institution."

"I'm so glad to hear that," Naomi said coldly. "So do your damn job. Sir."

"I'm going to need to call the police into this," the manager cautioned.

"By all means. I hope you'll be able to explain to them how this happened? Your colleague here"—she gestured to the banker, who was looking more uncomfortable by the moment—"said the name on the ID used to open this account was mine, but the photo was not. She said she couldn't show me the photo. I suspect that's not true, that she simply didn't want to. But you will show the police that photo and then we will hopefully get to the bottom of this."

She hoped Antoine had seen the woman's monitor. She did not want to leave the bank without a solid lead.

The manager frowned down at the banker. "You wouldn't show her?"

The banker blinked, at a momentary loss for words. "But . . ."

The manager skewered Naomi with a glare. Or he tried to, anyway. He was behind the eight ball and Naomi held the reins.

She liked this feeling of power.

"Why do you want to see the photo, Miss Cranston?" the manager asked.

"So I know who to blame," Naomi said, as if this man was stupid. Because he was. "I'm sure that's not terribly difficult to understand."

The manager's cheeks darkened. He knew when he was being insulted.

Good.

"Do you think you know this individual?" he asked. "The one who fraudulently opened this account?"

"Maybe, maybe not. But I do know that my ex-husband is a devious man and our divorce was messy after he cheated on me with a nineteen-year-old bimbo. It's entirely possible that he is behind this. Maybe he's hiding assets from the new wife, in case he leaves her for a younger woman. I know you wouldn't want to be an accessory to anything like that. Would you?"

Oh. Her thoughts skittered when Burke began massaging her stiff shoulders.

The man had very nice hands. Which she'd think about later.

Because the bank manager's expression had become cagey. "Maybe you can help us get to the bottom of this." Abruptly, he turned the screen so that she could see it. "Do you know the woman in this photo?"

At first glance, Naomi thought it was her own photo. The woman had black hair, just like Naomi's. But, with closer study, the differences became clear and it was all Naomi could do to keep her fury in check. Her mind was thrown back to that night six years before when she'd stopped to help a young woman broken down on the side of the road.

"Yes, I do. Her name is Winnifred Timms."

The Central Business District, New Orleans, Louisiana

TUESDAY, FEBRUARY 25, 5:15 P.M.

A brisk knock on his office door had him lifting his gaze from the numbers he'd been running. If this week went as anticipated, he'd make enough of a profit to meet all his financial obligations and still have cash left over.

"Come in."

Wayne Stanley entered, his expression tense. "I thought you told Gaffney to have Freddie close down the Cranston bank accounts."

Fury geysered within him. *Fucking hell.* Both Gaffney and Winnifred had much to answer for. "I did."

"Well, I just got alerts from all three accounts saying they'd been frozen. We've lost half a million dollars."

"Broussard," he muttered.

"I assume so."

"Where is Gaffney?"

"At the warehouse," Stanley said with a sneer. "Probably helping himself to the inventory again."

"Again?" His hands clenched into fists. "He's been having sex with them?"

"He has. I told him to stop and he told me to mind my business and do my job."

"You should have told me."

"I just did. But you can deal with him later. Freddie just used her credit card for a one-way flight to Quito."

"Ecuador," he said grimly. Because they had no extradition treaty with the United States. "She can't be allowed to leave."

"You want me to take care of her?"

Stanley wasn't a sharpshooter, but he was damn close. "Yes. And then find out how she knew to run."

"I already did. I accessed one of the street cams facing the bank. It seems like it was a fluke, that she just happened to go to the bank when Cranston was there."

"So we lost five hundred grand because she waited an *entire day* to follow instructions?"

"Pretty much. Are we at plan Z yet?"

"Not yet." Killing Broussard was a last resort that he wasn't ready to execute. The man had friends in the NOPD who wouldn't rest until his murder was solved.

Freddie Timms, on the other hand, was expendable. Which was one of the reasons he'd chosen her. That she looked like Naomi Cranston was another reason, but Freddie hadn't understood that. She thought she was important to him, that her behavior would be excused.

"Take care of Freddie and then we'll discuss next steps."

Stanley gave him a salute before going to do his bidding.

He called Gaffney, grimacing when the man seemed out of breath when he answered. "You said that you told Winnifred to close those accounts."

"I did! Are you saying that she didn't?"

He could hear a slight whimper and wanted to strangle Gaffney with his own two hands. You didn't use your own drugs and you didn't fuck your own whores. It was the most common-sense rule.

"She did not," he said evenly. "And now those accounts are frozen."

"Broussard," Gaffney spat. "Tell Stanley to kill him. He's wanted to for years."

It wasn't that easy. "We've had this conversation, Detective."

"I know, I know. It'll bring down the wrath of André Holmes. I have a shift to get to, so I need to go."

Gaffney was a weasel and a coward, but he was still useful in his detective role. "Fine. This way you'll have an alibi in case anyone accuses you of killing Freddie." He ended the call.

He didn't care about Freddie, who'd only been a nice distraction over the years. However, if he lost any more people, he'd have to borrow a few more from Ortiz to manage the warehouse and its occupants.

He'd try nearly anything else before he did that. He didn't want to give the gang leader any more of a toehold in his organization.

This was all because of Broussard. Plan Z was looking better every day.

15

Metairie, New Orleans, Louisiana
TUESDAY, FEBRUARY 25, 6:00 P.M.

YOU CONTINUE TO surprise me, Naomi," Antoine said from the back seat of Burke's SUV as they left the parking lot of the fast-food restaurant. They'd all been starving so they'd stopped for a bite before heading back to the Quarter.

Burke was in agreement with Antoine's statement, but hopefully not for the same reasons. Watching Naomi deal with that bank manager and the police who'd shown up at the bank to take their statements had been something else.

Okay, fine. It had been damn arousing.

Until the manager had shown them the photo of Winnifred Timms. That had felt like a bucket of cold water. He'd been certain that Winnifred was complicit in Naomi's arrest, but to have her continued involvement confirmed had him kicking himself for not making her a higher priority in the investigation. He should have interviewed her himself.

But so many things had happened that had distracted him. It had been less than two days but it felt like two weeks.

At least the bank accounts were secure for now. The bank manager had called the NOPD, who'd frozen the other two bank accounts opened in Naomi's name. Now all three were frozen. Nobody would be able to touch that money.

And that it was Winnifred Timms who had opened the accounts—with a fake ID featuring Naomi's name—was a checkmark in Naomi's favor. It established a connection between her previous arrest and this latest effort to frame her. It established a conspiracy.

Burke wondered when Gaffney would realize what they'd done with the accounts. He wondered what Gaffney's reaction would be. He'd already tried to steal their children and had shot up the flower shop where Naomi worked. Any retaliation would be scaled up from there.

Naomi was not safe.

At least this SUV had bullet-resistant windows.

Naomi twisted around in the front passenger seat, looking at Antoine. "How do I surprise you?" she asked.

"I've seen you defeated, scared, riled up, and sweet. But there, in the bank, you sounded like every rich person I've ever had the misfortune to cross."

Naomi chuckled. "I was channeling one of the inmates on my cellblock. She was *very* wealthy before being sentenced for murdering her business manager after he stole all her money. I stayed away from most of the women in for murder. They were scary as hell, but Nessa freely admitted that she deserved to be in there and that she felt no remorse for killing him. I was nervous about her at first, but she really wasn't interested in hurting anyone else."

"And you became friends?" Antoine asked.

"We did. She was the first person who befriended me when I came out of isolation. I was so scared, you know? I'd gone into protective custody because I'd been stabbed. I didn't know what would happen when I was integrated into gen pop."

It was the first time Burke had heard her use prison slang, and it was startling. "You weren't hurt again, were you?"

"No. Had a few skirmishes. Broke a woman's nose and another's arm when they kept putting their hands on me. That sent me into the hole for a week."

She recounted it lightly, but there was tension in her tone.

"What happened when they let you out of solitary after that?" Burke asked.

"Nobody put their hands on me again."

"Good," he said fervently.

"How did you become friends with the rich woman?" Antoine asked.

"When I was in PC, I'd crochet. Kept me sane. My mom sent me the yarn and at first I made hats for preemies. Mom would take them and distribute them. One day one of the guards asked if I'd make a scarf for one of the aging inmates in gen pop. I couldn't even fathom wearing a scarf because it was always so hot in my cell. No windows and no A/C. Just a fan. But I figured older people get cold, so I made a scarf and a hat. The day I got out of isolation, I went to the cafeteria with everyone else. I was shaking, because that's where the stabbing happened, you know?"

"No," Burke said, "but I can imagine."

"Well, I was trying to fake being brave. And there was this old lady wearing the scarf and hat I'd made. She was watching for me and patted the seat beside her. She was grateful and told me to stick with her. So I did."

"I'm glad you had her," Burke said.

"Me too. We talked every day. I really miss her." She sighed, the sound fond. "She made things bearable and I'll always be grateful. So today, when that bank manager was giving me a hard time, I thought, what would Nessa do? And that's what I did. That manager was a jerk. I got the feeling that had I been alone, that conversation would have gone a lot differently. The way he looked me up and down? It felt predatory."

Yes, it had. Burke had wanted to smash his face. "Well, you don't have to talk to him again. In fact, you shouldn't leave my house again until this is over. I think that Gaffney will be angry when he can't get to his money. I don't want you shot at again."

"I'm not keen on it, either. I guess this means no more investigating for me. I really wanted to question Winnifred Timms, too. That bitch has some explaining to do."

"We never got the chance to talk about her financials because we went to the bank," Antoine said, "but she gets a hefty allowance every month. Comes from what's supposed to look like a corporation, but I think it's a front. It's set up to look like a scholarship fund. I'm still trying to track where the money is coming from."

"Did you find any of Winnifred's social media?" Naomi asked. "I looked, but never found a thing."

"She has no online presence," Antoine confirmed. "Which is weird for someone her age. I even ran a reverse image search in case she had social media under another name, but that was a dead end. Only thing I found was a Facebook account from when she was in high school, under Winnifred Timms, so it seems like that's her real name. Her Facebook was sparse, though. She rarely posted. Mostly just photos of her dog. Is Devonte still watching her?"

"He is. Let me call him and see what's going on." But he was interrupted by an incoming call. "Speak of the devil. It's Devonte." He hit accept. "You're on speaker," he told the man. "Antoine and the client are in the vehicle with me."

"Winnifred is on the move. She went home, so I was sitting in the parking garage of her condo. I was about to text you with an update when she came out with a suitcase and got in her car. I think she's headed for the airport."

Burke's pulse ratcheted up. "We're on our way. Where are you?"

"Almost to the Superdome."

"We're just leaving Metairie. We can get to the airport before you, so let me know when you know where she's parking her car." He ended the call and turned to Naomi. "You stay in the car, and if bullets start flying, you duck, y'hear me?"

She nodded, her expression now grim. "I hear you. But I'm going to talk with her, Burke. Don't take that away from me."

He wanted to tell her no but he couldn't. "Let's see."

"Yes. Let's."

Louis Armstrong International Airport
Kenner, Louisiana
TUESDAY, FEBRUARY 25, 6:30 P.M.

Burke had driven them to the entrance of the long-term parking garage at the airport, where they sat waiting for Winnifred Timms. Long-term parking had made the most sense, considering Winnifred appeared to be fleeing to . . . somewhere.

She pulled into the parking garage, Devonte directly behind her.

That she hadn't diverted her path spoke to Devonte's skill in tailing—or Winnifred's distracted frame of mind.

Likely both.

Naomi's heart pounded as Burke pulled in after Devonte, taking a ticket from the machine.

"Naomi, you stay in the SUV," Burke said. "Promise me."

She was saved a reply by Devonte. She wasn't going to promise any such thing. She needed to talk to Winnifred Timms.

"She's finally found a spot," Devonte said through the phone. "What do you want me to do?"

"Park as close as you can," Burke said. "I'll park behind her so she can't drive away. Then I have a great many questions to ask her."

Burke pulled into a space, allowing Devonte to follow Winnifred as she went around another curve before pulling her car into a parking place. Devonte parked his car a few slots away.

Burke slowed to a stop behind the first car in the row. Winnifred's car was visible to them, but they were not visible to her.

Burke waited until she'd retrieved her suitcase from the trunk, then sped up, coming to a stop directly behind her.

Winnifred looked up, shock on her face. She reached for her phone, but Devonte stepped up behind her and took it from her hand as Burke got out of the SUV, leaving the door open so that Naomi could hear him.

Or so that he could quickly get back in and drive away if this was some kind of a trap.

Winnifred paled. "I'll scream."

Burke shrugged. "Go ahead. I'm sure the cops will be happy to respond, considering you're now wanted for bank fraud. Devonte, can you make sure she's not armed? Antoine, can you inform NOPD that we've detained Miss Timms? And specifically let André know?"

"On it," Antoine said from the back seat.

Devonte patted Winnifred down with quick, impersonal movements. "She's clean."

"I have no idea who you are or what you're talking about," Winnifred insisted. "I'm not wanted for bank fraud. You have me mixed up with someone else."

Naomi had heard enough. She got out of the SUV, moving to stand beside Burke, noting the sneer that briefly twisted Winnifred's face.

"We do not have you mixed up with anyone else," Naomi said. "Hello, Winnifred. I wish I could say that it's good to see you again."

Pursing her lips, Winnifred said nothing, and Naomi was reminded of Cresswell that afternoon. It was entirely possible that this woman would also remain silent, but Naomi had to try.

"Why?" Naomi asked quietly. "Why did you participate in framing me? What did it get you?"

Malice glittered in the younger woman's eyes. "You can't prove anything, so don't even try."

"I don't have to," Naomi said, proud that she was maintaining her calm. "You used a fake ID with my name and your face to open at least one bank account. That's irrefutable. Pair it with the fact that this happened six years after you conveniently discovered a bag of drugs—that turned out not to be drugs—under the back seat of my car and it doesn't bode well for you. We saw Cresswell in prison today," she added, wondering at the reaction she'd get from the abrupt topic change.

Fear passed over Winnifred's face. "I don't know who that is."

"Liar," Naomi said softly. "You're still young enough that you probably don't have any children Gaffney can threaten. How else will they ensure your compliance?"

Winnifred swallowed hard, then pasted on a smile. "I don't know what you mean."

"I think Cresswell is still alive because he's a high-profile prisoner," Burke said. "Him dying in custody would raise too many questions and there would be investigations. But you are not high profile. No one will launch an investigation if you mysteriously die in prison. You are expendable."

Winnifred glanced up over their heads before her sneer returned. "So are you, Mr. Broussard. You've been living on borrowed time for years."

Startled, Naomi glanced up at Burke, who was frowning. "What the hell is that supposed to mean?" he demanded.

But Winnifred just smiled, no trace of fear remaining. She looked . . . cocky. "I think your time is up."

Burke had reached out a hand toward Winnifred, but Naomi never got a chance to know what he'd planned to do. Turning, Naomi looked in the direction that Winnifred had just glanced and froze.

There, on the deck above them, was a man with a rifle. Pointed at them.

"Gun!" Naomi shouted as she grabbed onto Burke's jacket. "Get down!" She dropped to the pavement, dragging Burke down with her, then grunted when he landed on top of her.

Protecting me.

Naomi struggled, partly to see and partly to breathe. Burke shifted, lifting himself a scant inch that allowed her to do both. To her relief, Devonte had dropped as well, but he'd drawn his gun and was looking around frantically.

Only Winnifred remained standing, her sneer becoming the same smirk she'd aimed at Naomi the night of her arrest.

But then Winnifred's body crumpled to the garage floor, a neat bullet hole in the center of her forehead.

"Oh my God." Naomi sucked in air, trying not to let panic overtake her because there was a dead woman mere inches away.

And then there were more shots. Four of them in rapid succession, the bullets hitting the cars around them. Two more shots hit the SUV.

Above her, Burke froze.

Beside her, Devonte swore.

Behind them, the back door of the SUV opened and Antoine shouted, "Get her in here!"

Burke scooped Naomi up and tossed her into the back seat with Antoine, who covered her body with his.

Burke got in the driver's seat, Devonte in the front seat beside him, both hunkering down. Because the SUV was bullet resistant.

They waited in tense silence, but nothing happened. No more shots, no shouts. No approaching footsteps. Nothing.

Still, they remained hunkered down until they heard police sirens approaching. Until they were surrounded by cruisers.

Until cops yelled at them to exit the vehicle with their hands up.

Naomi sighed. It was going to be a long evening.

The Quarter, New Orleans, Louisiana

TUESDAY, FEBRUARY 25, 8:25 P.M.

"You guys," André said as he shut the door to the interview room where Burke was sitting.

Naomi, Antoine, and Devonte had all been put in separate rooms.

It was standard operating procedure to be interviewed separately, but Burke was still annoyed. Naomi shouldn't have to be interrogated again.

Not after everything she'd been through. He wondered if she'd ever seen anyone murdered before. He hoped she was all right.

He wanted his eyes on her. He wanted to run his hands over her, to prove that she still breathed.

She'd saved his life today.

"We guys what?" Burke asked wearily. He had blood in his hair and on the back of his neck. It itched something fierce.

"You're trouble," André growled, taking the seat beside him. "I muted the speaker. No one can hear us. You okay?"

"Other than seeing a woman shot to death in front of us and being frisked like we were criminals? Sure."

"I got there as soon as I could. I told the responding officers to treat you gently, that you were not at fault."

"They were gentle," Burke acknowledged. "I know they were doing their jobs. It still sucked."

"Tell me again what Winnifred said."

"That I was living on borrowed time. And that my time was up. I think she believed the shooter was going to kill us. But he shot her instead."

"We got it all from the security cameras. The shooter left via one of the stairwells and got into a waiting vehicle."

"Let me guess," Burke drawled. "A black SUV with darkly tinted windows and stolen license plates."

"Yep. What do you think she meant? That you were living on borrowed time?"

"I don't know." And it was eating at him. "It might be that my reprieve from consequences after rejecting Gaffney's offers and threats has come to an end. That my bluff against Cresswell is no longer going to protect me. It could be any number of things."

André went still, and Burke knew that expression. Something had happened and André was hesitant to share.

"Just tell me," Burke said. "I wanna go home and wash my hair."

André sighed again. "Cresswell's dead."

Burke reared back. "What? How? When?"

"Poison, probably cyanide, but the ME will confirm. Sometime this afternoon."

"How did he ingest the cyanide?"

"Pills. Prison officials found a bottle hidden inside his mattress. No idea how long he'd had it."

"Suicide, then. Or that's what we're supposed to think."

"You got any proof that it wasn't suicide?"

"No. And it might have been. He was twitchy today. Depressed. Terrified."

"He came close to talking to you."

"To Naomi, anyway."

"I saw the footage. She was good at interrogation. We lost a good cop."

"When NOPD framed her?" Burke snapped.

André winced. "Not gonna deny it, even though I had nothing to do with it."

Burke sighed. "I'm sorry. That was a low blow and you don't deserve it."

"Thank you," André said quietly. "Sometimes you get so angry with the NOPD that I fear you'll lump me in with the others."

"I know you're a good man. A good cop. I trust you with my life. I trust you with hers."

"Naomi's?"

"Yeah."

André's lips turned up. "Look at you. I think you've got a crush."

Burke's cheeks heated. "Are we twelve?"

"Farrah says I act like it sometimes. But I think wives are supposed to say that we act like children. Keeps us humble. She says to tell you hi."

Burke loved Farrah, but he wouldn't let André's attempt to distract him work. "What are you doing to find the shooter?"

"All the normal things. BOLOs, eyes on the airports, train stations. We put up roadblocks around the airport, but we were way too late for that."

"If he wants to get out of New Orleans, there are a million places he can do that out of the bayou," Burke said. "I assume you've alerted the Coast Guard."

"We have. Like I said, all the normal things."

"Have you brought Gaffney in for questioning?"

"Yep. He denied everything and called his union rep. We cut him loose a half hour ago. Smug fucker."

Burke met André's gaze. "One of my sources tells me that Gaffney was investigated by PIB after Cresswell's arrest."

"Antoine," André muttered.

"I have many sources," Burke countered. "What was the result of that investigation?"

"Nothing. Nobody found anything."

"And the investigators? Who were they?"

"Your source didn't tell you?"

"Only that he recognized the names and that he believes that they're good cops. But something stinks here, André. You and I both know it. Gaffney came to me *twice* to try to force me to steal and sell drugs confiscated during busts. I can't be the only one he did that to. There *has* to be evidence. He *can't* be that smart or that lucky."

"I'll look into the PIB cops myself," André promised.

That would have to be enough. For now. "Something's rotten there. Do you agree?"

"It seems so, but I don't want to judge until I know for sure."

Burke got that. André was careful. He did things by the book. But that hadn't gotten them the truth about Gaffney, and now Cresswell would never be able to confess, even if he'd been ready to.

"Was Cresswell offered WITSEC protection?"

André blinked in surprise, then nodded. "He was. He refused. Those were among the last words he spoke before going silent two and a half years ago."

"Did Mrs. Cresswell know what he'd been offered?"

"I don't know. We didn't tell her." André's brows lifted. "Why?"

"I was going to offer her protection for her kids. They're nearly adults, but Cresswell clearly feared for their safety. But now that he's dead . . ." He sighed. "I don't know if the threat to them will remain. She needs to be warned."

"The threat to you appears to remain," André said quietly.

"Borrowed time," Burke murmured. "Yeah, I know." And he still couldn't figure out what Winnifred had meant. "I thought that with Cresswell in prison, I didn't have to fear him anymore. Naomi also thought that she was free and clear. But I don't think either of us is safe."

"I don't, either. I'd like to put you in a safe house, but you're going to say no, just like Naomi did. She doesn't trust that NOPD will keep her safe, and I can't say that I blame her. She has one hundred percent trust in you, though."

Burke felt the burden of responsibility even as his heart again fluttered like he was a teenager. "I will do my best to be worthy of that trust."

"You always do. What are you going to do next?"

"Go home. Wash off the blood. Eat a decent meal. And go the fuck to sleep."

André just looked at him. "You know what I mean."

"I know, but those are the best answers I have because my brain is fried." He pinched the bridge of his nose because his head was aching from where he'd hit it on the pavement when Naomi had yanked him off his feet. *To save my life.* "Somebody tipped off Winnifred that the bank fraud had been exposed or she wouldn't have known to run. Do we know how she knew?"

"You guys tipped her off. Bank cameras caught her coming into the bank while you were there. She immediately turned and left. We confiscated her cell phone at the scene, but it was a burner, so requesting records isn't something we can do quickly. We're trying to break into it to see if she has emails or messages or received any calls around five this evening. Your 'source' can keep you updated." He used finger quotes and a very dry tone.

Burke only grinned. "Okay."

André scowled. "That was not supposed to be an endorsement of your source."

"Oh, I know."

"Then wipe that damn grin off your face."

Burke complied, suddenly feeling more tired than he had in a very long time. "Have you searched Winnifred's condo yet?"

"Not yet. We can't prove which unit she lived in, so we're getting a warrant for the building's security footage. The building's management was not cooperative."

"But we have witnesses who saw her going in and out of the building—Naomi and Devonte."

"I've noted this on the warrant, but they didn't see which unit she entered. I've got uniforms outside, noting who comes and goes. We need to do this by the book so that whatever evidence we gather is admissible."

Burke wanted to argue, but André was right. "When can we go?"

"Now. I just wanted to touch base with you and your people."

"Including Antoine?"

"Including Antoine."

"Is there going to be any issue with him getting his laptops back?"

"Of course not."

Whether the laptops would have been tampered with was another story. Luckily Antoine had everything backed up to his own cloud and had probably wiped his laptops with his phone as soon as the cops had arrived at the garage and told them to exit the SUV with their hands up. The man was very serious about security and Burke appreciated that.

He'd also shielded Naomi's body with his own while they'd waited in tense silence for more bullets to be fired. Burke appreciated that, too.

"What about the arson at the Delgados' home?"

"Under investigation. It was purposely set, but so far, no leads."

Burke forced his bouncing brain back to Winnifred. "Do you know where Winnifred planned to go?"

"Ecuador."

Burke studied his friend. André didn't lie, but there was something he was holding back. "What else aren't you telling me?"

"She had a handgun in the glove box of her car. A Bersa Thunder .380."

"Like the one the female driver pulled on Harrison when he saved Everett." But that wasn't what André was holding back. Burke had known him long enough to spot his tells. "So that's another connection to Pablo Delgado—and therefore to the sex trafficking ring, because Pablo was ID'd by the trafficking victim who nearly died during the Super Bowl."

Ah. There it was. Something flickered in André's dark eyes. Something profoundly sad. Burke leaned closer. "Tell me," he murmured.

André swallowed. "There were five bodies found in the Delgado home—Ernesto, his mother, his grandmother . . . and two teenagers."

Burke's heart hurt. More victims of trafficking was the most likely explanation. "Do you think his mother and grandmother knew they were there?"

"I don't know. So far, none of the neighbors will talk to us. I think you poached the only one who would have been willing."

"Eleanor wouldn't have talked to you. She doesn't trust the NOPD to keep her safe, either. I'm sorry, André, but that's the truth of it."

André nodded stiffly. "I have to fix this, Burke."

"I know. And I'll help you."

"I know you will." André stood, tugging his jacket hem. "Let's spring you from this joint."

Burke stood, groaning when his muscles protested. Dropping to concrete pavement hurt like a bitch. "Music to my ears."

16

The Quarter, New Orleans, Louisiana
TUESDAY, FEBRUARY 25, 11:30 P.M.

BURKE SANK INTO his BarcaLounger and let out a long, slow breath. The house was finally quiet. All the children were in bed. Probably not asleep, but in bed. Molly and Lucien were back on guard duty, Val and Harrison now sleeping.

Door locks had been checked, windows secured. Val's dog Czar slept in the bedroom with Jace and Elijah. Elijah's dog was up there, too, but Burke wouldn't depend on Delilah to protect the boys from harm. Czar would protect everyone.

His house was sealed tight.

He could breathe now. He'd finally gotten a chance to change his clothes, to scrub Winnifred Timms's blood from his skin, out of his hair.

Naomi had also been splattered with the blood and gore, but she hadn't complained, not even once. She had, however, spent a very long time in the shower when they'd finally arrived home after being released by the NOPD.

It was dark in his living room and he welcomed it. His head ached. But he had messages to check, so he braved the light from his phone as he ran through his texts. There were several from Molly, Lucien, and Val asking where they were and if they were all right. That they'd heard about the shooting on the news and were so worried.

He'd called them as soon as he'd gotten his cell phone back from the NOPD, so he ignored those messages. There was a new one from Jace, accompanied by a photo. That one made him smile because it was a photo of Burke himself at about seven years old.

Jace's message read: ***Found in yore mamas cook book. U were cute.***

The kid was getting better at texting. Diagnosed with dyslexia at fifteen, Jace had a lot of catching up to do, but Val, Kaj, and Elijah were constant supports.

Burke loved his people so very much.

He texted back: ***Thank you. I didn't know the photo was in that cookbook. And I was pretty cute.*** He sent it, unsurprised to get a reply right away, a laughing emoji.

He kept scrolling through messages, deleting the ones from the media. His name had been mentioned in the initial reports of the shooting, as it often was when he was in the thick of a case that went south.

There was a whole slew of messages from Joy Thomas, his office admin. They started out worried and quickly became scolding. He'd already called her as well, giving her a heads-up because the office would be inundated with calls tomorrow.

But there was no message from the person he'd most hoped for. Nothing from Kaleb. Not even an *Are you okay?*

It hurt. A lot. His work group was family, but not in the same way as Kaleb and Juliette. This situation could not continue.

His heart couldn't take it. He glanced at the clock. It was late, but Kaleb was a night owl. He'd be awake. He hesitated for a full minute, staring at Kaleb's name in his favorites list. Then he tapped the name and held his breath.

The phone rang five times. Which meant Kaleb was either asleep or was purposely letting it go to voicemail. Burke was about to hit end when Kaleb answered.

"Burke."

"Kaleb. I'm sorry to call so late. I needed to talk to you."

Kaleb sighed. "I've been meaning to answer your text. I'm just not sure what to say."

"That you forgive me?"

"I forgive you. I said a lot of things in the heat of the moment that I wish I could take back. But . . ."

Burke had released the breath he'd been holding, but his lungs froze up again at that tiny little word that held so much power. "But?"

"I still don't want you around the boys. You're a magnet for trouble and I . . . I'm sorry, Burke. I just can't risk their safety."

Kaleb did sound sorry, but that didn't keep Burke's heart from breaking at the thought of not seeing his godsons again. "I guess that's your right as their father."

"It is."

"Are they okay?"

"They are. Still shaken up. Juliette's found them a therapist."

"That's good. That's real good." There was a long moment of awkward silence that Burke had to break because it didn't seem like Kaleb was going to say any more. "Can we meet later this week? There are still some things we need to work through. All that stuff about me leaving the running of the company to you."

"I was angry, Burke. I shouldn't have said those things."

"But you did, so you must have been thinking them. In fact, it sounded like you'd been thinking about them for a long time.

You're . . . Dammit, Kaleb, you're the only family I have left. I can't breathe if you're this angry with me."

"I'm not angry anymore." Kaleb just sounded tired.

"Can we meet? Just for lunch. Anywhere you choose."

Kaleb made an exasperated sound. "You were just shot at, Burke. Someone shot at you." He sighed. "Look, I'll be blunt. I don't want to meet with you. I don't want to be seen with you. I don't want to draw the attention of whoever shot at you tonight. Because the next shot might be aimed at anyone they think they can use to hurt you."

Burke swallowed hard. "Okay." Because, again, what else could he say?

"We can do a Zoom call to talk about the business. Just until I find someone to take over as liaison to the owner of the company."

Hurt swelled. He was no longer Burke, or Kaleb's brother, or Kaleb's oldest friend. He was now *the owner of the company.*

"Is . . . Is Juliette in agreement?"

"No. She's on your side. So now you've not only put my sons in danger, you're affecting my marriage."

There was the bitterness Burke had heard the night before.

"I'm sorry. I don't want to come between you."

"Then stop texting her. Stop asking about the boys. You're only making things worse." Another heavy sigh. "Give me time, Burke. It's only been a day and I'm still dealing with the fright of nearly having my children abducted."

I've been selfish, making this about me. "Good night, Kaleb."

He ended the call and shuddered out a breath. Kaleb was right, even though the truth had been devastatingly hard to hear.

A noise from the kitchen doorway had him jerking his gaze in that direction.

Naomi stood in the shadow left by the night-light over the stove.

She held a mug of tea in one hand and, in the other, her bag covered in butterflies.

"I didn't mean to listen," she said quietly. "By the time I realized you were on the phone, it seemed too late to come out."

"It's okay," he said. "I'm not angry with you."

Never with her.

She approached cautiously. "Thank you. I just didn't know what to do. I tried not to overhear. I, um, made you a cup of tea." She set it on the table beside him.

He took it gratefully. "Can't you sleep?"

She shook her head. "Mom can't sleep with a light on and I can't sleep in the dark or with the door closed. PTSD from being in solitary all those months. Plus, I thrash at night sometimes, when I have nightmares. I don't want to hurt my mom." She held up her butterfly bag. "So I came downstairs to work."

"Take my room. I can sleep in the chair."

"That's very generous, but I'm not going to take your bed, Burke." Then she surprised him by brushing a wayward lock of hair from his forehead. "If you don't mind, I can go sit in your study. I might snooze on the sofa up there."

He didn't want her to go. "Or you could sit on the sofa here. And snooze if you want."

He didn't want her to be alone.

He didn't want to be alone, either.

"If you're sure."

"I am. Sit down, Naomi. Turn on that light." He sipped at the tea. "Thank you for this."

She sat on the settee and switched on the light, which was so dim that it didn't bother his headache. He wouldn't have cared if it had. He was realizing that he'd do a lot to make Naomi Cranston happy.

"You're welcome," she said. "And if you want to talk, I'll be happy to listen."

He studied her over the mug for a long moment. "Thank you. But there's really nothing to say. Kaleb doesn't want to be seen with me. He's afraid bad guys will shoot him. And he isn't wrong."

"He isn't right, either. Burke, cops walk this path every day. They deal almost exclusively with bad guys, but it's rare that anyone shoots at their children. You know this. Kaleb might not, but you do."

"He said he needs time."

"Then give him time. Maybe he'll come around. Or his wife will."

"I don't want to be a wedge between them. He says I'm affecting his marriage."

"Well." She pulled her knitting from the bag. "You can take this with a grain of salt, but I have been married before."

"To a jerk."

"True enough. But if they're fighting about you, there's a fair-to-middlin' chance they've been fighting about other things that have nothing to do with you. You might be a final straw, but I doubt that you are the only straw."

He shook his head. "They're rock-solid."

"Maybe. Maybe not. People thought Jimmy and I were rock-solid, too. I'm not saying your Kaleb is like Jimmy. That would be too mean. But I am saying that you don't bear the weight of all the problems in their relationship. Give them time and a little space. They might work things out on their own."

"Thank you. That helps." And it did. Not that Burke wanted Kaleb and Juliette to have marriage problems, but what Naomi said made some sense.

"Good." She knitted in silence for a few minutes while he sipped his tea. Then she sighed. "Sylvi had to hire someone to take my place. Temporarily."

"Are you okay with that?" He didn't think so, since she'd brought it up out of the blue.

"I think so. She promised me it was just to get her through Mardi Gras, which I understand."

"Who did she hire?"

"A woman whose florist business failed. The woman is an artist with flowers, just not good with the business parts."

"You sound worried," he said gently.

"Insecurities, I guess. The new woman isn't an ex-con who'll get Sylvi's shop shot up. If Sylvi kept her, I couldn't blame her."

"We seem to be in the same boat, our troubles affecting those around us."

She met his eyes in the dim light. "We are indeed."

Which was why she'd brought it up, he realized. Not so out of the blue. "You're very kind."

"It's no hardship to be kind. You deserve it."

Pleasure soothed some of the sting from his heart. "If Sylvi keeps the non-ex-con, you can come work for me."

"I've been thinking about that. I really do love working in the flower shop, but if I'm going to endanger Sylvi, I'll stay away until it's safe. Did Kaleb give you a time frame? Like, ten days without being shot at? Or a year?"

"No, but I'm not going to press him on it. A wise person told me to give him time and space."

A soft whir had Burke turning toward the lift. It wasn't audible during the day when there was activity, but tonight, in the quiet of his house, it was loud.

The lift door opened and Eleanor Jackson emerged, wearing a bathrobe that looked soft and slippers that shuffled against the floor.

Burke stood. "Eleanor, is everything okay?"

"It is." She shuffled to the sofa and started to sit, but Burke stopped her.

"Use my chair. It's got a lift feature." He pressed a button on the chair and the chair rose vertically. "It'll make it easier to get up again."

She eyed the chair dubiously. "It's covered in duct tape."

Burke smiled. "It's an old chair, but it's comfortable."

She lowered herself to the chair and made a contented sound when Burke lowered it to a normal seated position. "I've been meaning to get one of these, but I always think they're for old people."

Chuckling, Burke sat next to Naomi. She smelled like honeysuckle and the scent soothed him almost as much as her words had done.

Smiling, Naomi turned to him. "Why *do* you have a duct-taped BarcaLounger? I'm surprised your decorator let you keep it."

"My decorator was Juliette and she did throw my chair away. I rescued it from the curb."

"Juliette is his sister-in-law," Naomi explained to Eleanor. "But it still doesn't explain why you love this chair."

"It was my uncle Larry's," Burke said. "When he passed, he left me this house and all of its contents. I had the house renovated a few years ago when a pipe burst."

"I didn't see anything about your uncle Larry when I googled you," Eleanor said.

"He was a character," Burke said fondly. "More of a father to me than my bio dad, that's for damn sure. My father was a fisherman out on the Gulf. We had a little shack on the bayou that leaked whenever it rained, which was a lot. When I was thirteen, I told my uncle that my father was beating me and my mom, and he moved my mother and me into this house. That was the year I met Kaleb and his family."

"Who is Kaleb?" Eleanor asked.

"Son of my uncle's business partner," Burke said, but his throat closed and no more words would come.

"He and Burke were close," Naomi told Eleanor when he couldn't speak. "Like brothers."

Burke cleared his throat. "Kaleb still runs the business. He's the CEO. I'm the president because Larry left the business to me, but I haven't really been involved. Although I'm thinking that should change. I've saddled Kaleb with all the responsibility."

Eleanor narrowed her eyes and once again, Burke had the feeling she had it all figured out. Either that or she'd heard him talking on the phone from upstairs.

"Do you pay him well?" Eleanor asked.

"Very well."

"Then he should be grateful."

"She's wise," Naomi murmured.

"I really am," Eleanor confirmed.

Burke smiled at them both. "Can I get you some coffee, Miss Eleanor?"

"No, thanks. I just wanted to come down to tell you that I've called my neighbors and asked if they'd be willing to talk to you."

Burke sat up straighter. "And?" he asked.

"Six of them said they could meet after work tomorrow, but only if it's somewhere secure and discreet. No offense, but they don't want to be seen giving you information. The fire was bad enough, but seeing the wreckage is scaring folks to death."

"No offense taken," Burke said, trying to feel the same way about Kaleb, Juliette, and the kids.

"I think a few of them have information you might find helpful," Eleanor said.

"Oh, good," Naomi breathed. "Maybe we can finally start cracking this case."

"Spoken like a true PI," he teased, then turned to Eleanor. "Thank you. I hope you calling them hasn't put them in danger."

"I used a burner phone. That nice Antoine gave me one." She gave them a saucy wink. "I feel so badass, using a burner."

"You *are* a badass," Naomi assured her.

Burke nodded. "We need to get you a leather jacket and a motorcycle."

"The jacket will be sufficient. A motorcycle would likely kill me." Eleanor hit the button on the lift chair, sliding to her feet once the chair was fully extended. "I'm going to get me one of these chairs, for sure. Maybe someone's selling one on that Craigslist."

Burke had already decided to get her a brand-new chair once this was all over and it was safe for her to return home. Because it *would* be all over. He was going to make sure of it this time.

"Sweet dreams, Eleanor," he said and walked her to the lift.

"Thank you. You've made a bad situation bearable. You're a good man, Burke Broussard."

Touched, he watched her get into the lift and waggle her fingers in a goodbye before ascending to the second floor where she was staying. When he came back to the sofa, Naomi was putting her knitting away.

"I'll go up to your office," she said. "You can rest in your uncle's chair."

He didn't want her to go. "Or you could just stay where you are." He sat beside her. "If you want to snooze here, you can use my shoulder as a pillow."

Naomi regarded him solemnly for a long moment, seeming to sense this was more than a casual offer.

Because it was.

"I'd like that," she finally said and his heart settled as he stretched his arm across the back of the sofa. It settled even more when she laid her head on his shoulder with a contented sigh. "Thank you, Burke."

"You're welcome."

"What are we going to do tomorrow?" she asked. "We can't talk to Eleanor's neighbors until tomorrow evening. What will we do until then? Cresswell is dead." She'd paled when he'd told her what André had shared about Cresswell's death, but she hadn't seemed all that surprised. "Winnifred Timms is dead. The Delgado brothers are dead. Who's left to investigate?"

He'd wondered that himself, but in a disjointed way he knew came from mental exhaustion. "There's the couple who saved Harper."

"Bill and Donna Burrell from Galveston," she murmured. "Except their names are not likely to be Bill and Donna and they're not likely to be from Galveston."

"Antoine's been trying to ID them through his facial recognition software. Maybe he'll have some luck."

She hesitated, then exhaled. "There's the girl, the sixteen-year-old in the hospital who's 'coming around' after the induced coma. She ID'd Pablo Delgado as her pimp. Maybe she saw something else."

"You want to talk to her." It wasn't even a question.

"I do. Do you think they'll let me?"

"I'm pretty sure they won't. But your mother was a nurse in that hospital before she retired. Maybe she can put out some feelers."

"That's a good idea." She yawned. "You'll take me with you to see Cresswell's wife?"

"I don't want to. I want to keep you safe."

"Please, Burke. I'll wear a vest and a tactical helmet. Hell, I'll wear a full suit of armor if that makes you more comfortable with the risk. But don't tuck me away."

Once again, he found that he didn't want to tell her no. She'd demonstrated calm under duress. She'd saved his life. "All right. I won't tuck you away. Try to sleep now."

"I can turn off the light," she offered, but there was a quaver in her voice.

"No, leave it on. It'll be fine."

And it was fine. It was very fine. So fine that he was starting to let himself wish for more.

With her.

"G'night, Burke."

He gave in to temptation, brushing a kiss on her shiny dark hair. "Good night, Naomi."

And when he finally went to sleep, it was with the scent of honeysuckle.

The Quarter, New Orleans, Louisiana
WEDNESDAY, FEBRUARY 26, 9:00 A.M.

Naomi had been awake for hours, jostled out of sleep by Val's giant dog, who'd lumbered down the stairs with Jace at six a.m. The boy had taken the dog out to the courtyard, under the watchful eye of Molly Sutton.

Who'd grinned at Naomi with unabashed glee upon finding her on the settee with Burke. They'd fallen asleep sitting up, her head on Burke's massive shoulder.

Naomi had been comfortable, but Burke's head was tilted at an angle that was almost certain to leave a crick in his neck. So she'd eased his body down, lifted his feet, and taken off his shoes before covering him with a light blanket.

Naomi had spent two of the last three hours in the quiet solitude of Burke's second-floor study. She'd finished the pair of knitted knockers she'd been working on and started another.

She kept knitting as nearly all the adults in the house crowded into the study for a planning session. Antoine, Val, and Lucien had been joined by Naomi's mother and James.

Eleanor was also present, Burke hoping that she might hear a detail as they planned and plotted, a detail that might trigger a memory. Perhaps something she didn't realize was important.

Only Harrison and Chelsea had remained downstairs with the children. Harrison was on guard duty and Chelsea was supervising Harper and the three boys in kitchen cleanup after breakfast.

Even Everett was helping. Jace and Elijah had been good influences on him.

Naomi sat on the same love seat as the day before, her heart doing a little happy dance when Burke sat beside her.

"How much did you sleep?" Burke asked softly. He looked rested and calm, his eyes alert. He'd clearly benefited from a decent night's sleep.

"More than I usually get. I don't sleep a lot. Leftover from . . . you know. Guards would come by to do cell checks or one of the other girls would have a nightmare and scream. I used to sleep in two-hour blocks. Now I'm up to four."

He frowned but didn't say any more because it was time for their meeting to begin.

Molly had rolled in a whiteboard. The sight made Burke's team smile and tease her about her penchant for whiteboards.

Molly just rolled her eyes. "We need a place to post our notes," she said. "We've spent enough time cowering in this house, afraid for our children." She flipped the whiteboard over, exposing the other side, which was covered in notes and photos.

Photos of Cresswell, Gaffney, Winnifred, the Delgado brothers, and the woman who'd saved Harper. But it was the question that dominated the center of the board that had Naomi's attention.

WHY NAOMI? was written in all caps with a red marker. "We have still not answered 'Why Naomi?' and this really bothers me," Molly said. "I think it's fair to assume that Naomi is intended to be the fall guy for something."

"Just as she was six years ago," Ruthanne said. "I think a follow-up question should be: why did they want to keep her in prison? They threatened me to keep me from pursuing an appeal. Why? I thought this might be just petty mean-spiritedness on Gaffney's part, but the bank accounts and the stalking of Everett indicate it's much bigger than that."

"Good point," Molly said and added the question, also in red. "Both the planted drugs six years ago and the fraudulent bank accounts this year indicate time and planning. Why?"

"Naomi could have been a random choice," Val said. "But I have the feeling there's a stronger connection. We've been wondering about your job with NOPD. You handled evidence. We know that Gaffney and Cresswell stole drugs from evidence. We also know that at least once—when they framed you—they substituted ground-up Sheetrock for the cocaine. What if something went missing that you'd processed? Or something was substituted for real evidence? It could have been drugs or guns or even something else. Something big, something that once you saw it, made you a liability. The discovery of missing or tainted evidence would trigger an immediate investigation."

Naomi shook her head. "Well, not immediate. When evidence went missing, usually it had simply been moved or stored in a slot different than what the system had recorded, and we found it pretty quickly. But if the evidence *wasn't* found, then, yes, there should have been an investigation."

"*Should* have been?" Lucien asked. "Wasn't it always investigated?"

"I don't know," Naomi admitted. "I thought so six years ago, but I also didn't know drugs were being stolen out of the evidence room or that they were being replaced with ground-up Sheetrock so that no one suspected they were gone. Clearly someone was keeping those thefts from being investigated."

"Fair point," Molly conceded. "But we're still going to assume that whatever led to you being framed six years ago had something to do with evidence you either saw or processed. It might not even have gone missing. It might have been enough that you saw it. For now, let's assume that whatever that evidence was, it went missing and Gaffney needed someone to blame. That was you. Let's also assume that it wasn't drugs, because Gaffney had a system for keeping missing drugs from being investigated."

"Okay," Naomi said, mind racing. "So something other than drugs. That could be anything. But I think it has to have had something to do with John Gaffney. Or maybe Cresswell."

"Or both," Burke murmured.

"Or both," she agreed. "They were good at covering their tracks. Gaffney still is. This would have had to have been damaging enough that it could have brought them down."

"Real evidence," Burke said. "Not rumor like I used."

Naomi nodded. "Exactly. I also think it would have to have been something unique. Something I'd remember. Something I'd be able to swear in court that I definitely saw. Something that could be used to connect Cresswell and/or Gaffney to an actual crime. And it has to have been six years ago or longer."

"I'm betting closer to six years," Lucien said. "Not longer. Otherwise, why the push to get you out of the way?"

"True." Naomi drew a breath. *We might actually have something here.* "So we're assuming that I saw something that was connected to a crime that could have taken Cresswell and/or Gaffney down. You said whatever it was might not even be missing, but I can't imagine that it's still in evidence storage. If it was damaging enough for them to go to all the trouble of getting me out of the way, they wouldn't want to chance someone else finding it and using it against them—either legally or through blackmail. If I'd been Cresswell and Gaffney, I'd have taken that evidence and destroyed it so that no one ever saw it again."

"I agree," Burke said and everyone nodded. "Planting the drugs in Naomi's car could have been their way of getting her arrested and out of the NOPD, but it also served to destroy her credibility. If whatever she saw ever did come to light or if she figured out what had triggered all this and reported it, nobody would believe her."

Destroying my credibility certainly worked, Naomi thought. Except that it hadn't. The people in this room believed her. Enough that, when their children were targeted, they hadn't turned their backs on her.

"And that's why keeping her in prison was important," Ruthanne said quietly. "And why, now that she's out, they want to send her back. To make sure no one ever believes her again."

"We believe her," Molly said fiercely. "Let's run with this theory for now. Antoine, can you create a list of cases that might fit our scenario?"

"I can," Antoine said. "I'll start with investigations that happened in the year before Naomi went to prison. It might be a case that was either closed or went cold for lack of evidence. I'm betting we'll find a lot of those."

"Antoine," Burke asked, "can you access the evidence database and make a list of the evidence Naomi handled? We can exclude drugs and probably guns as well."

Antoine frowned. "Yes, but listing every piece of evidence Naomi handled won't tell us what's missing. We'd have to do an internal audit and we don't have that kind of access."

"Or that kind of time." Naomi was overwhelmed by the scope of the effort required. "Identifying a missing piece of evidence when we don't know which case, which defendant, or even which year it was processed? I handled somewhere in the neighborhood of five thousand pieces of evidence each year—so fifty thousand in all. This could be a true needle in a haystack."

Everyone turned to her with wide eyes.

"Fifty *thousand*?" Burke repeated.

"Girl," Val said. "You were busy."

Naomi shrugged. "Evidence gets brought in every day of every week of every year. It adds up."

Molly looked undeterred. "We'll start with the year before your arrest, cross-checking evidence entered with cases touched by Cresswell or Gaffney. Then we'll regroup and see where we are."

"But the answer to your question 'Why Naomi?' might not even be a piece of evidence, missing or not," Naomi cautioned.

"Then we'll regroup," Molly said patiently. "An investigation doesn't normally involve getting shot at in a flower shop or witnessing someone being murdered. Most of the time it's dull, boring data analysis."

"At which Molly excels," Burke said with a smile. "Does anyone have anything else? Because I have a few next steps to assign."

Eleanor waved her hand. "I do. I've seen that woman. The one who saved Harper."

All eyes turned to Eleanor in stunned surprise.

"Why didn't you say something?" Burke asked.

"Because Molly here was trying to keep you focused on the question in red marker. I figured my thing would keep."

"So where did you see her?" Molly asked.

"Coming out of the Delgados' house. I saw her at least once a week, sometimes several times. She wore a nurse's uniform—scrubs—so I figured she was home health care for Carmen, the grandmother."

"Anyone can buy scrubs," Val said. "She could have been trying to pass as a home health aide when in reality she was working for the Delgado brothers and/or Gaffney."

Burke's expression became grim. "According to André, there were two teenage girls in the Delgado house when it burned. He thinks they were trafficking victims. Maybe it was Donna's job to deal with newly kidnapped teens. Or maybe she really is a nurse and she was treating victims who became injured or sick?"

Naomi suddenly had a terrible, awful thought. "What if she *is* a nurse? What if she's a nurse at the hospital with the sixteen-year-old girl who was nearly beaten to death by her john? That poor girl would be a sitting duck."

Burke blinked. "That's a bit of a leap," he said slowly. "But not out of the question. Can we check the woman out, Antoine? Maybe find out if she works at the hospital?"

Ruthanne went to the whiteboard and took the photo down so that she could study it. "If she does work at the hospital, she's probably a recent hire. I worked there for more than twenty-five years and I don't recognize her face. I didn't know every nurse, but I do have a decent memory." She returned the photo to the whiteboard. "I can ask around if you want."

"Please do," Antoine said. "I haven't found her anywhere yet."

"Mom," Naomi said, thinking of that sixteen-year-old girl lying alone in a hospital, "I'd like to talk to the girl. She identified Pablo Delgado as her abuser."

"You want me to find out which room she's in?" Ruthanne asked, returning to sit beside James.

"Only if you can do it discreetly," Burke said.

Ruthanne nodded. "I know who to ask. Linda's my oldest friend in the hospital. She works in the office, so she'll have access to patient lists. I'll tell her that we want to visit, but I won't tell her why."

Eleanor dug into her pocket, bringing out a flip phone. "You can use the burner that Antoine gave me. Just in case someone is monitoring her calls."

Naomi couldn't imagine why Linda's calls would be monitored, but she said nothing because her mother's face had lit up like the sun.

"I've never used a burner before," Ruthanne said, sounding almost giddy.

"We can be badasses together," Eleanor said dryly.

Ruthanne laughed. "We can indeed."

Burke looked amused. "Okay, that was one of the items on my list, finding the young woman. Ruthanne, you have responsibility for that."

Ruthanne nodded once. "On it, boss." Then she grinned. "Always wanted to say that."

James kissed her cheek. "You are too darn cute."

Burke's lips twitched. "Thank you, Ruthanne. Moving on, Naomi and I are going to see Amanda Cresswell today. I'm going to offer protection for her kids. I don't think she'll accept, but it's the right thing to do. Children should not have to pay for the sins of their fathers."

"And maybe you'll create a bit of goodwill at the same time?" Lucien asked. "In case Mrs. Cresswell knows something about her husband's life of crime?"

"Exactly. I don't think she'll be happy to see me since we were involved in getting her husband incarcerated, but I'm going to try. Molly, can you summarize our next steps?"

Molly flipped the whiteboard over and started writing. "Antoine's going to pull cases that involved Gaffney and Cresswell, and Val and I will cross-reference evidence that was collected in each case against evidence Naomi handled."

"I will," Val said. "Molly and Lucien need to sleep. They were on night duty."

"Okay," Molly allowed. "But I'll help once I've woken up. I don't want to miss out on all the data-crunching fun. Ruthanne is going to find out if Donna is a nurse locally and also, if she can do so discreetly, the location of Delgado's sixteen-year-old sex trafficking victim. Burke and Naomi are going to visit Cresswell's widow to see if she knows anything about her husband's extracurricular activities."

"I've got a next step," Antoine said. "I want to know why Winnifred Timms told Burke that he was 'living on borrowed time.'"

"And that his time was up," Naomi added.

Molly wrote it on the whiteboard, then stood staring at what she'd written, a frown furrowing her brow. She turned to Burke. "Do you have any idea what she was talking about?"

"Not yet. But I'm betting it has something to do with Cresswell. Either retaliation for getting him arrested two and a half years ago or . . ."

Naomi looked up at him. "Or?"

"I always thought my leaving the NOPD was a little too easy. I wonder if Cresswell was just biding his time, waiting until I'd been off the force long enough that he could have me killed without it boomeranging back on him."

"That might be a topic to broach with the widow," Naomi said.

He nodded. "I figured the same." He cleared his throat. "I have one more thing. Eleanor has called her neighbors and found a few who are willing to talk to us this evening, but not here and not in our office. And definitely not on their own street."

"Understandable," Molly said, "considering that the neighborhood's had two arsons linked to the Delgados' enterprise. You need a meeting place, Burke?"

"Yes. I thought about asking Gabe if the private room at his restaurant was available, but, even if it is, he's too connected to us. I won't put Eleanor's neighbors in danger."

"I know a place, Burke," Val said. "There's a private conference room in the building where the QuarterMasters skate."

James perked up. "The roller derby team? I *love* them."

Naomi was surprised. She had no idea that James was a roller derby fan.

"We go to *all* the games," Ruthanne added.

Naomi stared at her mother. "Since when?"

Ruthanne hesitated, then answered. "Since you went away. James asked me to go with him to one of the games, and I had a great time."

"Val's a star on the team," Burke said proudly. "She's Val-Killer-Rie."

James looked starstruck. "We *have* to get your autograph."

Val laughed. "Of course. I haven't played in a while, though. I've been busy with work and Kaj, Elijah, and Jace, but I'm hoping to go back next season."

"But it's not the regular season," James said. "Won't Eleanor's neighbors stick out like a sore thumb, all their cars parked in the lot alone?"

"There's actually an exhibition game tonight," Val said. "We're sold out, but I can get Eleanor's neighbors tickets so they can get through the doors. The meeting room will be empty during the game. I'll be your security, Burke. It'll be fine."

"Thank you, Val-Killer-Rie," Burke said. "I guess we all have our marching orders. Molly and Lucien, go to sleep. Naomi, we'll leave to see Cresswell's wife in thirty minutes, if that's okay."

"I'll be waiting at the door."

17

Uptown, New Orleans, Louisiana
WEDNESDAY, FEBRUARY 26, 11:00 A.M.

"NICE PLACE," NAOMI murmured as they drove up the Cresswells' street.

Burke eyed the line of news vans. He'd had to bypass a few reporters outside his own house, but there were a lot more reporters here. That a former NOPD captain had taken his own life in prison was incredibly newsworthy.

Not that Burke was sure he believed that Cresswell had taken his own life, but the bottom line was that he was dead and would never be able to tell them why Naomi had been chosen.

Or why Winnifred Timms had said that Burke was living on borrowed time.

"It's not as nice as the house they had before Cresswell went to prison. That was one of the old mansions in the Garden District. After Cresswell's arrest, Amanda sold that house and moved here."

"I don't think she'll talk to us," Naomi said when he'd brought the SUV to a stop in the driveway. "She'll say we're responsible for her husband's death because we visited him yesterday, which we probably are, indirectly, of course. Were they happy together, the Cresswells?"

"I don't know. The rumors of him hiring prostitutes around the time I left NOPD were credible enough that he didn't deny them when I confronted him."

"That's how you got out, right? You held those rumors over his head."

Shame washed over him. "If I'd had the proof then, I would have used it. I would have gone to the press so that it couldn't be swept under the rug."

"But?" Naomi asked.

"But I should have searched for that proof when I was free. I didn't and he was allowed to continue playing his games. If I'd done something, he wouldn't have sent you to prison. Our kids wouldn't be scared and in hiding right now."

"You came right from the Corps into the NOPD, didn't you?" she asked.

He blinked, surprised by the topic change. "Yes, why?"

"How much combat did you see?"

"Two deployments."

"I understand that Phin's service dog is because he has PTSD."

Ah. He could see where she was going with this. "He does. But I don't have PTSD."

"Don't you?" she countered. "You lost your mother, your fiancée, and your uncle when you were eighteen. Went right into the military, where I'm sure you saw terrible things. Then you dropped right into Cresswell's clutches in the NOPD. You might not have PTSD, Burke, but you were living a chaotic life. Of *course* you'd crave peace and quiet. Of *course* you'd want to just live your life. That you continued in some form of law enforcement during the past six years is laudable. That you didn't fight back harder is understandable. Once you'd opened your PI firm, you finally had control over your life, and looking back was painful. You moved forward, which, at the time, was the exact right thing for you to do."

Her words were the balm he hadn't realized he needed. "You give me too much credit."

"I don't think you give yourself enough. I think you expect a lot more of yourself than you do of your people."

He didn't want to talk about this. "We should go in and talk to Amanda Cresswell."

Naomi grabbed his hand. "Burke, stop. You dishonor yourself by denying your integrity. Most people would be content with simply *not* committing crimes. You seem to think you should have done more."

"Because I should have."

"And now you are. Look at me, please."

He dragged his gaze to meet hers and saw compassion. Approval. Maybe even pride. It stole his breath. "We need to—"

"We need to go, I know. But first, tell me this. Do you push Phin to be an investigator?"

"No."

"Why not?"

"Because he's not ready."

"When will he be ready?"

Burke was annoyed. "He might never be ready. He's doing what he needs to do to exist within the limitations of his PTSD. He's starting to thrive."

"He's living his life the best way he knows how?"

"Yes."

"Then why is it different for you?" she asked gently. "Burke, you went through a lot of life-changing experiences. You went from job to job, but in every case, you were focused on service. On helping. That you didn't push yourself outside of your own limitations is not a bad thing."

He sighed. "You maneuvered me into that nicely."

She smiled smugly. "I did, didn't I? But I'm right. You needed the time and the sense of safety before moving against Gaffney and Cresswell, even if you don't want to admit it. That you continued a life of service while you were healing makes you a good man." She lifted his hand to her cheek. "You're a *good man*, Burke Broussard. Any one of your people will tell you this. Don't let your own mind tell you otherwise."

At the moment, he only cared that she thought so. He'd leaned toward her, the console separating them. She'd leaned toward him, his hand on her cheek.

He cupped her jaw. He caressed her lip with his thumb and her breath caught.

She was watching him, her warm, dark brown eyes now expectant. Hopeful.

Burke couldn't have denied her anything. He brushed his lips against hers in the lightest of kisses. He felt her lips curve, heard her contented sigh.

And then he remembered that they were surrounded by reporters. "I don't want our first kiss to end up online," he murmured, but he couldn't pull away. Honeysuckle filled his head and he wanted to sink into it.

He wanted to sink into her.

"I think it's too late for that," she said dryly. She was the one to pull away. He feared he might see irritation or even anger in her expression, but she was smiling. "But I've had my photo online before.

I think it'll be better to be seen kissing you than being led out of court in handcuffs."

"I'd give everything I own to erase that experience from your mind."

"The handcuffs or the kiss?"

He chuckled, which he suspected had been her intention. "The cuffs."

"Good." She tugged on the lower edge of the Kevlar vest she wore under a turtleneck sweater that hugged her body in all the right places. "Let's do this."

They ignored the barrage of questions from the reporters gathered outside.

Why are you here? What did Cresswell tell you yesterday? Who's your lady friend?

That last one made Naomi chuckle. "Your lady friend?"

"Do you want to be?" Burke asked when they'd stopped at the Cresswells' front door.

She looked up, studying him for the space of several hard beats of his heart. "Yes. I do."

He brushed his hand down her spine before resting it at the small of her back. "Good." With his free hand, he knocked once.

His knuckles were still touching the door when it was abruptly opened. A young man stood at the threshold, glaring at them.

"You've got a lot of nerve, Broussard," he gritted out. "Showing up here? Now? And making out in our fucking driveway?"

This would be Matthew, Cresswell's son. He was seventeen. "I'd like to speak to you and to your mother."

The glare became a sneer. "And what makes you think we want to speak to you?"

Burke purposely looked over his shoulder, his gaze taking in the reporters before he returned his attention to the young man's angry face. "I have information for you that I don't think you want reporters to hear."

"I don't want to hear it, either. And my mother definitely does not."

"Matthew?" came a voice from behind the door. "Let him in. I have some things I'd like to say, too."

Burke stepped inside the house, his hand sliding from Naomi's back to grip her hand. He spared a moment to glance at her face, to make sure she was all right.

Her jaw was set, her lips flattened into a thin line. But she wasn't trembling and she didn't look scared. She looked grimly determined.

He was in awe of her. She'd survived so much and kept on going.

How could he do any less?

"Mrs. Cresswell," Burke began once they were inside the house.

Amanda Cresswell was in her midforties and had once been a beautiful woman. But time and life had left her face lined and hard. Her eyes were cold and watchful.

But he saw no malice, so he let himself draw an even breath.

"Come with me," she ordered, leading them from the foyer to a small sitting room.

Naomi stiffened beside him. He followed her gaze and blinked. Amanda Cresswell wore a prosthetic device on her left hand. A mechanical finger. It appeared to be made of flesh-colored plastic, but the joints were steel, catching the light.

She hadn't had the prosthetic the only other time Burke had met her. That had been at a holiday party at the Cresswells' old house, shortly after Burke had had made detective.

They sat on the sofa Amanda Cresswell indicated.

"I'm so sorry," he said quietly.

"For what?" Amanda demanded, but her tone was not angry. It was cold and detached, but Burke could deal with that.

"I suppose it depends on whether you're mourning your husband," Burke said candidly, watching for her reaction.

Amanda dropped her eyes to her hand, the one missing a finger. "I'm not. I mourned the loss of what I'd thought was a marriage more than two years ago."

"This is my colleague and my . . ."

"His lady friend," Naomi said mildly when he hesitated. "I think that's what the reporters are calling it these days."

Amanda's lips twitched. Just once, but it made Burke glad that Naomi had come. She seemed to have a knack for soothing people, for knowing what they needed to hear. For drawing them in.

"Do you have a name, lady friend?" Amanda asked.

"Naomi Cranston. I was a cop until I was framed for stealing evidence and sent to prison for thirty years."

"You must have been released early," Amanda said, her tone as mild as Naomi's. "Or else you got your hands on some very good moisturizer."

Naomi's smile was placid, and that was when Burke realized the two women were dueling in a way in which he could not begin to compete.

"I was happy to get an occasional bag of potato chips from the commissary," Naomi said. "Moisturizer was out of my reach. I was released after five years when my sentence was overturned. I was accused of stealing cocaine that had been taken in a drug bust, but it was just powdered Sheetrock."

"I remember you now. Or I remember your case. Why are you here?"

"Because John Gaffney approached me last Friday and asked me to distribute drugs for him."

Amanda went still. Her eyes flicked down to her hand before rising to meet Naomi's. "And you said?"

"I said no. Then he threatened my son."

Matthew Cresswell frowned. "With what?"

"With harm," Amanda said quietly. "Isn't that right?"

"It is." Naomi purposely studied Amanda's prosthetic device before meeting the other woman's gaze once more. "Did Gaffney threaten you, too?"

Matthew frowned, first at his mother, then at Naomi. "Mom?"

Amanda shook her head. "I can't talk about that."

"About what?" Matthew pressed. "I can make them leave. They shouldn't be here anyway. You can tell me."

"No, son, I can't talk about it with anyone. Especially with you."

"Mom? What is this? Should I call Milly?"

"Milly is the Cresswells' fifteen-year-old," Burke murmured in Naomi's ear.

"Almost the same age as Everett," Naomi said, not in a murmur. She spoke loudly enough that Amanda was sure to hear.

Amanda was shaking her head. "No, Matthew. Milly doesn't need to know about any of this."

Naomi leaned forward. "Ma'am, Mr. Broussard and I met with your husband yesterday."

"I know," Amanda said quietly. "Why did you?"

"Because after Gaffney threatened me with harm to my son, someone tried to abduct him. I'd hired Mr. Broussard's firm to protect him and his bodyguard kept him safe. Then there were two more attempted abductions of children belonging to Mr. Broussard's employees. Another abduction attempt targeted the children of Mr.

Broussard's extended family. We wanted to know why I was framed and why Gaffney was trying to draw me back in."

"Why haven't you asked Gaffney himself?" Matthew asked, bristling. "Why go to my father when he couldn't have been involved? He'd been in prison for two and a half years." He looked at Burke angrily. "Because of *you*."

Burke opened his mouth to reply—what he'd have said, he didn't know.

But Naomi knew what to say. "No, not because of Mr. Broussard. Because your father was a criminal. Which is hard to hear, I know. And we're not here to argue that point," she said firmly when Matthew started to do just that.

Burke wondered why she didn't use this tactic with Everett.

Naomi turned back to Amanda. "Are you aware that your husband hadn't spoken a single word since his incarceration began?"

"Doesn't surprise me." She glanced at her hand again, her focus lingering on the prosthetic. "He didn't say a word to me the first and only time I visited him there."

Matthew's eyes widened. "You visited him? In prison? When?"

"Later," she said to her son. "Get to the point, Miss Cranston."

"We asked your husband what he knew. Then Mr. Broussard offered to protect your children if he'd talk to us. He never said out loud he'd been threatened with the safety of your children, but from his reaction, it seemed certain he had been." Naomi gestured to Amanda's hand. "I don't mean to be cruel or unfeeling, but did your husband's associates do that to you?"

Matthew shook his head. "She lost the finger trying to move one of my father's power tools. She slipped and it started up and cut off her finger." Then he looked at his mother, who'd grown pale. "Mom?" Matthew then paled as well. "It was an accident, wasn't it? *Mom?*"

Amanda stared at them all, misery in her eyes. She shook her head mutely.

"Mom?" Matthew whispered, horrified.

She gripped his hand. But she still did not speak.

"We came today to make you the same offer that we gave your husband," Burke said gently, because both Amanda and her son appeared to be on the verge of a breakdown. "But with no strings. If you know something, we'd be grateful to hear it, but I can't let your children be endangered for something their father did. I suspect our visit triggered your husband's death, whether by his own hand or someone else's. If there's a chance they could come after your children, too . . . well, I couldn't live with myself."

Matthew was still staring at his mother. "It wasn't suicide? He was murdered? Mom! Answer me!"

Amanda closed her eyes. "I can't afford protective services, Mr. Broussard."

"It's okay," Burke said. He'd expected that, courtesy of Antoine's research into the Cresswell finances. Amanda owned this home and not much else. "I can cover the expense. I can have someone here in less than an hour."

He'd put Devonte on alert that he might be assigning him here.

Amanda nodded, tears slowly sliding down her cheeks. "Matthew, you should go upstairs. I need to talk with Mr. Broussard."

"I'm not leaving you," Matthew declared, his voice much smaller than it had been, but no less sure. "I have a right to know. I'm old enough."

"Nobody's old enough," Naomi said wearily. "And no one is out of Gaffney's reach. He tried to kill my mother when she was appealing my conviction. He is a dangerous man, Matthew. It might be your right to know, but once you do, you need to understand what might happen if you were to tell anyone."

Matthew looked at his mother's hand. "I understand."

Burke sent a text to Devonte, who replied that he was on his way. "One of my employees will be here soon. Like I said, no strings. But if you give us any information, it will help us put this danger to rest and *all* our children will be safe."

Amanda sighed. "All right. I'll tell you what I know. Matthew, go get your sister. I wanted to shelter her, but that time is past. She should hear this, too."

Uptown, New Orleans, Louisiana
WEDNESDAY, FEBRUARY 26, 11:30 A.M.

"I didn't know what Arthur was doing," Amanda began. Matthew clutched her hand and Milly sat on the floor at her feet, holding on to her mother's legs.

The sight of them, clinging together, hurt Naomi's heart.

Amanda looked exhausted. "Do you believe me?"

"Yes," Burke said, but Naomi heard the words he'd left unspoken. *For now.*

Once other truths were revealed, he might change his mind.

"Thank you. He liked to play the horses. Came home one day with the keys to a new car. Said he'd hit a trifecta, that he'd had a huge payout. He said the car was mine. I was thrilled. I'd never had a nice car before. Arthur was a captain by then, but he was still a cop. Even after the promotion, his salary still wasn't enough to buy a top-of-the-line Mercedes. But I believed him."

"Of course you did," Naomi said, feeling for the woman. She could find compassion in her heart for Amanda Cresswell—unless the woman was lying to them. Then Naomi would see her punished. "He was your husband."

"He got calls at night and claimed they were from work," Amanda went on. "But I suspected there was another woman."

Milly made a wounded noise and Amanda stroked her hair, careful to lift the prosthetic finger out of the way.

"Did you ever discover who that other woman was?" Naomi asked.

"Yes. You've met her. Quite recently, in fact."

Naomi understood. "Winnifred Timms."

Amanda's nod was grim. "One night, when he'd gotten a call, I followed him. He went to a condo on Poydras. Stayed there for hours. Finally, around dawn, I gave up and came home."

"Did you confront your husband?" Naomi asked.

"I did. I parked my car around the block, called in sick to work, and sat down to wait for him. He came in about fifteen minutes after I was supposed to have left for work and I nearly gave him a heart attack when I came out of the kitchen to greet him. I wanted to smell him, to see if he smelled like another woman's perfume. He didn't. He smelled like whiskey and cigarettes."

"Did you tell him that you'd followed him?"

"Not that day, but I did a few weeks later when it happened again. He denied an affair. He said he was having a meeting with some undercover cops and that I was endangering them by following him."

"Gaslighting," Naomi murmured.

Amanda nodded. "He was good at that, in hindsight."

Milly made another wounded noise.

"I'm sorry, baby," Amanda said. "I hate that you have to hear this about your father, but I'd hate it even more if you got hurt because I didn't prepare you and one of your father's thugs came after you."

"He's dead," Matthew said, sounding numb. "He can't have thugs anymore."

"Gaffney's continuing his crimes," Naomi said. "When did you find out about Winnifred?"

"That would have been about six years ago, in December."

Naomi nodded. "That was the same month that I stopped to help Timms, whose car was wrecked on the side of the road. She was the one who pointed out to the cops that I had drugs in my car. Drugs I did not put there."

"Which was what sent you to prison," Amanda said. "I'm sorry."

"Don't be." *Unless you were in on it.* But Naomi didn't think Amanda had been. "How did you find out about Winnifred?"

"I started to smell perfume on my husband's clothing. So the next time he left the house in the night, I followed him again. Made it easier after I put a tracker under his car. He went to the same condo, but this time he met a woman outside and they went up together. That was Winnifred Timms."

Matthew stared at his mother. "You put a tracker under Dad's car?"

"I did. Because by then we were making a lot more money and I was worried. Rumors were everywhere. But, to be brutally honest, I liked having the money. We were fine on the day-to-day expenses, but we hadn't saved a penny for the kids' college. That changed. We had savings for the first time in our marriage. We both drove new cars and we'd bought the house on First Street. I loved that house," she added wistfully.

That would have been the first home they'd owned in the Garden District, Naomi thought. The one that was far nicer than this one. And this one was still nice.

"How did your husband explain the sudden income?" Burke asked.

"He said he'd had another huge win at the track and had invested it. I believed him. I guess I wanted to."

"When did you discover that your husband was involved in a criminal enterprise?" Burke asked kindly.

"Not until he got arrested. I should have figured it out. I worried sometimes that the money was too good, that he couldn't have won that much at the track. I should have listened to my gut."

"Did your husband ever tell you about his activities?" Naomi asked.

"No. I found out about them at the same time the rest of the world did. I was . . . devastated. Appalled. Ashamed. I immediately put the house up for sale. I knew we couldn't afford to keep it."

"I'm surprised that the court allowed you to do so," Burke said. "That the house wasn't seized as part of his restitution."

"It was in my name and I was cleared by the NOPD. I wondered at the time why Arthur put the house in my name."

"When did you get a visit from Gaffney?" Naomi asked, glancing at the prosthetic.

"A week after Arthur went to prison. I hadn't planned on visiting him there. I was so angry. I still am." She swallowed hard. "I was packing dishes and heard a sound from out back. There was an old carriage house that we used for storage. I thought there might be intruders, looking to steal things after reading about Arthur's conviction. So I went out there." She swallowed again, her breathing growing shallow and rapid. "It was John Gaffney and he was leaning against a table saw that I'd bought Arthur for his birthday years before. Arthur never actually used it and I'd already put it up for sale. Gaffney was . . . Well, I never liked him."

"Me either," Naomi said dryly.

"Same," Burke said. "You don't have to tell us what he did if it's too painful to share."

"I need to. He grabbed my hand and told me that I wouldn't be saying anything about Arthur to anyone. That I'd keep my mouth shut. I told him that I didn't know anything and he said that it didn't matter. He was there to give Arthur incentive not to say anything, either. Then he . . ." She exhaled heavily. "He put tape over my mouth and . . . did this. With the table saw. I was screaming, but the tape made it so that no one could hear me. He took the finger with him and left me there, bleeding."

Naomi shuddered. "I'm so sorry he did that to you."

Both of Amanda's children were crying.

"Mom," Matthew choked out, "why didn't you call the cops?"

"Because Gaffney said if I did, that he'd be back and the next time it would be you or Milly. I did what he said. I told the hospital that I'd been trying to move my husband's saw, but I hadn't put on the safety. They asked where the finger was and I told them that I didn't know. Someone came to the house to search, but it was gone. I was too terrified to say anything else."

"I don't blame you," Naomi murmured. "I let Gaffney send me to prison for five years so that he wouldn't go after my son. So I don't blame you a bit."

"You said you went to the prison once to see your husband," Burke said. "When was that?"

"About a week after Gaffney hurt me. I wanted Arthur to know. I wanted to see if he even cared. So I went to the prison and they brought him to a private visiting room. They said it was because he was in protective custody. There was a guard in the room. When Arthur sat down, he wouldn't even look me in the eye."

Amanda had begun to cry, whether from grief or rage, Naomi didn't know. Probably both. She slid a box of tissues across the coffee table.

"Thank you," Amanda said, drying her eyes. But the tears kept flowing, becoming sobs. "I said, *'Look at me!'* I said, 'Your friend came to the house.' And then I put my hand on the table and demanded again that he look at me. He wouldn't. So I got up and leaned over the table until my hand was in his line of sight. The guard rushed over to pull me back, but that was okay. Arthur had seen it. He looked up and I don't think I'll ever forget it."

"He was shocked?" Naomi asked.

"No. The opposite. He wasn't surprised at all. He looked guilty, but not surprised. He cried, but I don't know if those tears were for me or for him, because he got caught. When I realized that he'd already known about my finger, I figured someone had told him. That that was why he was saying nothing, because they'd threatened him, too. He loved our children. I don't know for sure that he loved me, but he did love the kids. If they were threatened, he would have kept his mouth closed."

"He did keep his mouth closed," Naomi said. "He never said a word. I think he wanted to. I think he wanted to accept Burke's offer of protection for you all, but he never spoke a word. He was too terrified."

Amanda nodded at that. "There's one more thing. I should have handed it over to the police, but after Gaffney . . . I just didn't." Rising, she went to a desk in the corner and brought out a fire safe. She unlocked it and took out a three-ring binder, which she set on the coffee table between them. "Our important papers. Birth certificates and the like. They were in my safe-deposit box, in my name. Again, Arthur made sure most of the important things were in my name. I should have been suspicious that he was so hands-off about all those important things, but he said that because I paid the bills, it made sense that I should keep all the records, too. I managed everything except his gambling winnings. Looking back, I was naive."

Amanda flipped through the plastic sleeves until she came to what she'd been looking for. She withdrew a plain white envelope and handed it to Burke.

Burke took it hesitantly. "What is this?"

"I don't know. I found it in the safe-deposit box. I'd never seen it before. Arthur came into the bank vault with me only once. I'm thinking he put that in the box then. Since it's in my name and I wasn't accused of anything, there was no warrant for it. I'm sure they checked my bank accounts. You've probably checked, too. But they didn't know about my safe-deposit box and I didn't offer the information."

Burke ran his fingers along the edges of the envelope. "An SD card."

"I know. I've never even opened the envelope. I was afraid to know what's on the card. I didn't want to lose another finger. Or have anything happen to my children. But now Arthur is dead and your children are being threatened, too. If you protect my kids and can use whatever's in there to make this stop once and for all, then please take it."

Burke took a plastic evidence bag from his jacket pocket and put the envelope inside before slipping the bag back in his pocket.

Once a cop, Naomi thought affectionately.

"Thank you." Burke checked his phone, where a new text was displayed. "Devonte is here. He'll be your bodyguard for the time being. I'll create a staff roster and send it to you, so you'll know who else to expect. Can your kids stay home from school for the rest of the week? That will make our job easier. Next week they have vacation."

"We're homeschooled," Milly said. "I can't go back there. Every day there were . . ." She trailed off, shrugging thin shoulders.

"Kids can be cruel," Amanda said. "And I was afraid to let my kids out of my sight after this." She held up the hand with the prosthetic. "We've been living under a dark cloud."

"We're going to put a stop to that," Burke said. "For all of us." He went to the front door and returned with Devonte. "Meet your new bodyguard."

18

The Quarter, New Orleans, Louisiana
WEDNESDAY, FEBRUARY 26, 1:30 P.M.

WHAT IS IT?" Naomi asked, eyeing the envelope Burke had set on the desk in his office. The envelope that had been burning a hole in Burke's pocket.

It would be important. Which was why he'd waited until his available team members convened in his home office. At this point, it was just him, Naomi, Val, and Antoine. Molly and Lucien were still asleep, and Harrison was on guard duty, but he'd fill them in later.

"Let's find out." Pulling on a pair of disposable gloves, he sliced the envelope with a letter opener and shook the SD card into his palm.

It was tiny, yet he felt the weight of it. He slid the card into the slot of what Antoine called his "trash" laptop, the one that had no internet connection and was not connected to any of his other work. If whatever was on the card corrupted his machine, none of his files would be impacted.

Antoine tapped his keys, then squinted as he scanned whatever filled his screen. No one said a word until Val broke the silence.

"By all that's holy, Antoine, tell us what you see."

Antoine looked up, frowning. "There's only one file on the SD card. It appears to be a ledger. A record of payments. Dates and amounts only. No indication of who the recipients were or what the payments were for. The last date was two weeks before Cresswell was arrested."

"How many entries?" Naomi asked. "And when was the first payment?"

Burke had been about to ask the same things.

"Just over a thousand entries. The first was in July, ten years ago."

"Are there any repeating entries?" Val asked. "Like regular payments?"

"Yes. Several appear to be repeating." Antoine's eyes darted back and forth as he analyzed the numbers. "At first glance, I'm seeing ten payments on the first of every month, ranging from a few hundred to a thousand dollars each. In the final year before his arrest, he was paying out seven grand a month just in these recurring payments."

"Payoffs," Naomi murmured. "Or blackmail payments."

Burke agreed. "But to whom?"

Naomi bit at her lower lip. "For years, he and Gaffney were Teflon. Nothing stuck until Cresswell killed a suspect in front of witnesses. Gaffney is still somehow avoiding justice. Every investigation into him turns up nothing at all. Could we be looking at payments to PIB investigators?"

"It's likely," Antoine said. "I compiled a list of PIB officers who investigated either Cresswell or Gaffney at some point in the year before your arrest. We can start with them, looking into finances, et cetera. Are you going to turn this file over to André?"

Burke shook his head. "Not yet. Not until we know who in PIB is on the take. I've put protection on Amanda Cresswell and her kids, but I don't want to put her in Gaffney's crosshairs again."

Val and Antoine frowned in question, so Burke explained about Gaffney's mutilation of Cresswell's wife.

"Oh my God," Val said, horrified. "Who could blame the woman for not giving this file to the cops?"

"They've bullied so many of us." Naomi's jaw tightened. "We need to end it. Exactly how is still the question."

Burke studied Antoine, who'd gone still. "Antoine? What do you see?"

"A few large payments. One is fifty thousand dollars. It was paid out two weeks after Naomi was sentenced to prison. And it's the same amount as her ex-husband's mortgage, which Jimmy Haywood paid off at that same time." He looked over at Naomi, his expression both sorrowful and angry. "I'm sorry, Naomi. I only checked that time period because I'm still pissed off at your ex for testifying against you. This isn't definitive, but it sure looks like a bribe."

Naomi blew out a breath. "Thank you for checking. I hated Jimmy for cheating on me and lying about me, but I honestly thought he lied on the stand to get full custody of Everett. His taking bribes never entered my mind."

"I'm not surprised," Burke said, scowling. "The man is an asshole. But how the hell did he only owe fifty grand? He bought that house after your divorce, right? He would have only owned it a year when he paid it off."

"James helped him," Naomi said. "He'd sold his own house because he wanted to downsize. James had added Jimmy to the deed, so he got a sizable chunk of the proceeds. With that, plus his half of the sale of the house we owned, Jimmy was able to put a large down payment on his new place with his new wife."

"While you had to sell the house you'd bought after the divorce to pay Mason Lord for shitty legal advice," Burke said, barely managing not to growl.

"Pretty much," Naomi said, then softened her next words with a smile. "And while I'm grateful for your ire on my behalf, none of that is relevant now." She turned to Antoine. "How can we find out who the other payments went to? And if Gaffney has continued to pay these recurring amounts?"

Burke sighed. "We need to zero in on Gaffney. We've—*I've*—danced around talking to him for far too long. We know that he's connected to Pablo Delgado, who's a human trafficker. I don't think that assuming Gaffney is also a trafficker is that big a stretch. We know that at least two of the teenagers they were selling for sex were being held here in the city. We suspect the two young women found dead in the Delgados' house were also victims. Gaffney's got to be keeping more somewhere in the city—teenagers he plans to sell for sex. I think I do have a little PTSD when it comes to Gaffney and Cresswell. The last time I talked to Gaffney, he threatened to send me my godsons in pieces. But I need to get past that because he has to be stopped."

Naomi nodded. "But talking to him would be pointless in terms of getting him to admit something and would only show him our hand. So far most of what we're learning has to do with Cresswell. Gaffney could just shrug it all off. He could say he wasn't involved and that every internal investigation has proven that. What can we do when he's made of Teflon?"

Burke squeezed her hand. "We need to start looking harder at PIB. We need to follow the money and expose their bribes. That will scrub Gaffney's Teflon away."

"I agree," Antoine said. "In the meantime, Naomi, Val has that list of evidence items you processed that are connected to Gaffney and/or Cresswell. If you could go through them with her, that would be great."

"Bring it," Naomi said simply. "But I need some coffee or something first."

"Your mom will have some in the kitchen," Antoine said. "She's been keeping us caffeinated all morning. She and Miss Eleanor have been baking, too. Keeping the kids busy. Your mom found some sugar-free recipes for Elijah."

Naomi's smile was wistful. "Mom and Everett used to love to bake together, back before everything went wrong."

"Everett's been right in the kitchen with them," Antoine said kindly. "Maybe he just needs to get away from your toxic ex."

"You really don't like Jimmy Haywood," Burke said. "And neither do I. Do you have reasons other than what we've discussed?"

"No. I just hate weasels, and Jimmy Haywood is a total weasel."

Burke couldn't agree more.

"I need coffee, too," Val said. "I just texted Ruthanne to see if there's coffee left. She says give her a few minutes and she'll make a fresh pot. I'll go down and get it."

"Sounds good to me," Naomi said. "What are we going to do with that list of payouts? Other than fish around for cops in PIB whose bank accounts are bigger than they should be?"

"I've been thinking about that," Val said. "Cresswell was sent to prison for a lot of different crimes. He murdered a man in cold blood to keep him from spilling his secrets."

"He did," Burke said, remembering that day. "I was there."

Naomi turned to him with wide eyes. "Really?"

"Really. It was the case that brought Molly and Gabe together. Gabe's dad had been murdered and Cresswell's crimes came out during the investigation. Val's point is a good one. There's a lot of information out there about Cresswell's various crimes. We can check this payout ledger against the things we already know he did. If we can connect any of those payments to known crimes, we can eliminate them and focus on the crimes we don't yet know about. Antoine and I can work on this together."

Val looked pensive. "We haven't had a single issue with Gaffney's people coming after the kids since Monday. I'm thinking that two of us on duty at all times may not be required. Put me back into rotation for going out to interview and investigate. Harrison can stay here on guard duty, especially since Molly and Lucien are here. They sleep lightly and are trained to wake up and be instantly alert. If something goes wrong, you'll still have three bodyguards in place." Her jaw tightened. "I think we played right into Gaffney's hands. We've all hunkered down to protect our kids and we're not out investigating him in full force."

A knock on the door had Burke springing to his feet. Ruthanne stood in the doorway holding a tray.

"Someone rang for a snack?" she asked.

Burke took the tray from her hands and set it on an end table next to the sofa where he and Naomi were sitting. "You didn't have to bring it up here. One of us would have come down to get it. This is too heavy for you."

"I'm capable of carrying a tray up the stairs, but I used the lift, so it's moot." Ruthanne turned to Naomi. "I just got off the phone with my friend at the hospital. She was hesitant at first, but I finally convinced her that you needed to talk to the girl who was nearly beaten to death. She has a police guard on the room, though. You'll have to either convince them or find a way to get past them."

"I'll ask André to accompany us." Burke went to Molly's whiteboard and flipped it from their to-do list back to the side with photos, names, and questions. "We can take these photos with us, to see if she knows any of the players other than the Delgado brothers."

"But first, coffee," Val announced. "Except there's no cream on the tray. I'll go down and get it."

"I brought it," Everett said from the doorway. "I saw you forgot this, Grandma." He held a carton out to Ruthanne, who gave him a kiss on his cheek.

"Thank you, Ev. That was sweet of you to bring it up."

Shrugging, Everett looked around the room curiously. Then he froze for a moment before hurrying to the whiteboard. "Why do you have that picture of Winnie?" he demanded, pointing at Winnifred Timms.

Naomi stiffened. "She was the woman driving the SUV when Pablo Delgado tried to abduct you. Why? Have you seen her?"

The boy turned to stare at his mother, confused. "She's McKenzie's best friend. She comes to the house all the time. *She* tried to take me? No way. Why would she do that?" He shook his head. "No way would Winnie do that. You're either lying or you're wrong. But, either way, that's not true."

Burke wanted to answer but gave Naomi time to gather her thoughts. She should be the one to tell her son the truth. And if the kid got an attitude, Burke would step in.

"Wow." Naomi lifted a trembling hand to her hair, pushing it behind her ear before changing her mind and pulling it to cover the scar on her neck, even though it was already hidden by the collar of the turtleneck sweater she wore.

"Um," she started again. "There's a possibility that Gaffney, the detective who threatened us—you and me—is involved in sex trafficking."

Everett blanched. "*That's* why they wanted me? Oh my God. And Jace? And Harper? She's only ten years old. That's sick. But if you say that Winnie is part of that, then you're wrong. There's no way."

Naomi exhaled. "You know that last night we witnessed a woman get murdered, right in front of us."

Everett was already shaking his head, the rest of the color draining from his face. "No. You're wrong."

"Everett," Naomi said gently. "Winnifred Timms is dead. She was identified as the woman who fraudulently opened three bank accounts in my name. When her involvement was exposed, she tried to escape. She was in the airport long-term parking garage. Whoever killed her did so to keep her from talking."

Everett looked at Burke in desperation.

Burke nodded, saying nothing.

"She's right," Antoine said from Burke's desk. "I saw it all. I recorded it all, but I'm not going to show it to you."

Everett was still shaking his head. "The news would have been online."

"It was," Naomi told him. "Just not her name. Not yet. The police generally withhold the names of victims until their family can be notified."

"The news story is online now," Antoine said. "No gory video, just her driver's license photo. Go ahead and look, Everett."

Everett was already searching. "Oh my God. It's true. She's dead."

"It is true," Naomi agreed solemnly. "And her death—along with the trafficking she was involved in—is what Burke and his team are investigating."

"Your mother, too," Burke added, needing Everett to be aware that his mother was a team member as well. "She's far more than a glorified UberEats driver, Everett."

But Burke wasn't sure that Everett had even heard him. The boy was stunned. Shocked.

But Naomi's small smile was grateful. "Thank you, Burke." The small smile dimmed as she turned back to her son. "You might as well know it all now. Antoine also believes your father might have been paid to testify against me in my trial."

Shaken, Everett stared at his mother. "He wouldn't do that. You're lying." He turned to Antoine. "You're lying."

"I could be wrong," Antoine said. "But we found evidence that one of the men who framed your mother made a payment that was close to the amount your father owed on his mortgage. That payment was made shortly after the trial and the day before the mortgage was paid off. It *could* be a coincidence."

Everett stood there, motionless, a complex wave of emotions washing over his face. The room remained silent as the boy processed what he'd heard.

Finally, Everett exhaled. "Dad had a party a few days after Naomi went to prison. Told his friends that he was celebrating because he'd paid off the mortgage with some winnings at the track."

"Lots of people winning money at the track," Burke murmured, thinking that Everett was, once again, shoring up the emotional walls he'd built by calling his mother by her first name.

Naomi never even flinched. Burke found he had to take a deep breath to keep his voice calm because he wanted to yell at this boy. But Everett was a sixteen-year-old kid who'd been lied to and, in his own teenage mind, abandoned by a mother who'd gone to prison because she'd been so greedy that she'd stolen drugs she should have been safeguarding.

So Burke kept his voice level. "Did you believe him?"

Everett nodded. "I mean, he's my dad, and he wasn't the one who went on trial. So, yes, I believed him." He hesitated, then looked away. "But I don't think his friends did. One of them said that Dad had killed two birds with one stone—he'd gotten rid of his mortgage and his alimony with one incredible deal."

"What did your father do?" Burke asked.

"He got super angry. Got in the guy's face. The guy backed down."

"Do you remember who that was?" Naomi asked, her tone patient and encouraging. Loving. And yet so very sad.

Burke didn't know how she could pack so many emotions into so few words.

"It was Mr. Miller." Everett glanced at Burke. "He's my dad's best friend."

"We'll have a conversation with him," Burke said. "Thank you, Everett."

Everett nodded uncertainly. "Don't tell him it was me who said anything. His son is one of my friends."

"We'll be discreet," Burke promised. But he would find out. If Winnifred Timms was McKenzie Haywood's friend, that might mean that husband and wife had been actively working with Gaffney all this time.

That Naomi's ex was in on the frame from the beginning.

He couldn't fathom the betrayal.

Burke put his arm around her shoulders, ignoring the narrowed eyes of her son. "Jimmy might not be guilty of anything, Naomi."

She rested her head on his shoulder, accepting the comfort he offered. "I don't believe in coincidences any more than you do."

Tulane-Gravier, New Orleans, Louisiana
WEDNESDAY, FEBRUARY 26, 3:00 P.M.

"You can only have five minutes," the nurse said as she led Naomi and Burke to the ICU room in which Susan Snyder was recovering. André and Val brought up the rear, André having coordinated the interview and Val insisting that Burke and Naomi needed protection, given the shooting the night before. That they should have taken a bodyguard to the Cresswells' house.

It was fair, Naomi thought.

You've been living on borrowed time for years. I think your time is up.

Someone wanted both her and Burke dead. So she'd gratefully accepted Val's insistence that she join them. With a sigh, Burke had agreed.

"We had some . . . excitement right before you arrived," André said, his voice a quiet rumble, pitched so that only they could hear. "A woman posing as a nurse tried to get into Susan's room. The officer at her door turned the woman away."

Burke paused to stare at André, making them all stop. "Did you ID her?"

"She's the woman your friend saw leaving the Delgados' house," André said. "The one dressed in scrubs. She had on a dark wig today, but the cop at the door saw her face and ID'd her from the photo you sent me, Burke. We don't yet have a name."

"Did you arrest her?" Naomi asked.

"No. The cop at Susan's door was calling it in when the woman ran to one of the stairwells. He didn't want to leave his post, in case it was a diversion, so he stayed put and called hospital security. But the woman had disappeared before they could lock the hospital down."

This wasn't good, but there was something more that André wasn't saying.

"But?" Naomi asked. "What's wrong, other than the woman is at large?"

"The officer who made the call was a last-minute replacement on my part. The cop who'd been on duty had been the subject of rumors.

Like, he spent too much money for what he earned. I erred on the side of caution and made a schedule adjustment. I'm glad I was right, but now I've got another compromised officer to deal with."

"You may have saved Susan's life," Val murmured. "Did you recognize the intruder?" she asked the nurse.

The nurse, whose name was Shannon, shook her head. "I've not seen her before. We've kept tight control over Susan's room and her treatment. I don't know what the woman had planned. One of our nurses confronted her as she entered the floor because she didn't recognize her." The woman's lips pressed together grimly. "We found our nurse unconscious in one of the unoccupied rooms, but that wasn't until after the intruder had disappeared. The woman hit her with something blunt and then injected her with an opioid. We don't know which one yet. Our nurse will be all right because we got to her in time. Had to use Narcan to revive her."

"We think the intruder was planning to kill Susan the same way," André said.

"Has anyone else tried to get in before today?" Burke asked.

Again, Nurse Shannon shook her head. "But Susan's only been awake for a few days and only able to talk since this morning. We didn't even know her name before Monday. She was a Jane Doe until we used an alphabet card to find out her name. But we all knew what she'd been through and none of us were going to let her get hurt again on our watch."

"It was the first time the cop I suspected had been put on the guard roster," André said. "That was the other thing that drew my eye. I've kept a tight rein on who was standing outside Susan's door. She's our only witness right now."

"She's wary," Shannon said. "She didn't trust us at first, but it's getting better. I don't know what you'll get out of her today, but do not press her. Her vitals still aren't stable and her throat is sore, so talking will hurt. She just had her breathing tube removed."

"We'll be gentle," Naomi assured her. "We just want to know what, if anything, she heard that can help us find who took her. Who hurt her."

Shannon's expression softened. "We want that, too."

"Did the nurse have a badge?" Val asked as they resumed walking to Susan's room. "One that let her into the ICU ward?"

"She did." André scowled. "Stole it off one of the nurses who'd clocked out. The nurse was shocked when I called her to find out if she still had her badge. She said that she bumped into someone coming off the elevator but had no idea that her badge had been taken out of her purse."

Shannon stopped at a closed door, where a uniformed officer stood.

"No activity, Captain," the officer said to André.

André gave the officer a nod. "Thank you."

"Five minutes," Shannon reminded them as she escorted them into the girl's room.

Naomi's heart hurt when she set eyes on Susan Snyder. The girl looked so young. So frail. So scared.

"These are the people I told you about," Nurse Shannon said. "This is Naomi, Burke, and Val. They're private investigators. They're working with Captain Holmes, who you've also met. You can tell them whatever you like or you can say nothing. No one will force you. And if it gets to be too much, I'll make them leave."

Susan gave them all a thorough inspection. She was indeed wary. But she nodded. "Okay."

Naomi patted the plastic chair that sat next to the bed. "Is it okay if I sit down?"

A wordless nod was Susan's answer, so Naomi lowered herself into the chair. "I'm Naomi. The people who hurt you framed me for a crime I didn't commit," she said quietly. "I went to prison for five years."

"I'm sorry," Susan whispered. "That you went to prison."

"And I'm sorry for what happened to you."

Susan's eyes filled as she turned her face away.

Naomi took her hand. "Is this okay? If I hold your hand?"

Susan's nod was slight. "Is that why you're chasing them? Because they put you in prison?"

"No. I'm chasing them because they threatened to hurt my fifteen-year-old son if I didn't sell drugs for them."

"I can believe that," Susan said bitterly.

"Did they ask you to sell drugs for them?" André asked from the foot of her bed.

Susan swallowed again. "Yeah. I hated it. Made the men worse. You know, the men who paid to . . ."

"We get it," Naomi murmured. "They tried to abduct my son on Monday afternoon. They weren't successful."

"Good," Susan whispered harshly. "They would have done to him what they did to me." She glanced at André. "They have boys there, too. Not only girls."

Naomi's gut twisted. *Thank you, Harrison. Thank you for keeping my son from a similar fate.*

"Thank you, Susan," André said. "We thought they might, but we weren't certain."

"Did you check for missing kids?" Susan demanded.

"I have," André said, his tone grave. "Since we found out that you went missing out of the foster care system, I've had my teams running searches for other missing kids."

Which is something we should have been doing, Naomi thought. They'd been distracted by Gaffney and his people at every turn. Shootings, abductions, burning homes . . .

But it seemed Captain Holmes had been focused on the right things.

"Did you find any?" Susan asked.

"Too many," André admitted. "I've got photos that I'm going to ask you to look at when you're ready. Maybe you've seen some of them."

"Okay. I can do that." Susan turned back to Naomi. "What do you want to know?"

"Do you know where they were keeping you?" Naomi asked. André had said that Susan hadn't been able to answer that question using the alphabet card when she'd first awoken from the coma, but if her thoughts were getting clearer, it was worth a second ask.

"No, but it was really nice." Susan tightened her hold on Naomi's hand. "It was a mansion. There were five of us in our room, but it was still nicer than anywhere I've ever lived. We got to sleep in nice beds. During the day."

"But at night?"

Susan looked away. "At night it was bad."

"But you were found in a motel room," Val said. "Were you assaulted in the mansion or in motel rooms? Or both?"

"Both. Some of the customers didn't trust coming to a fancy house, Pablo said. That they thought it was a police trap. So there were a few of us who got taken to the motels to meet customers." She fussed with the sheet, distressed. When she spoke again, it was to change the subject. "Did you get . . . hurt? In prison?"

"No. Well, yes. I was stabbed in the neck and nearly died, but I wasn't sexually assaulted, if that's what you're asking."

"Then you don't really get it."

"I don't," Naomi agreed.

"I do." Val stepped up to the other side of the bed. "I know what you're talking about, Susan. I was raped years ago. Not the same as what you experienced, but I do understand the basics."

Susan met Val's gaze. "I wish you didn't. I don't wish that for anyone."

"I understand that, too," Val said gently. "But you can trust me and my friends. You can trust Captain Holmes. And when this is all over, you have my word that I'll help you get back on your feet, whatever that looks like."

"I'm sixteen," Susan said bitterly. "They'll put me back in the system."

"I know good people in the foster system. We can help you have a good life."

Tears streaked down Susan's face. "I can't think that far."

"I know," Val said, plucking a tissue from the box on the nightstand and drying Susan's cheeks. "But we can. So let us do the thinking. All you need to do is get better."

"And help you find the people who did this to me," Susan said, her jaw set in determination. "To all of us kids."

"Yes," Naomi said. "Who did you see at this mansion where you stayed?"

"They wore masks, all the time. Fancy masks with feathers. For Mardi Gras, you know."

"That sounds creepy," Naomi said.

"It was. I heard voices, but I didn't see most of their faces. Just Pablo, and I already told the police about him. I'm sorry."

"Don't be sorry, honey," Naomi said quietly. "How many adults did you see? Even the ones wearing masks."

"Three women. Three men, plus Pablo. He was the only one who didn't wear a mask in the mansion. The others did."

"What were their roles?"

"Only one of the women was there all the time. She served us food in our rooms, washed the clothes." Susan closed her eyes. "Made sure we got condoms. Made sure we used them. One of the other women called her Maya. She said she was our '*housemother*.'" She spat the word. "Like she *cared*."

"How old do you think she was?" Val asked.

"Not too old. Maybe college aged? Not as old as either of you."

Naomi gave her hand a light squeeze. "What about the other two women?"

"One was our recruiter. They called her Elaine. She was older. Maybe your age. I never saw her face, there in the mansion, but I think I knew her."

"You only have another minute," Nurse Shannon said. "Sorry."

"No." Susan shook her head. "Let them stay. I want to tell them. I want them to catch those bastards." Her pulse monitor started to beep and it looked like Shannon was about to throw them all out.

"Deep breaths," Val said. "Gotta bring down your blood pressure or Nurse Shannon's gonna be unhappy with us."

Susan complied, breathing with Val until both her pulse and blood pressure had decreased.

"How did you know the woman they called Elaine?" Naomi asked.

"You're not going to believe me," Susan muttered.

"I think you'll find we will," Naomi said, taking her phone from her pocket. They'd all downloaded the photos that had been posted on the whiteboard in Burke's home office, so that anyone who got the opportunity could show them to Susan.

"She was my social worker. Back in Baton Rouge."

"Oh no," Naomi murmured. "That's why so many kids came out of foster care."

Susan nodded, her lips trembling. "I didn't think you'd believe me."

"We do." Naomi showed Susan her phone. "Do any of these women look familiar?"

Susan shook her head at the photo of Winnifred but then went stiff at the photo of the woman who'd been seen coming and going from the Delgados' house, posing as a nurse. The woman who'd helped bug both Molly's and Val's cars, and—for reasons they did not yet understand—had kept Ernesto Delgado from taking Harper.

"Her," Susan whispered. "That's her. You have to find her."

"I've sent my computer expert her first name," Burke said, "and that she was a social worker in Baton Rouge. We'll have a full name in a short while. Thank you, Susan. That's helpful."

"I want her to die." Susan began to cry again. "She said she was moving me to a better house. Somewhere I could have a real family."

Naomi's heart broke. "She lied."

"Yeah. She must have drugged me because I woke up later and I was trapped."

"In the mansion?" Val asked.

"No. Not then. That's when I was twelve. It was a man's house, out in the country. Just one man. His name was Charles Hanson. He made me . . . do things."

Naomi brought Susan's hand to her cheek. "You don't have to say any more about that. How did you get to the mansion?"

"Elaine came to see Charles one day. Said she'd trade him for me. Said she'd give him another girl who was younger. He liked them younger. I was too old, he said. She drugged me again, and that's when I woke up at the mansion."

Behind Naomi, Burke drew a deep breath. "My computer guy's already found her name. Elaine Billings."

"I'll get out a BOLO on Elaine Billings and Charles Hanson," André said and began tapping his phone screen.

"You're doing so well," Naomi said, brushing the girl's hand against her cheek. "Can you answer a few more questions?"

Because Susan was looking more tired by the moment.

"Ask."

"What about the other woman whose face you didn't see?"

"She was young, too, like Maya. College-aged, maybe. They called her Freddie."

Winnifred, Naomi thought with a jolt of satisfaction. "Well, you don't have to worry about her anymore. She was killed last night."

Susan's eyes widened. "Are you sure?"

"Very sure. I saw it happen."

"Good," Susan hissed out. "I'm glad and I'm not sorry."

"Which is perfectly understandable." Naomi put their joined hands back at Susan's side. "What was her role?"

"She handled the money. Took the cash to the bank. I think it was cash from drugs, too. Pablo took the money from the . . . customers. And if we got a tip, he took that, too." She met Naomi's eyes. "I'm glad he's dead, too."

"He was the one who tried to take my son, so I'm going to have to agree with you. What about the other three men? The ones who stayed masked."

"One was the scheduler. I never heard his name. But he dressed really well. Better than the others. The other man also wore expensive suits, but the scheduler, his were . . . put together. He accessorized really well."

"Do you remember any specifics?" Burke asked.

Susan bit her lip as she thought. "He had beautiful shoes. We weren't supposed to look up when the bosses came in. We were supposed to keep our eyes down. So I noticed his shoes. They were brown and looked like soft leather. The kind you slip on. Loafers?"

"That could be an important detail," Naomi praised her. "Did you hear him speak?"

"Yes. He sounded like a butler, the ones on TV. But he was a local. Sounded like a New Orleans accent, anyway. They all sounded Southern. The guy with the shoes called one of the other guys 'sir.' He was the big boss. At least everyone called him 'Boss.' Except for the Freddie lady. Once she called him Romeo. But he didn't like it."

Behind her, Naomi felt Burke twitch and made a mental note to ask him why once they were done. "What did the boss do to Freddie?"

"Grabbed her wrist. Told her to never call him that again. Really mean voice. I think Freddie's feelings were hurt. She took that out on us. After the boss and the shoe guy were gone, she told us we weren't earning enough. That we needed to be 'more productive.' I must have made some kind of face because she slapped me, hard. I'm glad she's dead."

"So am I," Burke said, his voice quiet. "What about the third man?"

"He handled the drugs. Brought them to the mansion so that Pablo could sell them to the customers. Pablo called him Gaffney."

"Perfect," André said, his tone gone cold. He was already tapping on his phone, hopefully getting a warrant for Gaffney's arrest before whoever was protecting Gaffney could sanitize the investigation. "Do you remember how many kids they kept, Susan?"

"Fifteen? Maybe more. There were four other girls sharing my room and there were boys in the room next door. More girls on the other side. They're the only ones I had contact with. We'd talk through the walls because they were thin."

"What do you remember about the mansion, Susan?" Burke asked.

"It was huge. Three floors. Maya grumbled about having to go up and down three floors. There were curtains covering the windows. They were nailed to the wall, so we couldn't look outside. There was music. Lots of music. Oh my God." She sucked in a breath, followed by a rasping cough. "There was a parade," she said after a sip of water. "What's today's date?"

"Wednesday, February twenty-sixth," Naomi said.

"Mardi Gras parades," Susan said, as if she'd just put everything together. "One was close. Maybe a few blocks away. It was before I got taken to the motel, but I don't remember exactly which day, so you can't know which parade it was."

"But we now know that the mansion's on a parade route," Burke said. "That is *incredibly* helpful, Susan."

"Good." Susan closed her eyes. "I don't remember much more."

"You really have to go now," Shannon said. "She needs to rest."

Naomi pressed a kiss to the girl's forehead. "I'll come back as soon as I can. We can just sit together."

"Me too," Val said. "You're not alone anymore, Susan."

Susan swallowed. "Thank you."

They filed out, André immediately dialing a number on his phone. "Hogan, it's Holmes."

The DA, then. André was going straight to the top. He requested a warrant, then said he'd have officers pick Gaffney up as soon as possible.

"That yielded more than I thought," André said when he'd ended the call. "She was a lot clearer just now than she was even this morning. You guys go on home. I've got some more calls to make before I leave here. I don't want to wait until I'm back in the office. I don't want Gaffney slithering away. Thanks, y'all. You were a big help."

Naomi thanked Nurse Shannon, and then together she, Burke, and Val made their way to the parking garage.

None of them spoke, both Burke and Val on alert.

Naomi let them watch for danger. Her mind was spinning with new information, her heart breaking over what Susan had endured. The girl was brave.

Naomi would make sure that they didn't let Susan and all the other kids down.

19

The Central Business District, New Orleans, Louisiana
WEDNESDAY, FEBRUARY 26, 3:00 P.M.

"IS IT FINISHED?" he asked after accepting the call from Elaine's burner.

"Not exactly."

"What does 'not exactly' mean?"

Elaine had been tasked with killing the girl in the ICU bed. Susan Snyder had been one of theirs, but Pablo had sworn she was dead. That he'd checked.

If Pablo weren't already dead, I'd kill him myself.

Wayne Stanley had been watching for her autopsy report, just to make sure nothing had been found that could link her to them, when—surprise, surprise—her name had popped up as a patient. She hadn't been dead after all.

One of his own cops was on guard duty at the girl's hospital door. Elaine was to have slipped into the girl's room and injected fentanyl into her IV, drugging her into a slumber from which she wouldn't wake.

Elaine had assured him that everything was under control.

It sounded like that was not the case.

"It wasn't our guy at the door," she said. "He got changed out at the last minute."

"Holmes," he said darkly. "He's getting closer."

The captain was highly involved in this case, running down leads on missing foster kids. A few of whom were currently housed in his new place of business.

"Yes. The cop on duty stopped me. Said I wasn't on the approved list. He made a phone call, so I ran."

"Did he chase you?"

"No. He stayed at his post. I got away."

That was good, at least. With Winnifred and the Delgados gone, he was quickly running out of staff, and the week for which they'd been preparing started tomorrow. "Where are you now?"

"Across the street from the hospital. I just saw Burke Broussard going into the hospital. Naomi Cranston was with him, along with Val Sorensen, the sister of the flower shop owner. I didn't get close enough to hear them say where they were going, but I'm betting it's got something to do with Susan."

"I agree. Are you safe to stay in the area?"

"Yeah. I've changed my wig. No one will be looking for this version of me. Do you want me to take care of Naomi Cranston?"

"Yes. If you can get a good shot, do it."

"And Broussard?" she asked, a little more warily.

He hated all this murder. But needs must. "Yes. Don't get caught."

"I won't."

He ended the call and dialed Stanley. "We're at plan Z."

"Broussard's gotten closer?"

"He's talking to Susan Snyder right now."

"Dammit. Okay, I can get over to the hospital, but it'll take me at least a half hour."

"Get started. I don't know how long Broussard and Naomi Cranston will be there, but you have a chance of getting to the parking garage before they come back. Elaine's there now, preparing to carry this out, but you're a better shot than she is."

Stanley had hit Winnifred right between her eyes.

He'd missed Broussard and the others, but he wasn't going to hold that against him. Stanley hadn't expected them to be there. He'd tried to get them, but Broussard and his team had ducked by then and Stanley had run. He could *not* get caught.

Of all his staff, Stanley was the most valuable.

"Will do, sir. On my way."

Tulane-Gravier, New Orleans, Louisiana
WEDNESDAY, FEBRUARY 26, 3:25 P.M.

"You should have just let me get the SUV and pick you up," Val muttered as she, Naomi, and Burke walked from the hospital to the parking garage.

But Burke hadn't wanted to wait out in the open, and it wasn't far to the garage. They would be fine. Still, Naomi was tense as they crossed the pedestrian bridge into the garage.

The parking garage was nerve-racking as well. It wasn't dark, but there were shadows lurking in every corner.

Val hurried them along. "I don't like this. Something feels wrong."

"We're hurrying," Burke said, lengthening his stride as his hand stroked up and down Naomi's back. It was really nice.

It almost made her forget to ask the question that had been lurking in her mind as she processed their conversation with Susan. What had bothered him about Winnifred calling the big boss Romeo?

That didn't make any sense.

"Hey, Burke?" she murmured as they passed between a dirty gray pickup truck and a bright blue sedan. The SUV was only another twenty feet away.

"Hmm?"

"Why—?"

Her words dried up at the crack of the truck's window close to where her head had been. The window suddenly pebbled, a tiny hole in the center of the damage.

Another ping had her jerking her head to stare at the bullet hole in the frame of the pickup truck, right next to Burke's head. And then she was being dragged down, her hands and knees stinging when they scraped against the concrete.

Burke shoved her under the pickup truck. "Stay there!"

She made a keening noise when her head hit the underside of the truck. Muttering a curse, she twisted her head in time to see Burke aim and fire. Unlike the gun that had narrowly missed them, Burke's weapon discharged with a loud boom that echoed throughout the space.

The difference in the sound was like night and day.

The shooter's gun was suppressed.

Where is Val?

Burke ducked down as two more suppressed bullets hit the pickup truck. When he popped back up, he fired only once. Through the echoing boom, Naomi heard a scream and hoped Burke had hit the shooter and not someone else.

"Got her!" Val yelled, and Naomi shuddered out a relieved breath.

Burke slowly rose to see over the hood of the truck that had sheltered them. "She alone?" he yelled back to Val.

Naomi's ears were ringing. She could barely hear Burke's shout, which was probably why both he and Val were shouting.

"Not sure," Val responded. "Stay down. I've restrained her. I'll sit here with her. Call André. Tell him we found Elaine Billings."

Naomi pulled herself sideways until she was no longer under the truck. She sat on the concrete floor of the garage, leaning against the pickup truck, which now sported four bullet holes.

She hoped the owner had good car insurance. Which was a ridiculous thing to be thinking about, but her mind had cleared of anything else.

Burke made his call to André, then turned to her, his face filled with fear. "Are you all right?" He ran his hands over her arms, down her sides, checking her out. "Were you hit?"

"No. You?"

"No."

She slid her arm around his neck and pulled him close so that their foreheads touched. "You kept me safe, Burke. We're fine."

"I shouldn't have let you leave the house."

Let me? But Naomi bit the words back. Burke was shaking, and though he continued to rest his forehead against hers, he was still touching her, running his hands down her legs now. He was scared, so she'd let him have one stupid statement.

He wasn't *letting* her do anything. But that was a conversation they'd have later.

They'd done everything as safely as they could. They'd brought Val with them for backup. And now they had one of Gaffney's people in their hands.

"I want to see her," Naomi said.

"When André gets here. When he says it's clear. Until then, stay with me. Please."

Her palms burned, so she used her fingertips to tilt his face so that she could kiss him. It was a hard press of lips, not the sweet kiss they'd shared that morning outside Amanda Cresswell's house. But it seemed to penetrate his panic. "I'm okay. You're okay. We're *okay,* Burke."

But they weren't okay. None of this was okay.

You've been living on borrowed time for years. I think your time is up.

She released Burke, holding him close when his head fell to her shoulder. He was breathing in great gasps of air. Very much the opposite of the way he'd reacted the night before.

Last night, in the airport's parking garage, he'd been grim, but in control. Today, he was literally shaking in his shoes. She stroked his dark hair, whispering comfort to him as he began to still.

By the time André rushed over from the hospital, five minutes had passed and four NOPD cruisers had pulled up, responding to 911 calls about the gunshots. One of the officers started to give them a hard time for firing in a hospital parking garage, demanding Burke's ID, but André's arrival quelled that.

At least Naomi could hear the officer's rant. The ringing in her ears was subsiding.

"It's a fucking hospital, Captain!" the officer argued. "He can't just shoot in here."

Naomi got the officer's concern. While a concealed carry permit was no longer required in most of Louisiana, there were still places, such as hospitals, where carrying a weapon wasn't okay.

"He's got a PI license," André told the officer. "Stand down." André crouched beside them, his face creased in concern. "You okay?"

Burke nodded. "They came close again, André. The Billings woman missed Naomi by less than an inch."

Naomi frowned. "They missed you, too. Don't make this about me, Burke. Elaine Billings was shooting at you, too."

"'You've been living on borrowed time,'" André murmured.

Naomi nodded, wincing when the movement hurt her head. "Exactly."

"What's wrong?" André asked. "You look like you're in pain."

"Bumped my head on the underside of the truck," Naomi said. "No big deal. Have you cleared the garage yet? I want to see the woman who shot at us."

André shook his head. "I don't think she'll say anything. She's been read her rights and cuffed. Val trussed her up with zip ties. Made our job easier."

"You're welcome," Val said dryly, walking up to where they still sat on the floor. "You got her in the forearm, Burke. Through and through. She dropped the gun, which made it easier for me to restrain her. That was good shooting."

Burke tried to smile, but it was clearly forced. "Thanks. Can we go home, André? I need to get Naomi home."

Naomi thought she was the one who needed to get Burke home, but she'd let him have a few caveman moments. He seemed to need the control.

"I'll need your gun, Burke," André said with regret.

Burke handed it over without any complaint. "Fired twice. There's still a bullet in the chamber."

André racked the gun and shook the chambered bullet free. "You'll get this back. Eventually."

Burke tried to smile again with the same forced result. "No problem. I have more."

"I know," André said wryly, then stood, offering his hand to Burke first, then to Naomi. "Do you need to get checked out? The ER's right there."

Burke shook his head. "No. I just want to get Naomi home. Where it's safe."

"Then let's go home," Val said, and then she flinched. "Oh, Naomi. Your hands."

Naomi studied her palms. They were scraped bloody. "I'll live. Get us home and I'll get my mom to clean and bandage me up. She was a nurse, you know," she added to Burke, because he was staring at her hands, guilt all over his face.

"You saved my life," she told him. "This is nothing. I had blisters you wouldn't believe working the farm in prison." She slid her arm through his and tugged him toward the SUV. "Let's go."

"Call me if anyone else shoots at you," André said, walking with them.

"Not funny," Burke snapped.

"I wasn't trying to be," André said. "Burke, you need to take a breath. Naomi is in one piece. You and Val are in one piece. You caught one of the bad guys. I'll need signed statements from all of you, but I'll come by for those later. Go home and relax."

Yeah, right, Naomi thought. *Like that's gonna happen.*

The Central Business District, New Orleans, Louisiana
WEDNESDAY, FEBRUARY 26, 3:40 P.M.

He scowled as Gaffney's cell continued to ring. It would go to voicemail in another—

"What?" Gaffney answered impatiently. "I'm busy."

The man was about to be considerably less busy. Forever. "Where are you?"

"At the warehouse. Why?" Gaffney added suspiciously.

"Because Elaine was arrested, and I'm going to need your help. Stay where you are. I'll be right over." He ended the call, then hesitated over his next move. Well, more like how best to accomplish the next move.

Elaine had been arrested, but he did not need Gaffney's help. Gaffney was compromised. He'd heard it over the call that Elaine had left open when she'd gone after Broussard and Cranston.

I should have told her to wait. Stanley wouldn't have missed.

And now Elaine was in custody. She wouldn't talk. Killing Cresswell had put the fear of God into his people. Elaine knew what happened to traitors. Plus, he'd have her taken care of before she'd left the holding cell.

Unlike Cresswell, Elaine had no family and no close friends. There was no one he could threaten to keep Elaine's mouth closed forever, and replacing her would be difficult. Still, he'd have to find a way.

If he continued this new business, which was becoming less profitable by the day. They'd lost four girls during Super Bowl weekend. Two had been beaten so badly by their customers that they'd died the same day. Their bodies had been taken out to the bayou and dumped in a swamp that he knew well, having spent several enjoyable vacations and holidays there.

Gators made cleanup a breeze.

The two they'd lost in the Delgados' house fire had already been on death's door. That the cops had their bodies wasn't ideal, but not a catastrophe.

The two who'd lived were problems, however. Pablo had sworn

that Susan was dead when he'd left her in that motel room to chase after the fourteen-year-old who'd slashed her john's face, but Susan had been found before he got back—and she'd survived.

The fourteen-year-old was back home in Baton Rouge now and he couldn't get anyone close enough to deal with her. He'd tried.

He'd expected to lose a few teenagers over the month. What he hadn't expected was having to eliminate his staff.

Winnifred was never going to last past next week, anyway. The moment that she'd shown up at the same restaurant where he'd taken his wife for lunch, she'd reached her expiration date.

The Delgado brothers were a bigger loss. They'd been very good at their jobs. Until they'd fucked up. And until Ernesto had gotten greedy.

"No children" had been the number one rule from the get-go. Kids under twelve would not be used in their business. Not even one. That Ernesto had broken that rule—and had wanted to keep the child for himself?

He'd deserved to die.

But Elaine's arrest was not as bad as the potential arrest of John Gaffney. The bastard would sing like a bird to protect himself.

So his song would have to be silenced.

The question was, who to do it? Stanley was a better shot, but Gaffney was in the warehouse, so it wasn't like he needed a sniper for the job.

He hit Stanley's name in his contact list. The man answered on the first ring because he wasn't an arrogant prick like Gaffney.

"Sir? I'm almost to the hospital."

"Too late. Elaine shot, failed, and got arrested."

An exasperated sigh. "Dammit. How do you want to manage this?"

"Have our guard at the holding cell in the jail serve her a meal or give her some water. Same as Cresswell."

"That might be difficult. There are more cameras in the holding area."

"Then figure out a better way," he snapped, then got hold of himself. "Apologies. Elaine is not the biggest problem. I told her to call me before she went into the parking garage so that I could send backup if required, so I was listening to everything. Broussard shot her in the arm. One of his people took Elaine down after that and was generously chatty. Told Elaine that Susan Snyder had ID'd her as her old social worker."

"Dammit."

"Yeah, well, it gets better. When Elaine said nothing, the Sorensen woman told her that Susan had heard one of our people call Gaffney by name. Tried to get Elaine to talk to her, to tell her who Romeo was."

And for that alone, he was glad Freddie was dead.

"Freddie was a fucking idiot," Stanley growled. "I don't know how many times I told her to stop using our names."

"Well, you took care of her. The question is how best to take care of Gaffney. He's at the warehouse now and is supposed to be there until midnight." It had been the Delgado brothers' shift, but with Freddie and the Delgados dead, they were having to double up on their duties.

"I know. I'm on duty with him. I'll go back to the warehouse now. It'll take me a while to get there, though. They're starting to close roads on the parade route."

"I'll head down there, too."

"But . . . you don't care for the dark side, sir."

He did not usually like murder, that was true. But . . . "Even I have fantasies."

Stanley chucked. "Understood."

"But seriously, we need to be sure that he doesn't have a confession somewhere that'll come back to bite us in the ass. We need to figure that out before we take care of him."

"I'll take him to the panic room when I get there."

The room that they'd soundproofed. Because sometimes their inventory screamed.

"Perfect. I'll see you there."

The Quarter, New Orleans, Louisiana
WEDNESDAY, FEBRUARY 26, 5:10 P.M.

Naomi knew that Burke was pacing outside the door she shared with her mother. She could hear the floorboards creak with his every step as Ruthanne cleaned and bandaged her skinned palms and knees.

"Burke's upset," Ruthanne murmured as she applied the last bandage.

Naomi studied her hands. "I look like I'm wearing oven mitts."

Her mother raised a brow.

Naomi sighed. "Yes, Mom, Burke's upset. I'm not sure why today was different from last night. He didn't seem so upset when Winnifred Timms was murdered right in front of our eyes. We got shot at last night, too."

"Maybe he's more emotionally invested today than he was yesterday." Her mother handed her phone to Naomi, who could only blink at the photograph on the screen.

"What the hell is this?"

"Looks like you and Burke kissing," Ruthanne said with mild amusement.

It had been taken while she and Burke were sitting in front of the Cresswells' house. Which had been surrounded by the press.

Well, it was what it was.

Their first kiss was making the rounds online, accompanied by the caption *Former NOPD turned PI "working" with disgraced cop.*

"Do you regret it?" Ruthanne asked, sounding genuinely curious.

"No. Not even a little bit. I . . . really like him, Mom. I haven't felt like this for a long time."

"Well, if the feeling is mutual, that could explain why he's so upset right now. Last night you were a client. Today you're . . . more."

Naomi wanted to hide her face. She must have looked like a tomato.

That the pacing outside her door had stopped made things worse. Burke had stopped stock-still when her mother had mentioned the online photo.

Naomi rolled her eyes. "Of course he has ears like a bat."

Ruthanne smiled. "If this is the start of something, I'm so glad for you. Even if it doesn't go anywhere, it's nice to feel appreciated. As a woman."

"Like James appreciates you?"

"He does." Then she sighed. "The worst day of my life was when you were sentenced. If I could go back and change that, I would, even if it cost me everything. But it's also how James and I grew closer."

"I'm glad for you, Mom. I've always loved James. I wish he'd used a little more discipline with Jimmy when he was growing up, but that may be simplistic. Jimmy could just be bad."

Ruthanne scowled. "Jimmy *is* just bad."

Naomi cocked her head. The floorboards began to creak again. Burke was on the move. She'd have to put him out of his misery soon and let him in. But she needed this time with her mother and hoped he understood.

"I won't argue with you there." Jimmy's role in her trial had been weighing on her mind. Had he merely been bribed to do something he would have done anyway—lie about her in court—or had he had a hand in the frame-up? Hopefully they'd find out. Hopefully Everett wouldn't be hurt in the fallout of whatever they discovered. "But on the shooting, I think Burke was more upset today because the bullets came a lot closer." She thought about the bullet that had come within an inch of her head. "A *lot* closer."

Ruthanne closed her eyes. "That terrifies me, Naomi."

"Well, I'm not terribly happy about it, either."

"I've often wondered why Cresswell and Gaffney didn't just kill you. Why they went to the trouble of the trial."

Once again, the pacing stopped. Aware that Burke was listening to every word, Naomi considered her answer carefully.

"If Molly is right, if I was specifically chosen to be framed, it's likely because of some piece of evidence I handled. It was my only job. There aren't many other things it could be, unless I saw something I shouldn't have seen that I'm not aware of. But evidence makes the most sense."

Her mother nodded. "Okay. And?"

"If they'd outright killed me, there would have been questions. Maybe an investigation. Maybe the evidence I'd processed would get a second look. I don't think that Cresswell, Gaffney, or this 'boss' that Gaffney's working with wanted that. So they got me convicted of a serious crime. If this piece of evidence happened to pop up, nobody would take it seriously. They'd destroyed my credibility."

Ruthanne shook her head. "I think that the plan all along was to silence you. Being convicted did damage your credibility, but you could have still talked in prison. Didn't you think it was suspicious that you were attacked the first week in prison? That you were wounded so badly that you nearly died?"

"Of course I thought it was suspicious. At the same time, I was an ex-cop in prison for stealing coke. Everyone knew that. Plus, I didn't have any major trouble after I came out of PC."

"Maybe they thought they'd made their point. Or that they'd beaten you down. You were at death's door, love. You'd lost so much blood. I still see your wounds in my nightmares."

Naomi frowned. "You saw my wounds?"

"You were in my hospital. The nurses on your floor helped me get in, pretended like I was supposed to be on your floor. The head nurse let me take your vitals every day for a while, just so that I could see you with my own eyes. The police guard never questioned it. I was there every day while you lay unconscious." She swallowed hard. "I thought you might never wake up."

"Oh, Mom. I'm sorry."

"You have nothing to be sorry about. My point is, Naomi, that now you're the genie who's escaped from the bottle. You're out there with Burke, investigating. And you're getting closer. So silencing you and Burke is in Gaffney's best interest. Or the best interest of whoever this boss guy is."

"Romeo," Naomi murmured. "That's what Winnifred called him."

"Well, this Romeo is scared. I think he'll keep trying until he gets you. And Burke, too."

"I don't think Burke's going to let me out of this house until it's over," Naomi grumbled.

"I kind of hope he doesn't," Ruthanne admitted. "But I don't think you'd sit still for that." She hesitated, but then raised her voice to make sure Burke would hear. "And I'm glad to see your fighting spirit again. It went into hiding when you were arrested. I'm glad to see my daughter taking control of her life once again."

Naomi chuckled. "Subtle, Mom."

Ruthanne kissed her cheek. "I'm proud of you, Naomi. I'm proud that you survived that awful place. I'm proud that you're thriving again. I'm proud that you're out there, holding your head high as you figure out who's behind this so you can drop-kick them into the sun."

Naomi's throat tightened. "I love you, Mom."

"I love you, too. Now, James and I have a date. We're going to watch a movie on the TV downstairs. Fred Astaire, I think. Burke's flat-screen is so big that it'll be like going to the movie theater."

Naomi rose to walk her mother to the door. "Have a good date, Mom. Do you need mad money so you can pay for a taxi home if James gets handsy?"

Ruthanne laughed, the sound tightening Naomi's throat even further. She didn't hear her mother laugh nearly often enough. "I don't think mad money would help, even if we were going out on an actual date. Taxis are stuck in traffic in the Quarter like everyone else."

Her mother opened the door, revealing a sheepish Burke. But he didn't apologize for listening, and Naomi appreciated that.

"You may see her now, Burke," Ruthanne said, lightly patting Burke's cheek. "I've checked her out and she's fine. A little bruised and scraped up, but fine."

Burke nodded. "Thank you." He tried to smile, but it looked more like a grimace. "Handy to have a nurse on-site."

"Glad to help. Don't come back bloody."

"I will do my utmost, ma'am. Enjoy your date."

"I will." Ruthanne threw a smirk over her shoulder. "Bye, Naomi."

Her mother disappeared down the stairs, but Burke stayed where he was, hesitating in the doorway. So Naomi gingerly took his hand in hers and drew him into the room, closing the door behind them.

She still hated closed doors, but she also hated being overheard by his people and her son. "You heard it all, I take it?"

"I did. I should apologize for eavesdropping, but I'm not sorry."

She cupped his face in both hands, his stubble catching on the gauze bandages. "What's really wrong, Burke? Was today closer than last night? Is that what has you all wound up like this?"

He stared at her for a long moment, his eyes darkening as fear morphed into lust. It was her only warning before he threaded his hands through her hair and took her mouth in a kiss that bordered on bruising.

But it wasn't bruising. It was fiery and passionate and perfect. Her heart was thumping in her chest and she drew him closer, her arms winding around his neck. His chest was hard against her breasts, a solid wall of muscle that made her feel safe. But it was so much more than that.

She felt feminine.

Wanted. Appreciated in a way she wasn't sure she'd ever been.

She made a noise in her throat that surprised her. She hadn't heard that noise in a very long time, not since she was a teenager who'd thought herself in love with Jimmy Haywood.

Burke's reply was a quiet groan that she could feel rumbling from his chest before it filled her ears. His hands were gone from her hair, sliding down her sides, hesitating just a fraction of a second at her breasts before continuing downward, one big hand stopping to cup her butt while the other flattened on her lower back. Continuing to kiss her senseless, he pulled her even closer until she could feel him.

Oh.

She could really *feel* him. He was big as he pulsed against her.

More than big. Heat shot to her core and she surged upward, needing more of him.

He ripped his mouth away, breathing hard. "Naomi?" he whispered against her lips.

"Yes." Whatever the question was, the answer was the same. *Yes.*

"I was terrified last night," he confessed. "But you were so brave, so . . . collected that I was able to hold myself together. But today I couldn't. That bullet was so close. I could have lost you and I've just found you." He winced. "I didn't mean to say that yet."

That made her smile. *Yet.* "You heard what I said to my mother. I haven't felt this way for a long time. I don't know what's going to happen with us. You might decide that I'm not what you want or that I'm too much trouble. I'm not a young woman anymore—" He started to say something, but she pulled his head down for another short, hard kiss. "I'm not finished."

"Sorry," he mumbled.

She kissed him again, slower and sweeter. "What I was going to say was that I'm not a young woman anymore, but even when I was, I wasn't the sort to tease. I want to be with you for as long as this lasts. I intend to enjoy every moment we have together."

One side of his mouth lifted in a sly smile. "Every moment?"

"Well, not the ones where we're being shot at."

"Noted." He started to sway, dancing her backward. She thought they'd land on the bed, but at the last moment, he swept her up into his arms and lowered them into the chair where she'd spent a sleepless Monday night. He snuggled her into his lap.

She wriggled, getting comfortable. And maybe so that she could feel the evidence of his desire hard against her.

He groaned quietly again. "I'm really trying here."

She looked up at him, admiring the sharp planes of his face. The depth of his eyes. The way his hair fell onto his forehead, making him look boyish.

"Trying to do what?"

"To be a goddamned gentleman."

She glanced at the bed, only a few feet away. It had been a very long time since she'd been touched. Since she'd felt alive in that way. And something told her that Burke Broussard would get her there. "What if I don't want you to be a gentleman?" Because she didn't. She really, really didn't.

He pressed his forehead to hers. "Naomi."

It was a plea. Almost a prayer.

She touched his lips, grateful her mother had left her fingertips unbandaged. His lips were soft and a little swollen from their kisses. "Okay. I'll behave."

"I didn't say that," he said, a distinct whine in his voice.

She wound her arms around his neck. "Then kiss me again."

He did, diving in with a combination of gusto and skill that stole her breath. She kissed him back, enjoying the sensation of sitting in his lap, of necking with a handsome man who wanted her.

His hands roved, up and down her back, pausing at her breasts again and again. She made a frustrated noise and he chuckled, not breaking the kiss.

He was teasing her. It was nice that he could be lighthearted, but that wasn't what she wanted. Years of deprivation had crumbled away, leaving a raw yearning for more.

For him.

She grabbed his hand and moved it to her breast. He froze for a moment, his lips going still on hers. Then he was kissing her again, more ferociously. He kneaded her breast, awakening nerve endings that had been dormant for far too long.

Finally, he lifted his head, his pupils blown, his eyes hungry.

For me. I could have this. I could have him.

It was more than she'd ever expected.

"I want you," he whispered. "More than anyone ever."

More than her? she wanted to ask. *More than the girl you loved?* But she held the question back. He was no longer eighteen. He was forty-three and knew his own mind.

So she accepted his declaration at face value. "You make me want all kinds of things, Burke Broussard."

"I want to give you all kinds of things."

"But?" Because there had definitely been a "but" in there.

He lowered his hand from her breast and she immediately missed his touch. "But we have work to do. I have a few errands to run before I meet with Eleanor's neighbors tonight."

"Right." She blinked, bringing the present back into focus. "Teenagers in danger. People shooting at us. Our kids in hiding." She sighed. "But you have one big thing wrong."

He winced as if already anticipating her answer. "What's that?"

"It's not just you going to see Eleanor's neighbors. It's both of us. You're not leaving me behind."

It was his turn to sigh. "Not a surprise. You and your mom really weren't subtle about reminding me that you're capable of making up your own mind."

"Is that a problem?"

"That you know your own mind? Hell no. That someone could kill you next time? Yeah. That's a problem."

"They're shooting at you, too, Burke."

"I know, but—"

"No. I know I wasn't facing danger every day when I was a cop.

Not like you did. Not like most cops do. But I can take care of myself. I survived in the general population of a women's prison."

"I know," he said and she knew she had him.

"What time are we meeting the neighbors?"

"Eight thirty," he said, sounding put-upon.

"Okay. What about these errands?"

"I need to talk to Kaleb. Everyone here in the house knows about the shooting attempts, but he might not know. I've tried calling him to warn him, but he's not taking my calls."

"What about his wife?"

"She's not taking my calls, either. I'm worried. They're my family, Naomi. I need to be sure they're okay. That they're warned."

Burke was loyal and that wasn't as common as it should have been. It was part of what made him special. "Take Val, then."

"Okay. That's smart."

She slid off his lap and offered him a bandaged hand. "Come on. We've had our respite. Time to get back to it."

He gave her hand a pitying look. "You do look like you're wearing oven mitts."

"Mom went a little overboard."

"She loves you."

"I know," she said with all the love she felt for her mother. "She's the best. And she's at risk, too." She scowled. "When we catch Gaffney, I want five minutes with him. Trying to hurt my mother . . ."

He came to his feet and kissed her exposed fingertips. "I wouldn't want to be John Gaffney in those five minutes."

"Damn straight. Come on."

"Um, I can't. You go first. I'll join you in the study in a few minutes. I need to . . . well, get things under control."

Despite the gravity of their situation, she glanced at his groin before grinning up at him. "Yeah?"

"Yeah." He tapped the end of her nose. "You don't have to look so happy about it."

"I'm a thirty-six-year-old woman who was in prison for five years and married to an abusive creep before that. I've had a long dry spell. So, yes, I'm extremely happy about it."

He glanced over her shoulder at the bed. "You need to go. Right now."

She giggled, clamping her hand over her mouth to quell the foreign sound. "I'm going, I'm going."

20

Carrollton, New Orleans, Louisiana
WEDNESDAY, FEBRUARY 26, 6:15 P.M.

ARE YOU SURE you want to do this, Burke?" Val asked as she pulled their SUV into Jimmy Haywood's driveway.

"Yes." He hadn't told Naomi about this part of his errand. She'd accepted that her husband was abusive, that he'd lied about her on the witness stand, that he'd cheated on her, but the possibility that he might have fully participated in the frame job that sent her to prison had hurt her.

She'd had enough hurt for a lifetime.

"And if Jimmy confesses?" Val pressed. "What will you do?"

"I'll call André and tell him to come get the bastard. Why, what did you think I'd do?"

"I thought you'd punch him in the face. It's what I want to do."

Burke chuckled. "Well, I won't hit him. If I have to restrain him, I won't be gentle, but I won't full-out hit him."

"Okay, boss. Don't open your own door. For now, I'm your bodyguard."

"But—"

Val held up her forefinger. "If you're about to say 'But Naomi isn't here and won't know that I'm being stupid and not letting Val do her job,' you should stop. If you get yourself shot because you won't let me do *my damn job,* then *I* will hit you, Burke."

"But I'll be shot," he whined. "You can't hit me if I'm shot."

She laughed because dark humor was their way to blow off steam. "Stay put."

Burke obeyed, taking the few seconds to check his phone one more time.

Val opened his door, her hand on the gun in its holster. "Did they answer?"

"No." Neither Kaleb or Juliette had responded to his calls or texts.

"Maybe they're just busy."

Wishing he believed that, Burke allowed Val to shepherd him to Jimmy Haywood's front door.

He rapped on the door, but no one answered. So he rapped again.

"I'm not leaving, Mr. Haywood," he called. "This is important. It's about Everett."

The door opened, revealing an annoyed Jimmy Haywood. "What's wrong with Everett? Did you let him get hurt?"

"No, sir. But he continues to be in danger." Which was true. Until they took down Gaffney and his team, Everett would be a target. "May we come in?"

Jimmy gave Val an appraising look. "Who's she?"

"My associate, Miss Sorensen."

"Are you doing her, too?" Jimmy demanded, his eyes narrowed.

It took Burke a second. *Oh.* Jimmy had likely seen the photo online of Burke kissing Naomi. Burke thought he saw jealousy in the man's eyes.

If you hadn't been such a prick, you wouldn't have lost her.

"May we come in, Mr. Haywood?" Burke asked. "I don't think you'd appreciate your neighbors hearing your business."

"Fine. Come in."

The living room was ostentatious. Burke's home was filled with antiques, but it was warm and comfortable thanks to his mother. He wondered who had decorated this room. It was white and gold and looked like something from a magazine.

A pregnant woman entered. "The kids are down for their nap," she said before catching sight of Burke and Val. "Oh. Who have we here?"

This would be McKenzie, the new wife. She appeared to be about six months pregnant.

"Burke Broussard and my associate, Miss Sorensen."

"So nice to meet you. Please, come sit down." McKenzie gestured to the living room.

Wondering if the woman knew who he was, Burke complied, choosing a chair that was even more uncomfortable than it appeared. Val took her place behind him, earning her a curious stare from McKenzie.

"Are you clients of Jimmy's?"

"He's the PI," Jimmy said curtly. "The one who took Everett."

"Oh." McKenzie's tone went frosty. "Then I'll leave you all to your conversation."

"Don't go," Burke said. "We have questions for you, too, Mrs. Haywood."

The woman's pregnancy did give him pause. He didn't want to upset her, but then he remembered the scant inch between Naomi's head and the bullet hole in that pickup truck.

He'd get the information he'd come for.

"Winnifred Timms," he said.

McKenzie flinched and Jimmy inhaled sharply. Then he lied. "Never heard of her."

Luckily Val had asked Everett if he had any photos of McKenzie and Winnifred together. He didn't, but he did have the password to Haywood's home security system. It kept video for thirty days, during which Winnifred had visited three times.

Burke pulled up a still on his phone and showed it to the couple. "Does this jog your memory?"

"Oh. Winnie," McKenzie said with a little laugh. "I met her in school."

"Before or after you started your affair with Mr. Haywood?"

McKenzie's mouth pursed as if she'd sucked a lemon. "You're very rude."

"Miss Timms is trafficking teenagers for sex," Burke said flatly.

The shock on Jimmy's and McKenzie's faces appeared to be genuine.

"What?" McKenzie finally demanded. "No. You're wrong."

"We're not wrong. And we know that you two have been friends for quite some time."

McKenzie's hand splayed over her belly. "Are you insinuating I was involved in this . . . this sex trafficking thing?"

"I don't know yet. I do know that Jimmy took payment from the same company that paid Winnifred's university tuition. Paid off your house with it."

Jimmy went still. "What are you accusing us of?"

"Right now? That you took money for false testimony in Naomi's trial. You claimed, under oath, that you'd witnessed her taking illegal drugs, including cocaine."

"I did," Jimmy snapped.

"You know that there were no drugs," Burke said mildly. "You know that what the NOPD claimed she stole turned out to be ground-up Sheetrock."

Jimmy's jaw tightened. "Doesn't change that I saw her snorting cocaine."

"Well, I suppose the IRS will be interested in the money that you used to pay off your mortgage, the money you said came from the track. Do you have receipts from the track?"

"No," Jimmy said. "I lost them."

"Did you know that the people who gave you that money are snipping off loose ends, Mr. Haywood? They've silenced several people who knew about their operation."

"I know nothing about that," Jimmy insisted.

"Detective John Gaffney has had three of his people killed in the past week. As I said, he's snipping loose ends."

The mention of Gaffney had both McKenzie and Jimmy going a few shades paler.

"You're lying," Jimmy said unsteadily.

"I witnessed one of the murders myself." Burke hadn't mentioned that Winnifred was dead because he wasn't sure if the couple knew. If they didn't know, he'd save the revelation in case he needed more leverage. "The victim was shot right between the eyes. Dead before they hit the floor. Do you think Gaffney won't come after you? His operation is unraveling and he's getting desperate. You represent a paper trail."

He waited to see if the couple would speak, but they did not, so he kept going.

"You could be next." Both were beginning to fidget. "Mrs. Haywood, your friend's false testimony helped send Naomi Cranston to prison. She's shown that she's willing to frame someone with a lie. Do you think she won't throw you under the bus with the truth?"

McKenzie was swallowing convulsively, so Burke went in for the kill. "If Gaffney doesn't silence you, the cops will be coming for you. Do you want your children, the baby you carry, to be raised by strangers, Mrs. Haywood? Because that's what will happen when the police show that you were involved in Winnifred's business from the very beginning."

"I wasn't!" McKenzie cried. "I just wanted Naomi gone."

Jimmy closed his eyes. "McKenzie, shut up."

"No. I won't go to prison, Jimmy. I won't."

"He's lying," Jimmy insisted. "And he's not a cop. You don't have to tell him anything." He rose, his movements shaky. "Mr. Broussard, it's time you left. You've overstayed your welcome."

Burke didn't move from the chair. "Call a cop. I'll be happy to tell them what I know. You might not be arrested today, but it will happen. They'll find the trail from Winnifred—a known sex trafficker—to the company that paid her expenses, up to the parent company and back down to another subsidiary that paid off your mortgage. Did you think Gaffney was just being generous? He *wanted* the paper trail. It was his way of keeping you quiet should anyone come asking questions about your ex-wife's conviction. Now that we know about the trafficking—and Winnifred—the jig is up, and the only way for Gaffney to ensure your silence is to kill you."

"What do you want?" Jimmy asked, teeth clenched.

"First, I want you to sit down." Burke waited until Jimmy had done so. "Now I want to know what happened between you two and Winnifred Timms."

"I met her at college," McKenzie said, voice trembling.

"Who initiated contact?" Burke asked. "And when?"

"She did," McKenzie said. "It was in November, six years ago. She asked if we could study together."

"When did she suggest that Jimmy lie during the trial?" Because that was the way he figured it had gone.

"The week before Jimmy was supposed to testify. At first, we said no, because we aren't criminals."

"And then?"

"And then—" McKenzie started.

"Shut up," Jimmy hissed.

"No," she snapped back. "I'm not going to prison because of your fucking ex-wife."

"And *then*?" Burke repeated, ignoring Jimmy.

"She explained to *both* of us that her boss wanted Naomi to go away. That he didn't want her dead, just disgraced. That the fact that no one had uncovered actual drug use on her part would make the defense's job easier, but if Jimmy testified that he'd seen her do the drugs, that would ensure that she went to prison for *years*. Decades, even. Winnie told Jimmy that he wouldn't have to pay alimony if Naomi went to prison. And he wouldn't have to share custody."

Everett's custody didn't seem to matter as much to McKenzie as not having to pay alimony.

"So you lied," Burke said, proud that he kept the contempt from his voice.

"*I* didn't," McKenzie denied. "Jimmy did."

Jimmy glared at his pregnant wife. "You fucking whore. You want to send me to prison? I'll make sure you're destitute. You won't see a penny of my money." His hands had balled into fists and Burke had a bad feeling that Jimmy would be hitting McKenzie right now if he and Val weren't in the room.

"I'm not a cop," Burke reminded Jimmy, hoping to calm him down. "I'm just a PI looking to close a case."

Jimmy turned his fury on Burke. "For the woman you're fucking."

"Whoa." Burke held up his hands. "I assume you saw the photo online."

"He has a Google Alert set up for her name," McKenzie supplied bitterly. "Any news on Naomi comes to him right away."

Jimmy closed his eyes. "Shut. Up."

"I kissed her," Burke said. "I'm not ashamed of it. But anything else isn't your business, Mr. Haywood. You lost that right when you cheated on her. When you lied about her under oath. So put your fists away. They might work on your wives, but they won't work on me."

Jimmy's eyes opened and in them Burke saw defeat. Jimmy was a bully and once confronted by someone bigger, he backed down.

"You're not a cop anymore, but you were one. You'll go straight to them and tell them everything," Jimmy accused.

"They won't hear any of this from me. It's possible that they'll follow the money and end up on your doorstep, but it won't be because of my visit today."

Jimmy didn't look convinced. "Then why are you here?"

"Because Naomi was devastated when she learned that your new wife and Winnifred Timms were good friends. She thought that the two of you had been involved in setting her up to go to prison. At least I can tell her that yours was a crime of opportunity, not planning."

Jimmy swallowed. "Okay."

"And—" Burke started, but Jimmy interrupted with a snarl.

"Of course there's an 'and.' You're going to shake me down."

"No. But I do want you to give Naomi full custody. That's the price for my silence."

Jimmy glared at him. "No."

"Do it," McKenzie ordered. "He's sixteen, for God's sake. He'll only be home for another two years anyway."

Jimmy slowly turned to stare at her. "What? No. At least another six. He's got four years of college."

"Somewhere else," McKenzie snapped. "You've got a new family now. Our family. We're running out of room for our real kids. Everett's just taking up space and eating us out of house and home."

Jimmy's eyes widened, like he was seeing her for the first time. "Ev said you'd be happy that he was gone."

"Well, Ev is right. I'm not going to lose everything because you won't give him to your bitch ex-wife." She gave Burke a defiant look. "Tell Naomi that Jimmy agrees to give her full custody. It won't matter. Everett hates her."

Thanks to you two. "Okay. Our agreement is set. I'd like to know a few more things. Mrs. Haywood, did you ever meet Winnifred's boss? The one who wanted Naomi disgraced?"

Was it Gaffney or Cresswell?

"No. She lived with him. That's all I knew."

"Where?"

"She had a condo on Poydras."

The condo where Naomi had seen Winnifred with the older man. Amanda Cresswell had seen her husband there with Winnifred as well. "Do you remember which unit?"

"It was on the third floor. I don't remember the number."

"Okay. Any other residences that she mentioned?"

Like the place they were keeping teenagers?

"No. Just the condo."

"Did you ever go there?" Burke asked.

"Once. She wouldn't let me visit. Said the guy she lived with wouldn't like it. We stopped there once because she'd ruined her clothes and needed to change. But all the other times, she came here."

"Did you meet anyone else at the condo?" Burke pressed. "And let me remind you that Winnifred Timms is involved in trafficking teenagers for sex. And that, had his abductors been successful, Everett might have ended up in their clutches."

Jimmy blanched. "Oh my God."

McKenzie blinked, seeming to have forgotten that detail. "Oh, right. No, I didn't meet—" She cut herself off. "I met her boyfriend's assistant. Just for a second. He was furious that I was there, so I backed out of the room fast and waited by the front door. He yelled at Winnie about bringing a friend over, that she knew that wasn't allowed."

"Did you notice anything about him?"

"Not his face. He was so angry that I kept my head down. But I saw his clothes. He had good taste. Nice suit. Really nice shoes. He'd taken them off next to the front door." She made a face. "The condo had white carpet, so everyone took off their shoes. Winnie and I hadn't and he yelled at her about that, too."

Shoes, once again. Susan Snyder had mentioned that the big boss's assistant had really nice shoes. "Can you describe the shoes?"

"Italian leather. Brown. Looked hand stitched. Expensive. But I didn't know the brand. Sorry."

"No, that's very helpful."

McKenzie exhaled quietly. "We didn't know about the sex trafficking. We never would have gotten involved in that. Please believe us."

Burke just gave her a nod. He wasn't sure whether he believed her or not.

"If you want to catch Winnie, I can call her," McKenzie offered. "I can arrange a meeting. That way, if the police do follow the paper trail to us, you can tell them that we were helpful."

"That's very generous," Burke said, then came to his feet. "But not necessary."

Jimmy slowly rose, his chin lifting angrily. "All of this was a lie?"

"No, sir," Burke said quietly. "I told you that I'd witnessed one of Gaffney's people being killed. That was Winnifred."

McKenzie gasped. "Winnie's dead?"

"She is, ma'am. I'm sorry to be the one to tell you." Except Burke wasn't sorry at all, even when McKenzie began to wail her grief. "We'll see ourselves out."

The Quarter, New Orleans, Louisiana
WEDNESDAY, FEBRUARY 26, 6:20 P.M.

"Thanks, Mom." Naomi looked up from the printouts she'd been reviewing to take the ibuprofen her mother offered. "I'm fine," she said to the concerned faces watching her from where they sat in Burke's study. "I hit my head on that pickup truck and I have a headache. Tell them, Mom."

Molly, Antoine, and Lucien turned to Ruthanne.

"She just has a bump," Ruthanne confirmed. "But I suspect trying to read that small print isn't helping."

It was true. There were pages of the evidence Naomi had processed while working for the NOPD. Antoine had narrowed it down to the year before her arrest and to evidence relating to Gaffney and/or Cresswell, but there were still hundreds of items.

She glanced up at the new whiteboard, purchased by Molly, of course. The woman did like her whiteboards.

On it was the other reason for Naomi's headache. In the middle of the new board, written in giant all-caps with a red marker, was *WHY NAOMI?*

Molly was an incredibly focused woman. Naomi couldn't fault her, of course. It was an important question.

Wearily, she flipped to the next page in the stack. "There has to be a better way than this."

She sounded irritable and fractious, she knew. But this was an overwhelming task and she was worried about Burke. He'd headed off for his errands and they hadn't heard from him in over an hour. He was with Val, so Naomi knew he was as safe as he could be, but she still worried.

"Maybe we should take a break."

The words came from the back corner of Burke's study, where Phin's wife Cora sat in a chair with her feet propped on an ottoman and one of Antoine's laptops perched on her pregnant stomach. Phin had slid pillows behind her back and under her legs, but she still looked incredibly uncomfortable.

Cora struggled out of the chair and pressed her fists into her lower back. "I texted Phin for snacks. That might help with your headache, Naomi."

Grimacing, Cora leaned against the sofa where Naomi sat with her mother. "I'm fine, Antoine," she insisted before the man could ask. "The kid's kicking, that's all."

Naomi remembered those days. She also remembered that Jimmy had been so attentive during her pregnancy. The memory of his tender care had been tarnished by the knowledge that he'd manipulated the first pregnancy and tried to manipulate her into another.

She loved Everett. She loved being his mother. She might have even wanted another child at some point, but not because Jimmy had tricked her into it. That was the part that hurt.

She thought about his new wife, already on baby number three.

Which made her wonder about McKenzie's relationship with Winnifred Timms.

Nobody in this small group was talking about her, and they had deftly changed the subject when Naomi had asked.

Which made her wonder if talking to McKenzie had been one of Burke's errands.

Phin arrived then, his dog at his side. Phin carried a tray filled with all kinds of snacks, offering it first to Cora, who just shook her head and pointed to Naomi. "She needs it more than the rest of us."

Which made Naomi roll her eyes, although the food did help. Her headache lessened, but the pages of evidence still overwhelmed.

"We do need to find another way. I'm going to miss the one tree we're looking for in the forest of all this." Naomi pointed to the stack. "Maybe we can work on some of the other questions."

"No," Molly said apologetically. "This is one of the two things we keep dancing around. Why you?"

"What's the second thing?" Naomi asked, grasping at straws.

"Gaffney." Molly's expression was grim. "We never approached him with questions and now he's gone."

"What do you mean, he's gone?" Naomi asked, the headache regaining ground.

"André said they've checked his house," Molly said, "and all the places he might go after you talked to Susan in the hospital. He's disappeared."

Naomi took a brownie from the tray because chocolate really did help stress. She'd missed chocolate during her years in prison.

"What about anyone from PIB who Gaffney might have been paying?" she asked.

"I'm running financials on the PIB investigators," Antoine said.

"So far no one I've checked has any outward signs of being paid off, but I've still got several investigators to go. Cora's been cross-checking Cresswell's ledger against the crimes he's known to have committed."

"I've been able to eliminate about a third of the payments so far," Cora said. "I'm trying to narrow down the unknown payments so that we can link them to PIB payoffs once Antoine identifies any investigators who might be compromised."

"And I'm looking into the ST gang," Lucien said.

That got Naomi's attention. "The Delgado brothers were part of that gang. They left to start working for Gaffney. And possibly Cresswell, too. I was wondering yesterday if they'd really left, because historically that's not been easy to do. Are you looking at Gaffney working with them to distribute?"

Lucien looked impressed. "I am. Cresswell was making a lot of money on the side, if his lifestyle was any indication. He told his wife that he'd won money at the track, but a win big enough to buy that house they used to own in the Garden District would have made some kind of news. Just thinking about his lifestyle—and the amount he was paying out every month according to his ledger—that's more money than he should have been able to make just selling drugs they skimmed from drug busts. I know a few guys who used to be in the gang from when I was a prosecutor. They turned state's evidence to get a plea deal. I've got messages out to them. They never gave up Cresswell or Gaffney, but to my knowledge, we never asked that question. This could be a lot bigger than the simple reselling of a few kilos of coke here and there."

"Not only cocaine," Naomi said. "We processed meth and ketamine and all kinds of pills that Gaffney could have stolen and sold."

"Which brings us back to my question," Molly said, pointing to the whiteboard. "What did you process that made you a target?"

Naomi wanted to groan. "Why are you so sure of this? And why is it so important?"

"Because framing you was a big deal," Molly said promptly. "And an expensive deal. Killing you would have been so much easier."

Ruthanne gave Naomi a smug look. "See? I told you."

Molly looked amused. "So the question is still, why you?"

"Fine." Naomi picked up the stack, then put it down. "I'm having trouble focusing on this. My brain is spinning too fast."

"I know that feeling," Cora said, patting Naomi's shoulder. "Let's go about this a different way. Did any evidence you processed ever go missing?"

"Sometimes, yes. I did a self-audit right before I got arrested. I discovered several things that were missing, but I found them. They'd just been stored in a different place than was listed in the database."

Molly's eyes narrowed. "You didn't mention the audits before."

Naomi had to fight the urge to shrink back. "I did self-audits all the time. It wasn't an isolated event."

"Back off, Molly," Ruthanne snapped. "You sound like you're accusing my daughter of holding back information on purpose."

Naomi gave her mother a grateful look. *I love you, Mom.*

Molly looked contrite. "I'm sorry. I didn't mean to sound accusing. I'm just surprised. Tell me about the audits, especially that last one."

That whole period was fuzzy, the week before her arrest.

Cora slid her hand around the back of Naomi's neck, squeezing lightly. "Breathe, hon."

Naomi realized she'd started to hyperventilate. She exhaled, then filled her lungs. "Okay. We were supposed to do formal audits annually. Those were done with varying degrees of frequency and thoroughness, so when I had free time, I did my own audits of the items I'd processed. There'd been an issue with the court calling up some evidence that had gone missing—processed by someone else. Big brouhaha ensued. Cops in the evidence room were investigated. So I wanted to make sure my items were where the BEAST said they should be."

"The beast?" Cora asked.

"That's the acronym for our database system: Bar-coded Evidence Analysis Statistical Tracking." Naomi rattled off the words that were forever stored in her mind. "There were some missing items, but most of them we found in the wrong bins, like I said." She forced herself to relive those final days of being in uniform. "I've blocked a lot of this out."

Her mother leaned her head on Naomi's shoulder, a comforting presence. "I'm not surprised."

"What kinds of things were missing?" Cora asked.

"A few handguns. Some jewelry that had been part of a department store theft. There was an old candlestick that was used to murder someone. It was an antique, solid silver." *Oh. Silver.* A detail clicked in her mind. "There was also a ring."

"What made it special?" Cora asked.

"It was beautiful. I remember the way it caught the light. A man's ring." She forced herself to think through each step of that day. Because the ring was the type of item that Molly had been searching for. "It came in a week before I did my last audit before my arrest. Some guy met me at the door as I was leaving for the day. He'd been waiting for someone to come out to give it to. Said he'd found it at the scene of a crime."

"That's not suspicious," Molly muttered. "What happened then?"

"It wasn't suspicious," Naomi said. "Not like you're thinking, anyway. He was a young guy. College age. CSI wannabe. We got those sometimes. Usually they called us on the phone, saying they'd seen something or found something. Usually they were asking if there was a reward. We referred those calls to the right department."

"But this guy came in person," Cora murmured. It was a soothing sound. Her hand on Naomi's neck was soothing as well. "He brought you the ring."

"He did. Told me where he'd found it. I recognized the address—the body of a known drug dealer had been found there the week before. I immediately called one of the detectives I knew to come and get it."

"Which detective did you call?" Molly asked.

"Not Gaffney, thank goodness," Naomi said. "I called Walt Edwards. He was Homicide. He'd been one of my instructors at the academy and we'd kept in touch." Sadness washed over her in a wave. "He died while I was waiting for my trial. Heart attack. Anyway, I escorted the guy who'd found the ring into the lobby of the evidence warehouse and waited until Walt got there. I had to maintain the chain of custody, so I didn't let the ring or the CSI wannabe out of my sight until Walt arrived. He took the ring and gave the CSI wannabe a receipt. He brought it back a day later and I processed it into the system."

"When was this?" Antoine asked from Burke's desk. "And where was the ring found?"

"About two weeks before I got arrested. One week before I did the audit. I checked the location of the crime scene where he said he'd found it. Down off Tchoupitoulas, near Napoleon. Like I said, the body of a known drug dealer had been found there the week before."

Antoine tapped the keys of the laptop in front of him. "Jeffrey Stacey. He was a known member of the ST gang."

"Like the Delgados." Naomi felt a flutter of excitement in her chest. That was a connection, and connections were good. "Like I said, I processed the ring, then stored it, but when I did my own audit, the ring wasn't in its bin. I told my supervisor and we all looked for it. One of the others found it and put it back, but when I double-checked on my next shift, it wasn't the same ring. I told my supervisor that if we couldn't find it I'd request a formal audit, as that was evidence tied to a homicide. My boss set everyone to looking again. The correct ring was found the next day and stored. I figured that was that. And then, a week later, I stopped to help Winnifred Timms, whose car was broken down on the side of the road."

"I wonder if that ring is still there," Molly said. "I'm betting it's not."

"Sucker bet," Lucien murmured. "What did it look like, Naomi?"

"It was silver, a fancy pattern. I think it's called filigree? It was definitely a man's ring."

"What happened with that case, Antoine?" Cora asked.

"Went cold, according to NOPD's records. And there's no ring listed among the evidence items linked to the case."

Molly went to the whiteboard and, underneath the *WHY NAOMI?*, wrote *MISSING RING.*

Lucien held up a hand. "Add that Naomi threatened to request a formal audit."

"Good point," Molly said and added that to the board. "We could be looking at either the threat of an audit or the ring itself or both. That the ring wasn't among the evidence linked to the case makes me think both."

"I agree," Lucien said grimly. "What evidence was collected from the scene, Antoine?"

"The dealer's wallet, emptied. No drugs. His gun was found underneath his body. He was holding a broken silver chain in his hand. He was shot in the gut and then once in the head. I guess they wanted to be sure he was dead. Where did the college kid say he found the ring, Naomi?"

"In a storm gutter, stuck in some trash."

"Fancy filigree," Cora said. "Can you think of specifics?"

Naomi closed her eyes and tried to visualize the ring but drew a blank. "There was a pattern in the silver, but I can't remember what it was. Sorry."

"Don't be," Molly said. "I think we've found the case we need to research. You called Homicide, but I wonder if they called Gaffney, since it was a dealer who got killed."

"They did," Antoine said, "but Homicide held on to the case. Here's something interesting. The homicide detective noted that word on the street was that the dealer had been transporting a big shipment from one of the cartels to the STs. The gang was not pleased when the shipment went missing."

"Send me any information you can find on that case," Molly requested. "I'll see what more I can dig up. This is a good lead, Naomi. Go get some rest."

That sounded like a really good idea. Naomi needed to be awake when she met with Eleanor's neighbors later.

21

Uptown, New Orleans, Louisiana
WEDNESDAY, FEBRUARY 26, 7:10 P.M.

VAL LOOKED AROUND admiringly as they approached Kaleb and Juliette's house. "This is a nice neighborhood, Burke."

Burke grunted his agreement. It was a nice neighborhood. Quiet and well kept. But he didn't care about that today. He was too worried about what they'd find at Kaleb's house.

After a lot of pondering, he'd texted his godsons. Yes, he'd promised to keep his distance, especially from the kids. But even the boys weren't answering his messages and he was becoming frantic with worry.

"They've only lived here for a few years. They used to live in Metairie, near the factory. I actually liked that place better. It was homier."

"Why'd they move down here, then?"

"Kaleb wanted a place 'befitting a CEO.' Juliette wasn't happy about leaving the old house. The boys had always gone to private school up there and she didn't want them to change. So she does the drive every day."

"Brutal, especially this time of year."

"It really is. But once his father passed and Kaleb became the CEO, he said he needed to be able to entertain customers. Which he does. Juliette throws amazing parties. I don't know if I'll be welcome at those anymore."

Val sucked in a startled breath. "You own the company!"

"But Kaleb runs it and he resents me not being more involved. He thinks I've made choices that put him and his family in danger. And he's not wrong."

"Burke."

He glanced away from the passing houses to her profile. "What?"

"I . . ." She swallowed. "If you did, then so did I. So did Molly. And Lucien. And André, even. He and Farrah are going to be parents and he's an NOPD captain. Of all of us, he's made the most enemies."

"Don't tell him that, please. He's enjoying the anticipation of fatherhood."

"I won't. You know I won't."

"But?"

"You remember when Elijah was in danger and Kaj was second-guessing being a prosecutor?"

"I have a vague recollection of the case, yes," Burke said dryly.

She pulled the SUV to the curb, a few houses away from Kaleb's house, and turned to face him. "Phin told Kaj the story of how a criminal had come after his family because his father was a cop. They were fine, but his father was thinking of quitting. His mother told him that situations like theirs—like ours—are like the one plane that crashes out of thousands of safe flights. That's how I'm going to choose to look at this week. And Jace is still a million times safer with me than he was with his brothers."

Jace's brothers had emotionally and physically abused him for his whole life.

"I agree with you. And so did Kaleb, the first time his boys were threatened, back when I was trying to leave the force. This time was the straw that broke the camel's back."

"That sucks. I'm sorry." She started to drive again, but Burke stopped her.

"If I just waltz up and knock and they're fine, I will have broken my word to Kaleb. If the boys see me, they won't want me to leave. And I won't want to, either." The thought of being so close and not seeing them hurt.

Her eyes softened. "Do you want me to knock on the door?"

"Would you?"

"Of course. You stay here and keep your head down."

"Just . . . hurry, okay? Call me if anything's wrong. I'll come running, but only if you call."

"Okay, boss."

Two minutes passed without a call from Val, then five. Then ten.

Burke had his hand on the door handle, ready to get out and check for himself, when he saw Val and Juliette walking quickly toward him.

Val opened the driver's door and Juliette got in. Val leaned her head in. "I'm going back up to the house so that the boys aren't alone. You two chat. Call if you need me."

"Wait!" Burke called. "Why are the boys alone? Where is the protection Kaleb hired?"

"When nothing happened yesterday, he sent the man away," Juliette said, her eyes cast down. "Thank you for watching over them, Val."

"You betcha." Val jogged back to the Marchands' house.

"I've always liked Val," Juliette said. "She's got a good head on her shoulders. And a good heart."

She sounded so sad.

"Juliette?"

"I'm sorry you were scared for us. I wasn't getting any of your calls. It seems that Kaleb blocked you on my phone."

"He did what?"

She nodded miserably. "He got into my phone and blocked your number. On the boys' phones, too. I checked before I came down here. The boys are livid."

"I bet they are," Burke murmured, stunned. "Why would Kaleb do that?"

"He really doesn't want you talking to us," Juliette said. "I thought this would blow over, but he's dug in his heels. I'm sorry, Burke."

"Not your fault," Burke said, his heart aching at the rejection. "He shouldn't have made that choice for you."

"No, he shouldn't have. It's also not the first time he's done something like this. He's searched my phone before. I've seen him do it."

Burke stared. "But why?"

"At the time, I didn't know. I . . . didn't confront him over it. But now I get it. He wanted to find out what I suspected because he's been having an affair with a much younger woman."

"No." He couldn't believe it about Kaleb. He'd known the man for thirty years and Juliette for nearly that long. She and Kaleb had been high school sweethearts. "I mean, I believe you, but . . ."

Her laugh was bitter. "I was stunned, too. But I saw them together."

Burke winced. "Together together?"

"No, but enough that it was clear they were lovers. She makes sales calls to Kaleb. He closes the door and they're alone. Sometimes for hours."

"Dammit, Jules. But that doesn't mean—"

"I hired a PI," she blurted out.

Burke wondered when the bombs would stop dropping. "What?"

"I hired a PI," she repeated. "He followed Kaleb around. And he took photos of the two of them, Kaleb and . . . her. He goes to her place nearly every day." She covered her face with her hands, sobs shaking her shoulders. "I don't know what to do."

Burke took one of her hands and held it tightly. "What do you want to do?"

"I don't know. I should want to leave him. I do want to leave him. But I think about the boys and I don't know what to do. I finally confronted him, but he denied it."

"When did you confront him?"

"Yesterday. We were fighting and it just came out."

Burke found himself wincing once again. "Fighting about me?"

"Only partly, so don't you blame yourself, Burke Broussard. None of this is on you. It's squarely on Kaleb. I . . . didn't tell him about the PI. I couldn't."

"Why didn't you ask me to help you?"

"I didn't want to put you in the middle. You're Kaleb's family. It didn't seem fair to drag you into it. But here we are."

"What else were you fighting about?" Burke asked, remembering Naomi telling him that nobody knew exactly what was happening in another couple's marriage.

She'd been so right. Burke hadn't seen this coming.

"His business trip. When I called to tell him about what happened—what *nearly* happened—to the boys, he was furious. And then I heard a woman asking him if he was all right. He was in his hotel room, so she was there, too."

Burke was terrified he'd say the wrong thing, but he had to try.

"Maybe it was a coworker and they were having a meeting in

Kaleb's suite. He always stays in the fancy places with boardroom tables and stocked bars. Maybe they were having a late-night meeting."

"I heard jazz music, Burke. I don't think he left the city."

"Dammit, Jules. What can I do to help you?"

She squared her shoulders. "When you've solved this case and everything quiets down, can you find out where he was this week? The PI never saw him kissing the woman, just hanging out all the time. Just Kaleb going to her apartment and staying until the wee hours of the morning. Which should be enough, I know, but I guess I need a smoking gun before I file for divorce. I need to know for sure."

"Okay. I'll also call the security company and get someone to cover your house until this is all over. I won't be able to think if I'm worrying about you being unprotected."

"Thank you. Can you call Val now? I think I've dumped enough on you for one afternoon. I know you're worried about whoever tried to grab Jace and Harper."

And Everett, Burke thought. He called Val and she was back at the SUV in less than a minute.

"I wish I could do more, Jules," he said. "I wish I could fix this for you."

"I know. You're a good man, Burke." She forced a smile. "Once I get through this, I'll get back to finding you a wife."

"Don't," he said, unable to stop his own smile.

"Did you meet someone?"

He thought of Naomi, of the kisses they'd shared. Of all the other things he wanted to share with her. "I did. I'll tell you all about her soon. She's a good person. You'll like her."

"I'm so glad. At least there's one piece of good news."

She got out of the SUV and Val walked her back to her house.

Burke texted Antoine. *Need a favor. Utmost discretion. Only you to see search results.*

Name it, was Antoine's reply.

When you get a break in the next few days, can you check flight manifests for Kaleb Marchand? He was supposed to have flown to Chicago on Monday morning.

Why?

He may be cheating on Juliette. So mention this to no one.

On it.

Burke hoped he was doing the right thing. If Kaleb found out, their relationship might be destroyed beyond repair, if it wasn't already.

He couldn't believe Kaleb had dismissed the bodyguard. That did not sound like his friend.

Maybe something was wrong with Kaleb. *A brain tumor or something.* Anything to explain this behavior away.

He called the first of the two protection companies he'd recommended to Kaleb. "Hey, Doug, did you get a call from a Mr. Marchand about protection? I recommended you to him. It would have been Monday."

Doug Burnham hesitated. "You know I can't tell you that, Burke. As much as I like you—and you know I do—I can't divulge a client's business."

"I know and I wouldn't ask if it weren't important. His house is unprotected right now and his sons are my godsons. I'm trying to figure out what to do about it."

"Well, you should call the other name on your list," Doug said kindly.

"Thank you. I'm sorry to have asked."

"No worries."

Burke stared at his phone for a moment before repeating the call to the other protection company.

The result was the same.

Kaleb hadn't called either of the companies Burke had recommended. Was Kaleb that angry with him? Did he really want nothing to do with him at all?

Who had he called instead?

He texted Lucien. ***Need your help. Can you do a few days at the Marchand house? Their protection didn't work out. But you'll need to stay out of sight of Kaleb.***

The three dots cycled for a long minute.

Why?

Burke sighed. ***Never mind.***

His phone buzzed with an incoming call from Lucien and he hit accept. "Hey."

"Burke, look. I know you're going crazy with this case right now. As long as Harrison and Molly hang around the house for Harper and the others, I can do the detail. I don't mind. But I don't like not knowing why I'm avoiding the homeowner."

"He's been acting strangely. That's all I feel okay sharing."

"Fair enough. I'll be over there as soon as I can."

"Thank you, Lucien."

Burke ended the call as Val got into the SUV. "Miss me?" she asked, her cheer forced.

"Always," he assured her. "Best get us back to the Quarter. You and I have to pick up Eleanor and take her to see her neighbors, and we're tight on time." They were meeting at eight thirty at the athletic center where the QuarterMasters played. "The Druid parade's probably only halfway done and Alta follows on its heels, so you should take the long way around."

"I hate Mardi Gras," she muttered.

Normally Burke would disagree. This was his favorite time of year in the best city on earth. But this year, his heart was full of fear and sadness.

Except Naomi was waiting for him at home. That lifted some of the sadness. The fear, however, remained.

The Quarter, New Orleans, Louisiana
WEDNESDAY, FEBRUARY 26, 7:15 P.M.

It was a dream. Naomi knew it was a dream because the door to her cell was wide open and there were no guards around. She wanted to stay where she was but she heard the screaming. It chilled her to the bone.

She was moving through the prison corridors, though she didn't want to be. She was looking, though she dreaded what she'd see.

Bodies. Everywhere. They lay on the floor in pools of blood. Rivers of blood. Her feet splashed in it as she walked. She looked for Nessa, for the women she'd known inside. But the bodies weren't adults.

They were teenagers. Teenagers whose faces were covered in blood as they reached out to her, screaming their terror and their pain. She wanted to scream, too.

But she didn't. She kept walking.

Until she saw a face she immediately recognized.

Everett.

He did not reach for her. He did not scream. He lay in the river of blood and did nothing at all. He was dead.

Her son was dead.

She began to scream then, but there was no one to hear. No one to help. She screamed and screamed and—

Naomi. Naomi. Naomi.

"Mom!"

She opened her eyes to find hands on her shoulders, shaking her awake. She stared up into Everett's face. He stared back, his eyes wide with alarm.

"You're not dead," she gasped out.

He was breathing hard, his hands trembling on her shoulders. "No. I'm not."

She sagged into the chair where she'd fallen asleep. Burke's duct-taped BarcaLounger. She'd sat down for a short rest and must have been more tired than she'd thought.

The chair smelled like Burke. Like his aftershave. That same scent had soothed her panic attack at the prison the day before. She drew in a deep breath, letting his scent fill her lungs.

Everett let go of her shoulders and straightened, but he continued to stare. He was genuinely shaken. "You were screaming."

"Bad dream."

"Must have been. Are you all right now? Do you need anything? Water?"

She smiled weakly. It was the first time he'd been anything but dismissive to her in years. Since her arrest.

His concern? It was everything. "Water would be nice."

He nodded once and went to the kitchen. She glanced up to see Jace, Elijah, Ruthanne, and James all watching her from the stairs. Molly and Lucien stood behind them. Apparently, they'd followed Everett down when she'd screamed.

Molly stood at the bottom of the stairs, holding them back. She gave Naomi a tight nod. "I couldn't stop Everett from running downstairs. You gave us a scare."

"I'm sorry," she said, embarrassed, but Jace gave her a little smile and a thumbs-up.

He'd said Everett would come around. She prayed he was right.

She drained the glass of water her son brought her. "Thank you."

He perched on the edge of the closest sofa. "What did you dream?"

She didn't want to tell him. Didn't want that image in his head. But she didn't want to lie, either. "I dreamed of the kids that are trapped in that house. The teenagers that Gaffney and his people are trafficking."

He swallowed. "That could have been me, huh?"

Her eyes filled with tears. "Over my dead body."

He winced. "Don't say that. Please."

"I won't let them touch you."

He hesitated, then sighed. "You went to prison to keep me safe."

Her throat caught. "I did. I didn't know where else to turn. What else to do."

He looked away. "Thank you," he whispered. "I'm still angry that you did it, but I understand why you did."

"That's fair," she whispered back.

"Gaffney needs to pay for what he did to you and what he's still doing to those other kids."

"And we're going to make that happen. Just you wait and see."

He looked over his shoulder. Everyone who'd gathered on the stairs had made themselves scarce. "Did they give you a bulletproof vest?"

"They did."

"Wear it, please."

"I will."

He went back upstairs and Naomi slumped into the chair.

Please, God. Let my son love me again.

It was almost too much to hope for, but she did anyway.

Gentilly, New Orleans, Louisiana
WEDNESDAY, FEBRUARY 26, 8:25 P.M.

"You shouldn't be here," Burke grumbled.

Naomi ignored him, studying the small track where the women's roller derby was playing their exhibition game. It was fascinating.

Burke didn't think it was safe for Naomi to leave the house. Naomi had, once again, reminded him that he was as big a target as she was. Bigger, because he was so much taller.

He'd begged Ruthanne to forbid Naomi to go with him.

Naomi's mother had laughed at him.

So, here they were—Eleanor, Naomi, Val, and Burke walking down a hallway to a meeting room.

Eleanor's neighbors had already gathered—three married couples. They hugged Eleanor hello. They were clearly close-knit.

Eleanor lifted a hand once everyone was seated. "We should make this short. Burke is nervous that Naomi is not in his house wrapped in bubble wrap."

Burke scowled at her, too. "You're not helping, Eleanor."

"I'm Team Naomi." Eleanor turned to her neighbors. "I told you all on the phone last night that the Delgados were involved in sex trafficking teenagers. These people here are trying to stop them. So if you can tell them anything, you'll be doing good."

An older man cleared his throat. His name was Zachary and he seemed to be the spokesperson for the group. "None of us wanted the Delgados in our neighborhood. They turned our lives upside down." He opened the folder he'd placed on the table in front of him. "These are stills I took from my security cameras. I'm happy to upload the corresponding recordings to your cloud account. We all brought stills and figured you could tell us if they showed you anything new. That way you could ask for the footage you wanted."

"That's amazing," Burke said, spreading the stills across the table so that everyone could see. He pointed to the first photo. "Her name is Elaine Billings. She was arrested this afternoon. She's a social worker. She drugged kids who no one would miss and held them captive."

"I hope she burns in hell," Zachary's wife spat.

Murmurs of agreement went around the table.

"And this," Naomi said, pointing to another photo, "is Winnifred Timms. She apparently handled the money. She was murdered last night."

"Shot in the head," Eleanor added. "Right in front of Burke and Naomi."

"Glad she's gone from this earth," a woman named Seema said. "I saw both those women going in and out of the Delgados' house. Elaine more than Winnifred. Elaine would be in and out a few times a week. Winnifred visited maybe once a week or once every two weeks. We had no idea what was happening in that house. We would have reported it. And those poor girls who died in the fire along with the Delgados." Her eyes filled. "It's heartbreaking."

"I know," Naomi said quietly. "We're going to do our best to save the others."

Because who knew what Gaffney, his "boss," and the assistant with the nice shoes would do to their captives now that she and Burke and the team were closing in? They'd killed their own people with what appeared to be ruthless ease.

She hoped they didn't find a house filled with more victims. She tried to stay positive and focused, but the nightmare had shaken her.

Blood and bodies everywhere. Teenagers. They were just teenagers.

And Everett had been one of those bodies in the nightmare, his face the only one that was clear. The only one she'd remembered when she'd woken up.

She needed to make sure that the nightmare never came true.

She began sorting the photos, putting all the stills of Elaine and Winnifred into separate piles. The next still was of a young Latina woman, her arms filled with folded clothes as she walked into the Delgados' house.

"Maya?" she said to Burke. "The woman Susan said took care of them in the house?"

"I'd say yes, but we should ask Susan to take a look at that picture tomorrow." He sorted a few more stills, then whistled. "This is new."

It was a photo of two men. Both wore suits and fedoras. The suits appeared to be expensive. The fedoras hid their faces. One of the men was about six feet tall and burly, the other a few inches shorter and lean. The boss and the assistant?

Naomi leaned in closer and nodded. "His shoes." The shorter man wore brown loafers which, even with the photo's low resolution, appeared to be made of soft leather. "Do you think we can get a clearer image of the shoes?"

"Antoine may be able to." He looked up at Eleanor's neighbors. "We want any footage you can provide, but we definitely want this one." He tapped the photo of the two men. "Whose security system captured him?"

The husband and wife of the third couple raised their hands. Eleanor had introduced them as RJ and Irma. "That would be ours," RJ said.

"Excellent," Burke said. "The shorter one has been mentioned to us twice already."

Naomi was startled. "Twice? It was only Susan. What do you know?"

He winced.

Val sighed. "You didn't tell her?"

Naomi narrowed her eyes. "Tell me what?"

"We went to see Jimmy and McKenzie today," Burke admitted.

"Her ex," Eleanor explained to her friends. "And his new wife."

"And?" Naomi prompted.

Burke's brows rose. "You don't seem surprised."

"I figured that's where you'd gone. None of your people would talk about McKenzie. They kept changing the subject. They're not subtle. What did Jimmy and McKenzie say?"

"Well, they did take money for testifying against you," he began, only to have Eleanor's neighbors erupt into angry chatter. Burke raised his hands placatingly. "Her ex is scum. You are correct about that. He was greedy and opportunistic, but he didn't plan to frame you, Naomi. Anyway, McKenzie said she visited Winnifred's condo one time and saw this guy." He tapped the shorter man in the photo. "She commented on his shoes."

Irma's brows lifted. "Those must be some shoes."

"I hope they're unique enough to be a decent lead," Burke said. He continued sorting the remaining photos, then stopped again. "Who is this?"

There were two men getting out of an Escalade with very shiny hubcaps. They'd made no attempt to cover their faces.

"Punks," Zachary said with a sniff.

"How often did they come?" Burke asked.

"Once a week," Zachary said. "You know them?"

"No," Burke said.

"Yes," Naomi said. Burke and Val stared at her.

"How?" Burke asked.

"While you were doing your *errands*," Naomi said, "Lucien said that he thought Gaffney might be working with the gang the Delgados supposedly walked away from. Antoine did a search on the gang after our work session and this guy is the leader. His name is Desi Ortiz."

The neighbors murmured among themselves, agitated.

"We've seen him, too," Seema said, and her husband nodded. "They come by once a week. On Sunday mornings."

"We knew they were drug dealers," her husband said. "We even called the police on them, but no one came."

"They were there when that little boy was shot," Irma said. "We told the cops that, too."

Burke sighed. "I'll pass that on to my NOPD contact. He's a good cop. He'll find out why no one responded."

"After calling three times we gave up," Seema said, her voice trembling with anger. "NOPD didn't care about us."

"That's when we got together as a community to try to get rid of the brothers," Zachary said. "But then Maisie Richardson—our leader—was killed when they burned her house down, so we backed off."

"André should be able to find these guys," Burke said.

"If André can't," Naomi said, "Antoine can."

The remaining photos were either repeats or too blurry, so Naomi and Burke thanked the neighbors, gave them email addresses to send the footage to, gathered all the stills, and let Eleanor bid her friends goodbye.

It had been a very long day and they still had a lot of work to do.

The Quarter, New Orleans, Louisiana
WEDNESDAY, FEBRUARY 26, 9:45 P.M.

"I found your shoes," Antoine said as Burke walked Naomi into his study, his hand at the small of her back.

All Burke wanted was to take her to his bedroom and continue what they'd started that afternoon, but his team was assembled and they appeared to have been working for hours.

Molly's second whiteboard was now filled with names and photos of PIB investigators and photos of men's wedding rings. Naomi had told Burke about the ring epiphany on their way to meet Eleanor's neighbors.

How they'd find the ring, and its significance, were still unknown.

"You got the shoes based off that photo I sent you?" Burke marveled. "I'm impressed, Antoine."

Molly and Cora were picking up papers from the love seat, making room for Naomi and Burke. Val took the papers from Cora's hands and shooed her away.

"Sit. You're pregnant. I'll do this."

Cora sighed. "Fine."

Burke smiled at her fondly. "They've worn you down about resting, haven't they?"

Cora nodded. "Yep. Tell us everything."

"I want to hear about the shoes first," Burke said. "Antoine?"

"I was able to get enough detail from the still to do an image search. Found it on the website of a custom shoemaker here in the Quarter. They're two-thousand-dollar shoes."

"Are they gold?" Burke demanded.

"Two thousand isn't that expensive for custom shoes," Naomi said. "One of the women on my cellblock got busted for selling counterfeit shoes for fifty bucks. She said the originals went for four or five grand."

"Wow." Antoine shook his head. "The shoemaker shop is called Hedden's, and it's open tomorrow. I'll try to break into their server, but I'll have a better chance in the morning if they open an email from me with a phishing link."

"La la la," Burke sang. "I don't want to know."

"Like what's in hot dogs," Val said to Naomi. "We don't ask."

Naomi laughed, and Burke's lips curved. She had a lovely laugh.

Sitting on the arm of the love seat next to him, Val snorted. "You're grinning like the Cheshire Cat, Burke."

"You really are," Molly said. "It's kind of cute. Let's get through this because Val's been on duty all day. She needs to sleep. And yes, Burke, I had a nice nap while you were gone. I'm good to go for the night. Val, Harrison, and I are going to overlap coverage, with two of us being on at all times. I'll show you the schedule. But we can't maintain this level of security for too much longer, especially with Lucien being assigned to your godsons. Either we solve this thing, or we'll need to bring in more people."

"Understood," Burke said grimly, wishing he knew why the hell Kaleb had dismissed the protection for Juliette and the boys.

Maybe it is *a brain tumor.* Because the Kaleb he knew would never leave his family unprotected.

"I found three PIB investigators who are living beyond their means," Cora said proudly. "Well, Antoine helped."

"Only with the first one," Antoine said. "You're a fast learner."

Naomi was watching Antoine. "Antoine, when do *you* sleep?"

"He catnaps," Molly said. "We've been telling him for years that he needs better sleep habits, but he does not listen."

Antoine's smile was wan. "I'm a stubborn cuss."

Few knew it, but Antoine had developed PTSD in the army, just as Phin had. Phin had anxiety attacks and Antoine struggled with endless, sleepless nights because of his nightmares.

The woman who'd trained Phin's service dog was training one for Antoine as well, but it would be another six months before the dog was ready. Antoine hadn't mentioned it to the team, so Burke hadn't, either. But there was hope for Antoine on the horizon.

Burke thought Naomi would ask Antoine more questions, but she didn't, and he felt a rush of affection for her for respecting Antoine's privacy.

"Who are the PIB investigators?" she asked instead.

Cora rattled off their names. "We got into the bank account of one of them, and he gets monthly deposits that match the dates and amounts in Cresswell's ledger. So that explains how he and Gaffney skated all this time. The fix was in from the get-go."

Damn. Burke would have sworn those cops were honest as the day was long.

He was starting to feel like he'd lost his touch. He hadn't noticed any stress in Kaleb and Juliette's marriage, either.

"You're not a superman, Burke," Naomi murmured. "No one's

caught them all this time for a reason. They've probably learned by investigating all the other dirty cops."

"You have a point," he admitted, feeling marginally better. "What about the rings?"

"We did some searches, Molly and I," Cora said. "We figure that none of the rings we found will be the ring you saw in the evidence room, but you can tell us if we're hot or cold. Then we'll go back and look for more rings until we find the design you remember."

"I might have a shortcut to that," Antoine said. "Another person who saw that ring is the guy who found it. I went back into the BEAST system and found your notes, Naomi. You entered his name and phone number, and I contacted him."

Naomi grinned. "That was smart of us—'past' me and 'present' you."

Antoine grinned back. "It was. Like I said, I contacted him. Told him I was a PI looking for input on a cold case. We'll see if he bites."

"You think he'll remember the ring design after all this time?" Val asked.

"I think he'll still have a photo of it," Naomi said. "He'd be in his late twenties by now, but then he was a fresh-faced college kid who really wanted to be a detective. I bet he's told the story to every girl he's taken on a date."

Burke chuckled. "I bet you're right." Then he startled when his phone buzzed. "It's André." He hit accept and lifted the phone to his ear. "Hey. I've got my team here. Should I put you on speaker?"

"Yeah," André said with a sigh. "Might as well only say it once."

That sounded upbeat. *Not.*

Burke put the phone on speaker and turned up the volume. "It's Antoine, Val, Molly, Cora, and Naomi."

"Cora?" André said warmly. "You're joining the team?"

"I'm on maternity leave and bored out of my mind," Cora said. "I have a feeling I'll be too busy taking care of a baby to join the team past this week."

"Good. Can't wait to meet the newest Burkette."

Burke groaned. "For the love of all that's holy, let it go."

"Joy, our office admin you met on Monday?" Val said to Naomi. "She coined the term. Burke and the Burkettes. I think we're fabulous."

Naomi pursed her lips, trying not to smile, but it was no use. She giggled. Burke would make himself get used to the stupid name if it would make her laugh like that.

"Best rock band name ever," Naomi said, then sobered. "André, what's wrong?"

"You know that Gaffney's gone under."

Everyone nodded. "We do," Burke said. "How did he know to run?"

"Because Elaine Billings had an open phone call when she shot at you this afternoon. If any of you said anything about Gaffney, whoever she was talking to heard it."

Val went still. "Oh my God. It was me."

"Tell us what happened," André said, kindness in his tone.

"I didn't know about the phone," Val said.

Burke took her hand and squeezed. "Of course you didn't. Did you tell Elaine that NOPD was going to arrest Gaffney?"

Val nodded, her expression miserable. "Yeah. That's exactly what I did. I was hoping she'd tell us who her boss was. I was so mad, Burke. I heard Susan talking and . . ." She swallowed audibly. "It took me back."

Back to her own sexual assault, Burke understood.

He didn't let go of her hand. "I imagine it did."

"I was so mad when I saw Elaine Billings in the garage." Val's eyes flashed fire. "She shot at you. She nearly killed Naomi. And she abused teenagers she was supposed to be protecting. I guess I lost control. I wanted to shake her until she spilled her guts. I did shake her, but she didn't say a goddamn word."

"She still hasn't," André said. "Val, don't beat yourself up. It wasn't ideal to spill those particular beans, but Gaffney didn't come in to work today. He called in sick. I think he's probably holed up in the house where Susan was kept."

"And all the others," Naomi said quietly.

André's voice hardened. "We *will* find those kids. We've got alerts out to all the airports, train and bus stations for Gaffney. The Coast Guard, too, in case he tries to escape via the Gulf. We weren't going to find him at home or work today anyway."

"Thank you," Val said, wiping her eyes viciously. "I'm still sorry."

"We all make mistakes," André said. "I trusted those PIB guys whose names appeared anonymously in my inbox. I don't want to know how you came by the information, Antoine. Nobody will know that those bank accounts have been accessed, will they?"

Antoine scoffed. "It's like you don't even know me."

They all smiled at that. Even Val. Antoine's wink let Val know that making her smile had been his intent.

"You're awesome, Antoine," Val said quietly.

"I know."

Burke loved these people. Like Kaleb and Juliette, they were his family. "André, what about the condo where Winnifred Timms lived? Have you searched it?"

"Huh." André sounded surprised. "I know something before you. Go me."

Burke was tired of bad news. "What happened?"

"My detectives got a warrant but the condo was on fire. Up in smoke."

Molly leaned toward the phone. "Was anyone hurt?"

"No, everyone got out, including their pets. It started in Timms's condo, which is a total loss. The arson investigators are waiting for it to cool down before they go in. The firefighters said that the fire probably started in the home office, and there were definitely accelerants involved."

Burke rubbed his forehead. "You're always the bearer of good tidings of great joy, André."

"Don't I know it," André said. "Well, that's all I needed to tell you. Y'all get some sleep. You had a busy day." He ended the call.

Val hadn't moved from the arm of the love seat, so Burke gave her a hard hug. "You are awesome, too, Val. We all make mistakes. I've made many. Get some sleep, everyone. All of you except for Molly, since she's on guard duty. Let's solve this thing quick. I want to enjoy the parades. Mardi Gras only comes once a year."

"Thank the good Lord," Val muttered before dragging herself to her feet. "I'm tired. See you all in the morning."

Burke stood, holding his hand out for Naomi. He wanted to pick up where they'd left off that afternoon. But she shook her head regretfully.

"Let me look at the rings. Cora and Molly spent so much time on them."

Burke shoved his frustration away. "Cora, do you have a ride home?"

It was late enough now that the roads should be clear.

"Phin's coming for me. He and Sylvi are just finishing deliveries from the flower shop."

"Then I'll let you ladies talk about rings."

"Meet you downstairs later?" Naomi whispered. "In the living room?"

He gave her a slow smile. "It's a date."

22

The Quarter, New Orleans, Louisiana
WEDNESDAY, FEBRUARY 26, 11:30 P.M.

BURKE TILTED HIS head when he heard the creak of the stairs. Naomi had been going over ring designs with Molly for the past hour. Phin and Sylvi had come for Cora and they were long gone. The kids were asleep, Val's dog lying in the hallway outside their doors. Everyone was where they were supposed to be.

Except Naomi. But soon she would be.

She'd be tired. Ruthanne had confided that Naomi had fallen asleep in his chair that afternoon, only to wake screaming because of a nightmare. It had been Everett who'd calmed her down.

That was good. Giving Naomi a chance to bond with her son was important. He hoped they'd continue building a new relationship together.

He hoped that for himself, too.

He smelled honeysuckle and patted the love seat cushion. "Rest."

She curled into the space beside him and put her head on his shoulder, making a contented sound.

"Did you find the right ring design?" he asked.

"No, but Molly said that I gave her good feedback so that she and Cora could look more tomorrow. It all could be for naught. The ring might not be missing or have anything to do with any of this. We'll check the evidence room, but we can ask André to do that tomorrow." She set her hand high on his thigh, giving it a light squeeze. "You okay?"

He stared at her hand that was so close and still so far away. "I'm fine. Why?"

"Because you looked like someone kicked your puppy when you came back from your errands earlier. You still look sad."

He sighed. "You were right."

"About what?"

He didn't even hesitate. He knew she'd keep his confidence and he needed someone to talk to. "Kaleb and Juliette. Their marriage is in trouble and Kaleb has . . . changed. He went into Juliette's phone and blocked my number."

"Which is why she hadn't called you back. That's not good. If he's violating her privacy like that, what else is he doing?"

"Apparently having an affair."

"I hate that for her. Is she sure?"

"She hired a PI. Didn't ask me so I wouldn't be dragged into it, but I guess we're past that."

"That's pretty serious. Did she get a definitive answer?"

"Definitive enough. The PI followed Kaleb all over New Orleans. Kaleb met the same woman several times at her apartment."

"I'm sorry, Burke."

"So am I, because now I *am* dragged into this. Kaleb was supposed to have left New Orleans on Monday for a business trip, but Juliette thinks he lied, that he stayed in the city. I asked Antoine to check. I figured I'd be able to show her that he'd gotten on a plane for Chicago, just like he said."

"But Kaleb didn't?"

"No. Antoine told me that he checked the airlines and there was no Kaleb Marchand on any of the manifests. He might have taken a private charter, but there'd still be a record of the flight."

"That's a problem. And, let me just add, I find it both fascinating and alarming that Antoine can get that information so easily."

"I agree with both of those statements. So now I have to tell Juliette that Kaleb lied to her."

"Maybe give it a few days. Antoine might find a chartered flight. Plus, you're kind of busy right now."

He kissed the top of her head. "Not as busy as I'd like to be."

She smiled up at him. "Why, Mr. Broussard," she said, thickening her accent, "whatever could you mean?"

He kissed her and she hummed her pleasure. She fit so perfectly against him. He'd dated over the years. Not much, but some. All the women had been too small. Naomi was just right.

I want to keep her. I want her to keep me, too.

He ended the kiss, nudging her nose with his before leaning back into the love seat, keeping her close.

"I'm sorry that your friends' marriage is in trouble," she whispered. "Does that . . . does it make you doubt the whole idea?"

"Of marriage?"

"Yes."

He hesitated, then thought, *To hell with this*, and he lifted her to sit on his lap. She snuggled right in. "I never thought I'd find anyone I'd even consider marrying," he admitted. "Not after Kyra."

"Kaleb's sister?"

"Yeah. We were both young, but I loved her."

"Young love can be hard, even when things go right."

He thought she was talking about her own marriage. "Was Jimmy your first?"

"He was. We were high school sweethearts, and back then we agreed on what we wanted. I wanted to be married, but I also wanted to be . . . I don't know. Part of something bigger than me. That's why I applied to the police academy."

"I get that. I'd toyed with the idea of enlisting for the same reason, but Kyra was against it, so I decided not to."

"Until she died."

"Yeah. Until they all died on that plane. So I joined up. Left Kaleb behind. That was wrong of me. He'd lost his sister. Maybe that's when the resentment started."

She kissed his chin. "You can't go down that road. Just be the good man that you are. He'll either come around or he won't."

"You're right, once again. And no."

"No, what?"

"No, their marriage falling apart doesn't make me doubt the institution. My mother's marriage sucked because my father was an abusive asshole, but I've seen good marriages and they're beautiful. André's parents, for example. They've been together for nearly fifty years and love each other. So I do believe."

"Good. It would be sad if you didn't. You should be happy."

"And because you're the marrying type?"

"That too." She met his eyes, hers intense. "Not . . . soon. I'm not trying to move too fast. And it doesn't have to be formalized. But the concept of monogamy is important to me. I felt that you needed to know that before . . ."

"Before?"

She smirked. "Before we get too busy."

He lightly gripped her chin and kissed her again, this one much more thorough. He kissed her until she was pressed against him, her arms tight around his neck. He kissed her until she straddled his lap, until her body surged and ebbed against him. Until his body responded and he was harder than he'd been in a very, very long time. Maybe ever.

He kissed her until she broke away, gasping for air. "Burke."

"Let's see where this takes us. I don't want anyone else. You're the first woman in a long time that I truly see. And who sees me."

She kissed him this time, a light, sweet kiss, then smiled against his lips. "I do see you, but I wouldn't mind seeing more of you. It's been a long, long time since I've actually *wanted* anyone. Assuming that's what you want, of course."

"I want you," he said gruffly. "Any way you'll have me."

"Then show me your room, Burke Broussard. Let's see where this takes us."

The Quarter, New Orleans, Louisiana
THURSDAY, FEBRUARY 27, 12:00 A.M.

Naomi thought she'd hidden her nerves very well as Burke led her to his bedroom, but he'd picked up on them.

She should have known that he would.

She wanted this. Wanted him. A lot. But it had been a very long time and she wasn't the young woman she'd once been. Plus, he was going to have to close the door. She hadn't considered that when she'd been so bold in the living room.

Holding her hand, Burke glanced at his door before he closed it. "Will you be all right if I shut the door?"

She made herself nod. "Yes."

He studied her for a moment, then closed the door. "I suppose I could find a way to take your mind off whatever's making you nervous."

She smiled at him. She'd expected him to offer her a way out, to say that they didn't have to do anything she didn't want to do.

But he trusted her to know her own mind. "Like what?"

He led her to a chair in the corner of his room and she chuckled. "Another BarcaLounger? Was there a sale?"

He grinned. "If it ain't broke. They're comfortable. Sit. Stay awhile."

She sat and watched him cross the room, his big body fluid and graceful as he lit the candles that were placed here and there. He was a beautiful man. Soon she'd get to see just how beautiful.

For now, she looked around his room, wanting to know him better. It was a masculine room, but not too much. The bed was huge, but the room was large as well. She thought that at one time it might have been two rooms.

"Did you knock down a wall?"

He looked up from lighting the candle on his mantel. "My uncle did. He was big like me. Needed more space, he always said. This suite was three rooms. He turned one into a bathroom. The other two . . ." He waved at the space. "Took me a while to move in here after I came home from the Corps. It had always been his space, but over the years I made it mine."

He picked up a straight-backed chair from beneath a desk that was piled high with paperwork and books. He set the chair in front of her and lowered himself onto it. "Can I take the bandages off for a little while?"

She nodded, her heart tripping. "My mother only put them on so that I wouldn't pick anything up for a few hours."

He began to unwind the bandages her mother had applied, his lips tipping up into a rueful smile. "I'd really prefer we not talk about your mother right now." He met her eyes in the flickering candlelight. "I don't want to think about anyone else but you."

She swallowed, her cheeks heating. Being the center of his focus was heady. "Okay."

His cheek dimpled as his smile grew. "You're pretty when you blush."

Her cheeks grew even warmer. "I don't even know what to say to that."

He pulled away the last of the gauze bandage away from her left hand. There was still a large Band-Aid covering her palm and he kissed it softly. "You do have hands under those oven mitts."

"The better to touch you with," she said, her voice husky.

"I like that." He cleared the other hand of gauze and kissed that palm as well. "I want your hands on my skin."

She leaned forward, cupped his face, and brushed his lips with hers. "Take off your shirt, Burke. I want to touch you."

He made a sound in his throat, part moan, part growl. It made her tingle in all the right places. He pulled off his shirt and tossed it to the floor.

"Oh," she breathed. She trailed her fingertips over his chest, covered in just the right amount of hair. Enough to be sexy but not so much that she couldn't feel his skin beneath. His shoulders were broad, his pectoral muscles defined.

He held still, letting her look. Letting her touch.

She flattened her palms over his biceps, cursing the Band-Aids that kept her from the full experience. Next time.

There *would* be a next time.

Because he wanted this, too. Wanted exclusivity. *With me.*

It was more than she'd dared to hope for.

He slid his hand to the back of her neck and pulled her closer for another kiss, this one deep and much more intimate. She closed her eyes and lost herself in the moment.

This was perfection. She never wanted it to stop. Her hands wandered lower until they reached the top button on his jeans.

He froze. Then he shuddered.

"Do it," he whispered against her lips. "Please."

She pulled the button free, then the next, her breath catching as her knuckles caressed his length. She dropped her gaze to his groin and had to wriggle on the chair as her body responded to the sight of him. The tip of his erection was poking free of the waistband of his boxer briefs. "Wow."

His swallow was audible. "Don't stop."

So she worked her way through the buttons, revealing more of him with each one she freed. He was a big man. Everywhere.

She squeezed her thighs together, anticipating how good he was going to feel.

He didn't miss the movement, his slow grin smugly masculine. He rose, nudging the chair away with one foot as he held out one hand. "My turn. Stand up."

She rose, a shiver racing over her skin when he placed her hand on his erection. Then he was kissing her again, hot and hard and . . . perfect.

He pulled her sweater off and made a frustrated noise when he encountered the Kevlar vest. "Really?"

She was slightly out of breath. "Never got a chance to take it off."

He pulled at the Velcro tabs, releasing her from the vest and tossing it on the chair behind her. She was left standing before him in her bra and leggings.

The sound he made then was the greediest she'd ever heard. She shivered again. Hard.

"Naomi." He traced a finger from her throat to between her breasts, then followed the edge of her bra. It was her prettiest one. She'd chosen it that morning, hoping for a moment like this. But she hadn't known to hope for the way she felt at this moment.

Desired. Cherished.

"You're beautiful," he whispered reverently.

She wasn't. She was thirty-six years old and scarred. But he made her feel beautiful. "So are you."

He kissed her again, stealing the breath from her lungs. She linked her arms around his neck and pressed against his chest, moving side to side to give her nipples the friction she needed.

Groaning, he reached behind her and tugged at her bra strap. It fell away and he dragged the frothy lace down her arms and tossed it into the chair.

"Do the panties match?"

She found herself smiling cheekily. "You'll have to find out."

The dimple reappeared. "In a minute. I'm busy."

His hands covered her breasts and she closed her eyes. He was taking his time and, on one hand, she appreciated the care. On the other hand, she was impatient.

"Burke. Hurry."

He chuckled darkly. "Don't rush me. We only get a first time once. I'm savoring." He bent his head and licked her nipple, humming in pleasure when she threaded her fingers through his hair and pulled him closer.

"Burke."

He wasn't to be hurried, though. He explored her thoroughly until she was trembling. Needing more.

So much more.

She shoved his jeans down and slid her hand under the waistband of his underwear, gripping him firmly.

Hissing, he straightened abruptly, his dark eyes full of lust.

Lifting her chin, she met his gaze, wordlessly challenging him to hurry.

She gasped when he scooped her into his arms and carefully laid her on the bed. Like she was precious.

Tears pricked her eyes. "Don't stop," she whispered. "Please."

He seemed to understand her rush of emotion, because he kissed her softly. "Tell me if I do anything you don't like."

"I promise. But so far, I've liked everything."

The dimple was back. She hadn't seen it nearly often enough. But if it came out when he was aroused, she could accept that. Because then only she would be its recipient.

"What has you looking like the cat in cream?" he asked indulgently.

"Just thinking about how lucky I am."

He ran his fingertip over her lips. "Same."

She reached for the waistband of his boxer briefs and tugged, but the angle was wrong from where she lay. "Take them off."

"You're bossy," he said mildly, but he hooked his fingers in the waistband and pushed them down.

She swallowed. "Oh my." Because . . . *Wow.* She needed that in her. *Now.* She reached for her leggings, but he shook his head.

"Mine." He pulled them down her legs, leaving her wearing only a bit of white lace. "So pretty. I want to rip them off you, but I want to see them again."

She laughed breathlessly as he slowly pulled her panties off. "Burke. Please."

He bent to grab his jeans, going for his wallet.

She almost told him not to bother, that she hadn't been with anyone since her divorce, but there was always the possibility of pregnancy and she knew she wasn't ready for that.

Not now. But maybe later. When they'd seen where this thing between them went.

When he turned back to her, he wore a condom and a smile that rendered her speechless. She reached for him, sighing when he lowered his body to hers.

He touched her then, making another one of those lovely groans that vibrated from his chest. She felt it all over her body, lifting her hips at the way his finger felt inside her.

"God," he whispered. "You're wet."

"Want you."

He moved his hand to her hip, holding on as he slid inside her with one smooth thrust.

She closed her eyes. "Oh."

"Good?"

"So good," she breathed.

He kissed her again and she rolled her hips, needing more. His lips skimmed over her cheek to her throat.

It was her turn to freeze. She'd forgotten about her scar. How could she have forgotten?

"Beautiful," he said in a tone that brooked no argument. He pushed her hand away when she tried to pull her hair over the scar. "Don't hide from me, Naomi. Please. Let me see you."

He threaded their fingers together, moving their joined hands to the pillow beside her head as he kissed the scar. "Beautiful," he said again. He lifted his head so that he could see her eyes. "Tell me that you believe me."

How could she not? When Burke Broussard said she was beautiful in that low Cajun rumble, how could she not believe him?

"I believe you."

He started to move then, holding her gaze. It wasn't fast. It wasn't rushed. It was slow. It was . . . perfect.

It was beautiful.

More than she could have imagined in all those lonely years.

When she came, it was on a throaty sigh of satisfaction.

When he came, it was with a groan that she was sure the whole house could hear. She'd probably be embarrassed tomorrow.

Right now, she was too sated to care.

He pulled out of her and disappeared for a minute. She was on her way to sleep when he climbed into the bed and spooned her from behind, his hand closing over her breast. It was just right.

"Sleep, darlin'," he murmured in her ear. "I've got you."

She was already drifting off. But hearing him call her "darlin'" again made her smile.

The Quarter, New Orleans, Louisiana
THURSDAY, FEBRUARY 27, 6:45 A.M.

Burke stretched awake, feeling pretty damn good. He had his arms full of a beautiful woman who was warm and curvy and . . .

Mine.

The thought might have scared him before he'd met Naomi. But he *liked* her. Importantly, he also respected and admired her.

He admired all of her, from her courage to her tender heart to her inquisitive brain. And her breasts. She had very nice breasts.

He wanted her again. But she slept deeply, and he knew it was a rarity for her. So he enjoyed holding her, the honeysuckle of her shampoo soothing him.

Until his phone buzzed under his pillow with an incoming text.

He hadn't wanted a ringing phone to wake Naomi, but if any of his people needed him, the buzzing would wake him up.

He released his hold on Naomi and retrieved his phone.

Oh. He had two texts, both from Kaleb. The first one must have been what had woken him.

We need to talk. ASAP.

The second message read: ***Hello? I know you're awake. It's past six.***

Because Burke normally was an early riser. Today he thought he could have slept another few hours.

A third message popped up. ***HELLO????***

Burke slid his other arm out from under Naomi, freezing when she murmured in her sleep. But she snuggled back into the pillow with a sigh, so he swung his legs over the side of the bed and sat up.

I'm here, he texted back. ***Where and when do you want to talk?***

At the coffee house where we last met. ASAP. I'm halfway there now.

Burke sighed quietly. Of course Kaleb would want to meet now. But Burke had been the one to request a conversation. Before talking to Juliette, he would have readily accepted, understanding that he had a lot of groveling to do.

Now, not so much. Because Kaleb had cheated on his wife.

Or it could be a misunderstanding.

How Burke wanted that to be true.

For a moment, he considered declining, but another message popped up.

Well? You said you wanted to talk to me.

Burke started to type something snarky but stopped himself at the next message from Kaleb.

Please, B. I need your help. Please.

Burke sighed again. He couldn't refuse to help. Even if Kaleb had hurt Juliette with his affair. It was just that he couldn't reconcile the Kaleb he'd known for thirty years with the man who'd apparently cheated on his wife.

The brain tumor theory was looking better all the time.

Fine, he replied. ***I'll be there in 15–20 min.***

Thank you.

He needed to clean up first. Meeting Kaleb while he still smelled of sex seemed like a bad plan.

Burke wanted to meet somewhere else. He knew the coffee shop Kaleb meant. It was just over the border of the Quarter in the Central Business District. Even at this time of the morning, tourists would be roaming the streets, many of them still drunk from the night before.

He shuddered. There would be puddles of piss and puke. He loved New Orleans but hated the smell of it in the morning after a major event.

A hand lightly traced down his spine, spreading a shiver over his bare skin.

"You okay?" Naomi whispered.

"Yeah. Kaleb wants to talk."

"You want me to go with you?"

He kissed her softly. "No. You stay here and sleep."

"I like your bed," she murmured sleepily. "Smells like you."

He smiled down at her. "And now it will smell like you, too. Honeysuckle."

"Hmmm. Take Val. Please? So I don't worry?"

He started to protest, mostly out of habit. He didn't like not being able to go where he wished, when he wished, all alone. But these were not normal circumstances and her worry felt like a caress, not a rope around his neck. "Okay."

"Thank you." She closed her eyes. "Bring back beignets."

He chuckled and stroked her hair away from her face, away from her neck. Away from her scar. "Yes, ma'am."

She pulled her hair back over the scar, but he pushed it away again. "Don't," he whispered. "Don't hide from me."

Her sigh was resigned. "Okay. Be careful."

He checked the time. Now he'd be late and Kaleb would yell at him about that, too.

He made up a little time by taking a shower before the water heated, and that put him in a sour mood. He was scowling by the time he got downstairs, but there was coffee, which helped.

Val and Molly were at his kitchen table, each clutching a mug as if they were afraid someone would take it from them.

Like me.

But there was still some in the pot and he made a beeline for it. Yes, he was heading to a coffee shop, but his body needed caffeine first.

"I thought he'd be in a better mood, considering," Molly stage-whispered to Val. "They weren't quiet."

"Well, he *is* old," Val said sympathetically. "Maybe he doesn't remember."

Burke snorted. "Shut up." He fixed himself a travel mug of coffee. "I'm not old."

"You're one step from yelling at kids to get off your lawn," Val said. "At least with that face you're wearing."

"She likes my face," Burke muttered.

The two women laughed.

"What's wrong, Burke?" Molly asked, patting the empty chair beside her.

He shook his head. "Can't stay. Finally heard from Kaleb. He wants to meet for coffee."

Val stood up. "Not without me."

"I already promised Naomi I'd take you, but I figured you'd still be asleep, Val."

"Nope. I got plenty of sleep. Let me get my jacket."

Molly remained seated, watching him as Val ran upstairs. "What are you going to say to him, Burke?"

"I don't know. He's behaving so erratically, blocking my number on Juliette's phone—and the kids' phones—but he said he needs my help, so maybe . . ." He winced. "I'm hoping he has a brain tumor or something."

Molly choked on her coffee. "Burke! That's terrible."

"I know. But I don't want him to just be a selfish cur," Burke said. "I know that's stupid, but . . ."

"Not stupid. He's as close to a brother as you have. If my sister needed my help, I'd go. Just be careful."

"I know." He scowled. "I hate needing a bodyguard."

"Not for much longer, I hope. But kudos to Naomi for getting you to agree to one." She smiled up at him. "I'm happy for you, Burke. You deserve this."

He wasn't sure that he did deserve Naomi, but that Molly thought he did was nice. "Thank you."

Val jogged down the stairs. "You wearing a vest, Burke?"

"I am."

"Good."

They walked outside, the sun just peeking over the horizon.

"We need to hurry, because I'm already late. We're going down to Canal."

Val grimaced. "Hopefully the street cleaners have gotten all the puke and piss."

"Your mouth, God's ears. Look, I don't want Kaleb to see you. It'll just make his fears more real. I'd like him to let me see the boys again, and having a bodyguard won't help."

"I'll try to be discreet, but there aren't a lot of places I can hide and still have eyes on you."

"Once I'm in the coffee shop, I'll be fine. Just stand at the door." He hesitated. "That's an order, Val. I have to work this out with Kaleb."

She frowned at him as they race-walked, skirting around the tourists who were either early risers or still partying from the night before. "For the record, I do not like this. Not even a little."

"I know. Please do it anyway."

23

The Central Business District, New Orleans, Louisiana
THURSDAY, FEBRUARY 27, 7:15 A.M.

BURKE," VAL SAID when they'd stopped outside the coffee shop, "I should go in with you."

"I'll be fine," Burke insisted. "See, Kaleb is here already, just like he said he'd be."

There were two cups of coffee and a plate of breakfast sandwiches on the table where Kaleb sat. The place wasn't crowded yet. In an hour there would be a line around the corner.

"Fine. Just hurry. I don't like you being out in the open."

This has to end, Burke thought. By threatening their children, Gaffney and his boss had skillfully set them up to be the victims. Well, that and shooting at him and Naomi.

But at least he and his team now had a plan. If Antoine could discover the identity of the man with fancy shoes, they'd be a step closer to whoever had organized all of this.

They'd be a step closer to saving the teenagers who thought no one would miss them.

But now, he was going to take a moment for himself. A moment to reconnect with the man who was his brother in all but blood.

Kaleb wore a suit like he always did, but today he wore a hat. A fedora that covered his face. And sunglasses inside. In any other city, this would make people wonder. In New Orleans, during Mardi Gras, everyone just assumed he was another businessman with a hangover.

Burke hoped Kaleb wasn't hungover. He hated when Kaleb drank because he reminded Burke too much of his own father. Of the hitting and the yelling.

Kaleb had given up booze years ago. Burke hoped that he hadn't fallen off the wagon. But it would make sense given the cheating.

"Kaleb."

"Burke. Thank you for coming."

"You knew I would."

"Yes, I knew you would. Please. Sit down."

They sat down and Burke reached for the coffee at his place. "For me?"

"Yes. Light and sweet, just as you like it."

Burke took a sip and exhaled. It *was* exactly as he liked it. The coffee in the travel mug was fuel to make his body move. This was pure enjoyment.

"I'm sorry, Burke."

Burke wished that he could see Kaleb's eyes. "For?"

"For overreacting on Monday. I said some terrible things that I really didn't mean. It isn't your fault that the boys were targeted."

"I don't know. Someone was trying to hurt me by hurting them. We think we're close to neutralizing the threat, though. Hopefully the boys can go back to school when the break is over and never have to worry about danger again."

"You're close, then?"

"I think so, yes." He finished the coffee and set the cup aside and decided to confront the issue head-on. "I talked to Juliette yesterday."

"I know. She told me."

Burke tried not to seem judgmental. "Juliette thinks you're cheating on her."

"Because I was. I ended it. I don't even know what happened to me. That's not who I am."

"I know it's not. What did Juliette say when you told her that it was over with the other woman?"

"We're going to couples counseling. She's not sure she wants to save our marriage and, right now, I can't blame her. I . . . fucked up, but I'm trying to make it right. I told the woman that it was over. When we were in Chicago. I broke it off."

Chicago. Burke went still because Kaleb hadn't gone to Chicago. Not according to Antoine.

Maybe Antoine had been wrong.

But he rarely was.

"I'm glad you ended it," Burke said, wary now and not liking the sensation. This was Kaleb. His oldest friend. His only remaining family. "You asked me to help you. What can I do?"

"You're helping just by being here. Can we talk about the company?"

"I can do more. I never meant to dump it all in your lap."

"Well, you did dump it all in my lap," Kaleb said in a matter-of-fact tone. "Or my father's lap, I guess. He liked it, the fast pace. Making all the decisions."

"You don't?"

"I like parts of it. But I think I resent you taking home such a huge paycheck when you do none of the work."

Burke couldn't control his flinch. *Because . . . wow.* Kaleb took home a much greater percentage of the profits than Burke did. Now Kaleb wanted more?

"Okay. What part of the business do you want me to take on?"

Kaleb's brows lifted above the sunglasses he still wore. "I mean, what are you qualified to do?"

The sneer on Kaleb's face hurt. A lot. "Excuse me?"

"Well, you're not a scientist or an engineer." His words dripped with acid, each one burning Burke's heart. "You're not a businessman. You don't seem to understand that you should be charging people for your services, not giving them away to every beggar with a sad story. God only knows what would become of your firm if you didn't have Joy. She manages everything for you. You're not an accountant or a salesman. You don't know much about computers, which is why you hired Antoine. I suppose you could drive a delivery truck." For some reason that made Kaleb smile, but it was a cold and vicious thing. "Or be our night security. You know, a rent-a-cop."

Burke sat back, unsure of what to say to the vitriol coming from Kaleb's mouth. "How long have you . . ." He shook his head, disoriented. "How long have you resented me?"

"I think the better word is 'hate,' Burke. How long have I hated you? A very long time. Maybe always. Definitely since I turned eighteen and was told I had to follow in my father's footsteps. My life was already planned. But not yours. You got to do whatever the hell you wanted. You had a house, a company, and a fortune handed to you on a silver platter. You did nothing to earn any of it. You would have nothing were it not for me."

"Were it not for your father," Burke corrected, because that point seemed important even as Kaleb's words stabbed like knives. He wanted to strike back, to set the record straight. "Your father and my uncle built the company together. Your father grew it after my uncle died. You've maintained it since his death, but you haven't grown anything." He blinked hard when a wave of . . . something washed over him. The room was spinning. "Shit."

Maybe the coffee had been too sweet.

He reached for one of the breakfast sandwiches on the plate between them, but Kaleb pulled it away.

Everything went wavy, and Burke blinked again. "Was that not for me?"

"No." Kaleb lowered his glasses enough to peer at Burke over the rims. His eyes were so very cold. "No food for you. I don't want anything in your stomach. Slows down the reaction."

Reaction? Another wave of dizziness hit him and this one went on and on. *Something is wrong. Get help.*

Burke went for the phone in his pocket, but Kaleb reached across the table and gripped Burke's wrists. Hard. But no one watching them would see that. They'd only see two men holding hands.

"Keep your hands where I can see them."

Burke tried to free his hands, but his arms weren't working right. He tugged, but weakly.

Weak as a kitten.

His gaze dropped to the empty cup, then flicked up to meet Kaleb's cold eyes as realization dawned. "You drugged me."

"I did. Easier that way. So many drunks on the street. You'll just be one more."

He had to focus on forming the word on his lips. "Why?"

But his head was getting heavy and his chin dropped to his chest. *Shit, shit, shit.*

"Is the Sorensen woman taken care of?" Kaleb asked quietly, and Burke tried to lift his head, tried to ask *what* and *how* and *why, why, why*.

"Yes, sir," another man said. "She won't be waking up."

He'd killed her? The man had killed Val?

Val. Oh my God. Val. His heart was pumping but not fast. It was slow and plodding, like it was moving through molasses.

"Why?" he managed, but it came out slurred. Unintelligible.

And then he saw the shoes. The man who'd killed Val had come closer. All Burke could see was his feet.

Feet that wore fancy brown leather loafers. Handmade.

No, no, no.

It came together like a clashing of cymbals. The man's shoes. The fedora—just like in the footage of the two men entering the Delgados' house.

But . . . Kaleb? *No.* It couldn't be.

Kaleb was the boss of a sex trafficking ring? *Kaleb?*

He stared at his old friend in disbelief. This could not be true.

"No," he tried to whisper, but it sounded like a moan. His heart broke in two.

How could it be true?

Kaleb's labored sigh was followed by words that were spoken loudly. "You could never hold your liquor. You're drunk as a damn skunk. Dammit, man, aren't you ever ashamed? Help me get him to the car. We'll take him home and sober him up."

And then two sets of arms gripped him firmly, hoisting him to his feet.

"He weighs a frickin' ton," the man with the shoes muttered as he reached into Burke's pocket for his cell phone.

They propped his arms on both their shoulders and began dragging him to the door.

No, no, no. He thought he said the words aloud, but no one stepped in. The few gazes he met looked away, but not before he could see their disgust.

The other patrons thought him drunk at seven a.m.

He saw his cell phone fall to the street, tossed there by the man with the shoes. A moment later, he was thrust into the back seat of a black SUV that was parked at the curb.

Kaleb.

This has *to be a nightmare.* He'd wake up soon and have his arms full of Naomi.

But he didn't wake up. He just got sleepier.

"Where is the Sorensen woman?" Kaleb asked as Burke fell over to his side. He couldn't sit up. And then he was on the floorboard, Kaleb's hands rough as he pushed him down.

The SUV pulled away from the curb, the man with the shoes at the wheel. In the back seat, Kaleb patted Burke down, removing his gun from its shoulder holster. His backup gun from his ankle. The tool kit from his pants pocket.

He winced as his wrists were bound with flex-cuffs.

Kaleb had come prepared.

Kaleb was a criminal. A trafficker. A killer.

No. This can't be happening.

But it was.

"In one of the shops," the shoe man said. "My gun convinced the owner to open it early. He got the first syringe. She got the second. I locked them in the shop owner's office. There's an access alley behind a gate that I can drive into and load them up. As soon as we get

Broussard settled, I'll go back for their bodies. The shop doesn't open till ten, so we have time."

Bodies. Oh God. Burke wanted to scream, but he couldn't draw enough breath. *Val.*

"And the security footage?"

"Scrubbed everywhere that we were. Street cams, coffee shop cams, the shop owner's cams. Not my first rodeo, sir."

"Good."

No, not good, Burke thought, feeling the bumps in the road as they drove away. *Not good at all.*

"Drop me off in the next block," Kaleb said. "I need to create my alibi."

The Quarter, New Orleans, Louisiana
THURSDAY, FEBRUARY 27, 8:30 A.M.

Naomi sat on the edge of Burke's bed, dressed and ready to go downstairs. Her gaze was fixed on the bedroom door, which Burke had closed on his way out. She didn't like closed doors, but opening it meant leaving the room.

She was hesitating.

Not because she regretted what they'd done. She had no regrets whatsoever. What they'd done together . . .

It had been magical. And exactly what she'd needed.

Exactly what she'd wanted.

She'd missed the touch of a man who cared about her. She wasn't certain she'd truly ever had that, not even when she and Jimmy were first starting out.

Jimmy's abuse and manipulation had been wrong.

She'd deserved better.

She still did.

She shivered, remembering the way Burke had made her feel.

How he'd wanted her.

How she wanted him again.

So, no. She wasn't ashamed. But she was hesitant to go downstairs. Her son might know, and that would be awkward. It might even set back the small bit of progress they'd made.

But life was short and tomorrows were not guaranteed. She'd sacrificed her freedom for her son. For five long years she'd survived a hellhole of a prison. To keep him safe.

Maybe I'm entitled to a little pleasure.

Either way, she was going to have to face Burke's people at some point. She didn't think they'd be upset with her. Burke seemed happy and that seemed to make his people happy.

So she stood and headed for the bedroom door, only to veer away when the photos on the mantel of the fireplace in his bedroom caught her eye.

You're procrastinating.

True. But she was also learning more about the man whose bed she'd shared. He had a few photos on the mantel downstairs, mostly of his mother and uncle and his godsons, but the mantel in his bedroom was crowded with photos, all of which carried a thin layer of dust. He'd mentioned that a housekeeper came in weekly, but it didn't seem that his room was within her cleaning purview.

Naomi went to the en suite bathroom to get a damp washcloth, returning to the mantel to clean the frames as she studied each one.

There were several faded photos of a young woman with light brown hair and a joyous smile.

This must be Kyra.

In most of the photos, Kyra stood alone, but there were a few where she stood with others, including a very young Burke Broussard. In those photos she gazed up at him with shining eyes. She'd loved him, too.

Naomi gave the frames some TLC, setting each one down with the reverence they deserved. Burke's first love.

I'm sorry you didn't live to see the man he is today.

Because that man is special.

She checked out the rest of the photos, cleaning each frame as she went. There were several of the godsons he was missing so much.

She hoped his meeting with Kaleb was going well. She hoped that Burke would soon be allowed to see the boys who he so clearly loved.

She returned the photos of the boys to the mantel and picked up the next photo. It was of Burke with a couple. All three appeared to be in their twenties. The woman was pregnant and looked so happy. She'd laid her head on the shoulder of the man standing on her other side.

Naomi frowned. The man looked familiar.

Her heart began to race. *Very familiar.* But it couldn't be.

No.

She set down the photo and snatched up the next one. The couple was a few years older. They were at the beach, a setting sun behind them. The woman wore a modest swimsuit, the man a pair of trunks. He was shirtless, the silver chain he wore around his neck contrasting with his bronzed skin.

There was a ring on the chain, but she didn't look at that.

Not yet, even though she knew, deep down, that it was *the* ring. The one she'd seen before.

For this one horrible moment in time, she stared at the man's face.

This is Kaleb.

Oh my God. This is Kaleb.

But it can't be him. Because . . .

"Burke," she whispered, horrified.

No, no, no.

Frame in hand, she ran to the bedroom door and threw it open. "Molly! Val! Antoine!" she shouted. *"Molly!"*

Molly ran up the stairs, meeting her at the second-floor landing. The woman had her gun drawn and was looking around for a threat. "What's wrong?"

She thrust the photo at Molly. "Who is this man?"

Because maybe I'm wrong. Please let me be wrong.

Molly frowned. "That's Kaleb Marchand, Burke's best friend. He's the CEO of—"

No. "Molly, listen. I *saw* him. He was with Winnifred Timms. They went to dinner together. He went to her condo on Poydras. They were kissing, Molly. This man was with Winnifred Timms."

"Oh no." Molly paled, instantly understanding. "Are you sure?"

"What's wrong?" Antoine asked, rushing from the second-floor study.

"Kaleb Marchand," Molly said tightly. "He's involved. Dammit, Antoine. The guy we're looking for is Kaleb."

"That can't be," Antoine protested. "Not Kaleb. We know him."

Heart pounding, Naomi grabbed the photo and held it to her face, squinting to better see the ring around the man's neck.

It was silver filigree.

It was a wedding band.

It was exactly as she remembered from six years ago.

"This is the ring," she said, feeling suddenly numb. "This is the ring I saw in the evidence room. We need to warn Burke."

Kaleb's ring had been put into evidence the week before she was arrested.

Antoine already had his phone to his ear. "He's not answering. Where is he?"

Molly met Naomi's gaze. Naomi saw her own horror reflected there.

"He went to meet with Kaleb," Naomi whispered. "I don't know where."

"He took Val," Molly said, visibly trying to hold herself together. "He'll be okay." She dialed on her own phone. "I'll warn Val. You keep trying Burke, Antoine."

Antoine nodded grimly.

But it was no use. Neither of them was picking up.

"Can you track their phones?" Naomi asked.

Antoine nodded again. "Burke's is at a coffee shop on Canal. Val's is . . . next door in a souvenir shop."

"I'll go," Molly said. "Stay here, Naomi. He needs you safe."

She wasn't sure she could even move. "Hurry."

The Quarter, New Orleans, Louisiana
THURSDAY, FEBRUARY 27, 8:45 A.M.

"Can I get you anything else, sir?" the coffee shop server asked Kaleb politely.

Translation: You're taking up a table and you need to leave.

Exactly as Kaleb had intended.

"I'm so sorry. I've been waiting for a friend and he never showed up."

The server glanced at the line that had formed at the door. "Well, if I can't get you anything else . . ."

Kaleb sighed heavily. "Let me send my friend a text and I'll be going."

"Thank you," she said gratefully and headed to the next table.

Kaleb typed a message to Burke's phone. *I've been waiting for you for 90 mins. Where the hell are you? I can't wait any longer. I guess you don't want to help after all.*

He hit send, pleased. If someone hadn't taken Burke's phone from the street, his people would find it soon and read his texts. He'd been sending increasingly impatient texts to Burke for the last hour.

Even if someone had stolen Burke's phone from the street, Kaleb had no doubt that Antoine would be able to hack into Burke's phone records and see the texts.

He tossed a large cash tip to the table and paused at the counter where the manager was assisting the barista through the morning rush. "Sir? Do you know Burke Broussard?"

Of course he does. Burke was well known here. This was his favorite coffee shop.

"I do, yes. Why?"

"I was supposed to meet him here this morning, but he didn't show. If he does come in, can you tell him that Kaleb was here?"

The manager smiled. "Of course, sir. Have a nice day."

Kaleb walked out of the shop and drew a deep breath before arranging for an Uber. He'd head to the company parking lot where he'd left his car.

Then to the warehouse where Stanley had dumped Burke.

Part of him hoped that Stanley had killed him, that he'd find Burke's body and wouldn't have to talk to him again. The betrayal in Burke's eyes had hit him harder than he'd expected.

But that was Burke's own fault. *Shouldn't've poked his nose where it didn't belong.*

Stanley had likely followed his instructions, though. The former Marine still took orders seriously, despite having been dishonorably discharged ten years before.

Besides, Stanley would want to take his time with Burke, to make sure his old commanding officer suffered. Stanley had a lot of anger to work through.

His cell phone rang while he was in the Uber, on his way to his own car. It was a number he didn't recognize, but he did recognize the caller's voice.

"Kaleb Marchand?" the man asked.

"Yes. Who is this?"

"André Holmes. I'm calling because Burke Broussard has gone missing."

Ah. The call he'd been expecting, just not from the person. He'd expected it to come from Molly Sutton or Antoine Holmes. Not from Lucien Farrow, because he was sitting outside Kaleb's house. But that they'd called André Holmes wasn't a huge surprise. Burke and André had been tight for years.

He answered with the concern he'd practiced. "Missing? When? How?"

"This morning. He told one of his people that he was meeting you."

"He was supposed to, but he never showed. I just left the coffee shop on Canal. I waited for over an hour."

"I know the place. It's Burke's favorite. I'll check it out. Thank you, Kaleb."

"You're welcome. Keep me up to speed. It's not like Burke to just . . . disappear. He knows his people will worry."

"And they are worried. Be careful. Whoever has been after him—whoever tried to grab your sons—is still out there and has tried to kill Burke twice now."

And been unsuccessful, dammit.

"I'll be careful. Let me know when you've found him."

"Will do."

Kaleb ended the call and smiled. Things were going according to plan.

The Quarter, New Orleans, Louisiana
THURSDAY, FEBRUARY 27, 9:40 A.M.

They'd all gathered in the living room, waiting for Molly's call. Antoine had called his brother, who'd sent officers to assist Molly.

Jace sat with Elijah, the older boy's face sheet-white. Val was still not answering her phone.

Naomi sat on the settee where she and Burke had sat just the evening before. Where they'd said they wanted to see where the thing between them would go.

Stay alive, Burke. I'm not done with you yet.

But the words fell flat. She was frozen with fear. She'd felt like this before, as she'd sat in the NOPD holding cell awaiting booking. As she'd entered prison, terrified of what the next thirty years might bring.

As she'd contemplated the Glock after Gaffney's visit last week. Six days. It had only been six days since she'd sat frozen, thinking she had no one. Wondering if anyone but her mother and Sylvi would miss her if she were gone.

James and Ruthanne sat on the love seat across from her, grim and silent. Eleanor sat in Burke's duct-taped BarcaLounger, clutching her rosary beads.

Chelsea sat on the floor with Harper on her lap, the child's eyes having gone distant again.

Naomi wanted to give comfort but she couldn't. She had no comfort to give herself, much less anyone else. Only panic.

Antoine sat beside Naomi, his hands clenching and relaxing, over and over, before he offered her his hand, palm up. She took it and held on.

She had no words and it didn't seem like anyone else did, either. They simply sat, tensed and waiting.

It had been nearly an hour with no call from Molly. Antoine could see her phone and was tracking it with one of his laptops. She was near Burke's phone, but they hadn't heard anything. Not yet.

Footsteps on the stairs had Naomi turning to see a frowning Everett descending.

"What's going on?" he demanded, his voice loud and strident.

"Burke's gone," Harrison said, following him down.

Everett turned to glare at him. "What do you mean, he's gone? Like he left?"

"Like he disappeared," Antoine snapped. "The ringleader of this shit show has him. And maybe Val, too."

Jace whimpered, a devastating sound.

Naomi wanted to go to Jace. To put her arms around him.

But she couldn't move. She was frozen.

Elijah put his arms around his friend. "I got you," he said when the older boy began to cry. "I got you."

Naomi's throat closed and she struggled to breathe. "He didn't know," she said to Everett when her son came to stand before her, his expression bewildered and sad. "He didn't know it was his best friend."

"Oh man," Everett muttered, then glared at Harrison again. "Why didn't you tell me?"

"I didn't know you were invested," Harrison said calmly.

Everett flinched. "I'm not a monster. Of course I'm invested. Of course I care." He looked around the room, searching faces. "What can we do?"

"Molly's gone to see if she can find them," James said heavily. He hadn't been the same since he'd learned that Jimmy had taken money to help frame Naomi.

Naomi wanted to comfort him, too.

She closed her eyes, fear and grief overwhelming her.

Don't grieve. You don't know anything yet.

But part of her did know. Something terrible was happening to Burke right now. Kaleb had him. Kaleb, who'd hurt so many people.

She thought of the bullet hole in Winnifred's forehead. Of the dead Delgado brothers and their mother and grandmother. Of the two innocent girls who had died in that fire.

Burke could be dead, too.

Her free hand was enclosed in a pair of warm ones, and she opened her eyes to see Everett kneeling in front of her, his eyes filled with misery.

She tried to smile at him, but a sob burst out instead. She clamped her lips shut. She would not break down. Not with Jace already crying.

"What can I do?" Everett whispered.

"Nothing," Naomi whispered back. "Just . . . wait with us. Please."

"Okay." Everett hesitated, then rose to sit on the arm of the settee. Tentatively, he put his arm over her shoulders, as if unsure of his welcome.

Oh, she thought, unable to hold back the tears. *My son.*

She leaned into him, taking the comfort he offered. His arm tightened. "He's smart, Mom," Everett said softly. "He's strong and he's smart."

"Thank you," Naomi murmured.

And they waited some more.

Until Antoine's phone buzzed. Startled, he fumbled it before grabbing onto it. He hit accept and put the phone on speaker. "Molly?"

"I've got Val," Molly said.

Jace lifted his head, his face tear-streaked. "Alive?"

"Yes, Jace," Molly said. "She's alive. On her way to the hospital. She was being held in the shop next to where Burke met Kaleb. She was dosed with some kind of opioid. Which I only know because the officer André sent to help me had Narcan. We found Val and the shop owner unresponsive. We tried the Narcan because it wouldn't hurt them, even if it didn't help. But it helped. Both of them were conscious when they were loaded into the ambulance. Kaj is on his way to the hospital. He'll come back and get Jace and Elijah when it's safe to do so."

"Thank you." Jace's voice croaked. "Thank you for saving her."

"You're very welcome, Jace," Molly said. "Burke's nowhere to be found. The people in the coffee shop said he sat down with a man but he and another man had to practically drag him out. They thought he was falling-down drunk."

"They drugged him," Naomi said.

"Yeah," Molly said shortly. "And there's no security footage. It's all scrubbed. Nobody saw the guy's face. Just that he wore a nice suit and a fedora."

"Like the two men going into the Delgados' house," Antoine said, his jaw tight. "We're going to find him."

"I found his phone," Molly said. "It was in the street, in front of the coffee shop. The officer André sent is taking me to the hospital. I'll stay there until Kaj arrives, then I'll come back. We'll figure out where they took him. It's what we do."

"All we know is that it's a house on one of the parade routes," Antoine said. "Goddamn needle in a haystack."

"We will find him," Molly said firmly, then sighed. "André called Kaleb."

"And?" Antoine asked sharply.

"He said that Kaleb claimed to have been waiting for Burke at the coffee shop on Conti, but that Burke never showed."

"He's a liar," Antoine spat.

"I know," Molly said, "and so does André, but Kaleb's story checked out. André went there himself. Kaleb waited for over an hour and that shop had security footage. He'd changed his clothes. No suit or fedora. He wore a polo shirt and a baseball cap. The manager said that Kaleb even asked that they tell Burke that he'd been waiting when Burke showed up. Burke's phone shows a number of texts from Kaleb that seem to back his story as well."

"He's lying," Antoine insisted.

Rage made it hard for Naomi to breathe. "Kaleb planned this."

"I know," Molly said again. "He's clever, but so are we. And he doesn't know we suspect him. We *will* find Burke."

"Yes," Naomi agreed, proud that her voice no longer trembled. "We will."

How, she didn't know.

24

Uptown, New Orleans, Louisiana

THURSDAY, FEBRUARY 27, 12:30 P.M.

BURKE SLOWLY WOKE, becoming aware of several things.

His body hurt, a dull ache that meant he'd been stationary for at least a few hours. The floor where he lay was hard. Concrete.

The room was completely dark, which was disorienting. Not a sliver of light came in from anywhere. So probably no windows.

The air was thick and heavy. So probably no ventilation, either.

He could hear music, but it was muffled. The room was soundproofed, too.

He felt sick, like his head had been stuffed with cotton.

Like he had a hangover.

Had he been drinking?

And then he remembered.

Coffee. He'd had a cup of coffee.

With Kaleb.

Burke's mind stuttered to a stop as his chest seized tight.

Kaleb.

He drugged me.

He hates me.

The memories continued to return, each one more hurtful than the last.

He's always hated me. Since we were kids.

Unless that had been a dream. He wanted it to be a dream.

But it hadn't been. The concrete beneath his body told him that.

Where am I?

He tried to move, but his wrists were bound behind him.

Flex-cuffs. Kaleb had come prepared.

I was clueless. A fucking lamb to slaughter.

He didn't ask himself how he hadn't known, how he hadn't seen. Didn't beat himself up for being caught unaware. Because this was Kaleb.

Clearly Kaleb was not the man Burke thought he was.

Kaleb was a criminal.

The man with the shoes had been in the coffee shop, connecting Kaleb to Winnifred Timms and human trafficking. *Teenagers.* Kaleb had stolen and sold teenagers for sex. He'd also framed and imprisoned Naomi.

He'd murdered people.

Rage boiled up from Burke's gut, giving him the strength to jackknife into a sitting position. His head fell forward, that small motion tiring him out.

He was not in good fighting form.

He closed his eyes, the room spinning even though he could see nothing. If Kaleb or the shoe guy came back now, he'd be at their mercy.

He'd been here at least a few hours. His people would know he was gone. They'd be looking for him. His people wouldn't let—

And then another thought came crashing into him, sucking the air from his lungs.

Val. The man with the shoes was going back for her body.

Oh, Val. I'm so sorry.

Burke couldn't hold back the tears.

They'd killed Val. Sorrow overtook him and for a moment he could only sit there and cry. But then the rage returned and he drew a deep breath of the stale air.

He needed to escape. He needed to find Kaleb. He needed to make him pay. For everything.

It can't be true. Part of him still rejected the notion that Kaleb could be involved in anything so vile.

He's more than involved. He's the boss.

Kaleb had done so many things for which he'd have to pay. Kaleb and John Gaffney, wherever that prick was.

Using his legs, Burke scooted backward until his back hit a wall. Clenching his teeth, he pushed himself to his feet, using the wall for balance. He paused when he was upright, his heart pounding and his head light. He closed his eyes and waited for the dizziness to pass, cursing Kaleb in his mind.

Cursing himself as well, because it seemed like he could blame himself after all. *Why didn't I see it?*

Kaleb didn't want you to.

Burke took shuffling steps sideways until his shoulder hit another wall. He repeated the motion until he'd circled the perimeter of the room.

Ten by ten. Not so big.

Only a little bigger than the cell where Naomi had spent five long years because someone—*Kaleb*—was a criminal asshole.

There was one door with no handle on this side of it. Just a lock that required a key.

He wondered what this room was for. He wondered if there was anyone in there with him.

"Hello?" he said quietly, but there was no reply.

He'd hoped his eyes would become accustomed to the darkness, but it was absolute. He couldn't even see shadows.

If there was anyone in there with him, they were likely unconscious.

Val. Maybe she wasn't dead. Maybe they hadn't killed her.

The man with the shoes had said that he'd given her a syringe of something and that he'd be going back for her body, but if she was in here, Burke needed to know. He needed to save her.

He began shuffling sideways again, his foot testing for obstructions before he made the next step.

He found the body on his third pass. The person was lying in the middle of the room.

"Val?" he whispered.

He slowly lowered to his knees, turning his body so that his bound hands could touch the person's face. It was stone cold.

Whoever this was, they were dead.

Burke twisted so that he could search for hair. Val's long white-blond hair.

But there was no long hair. Just a short buzz.

He trailed his fingers back to the face, lightly touching the features.

A man. This was a man. And he was dead.

Not Val.

But there had been a shop owner. This could be him. Val could still be here, too. So Burke rose to his feet and continued to shuffle sideways until he'd mapped the room.

No other bodies. Just him and the dead man.

Now what?

He had no idea how long he'd been out, so he could be far away from the city. He wondered if this was the house where Susan had been brought. Where Kaleb was holding the other kids. *I need to save them.*

A light came on, so abruptly that Burke staggered back a step. He peered up at the single lightbulb hanging from the ceiling. Someone had just turned it on from outside the room.

Shit.

Burke's gaze landed on the dead man.

John Gaffney.

The bastard had been dead for hours, at least. *No wonder André couldn't find him.*

To his left, Burke heard something scraping the floor.

The door. Someone was opening it.

Burke straightened his back against the wall, waiting.

Loud music rushed into the room as the door opened. There was a party going on outside. He debated rushing the door, but he wasn't strong enough. Not yet.

Kaleb came into the room. "You're awake." He shut the door and the music abruptly grew muffled again.

Whoever had soundproofed the room had done an amazing job.

Burke said nothing. Waited for what he'd do.

And noticed the gun in Kaleb's hand. It carried a suppressor, just like the gun Elaine Billings had used when she'd tried to kill Naomi. *And me.*

Naomi had been right. Burke had been as much a target as she was.

"Are you going to kill me?" Burke asked, his voice raspy.

"Yes. But not yet. You were brought here during a lull in our business day. I'll need to wait for another lull to get you out. It might be a day or two as I'm now short-staffed. I don't want you to start stinking."

"Like he will?" Burke asked, gesturing to Gaffney with his chin.

"He doesn't weigh as much as you do. We'll be able to get him out more easily."

"Out of where?"

Kaleb smiled. It was such a familiar sight. Burke had seen Kaleb smile hundreds of times. Thousands. He wondered why he'd never seen the malevolence lurking beneath.

"I'd say nice try, but it really wasn't. I'm just giving you the courtesy of letting you eat." From his pocket, Kaleb pulled out a wrapped sandwich.

Burke's nose told him it was a burger. His stomach growled.

But he thought of the drugged coffee and shook his head. "No, thank you." He wasn't trusting any food or drink that he'd be given. And then a thought occurred to him. "Did you murder Cresswell, too? Or did he really have a cyanide pill in his cell?"

Kaleb pocketed the sandwich. "I had him killed."

His old friend sounded so proud. "You have reach, then. Guards at the prison?" Details started to click in his mind. "Amanda Cresswell said that her husband was unsurprised at the loss of her finger. Did a guard tell him?"

"Cresswell's attorney hand-delivered a package with her finger."

"So his attorney is working for you, too."

Kaleb lifted a shoulder, apparently all the confirmation Burke was going to get.

"What about the guy who helped you carry me out of that coffee shop?"

"My assistant. He's very loyal."

"Are you having an affair with him, too?"

Kaleb chuckled. "No. I can thank you for him, actually. Him and Cresswell. I began working with both of them because of you."

Burke searched his mind. "That holiday party at Cresswell's house. I took you and Juliette with me. That's how you met Cresswell."

"Not bad. Not correct, but not bad. That's where I met him the second time. The first was at a poker game. Both your former captain and I lost badly that night. I was upset, but he just laughed it off. Said he had more money than he knew what to do with. I didn't know he was a cop at the time. When I met him again later, I wondered where he was getting the money."

"You blackmailed him?"

"Didn't need to. I just wanted in on his side business."

"Why did you need the money? You make more from our company than I do." Then Burke understood. "You have a gambling problem."

Kaleb gave Burke a look filled with contempt. "I had to run your company while you were in the Marines. Lots of stress."

"Does Juliette know?"

"No, and she won't. We'll go to couples therapy and we'll be fine."

"And you'll go on cheating on her."

Kaleb looked amused. "Not with Winnifred, I'm afraid. But there will be others."

"Why Winnifred?"

Burke wasn't sure if he'd get out of there, but if he did, he would take with him whatever information he could get. Unfortunately, the fact that Kaleb was so freely sharing was not a good sign.

"With a wig and the right makeup, she looked just like Naomi Cranston."

"For the bank accounts," Burke guessed, then shook his head. "That can't be right. You brought Winnifred into this years ago. She didn't open the bank accounts in Naomi's name until September."

"Your mind is quick. You could have been my second, but you said no."

Burke's gaze flew to Gaffney's body once again. "You had Gaffney approach me? Tried to get me to steal drugs for you?"

"No. I told Cresswell and Gaffney not to approach you. That you'd say no. They thought they knew best and did it anyway."

"But . . ." Burke returned his gaze to Kaleb's face. "Gaffney threatened the boys. Your children."

"He thought that would work. I did, too, to be honest."

"And you were angry when it didn't. When I still said no."

"You don't care about my sons, Burke. You made that fact abundantly clear when you risked their lives."

"But Gaffney wouldn't have harmed them."

"You didn't know that."

No, Burke hadn't. "And if I'd said yes? Would you have revealed yourself to me then? As my new master?" He said those last words bitterly.

Kaleb's lips twitched. "Your new master. I like that. No, I wouldn't have 'revealed myself' to you. I would have thought you were gathering evidence against us. But I would have allowed you to participate. Enough to get you arrested, at least. Put away in prison. Where you would have been killed."

"Like you tried to have Naomi killed. You put that inmate up to stabbing her." Six times.

"She's remarkably resilient. But she will die. Especially," Kaleb added mockingly, "since you're no longer around to protect her."

Burke fisted his hands behind him. He wanted to rush Kaleb, wanted to take him down, but he had no illusions that the man wouldn't kill him if given the provocation.

So he stayed put until his thoughts settled. "The assistant. How am I responsible for him?"

"You know him. He hates you nearly as much as I do. Stanley's wanted to kill you for years. Ever since you got him tossed out of the Marines."

Stanley? He didn't remember—

Oh. Wayne Stanley. He'd killed another Marine in a fight. Not intentionally, but Stanley had been convicted of manslaughter and dishonorably discharged. Burke had broken up the fight and held Stanley down until the MPs had come to take him away.

Stanley had been a mean, arrogant SOB.

And then Kaleb's words registered. Stanley had wanted to kill him for years.

You've been living on borrowed time for years. Was that what Winifred had meant? Had she been talking about Wayne Stanley? *No, not only Wayne Stanley. Kaleb, too.*

More details were slotting into place. "You let me get away from Cresswell and Gaffney. You let me survive leaving the NOPD. Cresswell never called my bluff when I confronted him about hiring male prostitutes."

"Number one, you didn't have actual proof or you'd have used it. You wouldn't have let Cresswell continue being a dirty cop. Number two, yes, I let you survive leaving the NOPD. Your death would have raised too many questions. Your partner would have kicked up a fuss."

Burke's partner, who'd been a good cop. A good man. Who'd later been murdered for doing the right thing after Burke had left the force. "Were you involved in his murder, too?"

"No. I had nothing to do with his death. Wish I had, though. It tore you up."

Burke swallowed. "You went with me. To his funeral."

"It was always nice to see you fall apart."

"Did you kill my uncle? My mother? Kyra?"

Kaleb's jaw tightened. "Of course not. She was my sister. And too good for you."

Burke believed him. It was a relief that Kaleb hadn't killed his mother and uncle. Hadn't killed his own sister. "On that we can agree." Another terrible thought presented itself. "Your father?" Something flickered in Kaleb's eyes. Guilt? "You did. You killed your father. Did he find out about your gambling problem?" A twitch in Kaleb's jaw told Burke he was right. "You sonofabitch."

"Careful," Kaleb said lightly. "I can still kill you."

But Kaleb could have had Burke killed hundreds of times over the years and hadn't. Kaleb didn't want to kill him.

There was still something there. Some semblance of a relationship, even if Kaleb didn't want that to be true.

Burke hoped it was enough to keep him alive until his people found him.

Kaleb took a step backward. "Try to make yourself comfortable. It won't be long."

Burke had so many questions, but one rose to the top when he saw Kaleb lift his left hand, a key clutched in his fist. The dim bulb reflected off the band on Kaleb's ring finger.

"Your ring."

Kaleb paused. "Excuse me?"

"That ring you're wearing. That's the ring Naomi saw, isn't it?"

Burke, as best man, had held that ring during Kaleb and Juliette's wedding.

But he'd never paid attention to what it looked like.

Kaleb put his key in the lock, as that was the only way to open the door from this side. "Her and her stupid audit," he said. "If the NOPD had done a formal audit, it would have turned up a lot of missing drugs."

"And if she'd reported the missing ring, it would have connected to you," Burke said bitterly.

"That too. My wedding ring was one of a kind. Juliette had it custom-made for me."

"So it was identifiable as yours. And you'd likely left some DNA on it."

Kaleb's smile was cool. "That was a major concern, yes. We had to put the ring back long enough for her to report that it wasn't missing anymore. Otherwise, she would have made a fuss. Requested a formal audit. I couldn't afford an audit."

"So you ruined her life."

Kaleb met his gaze, his eyes cold. "You've ruined your share of lives, Burke. You have no room to talk."

Kaleb opened the door and made his exit.

The door closed and the light went off.

Burke was once again trapped in the darkness.

He slid down the wall until he sat on the cold floor.

Had he ruined lives? Yes, if you called putting criminals away ruining their lives. He'd never ruined an innocent life.

Kaleb had ruined many innocent lives.

So fuck you, Kaleb.

His "brother" had gaslighted him for long enough. The next time Kaleb came in, Burke would end his life.

He just needed to free his hands first.

With the proper tools, even flex-cuffs could be broken.

Luckily he had those tools. Kaleb had taken his guns and his knives and his toolkit, but he'd left Burke his boots.

He grimaced as he rolled to his stomach and kicked his feet up so that he could begin removing his bootlaces. He remembered the conversation he'd had with Naomi. She still hoarded food after prison. He still carried a tool kit with a lock pick and laced his boots with Kevlar kite string.

He was grateful that old habits died hard. Kaleb had taken his toolkit but had left his bootlaces alone.

He had a way to break free, but it was going to hurt.

Uptown, New Orleans, Louisiana
THURSDAY, FEBRUARY 27, 1:05 P.M.

Kaleb closed the door to the soundproofed room and leaned against it. He'd intended to shoot that sonofabitch in the head.

But he couldn't do it.

And Burke knew it, the smug bastard.

Every time Kaleb had considered pulling the trigger, he'd seen them as kids. Lying on the grass in that damn courtyard at Burke's house, looking at the stars and dreaming of what might be.

As much as he hated Burke, he had to face the fact that he could not be the one to kill him. If he'd really wanted to, he would have done so years ago.

Stanley was eager to do the job and Kaleb had promised him that, when the time was right, it would be Stanley's responsibility. More like Stanley's pleasure.

I should have let him do it this morning.

But he hadn't and Stanley had known why. The man's gaze had been filled with contempt for Kaleb's weakness.

Killing his own father had been so easy. Killing Burke was not, and Kaleb wasn't sure of the reason.

Wayne Stanley could do it when he returned. Which should be soon. He'd gotten a text from Stanley three hours ago saying he had picked up the two bodies in the souvenir shop and had just dumped them deep in the bayou where they'd never be found.

The trip was two hours each way in the best of traffic. Today, it could take twice that long. So Stanley would return soon and he'd kill Burke and that would be that. Burke's people might make noise about his involvement, but there wasn't a speck of evidence to back them up. And if they found evidence, he had enough people on his payroll in the NOPD to make any investigations go away.

He stared at the ring on his finger. Naomi had remembered it. They'd figured out why she'd been targeted. *But Naomi doesn't know it's my ring.*

Kaleb had no compunction about killing Naomi Cranston. She was probably hiding in Burke's house after being shot at the day before. If he had to burn Burke's fancy house to the ground, he'd smoke the bitch out. He'd kill them all.

"Marchand."

Kaleb looked up to find his new partner approaching. He hated that he'd had to cut Desi Ortiz in. He didn't trust the gang leader as far as he could throw him. But he didn't have much of a choice. He needed more hands to manage this weekend's business.

Kaleb dipped his head in acknowledgment. "Desi."

"We have some dead space in the schedule."

"I told you that we would. Clients want to see the parade and they'll be jockeying for the best viewing position." People had been lining up for hours for the Krewe of Babylon's parade. "We'll be full again afterward. Every slot is booked. Maya is taking this lull to prep the rooms and the inventory for the next round."

"Okay," Desi said. "They're paying up front?"

"Cash or their appointment goes to the next person on the waiting list."

"I'll want to count the cash with you at the end of the night. To make sure there are no errors in the splitting of the profits."

Kaleb rose to his full height, annoyed when Desi looked bored. "Are you suggesting that I'd steal from you?"

Desi smiled. "Of course not. It is standard operating procedure. Forgive my insistence, but I need to be sure that *our* business shows a profit."

"It will." *It'd better.*

"I want to see your expenses. I'm not pleased with how much money you've spent on this warehouse. Clients who wish to purchase inventory such as ours don't need fancy trappings. They simply want to fuck kids. There are cheaper ways to do this."

"This is not a low-class establishment."

"Then you'll have to charge more. It appears that you don't want me to see your P&Ls."

Kaleb felt himself bristling, even knowing that this was Ortiz's power play. "Not at all." He kept his tone level. Civil. "If you'll follow me to my office, I'll be happy to review our expenses."

"Thank you. Is that also where you keep the cash?"

The cash was Ortiz's bigger concern, Kaleb knew. "It is," he lied. He only kept a small part of the cash in the office. There was no way he was sharing everything he brought in with Ortiz, or he'd never turn a profit. "This way, please."

25

The Quarter, New Orleans, Louisiana
THURSDAY, FEBRUARY 27, 3:00 P.M.

NAOMI WANTED TO scream in frustration.

They'd been gathered in Burke's study for hours, looking at maps and checking properties owned by the companies who'd paid Winnifred Timms's expenses and who'd paid off Jimmy's mortgage.

Well, it was mostly Antoine and Molly doing the work while Naomi, Eleanor, Ruthanne, and James watched in tense silence. Naomi felt useless. Helpless.

Hopeless.

Because other than the condo that had been destroyed by fire, the companies appeared to own no property. They were no closer to finding Burke.

André had been unable to get search warrants for Kaleb's home and office. Naomi's recognition of both Kaleb and the ring in the photo hadn't been nearly enough for the judge.

His coffee shop alibi checks out. And weren't Kaleb's own sons targeted? the judge had asked. *Surely he didn't try to abduct his own children.*

The abductions had to have been faked, at least the attempted abduction of Braden and Trent Marchand.

Faking the abduction of his own children had been brilliant, Naomi had to concede. It had put Burke on the defensive, had made him second-guess himself and his career choices. And, perhaps worst of all, his own integrity and loyalty. Still, Burke had managed to investigate the case so thoroughly that he'd made himself a target.

Molly had taken it upon herself to search Marchand's office and the factory. She'd called up all of Burke's part-timers and, using the keys they'd found in Burke's bureau drawer, they'd searched the factory top to bottom.

But there was no sign of Burke or of any teenagers being forced into sexual slavery. The searches were a total bust.

There were two silver linings to the dark cloud that hung over them.

Everett, in a move that had surprised everyone, had taken charge of the other kids, choosing the movies and making snacks that Elijah could eat.

And Val's prognosis was good. She'd been alert enough to tell Molly that she'd been standing outside the coffee shop, waiting for Burke as he met with Kaleb. She'd chosen a secure location—directly in front of a locked gate that closed off the alley between the coffee shop and the souvenir store. The gates were common all over town. Without them, locals and tourists alike would use the alleys as shortcuts, places to deal drugs. Places to pee. So the property owners kept the gates locked.

But the gunman had opened the gate behind her, shoved a gun into her neck, and pulled her through, growling that if she went for her weapon, he'd shoot. She was wearing Kevlar, but it didn't cover her neck.

He'd pushed her into the souvenir shop, where he injected her. Before she passed out, she noticed the man's shoes.

It always came back to the man with the shoes.

"We need to ID the man with the shoes," Naomi said abruptly, interrupting Molly and Antoine, who were staring at one of the whiteboards.

Antoine continued studying the map. "I did. His name is Wayne Stanley. The shoe store clicked on the phishing link I sent to their email, so I was able to access their sales records. I got a list of their customers, and Molly recognized Stanley's name. He's the same general size as one of the fedora-wearing guys entering the Delgados' house."

"I knew Stanley," Molly said, also staring at the map. "He served under Burke in the Corps. Killed a man and was dishonorably discharged. He *hated* Burke. Blamed him for turning him over to the MPs. Like Burke had a choice."

Naomi had to bite back her anger. "Why didn't you tell me about Stanley?"

Antoine faced her then, his expression a mix of frustration and fear. "Because there's nothing on him. He owns no property, has filed no taxes, has no income. He has no current address, no car, no driver's license. He's a ghost. I dug into him and I got nowhere."

"This isn't getting us anywhere, either," Naomi said, gesturing to the whiteboard. "It's been eight hours."

Molly turned and Naomi couldn't hide her wince. Molly's face was dangerously pale. Her eyes were dull. Her hands trembled. "I know exactly how long it's been, Naomi," she said quietly. "Down to the second. But I don't know what to do next."

Not knowing was probably one of Molly's greatest fears. The woman was calm efficiency personified. Burke's people were running scared.

So am I.

"Come, sit down," she said to Antoine and Molly. "Let's go over what we do know."

"I have," Molly said, her voice strained. "Over and over. It's no good."

Molly was on the verge of spiraling. Naomi knew what that felt like. She asked herself what Burke would do, were he there.

He'd take charge.

"Molly, sit down," she said firmly, using her mom voice.

Blinking, Molly obeyed. Antoine sat next to her. Both looked wrung out.

"Thank you," Naomi said. "We *will* find him." They had to. "Tell me what else you know about Wayne Stanley. What was his skill set?"

"He was a demolition expert," Antoine said. "He trained with the firefighters, but he didn't make the final cut."

"So the fires in Eleanor's neighborhood and the condo make sense," Naomi said.

"They do," Molly said. "But they bring us no closer to finding Burke."

"But we will know what we're up against when we do find him," Naomi said.

Molly nodded. "Okay. What do *you* think we should do?"

It wasn't said with any sarcasm. Only exhausted defeat.

"Let's go over Kaleb again. What do we know?"

"He's forty-two," Molly said. "He's been married to Juliette for twenty years. They have two sons, Braden and Trent. He started working for the Fontenot company at age eighteen, working his way through college. After college, he was hired into an entry-level manager position."

Naomi considered the dates. "He told Burke that he resented him for going into the military, then becoming a cop. Burke would have still been in the Marine Corps when Kaleb graduated and started at the company."

Molly and Antoine stared at her.

"How do you know that?" Molly asked.

"Burke told me." Naomi felt her cheeks heat. "We'd meet in the living room and we'd talk."

"And canoodle," Eleanor added in a singsong, trying to lighten the mood. "I saw it with my own eyes."

"So did I," James said. "I was coming downstairs for some water and turned myself right around. There was a lot of canoodling."

Molly almost smiled. Antoine looked slightly less tense for a heartbeat.

"There was *some* canoodling," Naomi allowed. At least in the living room. What she and Burke had done in his bedroom was private. And she would have that again because they would find him. "But mostly talking. Kaleb called him right after his sons were fake-abducted. Gave Burke a lot of bullshit about him not caring about his family, about him taking risks and putting Kaleb's kids in danger. Told Burke that he didn't want him to see the boys anymore. That he was too dangerous."

"Oh, wow." Molly scowled. "What a gaslighting asshole."

"It worked," Antoine said glumly. "We've been holed up here for days, not out looking for Kaleb's sorry ass."

"Now we *are* looking for Kaleb's sorry ass," Naomi said. "What else do we know, other than he was cheating on Juliette with Winifred Timms?"

"That still shocks me," Molly confessed.

"It shocked Burke, too," Naomi murmured. "He didn't know it was with Winnifred, though. Juliette had only told him that Kaleb was cheating."

"How did she know about the cheating?" Molly asked. "When I called her to tell her about Burke being missing, she said that she knew Kaleb had cheated, but she wouldn't believe he'd done all the other stuff—not the trafficking or the murders. She said we'd lost our minds."

Naomi had been too numb to even think about talking to Kaleb's wife. Molly had taken it upon herself to contact Juliette, both to warn her that Kaleb was dangerous and hoping that the woman would know where Burke was being held, but they'd only gotten her forceful denial of Kaleb's involvement.

"She hired . . ." Naomi stopped, the words bouncing around in her mind. "A PI. *She hired a PI.* I can't believe I didn't think of this. What if the PI followed Kaleb to the house he's using to traffic those kids? What if that's where he took Burke?"

Molly seemed suddenly energized. "That's a lot of ifs, but let's go with it for now. We need that PI's report. Someone else needs to ask. I don't think she'll talk to me again."

"Let me try." Naomi took out her own phone. "Give me her number."

Naomi dialed, then held her breath. The call was answered on the first ring and Naomi put it on speaker.

"Kaleb?" Juliette sounded like she was crying.

"No," Naomi said quietly. "My name is Naomi Cranston."

"You." It was said with contempt. "You're the one who started all this. You're the one who got Burke all tangled up in your business. This is all your fault."

"No, it's not!" Everett shouted from the doorway.

Naomi turned to her son, shocked. "Everett?"

Everett's face was red, his fists clenched at his sides. "She says it's your fault, but it's not. Those men threatened you. They put you in prison for five fucking years. They framed you. Her husband framed you. And he tried to kill you twice this week. Lady, you can't talk to her that way. It's not her fault."

Naomi reached out a hand to her son, barely able to swallow the sob of relief that rose when he took it. "Thank you, Everett."

"I'm sorry. I should have believed you." He pointed to the phone. "She should believe you."

"But you have the facts now," Naomi said gently. "She doesn't. Not yet. Mrs. Marchand, I apologize. My son is defending me, but there is some truth in your words. I came to Burke for help. My son was being threatened. His was the first attempted abduction on Monday."

A beat of silence. "I'm glad he's okay," Juliette said stiffly. "What do you want?"

"First, I don't expect you to believe everything Molly told you. Not yet. But I have a few questions for you."

"I don't have anything to say to you."

"Wait," Naomi pleaded before Juliette could hang up. "Did your husband lose his wedding ring six years ago?"

Another moment of silence, this one longer. Naomi clutched Everett's hand tighter. He lowered his forehead to her shoulder. He was shaking.

Feeling like she was walking a tightrope, Naomi put her arm around him and kissed his temple. She was holding her son. He was letting her.

"It'll be okay, honey," she murmured. "Mrs. Marchand? Are you still there?"

"Yes. How did you know Kaleb lost his wedding ring?" The question was accusatory. "Were you having an affair with him, too?"

"No, ma'am," Naomi said quickly. "I was a cop, working in the evidence room. A ring was brought in one day by a college kid who'd found it at a crime scene. It was silver filigree with a pattern of tiny fleurs-de-lis. I think your husband wore it on a chain around his neck. The chain was somehow broken and the ring ended up in a storm pipe."

"He has allergies. His fingers would swell and he was afraid he wouldn't get the ring off in time. So he started wearing the ring on a chain. He takes antihistamines now, so he can wear the ring again." She faltered. "He said he lost it at the gym and they found it and gave it back." Then her defensiveness was back. "Are you saying he lied about that?"

Naomi understood denial. She'd felt it when she'd first learned the truth about Jimmy, so she proceeded carefully. "I only know that I processed the ring into the system, but it was missing a few days later. I reported it and another ring ended up where the silver filigree ring had been. A day later, the correct ring showed up, and I figured everything had been put right. But it's not in evidence anymore."

André had checked and the ring was gone.

"There are a lot of silver rings," Juliette said. "It wasn't my husband's. You have to be wrong."

"We have a photo," Antoine said. "The man who found it sent me the photo he took of the ring. I'll text it to you now."

A few seconds later, Juliette gasped. "Oh my God. This isn't possible."

"Is that your husband's ring?" Naomi asked.

"Yes. But that doesn't mean that Kaleb killed anyone like Molly said he did."

Naomi hated to do this, but they needed Juliette's cooperation. "Do you know a man named Wayne Stanley?"

"Yes. He's one of my husband's customers."

"He's not," Naomi said. "He's your husband's assistant in his illegal enterprises and he's been identified by three different people as being connected to this case. One of the IDs came from a sixteen-year-old girl who escaped her captors during Super Bowl weekend. She was being sold for sex."

"No," Juliette whispered. "That doesn't mean Kaleb was involved."

Naomi realized that Everett had stopped shaking. When she turned to look at him, he lifted his gaze to hers. He was interested. Respectful.

Her heart squeezed painfully. It was difficult to contain the joy, sadness, and fear she felt, all at once.

"This young woman identified four people. One was Elaine Billings, who's currently in custody. One was Wayne Stanley, who's still at large. The third was murdered Tuesday night. Her name was Winifred Timms. Can you google her name for me? Find her photo?"

Another gasp. "I know her. She's my husband's . . ."

"The woman he was having an affair with," Naomi said, keeping her tone gentle. Juliette was brittle. Too much pressure and she'd break.

"Yes," Juliette whispered. "Oh my God. Is this true? She's dead?"

"Murdered right in front of us. They shot at us, but we'd hit the floor already."

"This can't be happening."

Naomi hated to hurt this woman. "Juliette, the sixteen-year-old said that Winnifred called him Romeo." She remembered Burke's little jolt of surprise, but Romeo wasn't an uncommon nickname. "Was that your pet name for him? Because you're Juliette?"

Juliette's sob was heart-wrenching. "Why are you doing this to me?"

"Because you could be in danger," Naomi said. "Your husband is not the man you thought him to be. When he realizes he's cornered, he might come home and try to use you all to escape. Willingly or not."

Juliette said nothing, her sobs echoing through the phone.

Naomi let her cry for another minute. "Mrs. Marchand, Burke met with your husband this morning and we believe Kaleb drugged him. Patrons at the coffee shop said two men dragged him out because he was drunk. It was only seven in the morning."

"Burke never drinks too much," Juliette whispered.

"Which is why we believe he was drugged. Wayne Stanley drugged Val, too. Overdosed her on a fentanyl mixture. She nearly died. Molly found her in time."

"Oh." It was a mournful sound. "She'll be okay?"

"She will. But now I need to ask you for something that I'm not supposed to know about. Burke was devastated on Monday when Kaleb told him that he was no longer welcome in your lives. He needed someone to talk to, so he talked to me. Last night, he was even sadder. You'd told him that you suspected Kaleb of having an affair. That you hired a PI."

"He *told* you that?"

"He did. I'm sorry. I wouldn't have told a soul, but that PI could be important. His report could tell us where Burke is now."

One last, long silence. "I don't believe that Kaleb has done any of the things you're accusing him of," the woman finally said stubbornly. "There has to be another explanation. This man, this Wayne Stanley, has to have deceived Kaleb. Kaleb would never hurt Burke or anyone else. But I've sent the PI's report to Antoine. Burke hasn't been behaving like himself, either, so maybe he *was* drunk at seven this morning. He could be sleeping it off somewhere. Kaleb would watch over him until he was sober."

Naomi wanted to argue but she understood. It had been difficult for her to believe the worst about Jimmy for a long time, too. She glanced at Antoine, who held up his phone, nodding.

"I've got the report," he said into the speaker. "Thank you, Juliette."

"Find Burke. And when you do, tell him that Kaleb was right. His life is filled with too much drama. It's better if he doesn't come around anymore."

The woman ended the call and for a moment, they stood in stunned silence.

"She is in major denial, isn't she?" Everett said quietly, like he knew what that was like.

"She is." Naomi laid her head on Everett's shoulder, her eyes stinging when his arm came around her waist, holding her up. "But she and Burke can hash all that out when we find him."

Uptown, New Orleans, Louisiana

THURSDAY, FEBRUARY 27, 3:15 P.M.

Burke struggled to sit up, then dropped his face to his knees to wipe the sweat from his eyes. The last time he'd done this maneuver was on a dare with Antoine.

He'd been successful then. He'd be successful today, too.

He rolled to his stomach once again, having looped his Kevlar kite-string bootlaces through the flex-cuffs restraining his hands. At one point, he'd been able to complete this escape in under three minutes.

Today, it had taken him hours. And he wasn't done.

To be fair, when he'd done it on a dare, he hadn't been recently roofied. Nor had he been in absolute darkness. He'd been bound with zip ties, not flex-cuffs.

They were harder to break.

Had Kaleb used zip ties, Burke could have broken through already. It was possible to use the body as a wedge to snap the plastic. He'd learned that skill during survival training in the Corps.

But flex-cuffs were stronger. Kaleb had done his research.

Or Wayne Stanley had. The man had been a shitty human being, but he'd been a decent Marine.

Not gonna think about them now. Thinking about Kaleb and Wayne Stanley and Gaffney tensed him up and he needed his body to be relaxed.

He fumbled for the bootlace, now draped around the middle of the flex-cuffs. Kevlar kite string was a handy survival tool. It could cut through wood in a pinch. And, with enough elbow grease, it could cut through plastic flex-cuffs.

He found the end of the bootlace and formed a loop. It would go over the toe of his right boot.

He wasn't sure how long it took to secure the loop, but he was panting and sweating again by the time he'd done it. This room had no ventilation. No fresh air. He blinked to clear the sweat from his eyes. It didn't work, but now that he was securing the kite string to his boots, he couldn't sit up to properly wipe his eyes.

It was just going to have to sting.

One more boot.

He got the other end of the kite string looped over his left boot and stopped to rest. He wondered again what Kaleb used this room for. He wondered if it was where he put people to die.

It was more likely that this was where they put people who had died. He thought of the kids like Susan Snyder. He wondered if they were trapped in this place along with him.

Once he escaped, he'd find out.

Okay, break time's over. The Kevlar kite string he'd looped through the flex-cuffs would act like a saw once he got his feet moving.

So move, feet.

It was like swimming. Kicking the water. He pumped his legs as fast as he could. The heat generated by the kite string would melt the plastic and—

Yes. The plastic snapped and his hands flopped to his sides.

He lay there for a moment, catching his breath. Then he rolled to his back, staring up into the darkness before finally sitting up. He touched his wrists and his fingers came away sticky. He was bleeding, but he'd had a lot worse.

His hands were free.

It was time to escape this room.

The Quarter, New Orleans, Louisiana
THURSDAY, FEBRUARY 27, 3:55 P.M.

Naomi stood at the whiteboard with Molly and Antoine. They were alone in the study, everyone having dispersed after Naomi's call with Juliette.

Everett had been the last one to go, and only after he'd asked her several times if she was okay. She wasn't, but she thought that maybe, with him, she would be.

Once Antoine had read the PI's report, he'd marked the addresses Kaleb had frequented on the map they'd taped to the whiteboard.

There were nine addresses. Seven houses and two warehouses.

She wondered why Kaleb had gone to all these places. She wondered which were part of his drug business and which were tied to human trafficking.

"We should go to these two," Molly said, pointing at two houses on Magazine Street.

Both were on the parade route and both were three stories tall, exactly as Susan Snyder had said.

"I don't know," Naomi said, trying to figure out what was bothering her about the two houses.

"None of the other homes are on the parade route," Molly said. "These houses are exactly as Susan described, aren't they?"

"They are," Naomi conceded. "But . . ." She pointed at one of the warehouses. It was between the Mississippi River and Tchoupitoulas Street. "This one is also three stories."

"But it's not a house," Antoine said. "And it's not on the parade route."

That was true as well. "It's only four blocks away. Susan could have heard the music."

Antoine shook his head. "We're looking at *houses*."

He and Molly continued laying out their strategy for approaching, entering, and searching the houses.

But there was something about the warehouse. Naomi brought up its street view on Google Maps. The building was solid brick. Three stories. Very few windows.

It was situated near some self-storage places and a few open lots that stored containers carried by ships into the port of New Orleans. It was isolated, with river access, which made it perfect as a sex trafficking den.

But it was not a house.

Maybe Susan had been wrong.

"She never saw the outside," Naomi said, interrupting Molly and Antoine.

"What?" Molly asked. "Who never saw the outside of what?"

"Susan. She never saw the outside of the place. She was drugged before she got there, blindfolded when she was taken out to the motels."

"Okay," Molly said slowly. "And?"

"And . . . what if it only looks like a house on the inside? What if it's a warehouse on the outside?"

Both Molly and Antoine looked surprised. "I don't know . . ." Antoine said.

"It's possible, right?" Naomi insisted.

"Yes," Molly said. "If we strike out with these two houses, we'll check it out. But we're looking at the houses first."

The two went back to discussing their plans.

Naomi wanted to scream once more, but this time was because it felt like they were patronizing her. Burke had never done that. Not even once.

"Think about the traffic," she blurted out.

"Cars?" Antoine asked.

"No," Naomi snapped, then drew a breath. "Sorry. I mean people. They'll have customers at all hours. You think that can happen here in a residential neighborhood? The neighbors would go crazy."

"She's got a point," Antoine murmured.

"I know," Molly said. "Like I said, we'll check it out."

"But only after you look at these two houses," Naomi said, trying to rein in her irritation.

"Yes," Molly said firmly.

"Fine. I'm going, too," Naomi said.

Molly shook her head. "You're not. You're not trained, Naomi. I'm sorry."

Naomi stared. "You're kidding, right? I was a cop."

Molly winced. "In the evidence room."

Naomi closed her eyes and tried not to seethe. "I am going."

"Sorry, hon," Antoine said, giving her a one-armed hug. "Burke wants you safe. We can't be worrying about you when we go into these places."

Naomi thought that Antoine rarely went on missions like this one and that he was probably less trained than she was, but she bit her tongue.

Molly squeezed Naomi's shoulder. "We'll keep you up to speed."

Naomi watched them leave through narrowed eyes.

"I can't believe this," she muttered, then stared at the one address on the map that met all their criteria, except for being an actual house.

"What's going on?" Eleanor asked from the doorway. She was leaning on her walker, a sure sign of her fatigue.

"Molly and Antoine are being . . . well, they're not listening to me."

"I know," Eleanor said. "I could hear you from my room. What are you going to do about it?"

Naomi heard the roar of Burke's SUV as Molly and Antoine departed. They'd be lucky to get out of the Quarter at this time of day. They'd be closing down the roads on the parade route in fifteen minutes. Traffic had been snarled for hours.

"I don't have a car and I don't think one would be all that useful anyway."

Eleanor nodded. "True enough."

"But . . ." She remembered Burke's bike, leaning against the wall in the mudroom. She felt the first spark of control. She was not hopeless *or* helpless. "Burke has a bicycle."

"So what are you going to do with it?"

"I'm going to the warehouse." She nodded toward the whiteboard. "On Burke's bicycle. It's probably the fastest way to get anywhere right now."

"Stick to the roads at least three to four blocks off the parade route," Eleanor cautioned. "Any closer and you'll be stuck in wall-to-wall people."

Naomi abruptly deflated. "I don't have a weapon and I don't know the combination to Burke's gun safe. I'm not going after him unarmed. I'll have to guess the combo."

"Or you could borrow mine." Eleanor reached into the pocket of her cardigan, which Naomi only just noticed was hanging inches lower on one side. The older woman brought out a Glock 19. "You take care of this, y'hear? It belonged to my husband. I didn't want to leave it in the house in case those thugs broke in. It hasn't been fired in years, but my husband kept it clean."

Naomi took the gun, checked the chamber, then popped the magazine. It held seventeen rounds. "That should be enough."

Eleanor reached into her other pocket and brought out a fully loaded thirty-three-round magazine. "In case it's not."

"You're amazing," Naomi breathed. "Thank you."

"You're a good soul, Naomi. Go get your man. Just . . . be careful. And don't tell your mother that I gave you that gun."

"I won't." She kissed Eleanor's cheek and ran down the stairs to the mudroom where Burke kept his bicycle.

Where she gained the undivided attention of three boys and one gruff bodyguard. Harrison stared at her with knowing eyes. Naomi stared back.

"Naomi?" Everett asked, then grunted when Jace elbowed him in the gut. "Mom?" he corrected himself. "Shit, man, don't do that. It hurts."

"We talked about this," Jace said. "You've got a great mom."

"Yeah," Elijah added. "Treat her with respect."

Naomi wanted to hug them all. Instead, she cupped Everett's cheek. "Thank you. I'm proud of you."

He looked at his feet. "You shouldn't be. I was awful."

"You're sixteen and your father lied to you. I was thirty and I believed his lies until I caught him red-handed."

"He hit you. I remember that night."

"I'm sorry you had to see that."

He looked up, his eyes glassy with unshed tears. "I just wanted everything to be normal. For us to be . . . happy. Together."

"I know. But you and I are together now. And when I get back, I'll make you some cookies."

He looked a little green. "Everyone's been making cookies. I'm kinda sick of the sugar, to be honest. Rain check?"

"Absolutely." She kissed his cheek, thrilled when he didn't rebuff her. "I love you."

He didn't say it back, but he smiled. It was enough.

"Miss Naomi?" Jace said, poking at the bulge in her jacket pocket. "What are you doing with that"—he lowered his voice to a whisper—"gun?"

She winced. *Busted.* So she decided to be truthful. "Going after Burke."

She glanced at Harrison, expecting him to take the gun away. But he just stood there looking . . . satisfied.

Jace frowned. "Molly and Antoine are going after Burke."

"I don't think he's where they'll be looking." She took hold of the handlebars of the bicycle. "It'll take me at least half an hour to get there. I hope Burke has that much time."

You've been living on borrowed time for years. I think your time is up.

Elijah raised his brows, suddenly looking so very adult. "Are you going alone?"

"You *can't* go alone, Mom," Everett said, frowning. "It's dangerous. Harrison should go with you."

"I can't," Harrison said. "What if they're waiting for all Burke's people to leave so that they can get to you? My job is to protect you. That's what I'm going to do."

"He's right," Naomi said. "And I was a cop, honey. Even if I only worked the evidence room. I'll be okay." She hoped that she wouldn't need the gun, but she'd kept up with her firearms practice, both before and after she'd gone to prison. "And I'm not going alone." She made a split-second decision, once again glancing at Harrison. "I'm going to ask André to meet me there."

Harrison nodded once in approval.

To her surprise, her son hugged her, a full, two-armed bear hug. "Be careful."

She hugged him back. "I will. Bye, guys." She headed outside with Burke's bicycle, then dialed André Holmes.

"Naomi. Did you find Burke?"

"No, but I think I know where he is."

"Where?"

She gave him the address and he groaned. "That's only a few blocks from where the parade starts. Are you sure?"

"No," she admitted, "but it makes the most sense." She recounted what they'd learned from the PI's report.

"That actually does make a lot of sense that they'd put it on the river," he said thoughtfully. "Both for the customer traffic and river access. I'll go. You stay where you are."

She opened her mouth to say no, that she was going, but she knew they'd only waste time arguing. "Hurry."

The call ended and Naomi tucked her phone back into her pocket. Squaring her shoulders, she threw one leg over the bicycle.

Hold on, Burke. I'll be there soon.

26

Uptown, New Orleans, Louisiana
THURSDAY, FEBRUARY 27, 4:45 P.M.

KALEB WANTED TO snarl. Juliette had called five times in the last forty-five minutes and he did not have time to talk to her.

Things were not going smoothly with his new partner. Ortiz was unimpressed with the way Kaleb had been running the business.

Join the club. If this weekend didn't go well, Fontenot's board of directors would vote to remove him. They were too deeply in debt, because Kaleb had embezzled too much money. He'd had losing streaks at the gaming tables in the past, but never like this. He needed every penny of this week's projected income to prop up his legit business or face ouster.

His other concern was even bigger. Wayne Stanley still had not returned, nor had he answered Kaleb's texts. How long did it take to dump two bodies?

Something was wrong.

His phone buzzed again.

Ortiz lifted a brow. "Someone really wants to talk to you."

Juliette. Again. "I'll take this in the hallway." He shut the door behind him. "What?" he snapped when he'd hit accept.

"Kaleb." Juliette was crying.

"What's wrong? Is it the boys? Did someone else try to steal them?"

No one would, of course. No one had actually tried kidnapping them to begin with.

"No. It's . . . it's Burke. He's missing. He was supposed to be meeting with you."

"We had an appointment, but Burke never showed up," he lied. "I waited for over an hour."

"His people called me. They said he'd been seen in a coffee shop and was dragged out, drunk. I thought maybe you'd taken him somewhere to let him sober up."

The first part was exactly the plan, to have Burke appear to have been drunk. But not the second part. Kaleb was not supposed to have been connected with him. "I never saw him, Jules. I don't know where he is."

"His people . . . they . . ." She made a wounded noise. "They told me some things."

Kaleb's blood ran cold. "What kind of things?"

"That you were involved in . . . things. Terrible things, Kaleb."

"Such as?" he asked, trying to sound confused and not scared as fuck.

"Trafficking. Kids. Teenagers."

Kaleb's knees went weak. How? How did they know?

I should have killed Burke years ago.

"They're delusional," he managed.

"I know."

But she didn't sound sure. *Dammit.* "Do you? I cheated, yes, but that you could believe I did . . . those things? Maybe our marriage is past saving."

"No!" she cried. "I don't believe them. And . . . but . . ." She cried harder. "I did something terrible."

"What?" This wasn't going to be good.

"I hired a PI. Not Burke. I wouldn't do that to you. But I needed to know if you were cheating. So I hired a PI to follow you."

Oh my God. "And what did he find?"

"Just that you were cheating with that woman. The one who died this week. You never told me she was dead."

"I didn't know," he lied again, his heart pounding. "Freddie is dead?"

"That woman says so. Naomi. She knew about your ring, Kaleb. She knew that you'd lost it."

Kaleb closed his eyes. "What have you done, Juliette?"

"I gave them the PI's report. I thought that if you had Burke with you, if you were helping him get sober . . ."

"I see." And he did.

He could see that everything was lost. He had to get out of here. Had to destroy the evidence.

"I told them to tell Burke not to come around anymore, once they found him. You were right, Kaleb. We don't need his drama."

"Okay," he said numbly. "When was this?"

"Forty-five minutes ago. I've been trying to reach you. To tell you that Burke's people are trying to set you up."

It was still only circumstantial evidence. Once he destroyed this place, he could hire a decent lawyer. He could get away with it. The only people who knew the truth about Burke were Stanley, Burke's bodyguard, and Burke himself.

"Kaleb?" Juliette asked tearfully when he said nothing. "Are you still there?"

"Yes. I'll be home soon. Did they say anything else I should know about?"

"Just that they thought Burke had been drugged like his bodyguard. Val Sorensen."

Oh no. No, no, no. "Val was drugged?"

Val was dead. Her body was in the bayou. Stanley had said so.

"They said that she almost died. She's in the hospital."

Stanley had lied. Why? Why would he lie?

To buy time, Kaleb realized. Stanley knew they were fucked and he'd saved himself.

Kaleb had to fight to breathe. Stanley hadn't killed Val. He hadn't picked up her body and taken it to the bayou.

And now everyone would know. Everyone did know.

I have to get out of here.

"I need to go. I'll see you soon."

He left Ortiz in the office. He needed to get rid of this place. Ortiz could figure it out on his own. He would soon enough.

The smoke would be Ortiz's first clue.

He ran to the back, to where the trucks docked. To where they kept supplies.

He grabbed a box of flex-cuffs and a full can of gasoline and ran up the stairs. "Maya!"

Maya emerged from one of the rooms, closing the door and locking it with her key. "Yes, boss?"

"Get everyone into one of the trucks." He thrust the box of flex-cuffs into her hands. "Use these. Do it now."

Maya's eyes widened. "We're made?"

"Just do what I said!" Kaleb snapped, then began dousing the floor with gasoline.

Seemed like he'd be the one killing Burke, after all.

Uptown, New Orleans, Louisiana
THURSDAY, FEBRUARY 27, 4:50 P.M.

Naomi slowed her pedaling as she approached the warehouse. The muscles in her legs were screaming, but she ignored the pain.

If she could find Burke or those kids, it would be worth it.

There were no crowds down this way. They were all gathered a few blocks north, waiting for the parade to begin. There was music, though. She could hear the marching bands warming up.

She pushed the bicycle the last hundred yards, hoping to see André, but there was no sign of him. The warehouse seemed nearly deserted, but there was some activity in one of the loading bays on the right side of the building. A truck was backed up to an open bay and there was someone standing to one side of the truck holding a clipboard.

It looked just like a warehouse should.

She pushed Burke's bike to the rear of the building and gently leaned it against the wall. There was no activity here, either.

Maybe I was wrong. She'd expected to see perverted customers entering and exiting via the river, but it was just a warehouse.

Hopefully Antoine and Molly are having better luck at the houses.

And then she heard a scream. Leaving the bicycle, Naomi ran along the far side of the warehouse, halting abruptly when she got to the front right corner of the building, nearest the open bay. She eased forward, her hand on the Glock in her pocket as she tried to see what was happening.

If there were cameras, they'd probably already seen her, but she couldn't make herself back away. She stood, transfixed in horror, as a large man dragged a teenage boy from the street in front of the warehouse toward the open bay. The man lifted his arm and the gun in his hand glinted in the light from a streetlamp before he brought the butt down hard on the kid's head, making him stumble.

He shoved the young man, who looked to be Everett's age, up onto the raised loading platform. "Cuff him," he growled.

The person with the clipboard came forward. Naomi recognized her from the photos provided by Eleanor's neighbors. This was Maya.

Maya yanked the young man to his feet. Holding a handful of flex-cuffs, she dragged the kid to the truck and shoved him in.

Naomi couldn't hear what Maya was saying, so she edged closer.

"Anyone else want to try to run?" Maya snarled.

Anyone else? The kids they'd been searching for.

The large man with the gun heaved himself up on the raised loading platform and disappeared into the truck.

Whatever he was saying to the occupants was too low for Naomi to hear. Then the doors to the truck were slammed shut.

For a moment, Naomi held her breath. If they came this way, if they saw her, she'd be dead.

But they didn't approach. Instead, an inside door slammed shut.

Hands surprisingly steady, Naomi pulled out her phone and dialed André Holmes. "Where are you?" she hissed.

"Almost to the address you gave me. Where the hell are you?"

"At the address I gave you. The kids are here. In a truck. Two people were with them. One man, one woman. One has a gun, not sure about the other."

"Goddammit, Naomi," André said in a low growl. "You were supposed to stay at Burke's house."

She wasn't going to argue. "Hurry," Naomi urged. And then she smelled the smoke. *Oh no. Oh shit.* "They've set this place on fire."

Burke. He was inside, she was certain of it.

"Get back," André commanded. "I'm only a few minutes out."

"Drive faster." She ended the call, having already decided what she needed to do. Those two could come back any moment. They'd drive that truck away and take the kids with them.

Burke would have to hold on a few moments more. He'd want the kids freed first. She was certain of that, too.

Taking a running leap, she hit the raised platform on her ass. She spun and was on her feet in seconds.

They'd slid a padlock into the latch on the truck's doors, but they hadn't closed the lock. She pulled it out and opened one of the doors.

Ten teenagers huddled inside. Half quietly cried. All wore flex-cuffs, cuffed together in pairs.

Naomi's heart broke. "Come with me. I'm here to help you."

They looked at each other fearfully, and then one girl stood, pulling another girl with her. "You heard her. Let's go."

The girl dragged her cuff-mate through the truck's door and motioned for the others to follow.

One of the other girls faced Naomi straight on, blocking the path of the remaining kids. "Who are you?"

"My name is Naomi. I've been looking for the men who've been using you. I've spoken to Susan," she added, when the girl didn't look convinced.

The girl jolted in shock before she gulped on a sob. "She's alive?"

"Yes. Now, hurry, before they come back."

She got all the kids out of the truck, easing them off the platform and onto the pavement that led to the street.

The boy who'd been struck with the butt of the man's gun staggered, but two other kids held him up.

"The cops are on their way," Naomi said. "To help you," she added when fear flared in their eyes. "I know Gaffney is a cop, but the one I called is a good guy." She got her phone and googled André's name, relieved when a photo of his face popped up quickly. "This is him. His name is André Holmes. The parade is starting. If you run that way"—she pointed north—"you'll run into the crowd. Stay around people until you see this man. Are there other kids?"

"Yes," the first girl said. "Another ten at least."

Naomi felt sick. "That many?"

"There were more," the girl said, her lips trembling. "They died."

Naomi swallowed hard. "I'll try to find them. You guys run. *Now.*"

She didn't wait to see if they'd obeyed her, instead climbing back up onto the loading platform. She closed the truck door and replaced the padlock as she'd found it.

André, where the hell are you?

She couldn't wait. The place was burning and Burke could be inside.

Loud voices caught her attention and she flattened herself against the wall of the loading dock. But the voices were coming from outside. She crept to the truck and peeked around the corner.

Five men were running away from the front door of the warehouse. Some coughed. Four were dressed in black T-shirts and jeans. The one man who wore a suit screamed, "Marchand, you fucking bastard!"

Kaleb was still inside the building.

The five men scattered like rats. She wasn't sure if they were customers or if they worked there.

She hoped the kids she'd freed had gotten far enough away.

Find Burke. Find the other kids. Get them out.

And if Burke's not here?

Hopefully Molly and Antoine would have already found him.

Her heart was racing when she opened the door into the warehouse. She could smell the smoke, but there wasn't any in the air. Not here.

Not yet.

She slipped through the door and found herself in a long hallway. There were five doors on her right and just one on her left, at the far end. That far door on the left was in the same position as the front door, from which all the men had exited, so she ignored it.

She'd have to search room by room and hope she wasn't discovered.

And that you don't get burned up.

She'd entered the first door on her right when voices caught her attention. The room was filled with boxes, but no kids.

No Burke.

She peeked through the door to see the woman from the loading dock rushing another group of teenagers down the hall. Maya was barking orders for them to hurry. The man with the gun was nowhere to be seen, but Naomi figured he was coming.

Until Naomi saw the gun in Maya's hand. It appeared to be the same one the man had been holding. They could have had similar guns, so she couldn't assume the man wouldn't follow.

But he hadn't appeared when the kids passed by the door where Naomi was hiding. Maya was only about five-three, with a long, dark ponytail.

I can take her.

The ponytail would be useful.

When Maya had passed by, Naomi rushed from the room and grabbed the woman's hair, winding it around her own hand and jerking the woman to a stop. She shoved Eleanor's gun to Maya's head.

"If you scream, I will kill you," Naomi said quietly. "Drop the fucking gun."

Maya began to twist her arm, like she was planning to shoot backward at Naomi, so Naomi fired once, hitting the woman's arm.

Maya screamed and thrashed, but she dropped the gun. Naomi kicked it into the room with the boxes and tightened her hold on Maya's hair.

She looked at the teenagers, who stared. "Are there any more of you upstairs?"

A few shook their heads.

"Good. I set the others free. Do you know any of them?"

One of the teenagers nodded silently, her eyes wide.

"All right. Go through this door and out the loading bay. Go north, away from the river. Find the parade crowd. Hurry."

She forced Maya to turn toward the end of the hallway. "Move." Maya fought her, so Naomi shoved the barrel of Eleanor's gun under Maya's jaw. "I will kill you. Have no doubt. Now *move*."

Maya moved.

"Where is he?" Naomi demanded. "Broussard. Where did Kaleb put him?"

"I don't know," Maya said defiantly.

Naomi pulled the ponytail so that Maya was forced to her toes. "Try again. My son would have been trapped in here if your boss had been successful, so I am not inclined to be kind. Tell me."

"In the panic room."

"Take me there."

"No." Maya tried to shake her head, but Naomi held her in place. "It's burning. We'll die."

Naomi shoved Maya forward. "Then you'd better hurry."

Uptown, New Orleans, Louisiana
THURSDAY, FEBRUARY 27, 5:15 P.M.

Burke knew his time was running out.

You've been living on borrowed time for years, Winnifred Timms had said. *I think your time is up.*

It seemed that she'd been right.

Burke smelled smoke. Someone—probably Kaleb or his toady Wayne Stanley—had set the building on fire. He'd die if no one came to get him.

Kaleb wouldn't free him. He wanted Burke dead but had been either unwilling or unable to do it himself. Fire was a passive way for Kaleb to achieve his goal.

But Burke hadn't lost hope. He was ready if Kaleb did come to get him. He held the Kevlar kite string. If he wound it around a throat tightly enough, it would cut through skin. Possibly bone.

It would also cut Burke's own hands, but freedom would be worth the pain.

He stiffened when the light came on and he heard voices.

"Open it." The voice was muted but unmistakably female.

"No." Another female.

A *thump* made the door vibrate.

"I said *open it,* bitch."

Burke blinked. That sounded like . . .

No. It couldn't be.

It could not be Naomi.

There was another *thump,* harder and louder this time.

"I said *open it* or I will shoot you again. I'll start at your feet and fill you with holes. I still have sixteen bullets and an extra mag when those bullets are gone. Open the goddamn fucking door. *Now.* Or I will take your keys, free him myself, and leave you here to burn. Your choice. You have one second to decide."

It *was* Naomi. *Oh my God.*

He stepped away from the door when he heard the key in the lock. The door opened and . . . there she was.

Naomi. With Maya. He recognized her from Eleanor's neighbors' security stills.

Naomi had hold of Maya's hair and pressed a gun under Maya's jaw. Maya held a set of keys in her shaking hand.

Naomi looked like an avenging angel.

She simply took his breath away.

"Naomi?"

She flicked her gaze to Gaffney, dead on the floor, then grimly met his eyes.

"Hurry." She turned Maya, using her ponytail like reins. "Get us out of here if you want to live."

The lights flickered and the entire hallway went dark. Smoke filled the air.

They began moving slowly, the darkness impeding their progress. Panic scratched at the edges of Burke's mind.

Panic and awe and shock.

Naomi had saved him.

Again.

They came to a door that Naomi's prisoner opened, dumping them into another hallway, which was thick with smoke.

"Move! Open the exit door!" Naomi snapped to Maya, who took a stumbling step forward, feeling around until she got the door open.

They stumbled into what appeared to be a lobby. There were fancy sofas and a counter like at a hotel.

The door to the outside was just visible in the smoke. Burke's eyes burned and watered, but he could see light from outside. The door was open.

And then a figure stepped in front of it, blocking their exit.

Kaleb.

"What have you done?" Kaleb snarled.

For a moment Burke thought that Kaleb was talking to him, but the question had been fired at Maya.

There was no warning before fire flashed from the muzzle of Kaleb's gun. The woman cried out, then sagged.

Naomi grunted in surprise, but she was thinking on her feet. She hauled the woman's body back up, using her as a shield as she pointed her own gun at Kaleb and fired.

Kaleb stared at them for a moment, then looked down at his chest. Then he laughed.

Vest, Burke thought and was about to jump in front of her because Kaleb was aiming at Naomi's head.

But the woman who'd fascinated him all week fired again, hitting Kaleb's wrist.

Kaleb screamed and dropped his gun. Burke dove for it at the same time that Kaleb did—and came face-to-face with his oldest friend.

Burke grabbed the gun and pointed it at Kaleb's head.

And then he hesitated. He couldn't do it. Couldn't pull the trigger.

It seemed that Burke could no more kill Kaleb than Kaleb could kill him.

Kaleb scrambled backward, pushing himself to his feet. He turned and ran.

Burke wanted to scream, to berate himself for not shooting the man when he'd had the chance, but the fire was spreading. He could hear the roar of it now. Could feel the heat.

Naomi dragged the woman outside and dropped her to the pavement before kneeling beside her to check her pulse. "She's dead. We need to find him."

But they couldn't just leave. Not yet. Burke grabbed Naomi's arm. "We have to go back in. I think this is where he kept the kids."

"I set them all free." Naomi tugged her arm from his grip. "Move."

He wanted to ask if she was sure, if she knew for certain that all the captive teens were safe, but she'd grabbed his shirt and was dragging him away from the burning building.

"Wait. Val. They said they killed her."

"She's safe. In the hospital."

Relief made his knees wobble. "You promise?"

She gave his shirt another hard tug. "Yes. She's safe. Dammit, Burke, *move*."

She released her hold on his shirt and set off at a sprint with which Burke had a hard time keeping up. He still felt weak from whatever they'd given him that morning. But he pushed himself to follow her.

They ran for three blocks before hitting a wall of people. The parade had started.

Thankful for his height, Burke searched for Kaleb over the heads of the crowd. "There. He just pushed that family out of his way."

Kaleb was only visible because he was shoving through the crowd. If he'd stayed put, he would have blended in and Burke wouldn't have seen him.

Burke muscled his way through the people, muttering apologies. Naomi was right behind him.

She had his back.

She'd come for him.

She saved my life.

Burke was five feet from Kaleb when the man abruptly went down on one knee, reaching for his ankle.

Fuck. Kaleb had a backup weapon.

"Gun!" Burke yelled and launched himself into the air, coming down on Kaleb with a hard impact that knocked the breath out of them both. Kaleb squirmed and thrashed beneath him, but Burke had several inches and at least thirty pounds on the man he'd called brother.

Don't think of him like that.

Burke grabbed Kaleb's wrists and stretched their arms out like they were readying to fly, but Kaleb still had the gun. Burke's hand slipped on Kaleb's wrist. It was wet with blood.

He put pressure on the wrist and Kaleb screamed in pain.

Burke's heart hated the sound even though he knew what Kaleb had done.

His brain knew. His heart hadn't caught up.

Don't listen. Don't think. Don't feel.

Crouching, Naomi pried the pistol from Kaleb's hand.

She pointed an unfamiliar Glock at Kaleb's head, then turned to one of the people who were staring at them in shock.

Just beyond them, the parade kept moving, most of the revelers completely unaware of what was happening around them. Only the people within a radius of ten feet were paying them any attention at all.

"You," she snapped at the closest bystander. "Call 911. *Now.* This guy traffics teenagers for sex. *Move.*"

The man obeyed, dialing 911, but he seemed to have lost the ability to speak. He handed the phone to Naomi.

"We've detained Kaleb Marchand," she said to the operator. "There's a BOLO out on him." She gave them their location, then handed the phone back to its owner. "Stay with the operator, please."

Keeping her gun pointed at Kaleb's head, she took her own phone from her pocket and tapped her screen one-handed. "André, it's Naomi. I have Burke and we have Kaleb. Did the kids find you?"

Burke let her words wash over him. She was all grace and intelligence and . . . competence.

And I'm so tired.

Kaleb had stopped struggling, but Burke didn't dare move. Didn't dare give Kaleb an inch of breathing space.

If Kaleb took off again, Burke didn't think he had the energy—physically or emotionally—to hunt him down. So he stayed where he was, his body keeping Kaleb contained.

"Good," Naomi said. "There were twenty-two of them. You got them all? You're sure?" A moment passed as she listened. "Okay. We'll hold him here. There's a dead woman outside the warehouse. It's Maya. Gaffney's dead. His body was in the room with Burke. And there was another guy, big guy with a gun. I have no idea what happened to him." Another pause. "Thank you, André."

She ended the call, put her phone away, then exhaled. "You okay, Burke?"

No. He was not okay. He might never be totally okay again. But he lifted his head to meet her eyes. "You came."

"I did." She brushed a lock of hair from his forehead, then cupped his cheek. "I got your back."

He nuzzled into her hand for a heartbeat, then two, before dropping his head to rest on the pavement next to Kaleb's. He didn't want to touch Kaleb at all, but he was so tired, his head aching. He couldn't relax his body for fear that Kaleb would buck him off, but he could rest his head.

"Why?" he asked quietly.

Kaleb said nothing.

"Was it the money?" Burke pressed.

Kaleb let out a derisive laugh that ended on a groan. "Of course it was the money."

"Why didn't you ask me? I would have helped you."

"Didn't want your fucking money. Didn't want your fucking charity. Don't want anything from you except to see you dead."

The words hit hard and Burke wanted to crawl away and lick his wounds, but Kaleb made one last effort to wrench free. Burke bounced, knocking the breath from Kaleb once more.

After that, neither of them said anything.

Neither did Naomi. She just stroked Burke's hair, somehow knowing what he needed.

Minutes ticked by and Burke became aware that they were being filmed. More and more people realized that something momentous was happening on the ground, and dozens of phones were pointed at them.

Burke didn't care. His body hurt. His heart hurt. His adrenaline was already crashing and the pain of betrayal was like a knife in his back.

He'd hurt for Naomi when she'd found that her ex-husband had been paid to lie at her trial, but she'd already accepted that Jimmy Haywood was a bad man.

This was different.

He'd had no idea.

He'd loved Kaleb.

He'd trusted Kaleb.

Juliette would be devastated. The boys would be crushed.

But there was solace also. Naomi had come for him.

I'll be okay. Eventually.

Finally, André was there, directing his officers to take Kaleb in.

Burke sat back on his heels and let the officers pull Kaleb to his feet. He watched them slap cuffs on Kaleb's uninjured wrist. Listened as they read his oldest friend his rights.

Naomi remained at Burke's side until Kaleb was dragged away. André held out his hand and both Burke and Naomi surrendered their guns.

"Where did you get that?" Burke asked. "It's not one of mine."

"Eleanor," Naomi said, and Burke wasn't surprised. "I shot his wrist," she added to André. "Burke confiscated one of Kaleb's guns and I confiscated the other, but neither of us fired them. Kaleb killed the woman outside the warehouse with that one." She pointed to the larger of Kaleb's handguns. "I shot her arm to get her to drop her gun."

André put all the weapons in an evidence bag. "Okay," he said simply. "Molly and Antoine got to the warehouse a minute before I did. Harrison called them. They'd seen a bunch of kids without shoes huddled together walking up the street. Flex-cuffed in pairs. Twenty-two of them. They're waiting with them until we can get the kids transported to the hospital."

"I guess they were all barefoot," Naomi murmured. "I didn't even think about that. I only wanted to get them as far away from the warehouse as I could."

André smiled. "You did a fine job, Naomi. I think you'll find you have a position with the NOPD if you want one."

"I don't," Naomi said. "I'm gonna work for Burke."

Burke tried to smile, but his mouth wouldn't curve. "Good." It was all he could manage.

André leaned down and helped Burke to his feet, then wrapped his arm around Burke's shoulders to keep him upright. "I'm gonna call the medics for you."

"I just want to go home."

"Then that's where we'll go," Naomi said, giving André a stern look that brooked no argument.

"Okay," André said. "I'll take your statements, then I'll drive you myself."

27

The Quarter, New Orleans, Louisiana
FRIDAY, FEBRUARY 28, 8:30 A.M.

BURKE HAD BEEN awake for hours, but he hadn't opened his eyes.

As soon as he did, he'd have to start the day. And starting the day meant remembering the night before.

When he'd taken down his oldest friend.

His brother.

Who'd sold teenagers into sexual slavery.

Who'd tried to have the children of Burke's friends kidnapped.

Who'd had Naomi imprisoned.

Who'd tried to kill Naomi.

Who tried to kill me.

Who's hated me for a very long time.

He wasn't sure which of those things hurt the most. It was one big ache in his chest that made it hard to breathe.

It was shock, he knew. And grief. And betrayal.

The shock would fade and the grief would process. The betrayal, though . . .

He didn't know how long it would take for that to subside.

The only good thing to have come from this debacle was the woman in his arms.

She'd been awake for a long time as well. Not as long as Burke, but at least an hour. He'd known exactly when she woke. Her body had gone stiff, her breathing rapid and shaky.

She'd awakened from a dream.

He should have asked what it was about, but he just couldn't manage to break the silence. Instead, he'd gathered her to him, urging her to lay her head on his shoulder.

She'd come willingly, settling her hand over his heart.

They hadn't done anything sexual in the hours since André had brought them home. Burke had made sure that his people knew he was all right—physically anyway—before heading to his bedroom.

He'd seen their devastation on his behalf. And he appreciated their love and care. But he hadn't wanted to talk about it. He'd only wanted solitude.

Sleep.

Peace.

Naomi had put him to bed, sitting with him until exhaustion had finally pulled him under.

The next thing he'd known, she was in the bed beside him, sleeping with her hand in his. He'd held her hand like a lifeline.

And let the minutes tick by. Dawn had broken long before and he could smell coffee and bacon. His people were waking up. This would be their last morning together in his house. Now that the danger had passed, they'd all be going home.

It would be too quiet again.

Naomi lightly stroked the hair on his chest. "I need to get up, Burke."

He swallowed hard and continued to say nothing at all.

She didn't sigh. Didn't huff. Didn't nag.

She leaned up and kissed him softly on the mouth. "But you can hold the day at bay for a little longer. I'll keep your people from knocking on your door as long as I can."

She went to get out of the bed, but he tugged her back to him. "I don't want to go downstairs," he confessed quietly.

She kissed his forehead. "I know. It makes it real."

That she understood was no surprise. After all she'd been through, Naomi Cranston possessed empathy that left him in awe.

"I can't handle reality yet."

She kissed him again, sweet and comforting. It felt like a promise. "They know that. They don't want you to be their boss right now. They just want to show you that they love you."

His eyes stung. She gently swiped a fingertip across his eyelids, gathering the tears that managed to escape.

"He was your brother, Burke. And he hurt you. You're allowed to be sad. You're allowed to grieve. You're even allowed to hide in your room. Just not forever."

He cleared his throat, but no words would come.

"Molly was frantic yesterday when we couldn't find you. She stared at that whiteboard, looking so lost." Her thumb caressed his cheek as she added wryly, "I think she might even have wrinkled her blouse."

A snort of laughter bubbled up. How quickly she'd come to know his people. The people who never would have stopped searching for him.

The laughter abruptly changed, his chest heaving with a sob he couldn't hold back.

He'd often thought that Kaleb was the only family he had left, but he'd been so wrong. Molly and Antoine, Lucien and Val. Phin. Joy. They were his family.

Once the first sob broke free, it was like a floodgate opening and he could only lie there, gasping as he cried loud, ugly sobs he was sure the whole house could hear.

Naomi put her arms around him. He buried his face in the curve of her neck and cried.

She didn't tell him that it would be all right. She didn't offer a single platitude. Only comfort.

Finally, he shuddered out a sigh. "I'm sorry."

"Don't be. Not one person waiting downstairs will think an iota less of you. They think you are the strongest man they know, but they've all been through troubles. They know that strength isn't absolute."

She pulled away and he felt her wipe her own cheeks. She'd cried along with him. That finally made him open his eyes.

Her eyes were wet and slightly swollen, but she was still the prettiest woman he'd ever seen.

"Thank you," he whispered.

"For what?"

"All of it. Trusting me to keep you safe. Saving my ass."

"Twice," she said cheekily.

"Twice," he repeated soberly. "For knowing what I needed. For taking care of my people. You did that last night while I was asleep, didn't you?" Because somehow he knew that was true.

She nodded. "They were . . . agitated. Upset."

"What did you do?"

She chuckled. "We dragged Molly's whiteboard to the living room and brainstormed ways we wanted to punish Kaleb. It got a little dark, to be honest, but I think they needed to get it out of their systems. It was something we used to do inside. We'd talk about the people who'd hurt us and fantasize retribution. And then we'd talk about the people we'd hurt, fantasizing redemption. And then we'd make lists of all the things we'd do when we got out to heal ourselves and the people we'd wronged. A lot of us knew it was futile, that we'd never be forgiven. Some of us would never get out. I wanted to tell Everett everything, but I knew that he'd be nearly forty when I got out. He'd want nothing to do with me. I still fantasized. It . . . helped. But you don't have to fantasize about redemption. You didn't do anything wrong. You can think all you want about retribution."

"Kaleb's going to prison."

"For the rest of his life," she agreed.

"I don't . . ." He swallowed hard. "I should want him to suffer. He hurt so many people. All those kids. I should be fantasizing about him burning in hell. About what the other inmates will do to him. But I can't."

"That says so much about the good in you."

"You really believe that?"

"I do. It's easy to want someone to suffer. It's much harder to show compassion."

"Will I ever forgive him?"

"If you don't, I certainly won't think less of you."

"The boys." Braden and Trent. "They're going to need me."

"They will. And you'll be there for them." She kissed his forehead again. "First, gather your own strength, however you need to do it. You know that thing flight attendants say?"

"Put on your own mask before you help others."

"Yep." She gently tugged her hand free. "I'm starving. I couldn't eat last night, and I'll get cranky soon."

He drew her down for one more kiss. "Go eat. I'll shower and come down. I'm starving, too, now that you mention it."

"Good." She climbed out of his bed and he realized she was wearing a set of his sweats, with the sleeves and cuffs rolled up.

It made him smile. "You look awful pretty this morning, Naomi Cranston."

"Thank you, Burke Broussard. You're looking mighty fine yourself."

She crossed the room and he saw the shudder shake her when she opened the bedroom door. She lifted her face to the sun that flooded the hallway, and he was struck once again by her strength.

She hated closed doors, but she'd tolerated them because she'd wanted to be with him. Once everyone had gone home, he wanted her back in his bed and they'd keep the door wide open.

That was one benefit to a quiet house, he thought, then swung his legs over the side of the bed. He had his people to see to. Their comfort to receive.

His family to hug and love, and their love to accept in return.

And then he'd face Juliette and the boys and do what he could.

The Quarter, New Orleans, Louisiana
FRIDAY, FEBRUARY 28, 9:15 A.M.

Burke found his lead team and their families eating breakfast at his dining room table. On one side of the table were Molly and Gabe, Chelsea, Lucien, and Harper. Antoine and André sat side by side, for once not bickering.

Ruthanne, James, and Eleanor sat with Everett on the other side of the table. Naomi had taken her place next to the only open chair—the one at the head of the table that was his.

Czar and Elijah's dog, Delilah, lay at the front door, snoring. That made Burke smile.

He was relieved beyond measure to see that Val was back from the hospital, Kaj hovering protectively. Jace sat on her right, Elijah on her left. Both boys leaned into her, keeping physical contact as they ate. Sylvi had also joined them, and she watched her sister like a hawk.

Joy sat at the other end of the table, and Burke was so happy to see her face. He was happy to see each and every face.

Harrison and Devonte were off duty and both had gone home to their families to rest up.

The only people missing were Phin and Cora. He made a mental note to visit them. Phin was probably making Cora rest.

Chatter ceased as Burke stopped at his chair. He saw concern, sympathy, and, on the faces of the children, residual fear. He hated that.

"Mornin'," he said with a smile that was small but genuine. "You can all stop worrying about me."

But it didn't have the impact he'd hoped. There was a melancholy hanging in the air and he wondered if it was because they'd heard him cry.

Naomi was the only one who smiled at him, pride in her eyes.

Val slowly rose, her expression stricken. "I'm sorry, Burke," she said, her voice breaking. "I'm so sorry I let you get taken."

He wasn't having that. Not from Val. Not from any of the family who worried about him. Who loved him.

Burke opened his arms and Val met him halfway. For a long moment they clung to each other.

"I was so scared," Burke whispered. "They said they'd killed you."

Val shuddered. "Almost. Molly got to me in time." She loosened her hold and met his eyes. "You're okay? Really okay?"

"My body is fine. My heart's going to take some time." He turned to the others. "Thank you for staying to make sure I'm all right. Thank you for searching for me. I knew you would be. I knew you'd find me."

Which was mostly true. He wasn't going to tell them that he'd feared he was going to die in that little room.

Molly stood, and in her eyes he saw guilt mixed with tears. He wasn't having that, either.

"It was Naomi who figured out where you were," Molly said miserably as her husband Gabe reached for her hand in support. "I didn't listen to her. If she hadn't gone off on her own to find you, I would have been too late."

"*We* would have been too late," Antoine corrected gravely. "It wasn't only you, Mol."

Burke frowned at Naomi. "What are they talking about?"

Molly and Antoine stared at Naomi. "You didn't tell him?" Antoine asked.

Naomi purposely forked some eggs into her mouth and did not say a word.

André shook his head at Molly and Antoine. "I told you two that you were not at fault, but y'all are addicted to guilt. Burke, they had three leads from that PI Juliette hired. Molly and Antoine went to check out the first two, which were plausible options based on what we knew. Naomi insisted on going to the third location and called me to meet her."

"She didn't tell you?" Molly demanded.

"She didn't," Burke said, giving Naomi a fond look. "But you all pitched in and I thank you all. Molly," he added lightly, "I heard you got an actual wrinkle in your blouse, so I know you were overcome by your worry for me."

Val turned to Molly with wide eyes. "A wrinkle? Say it isn't so."

Molly sat back down. "It isn't so. My clothes do not wrinkle."

"They're afraid to," Elijah said, making everyone laugh.

"Eleanor," Burke said, "thank you for loaning Naomi your gun. I don't think she would have found me in time had she not shot Maya."

It was Eleanor's turn to look at Naomi with wide eyes. "You *shot* someone?"

Everett looked impressed. "Mom?"

Naomi ate a huge bite of pancakes. Then gave her son a wink.

Everett was calling her Mom and not Naomi. That was a good sign.

Burke laughed and it felt good. "She shot Maya and Kaleb. Do none of you know what happened?"

"No," Ruthanne said primly. "Clearly we do not."

Naomi swallowed and patted her lips with a napkin. "Sit down, Burke. I'll get you some food."

"I'll do it," Ruthanne said. "You keep eating."

"Listen to your mama," Eleanor said.

"You shot Kaleb," Joy said. "I knew I liked you."

Naomi rolled her eyes. "I shot to wound. I don't know that I could have killed anyone."

Burke sat down, wondering if she'd forgotten that she'd shot Kaleb in the chest. Maybe she had forgotten, or maybe she needed to tell herself that she couldn't have killed anyone. He wasn't going to push her, either way. But he could tease. "That's not what I heard when you were threatening Maya. 'Open the door, b—'" He stopped himself when he caught Harper's wide-eyed gaze.

"You can say that word, Uncle Burke. I've heard it before."

Jace shook his head. "Not from us."

"Well," Burke said. "Let's just say that Naomi was very forceful in her demand that the woman working for Kaleb unlock my door. 'I still have sixteen bullets and an extra mag when those bullets are gone. Open the bleeping door. Now.' Then she said she'd shoot Maya and leave her to burn. 'You have one second to decide.' It was really quite masterful."

Naomi looked embarrassed. "I was channeling one of the other inmates. She was very Clint Eastwood."

Joy beamed at her from the end of the table. "You saved our Burke. You can channel whoever you darn well please."

Eleanor looked proud. "Good girl. I'm glad I had it to loan you." She glanced at André. "I *will* get it back."

"Yes, ma'am. As soon as it's no longer needed as evidence. I've got updates and I can fill in some holes."

"Please," Burke said. "Tell me you know where Wayne Stanley is."

"He's in a cell," André said. "He was caught trying to board a plane to Ecuador."

"Ecuador?" Jace asked.

"South America," Elijah explained. "They have no extradition treaty with the United States. The man could have hidden there."

"Well, he can't hide there now," André said. "We arrested him. We also have him on the hospital's security system approaching Val's room yesterday morning. He took one look at the guard at her door and turned around."

Kaj paled. "He was going to kill Val?"

"Likely," André said. "Chelsea? You might want to take Harper upstairs."

"I'm not a baby," Harper insisted. "Don't send me away."

Burke remembered that Chelsea's former in-laws wanted to claim custody of Harper because Lucien's job was so dangerous. This wasn't going to help. He made a mental note to hire the best attorney in the city to make sure Harper stayed with them.

Chelsea hugged her daughter. "We couldn't send you away. But why don't we go upstairs and watch a movie? Time for just you and me. You can pick the movie."

"Fine," Harper grumbled. "I hate being the youngest."

Elijah tickled her as she passed his chair. "Soon Cora and Phin's baby will be the youngest."

Harper brightened at that.

André waited until Chelsea and Harper were safely upstairs. "Gaffney's cause of death appears to be an overdose of the same drug they gave Val. Time of death is going to be a little more difficult as his body was damaged in the fire."

His people shuddered. Naomi's hand trembled as she set her fork on her plate. Because Burke would have been dead, too, had Naomi not come for him.

"Once we brought Kaleb in," André went on, "Elaine Billings chose to talk. She hadn't eaten or drunk anything for fear she'd be poisoned like Cresswell. She'll get a deal from the DA."

Kaj scowled. "I hate that. But she gave valuable information."

"She did," André agreed. "She'd only worked with them since the fall, but she protected herself by making copies of documents Kaleb kept in that condo. She's evil, but not stupid. She'd heard about Cresswell's drug ring. She'd already been selling kids from the foster system and pitched an organized prostitution ring to Cresswell and Kaleb. Cresswell said no. But once he was in prison, Kaleb reached out to her. From what she'd gleaned from the documents Kaleb kept, Cresswell and Kaleb had been partnered for several years already."

"I introduced them," Burke said grimly. "At a holiday party when I reported to Cresswell."

"I didn't know that," André said. "Elaine said that, at the beginning, Cresswell and Gaffney were skimming drugs from NOPD busts and Kaleb was selling them through a small network of dealers on the street. But there wasn't enough cash in that, so Kaleb and Cresswell stole a truck full of drugs that belonged to the STs. They fought with the driver, who grabbed Kaleb's necklace and broke it."

"Sending his wedding ring into the storm drain," Naomi said. "That makes sense."

"Kaleb killed the driver and searched for the ring, but never found it," André said. "When it was turned in by that college kid, Kaleb thought he'd be found out."

"So they framed my mother," Everett said, his jaw set.

"They did," André said. "But they're either dead or in custody now."

Everett's nod was grudging. "As long as they're punished."

"We'll make sure of it," Kaj said.

That seemed to be enough for Everett, who resumed eating—after he refilled his mother's plate. She smiled her thanks. Naomi and her son were going to be all right, Burke thought.

"Kaleb found Winnifred Timms through a modeling agency here in town," André continued. "He picked her because, with a black wig, she looked like Naomi. Winnifred told Elaine that Kaleb first hired her to plant the phony drugs in the back seat of your car and then to set up bank accounts, posing as you, so that they could implicate you if you didn't agree to let them railroad you into prison. But you did agree."

"Because they threatened Everett," Ruthanne murmured.

André nodded. "Exactly. At that point, Kaleb didn't need Winnifred to set up the bank accounts, so he used her to move drugs. He let her stay in the condo that he'd bought as an office for his illegal businesses, and he had an affair with her. According to Elaine, Winnifred was getting possessive, and Kaleb planned to get rid of her when Mardi Gras was over. They were counting on making a lot of money during Mardi Gras since Kaleb and Gaffney were forced to discontinue selling the drugs they stole from evidence after Cresswell was sent to prison two and a half years ago. PIB was watching Gaffney and the dirty cops he'd recruited, but none of the PIB investigators on their payroll wanted to risk covering for them right after Cresswell's arrest. Elaine said that Kaleb decided that enough time had passed. They'd recently restarted drug distribution and Kaleb decided to add sex trafficking."

Ruthanne scowled. "They used Winnifred to set up the phony bank accounts again after Naomi was released."

"Yes," André confirmed. "They were determined to send her back to prison. Where they were planning another hit."

Ruthanne paled. "So they planned the first one? Where she almost died?"

André nodded. "They did."

"What about the Delgado brothers?" Antoine asked. "Were they still in the STs?"

"Yes," André said. "This comes from Desi Ortiz, the leader of the gang. We picked him up running from the warehouse. After Kaleb and Cresswell stole the truckload of drugs from the gang—which was incredibly stupid on their part—they negotiated an agreement with the gang, mainly to save their own asses because the STs were pissed off. Cresswell and Gaffney used their contacts in NOPD to make sure the gang's most profitable dealers and pushers weren't arrested—up until Cresswell got arrested and PIB increased their scrutiny. Elaine gave up Desi Ortiz as working with Kaleb on the trafficking as well. Kaleb killed most of his staff this week, so he'd entered into an agreement with Ortiz to use his people to run the trafficking operation."

"I saw some of the rooms in that warehouse when Maya was taking me to Burke," Naomi said. "They'd decorated them to look like regular bedrooms. That's why Susan thought they were in a house."

"There are enough tourists in New Orleans and people coming all year for conventions that the business should have been very profitable, but Ortiz said Kaleb sucked as a businessman. I think he had plans to get rid of Kaleb and take over, but that's just my opinion at this point."

"What about Elaine?" Lucien asked. "We've been wondering why she helped Harper escape Ernesto Delgado on Monday night."

"Ah." André nodded. "Kaleb's one rule was no children. Teenagers yes, but no kids. So when Ernesto said '*para mi*' when he grabbed Harper, Elaine knew that Kaleb would be pissed. They would have taken Everett and Jace, but they mostly wanted to scare you into hiding."

"Which we did," Molly said grimly. "Score one for Kaleb."

"They did want to kill Burke and Naomi," André said. "Stanley at the airport garage and Elaine at the hospital garage. The kids were to scare you, but the bullets were to kill you."

"Who shot up my shop?" Sylvi asked.

"Two of the gang's people. They weren't supposed to do that, according to Elaine. Kaleb was displeased. He didn't want NOPD to be called in."

"My insurance company is displeased as well," Sylvi muttered. "But Phin replaced the glass at cost and his contractors cleaned up the mess and replaced the wall with all the bullet holes, so there's no long-term damage."

"I'll pay for it," Burke said.

Sylvi glared at him. "I don't want your money, Burke. It's bad enough that you took my best employee."

Burke grinned at her. He had a new full-time investigator and she was awesome. "Sorry, not sorry."

"I know," Sylvi grumbled. "But the new woman says she'll stay if Naomi doesn't come back."

"And the PIB cops who were taking bribes?" Molly asked. "What about them?"

André sighed. "That list of compromised PIB investigators that magically appeared in my email is being taken seriously."

Antoine looked pleased.

"And the teenagers?" Naomi asked. "How are they doing? Do they need anything?"

André looked pained. "All were treated and released except for the boy who tried to escape and got hit in the head. They kept him overnight for observation. He'll be released back into the system today. We have twenty-three traumatized teenagers to place, including Susan Snyder. It's not going to be easy."

Burke looked around the table. Several of his people had speculative expressions, like they were thinking of taking on a foster kid.

"Mom?" Jace said. "We've got room. I'll help."

Burke's eyes stung. What a fantastic kid he was.

Val smiled at her son. "We'll talk about it. Susan and I hit it off."

Eleanor seemed to be considering it as well.

A glance at Naomi told Burke that she'd already thought about it. "You too?"

"I'll need to rent a bigger place, but . . . they broke my heart, Burke."

He leaned in to kiss her temple. "It's a big heart. Strong too."

And he had a big house. There were possibilities.

"Any other questions?" André asked. "Because that's all I know."

"Yeah," Everett said. "Will my mother be cleared? Not just having her conviction overturned on a technicality?"

"My boss is already working on it," Kaj said.

"Okay," Everett said. "Thank you."

"Told ya," Jace said to Naomi. "He came around."

Everett looked embarrassed. "I'm sorry," he said to the table as a whole. "I was a dick."

"You're forgiven, Everett," Burke said. "At least by me."

"And by me," Naomi said quietly.

One by one, everyone around the table raised their hands. Eleanor gave Everett an approving nod.

"I have a question," Naomi said. "What about the other addresses in that PI's report? Why was Kaleb going to all those places?"

André hesitated, then closed his eyes. "They were either drug distribution centers, like the Delgados' house, or they were where Elaine Billings brought the kids who needed medical attention. We picked up three more teenagers. They . . . didn't make it."

The table fell silent for a long, sad moment.

"I wish Kaleb and Elaine were burning in hell," Everett said quietly. "What kind of deal did you give Elaine Billings, Mr. Cardozo?"

"We took the death penalty off the table," Kaj said. "She'll still go to prison for a very long time."

"Good," Everett murmured. He glanced at Jace. "That could have been us."

"But it wasn't," Jace said, trying to sound positive. "And look at it this way. You picked up some real friends right here." He pointed to himself and then to Elijah. "Remember us when you can't stop thinking about what might have been. It works for me."

"I'll try." Everett turned to Naomi, still sober-faced. "Thank you for protecting me even when I was being awful."

"I will always protect you," Naomi vowed. "We're going to be okay, Ev."

He smiled at his mother and bumped the fist Jace offered.

Burke was so damn proud of Jace. He had to fight the rise of emotion and was grateful when Eleanor waved at him from the other end of the table.

"When do you think I can go home, Burke?"

"Depends." Burke looked to André. "Can you ensure Desi Ortiz's people won't go after her?"

"No, but I've got people I trust stationed in Eleanor's neighborhood so the STs know to stay away. Eleanor, if you want to go home today, I'll drive you myself."

"And I'll go with you when you visit Juliette and the boys," Naomi murmured to Burke. "If you want me."

He squeezed her hand. "I do." He wanted her in so many different ways. In his business, in his life, in his bed. In his heart.

It was the best ending he could hope for, given the circumstances.

And then Burke's cell phone buzzed in his pocket. The text made his chest tight with new excitement. "We need to go to the hospital."

Naomi leaned in, concerned. "Why?"

"Cora's in labor."

It was the best possible way to end the worst possible day.

EPILOGUE

The Quarter, New Orleans, Louisiana
SUNDAY, JUNE 1, 10:45 A.M.

I HAVE TO WEAR a damn tie," Burke grumbled.

Naomi knew that his grumbling was due to nerves and not any real irritation. He'd been looking forward to the christening ever since little Jonas was born—almost exactly twenty-four hours after Burke had taken Kaleb down at the Mardi Gras parade. Wearing a tie for such an occasion wouldn't have made him this agitated.

She put down her knitting and went to the full-length mirror in Burke's bedroom where he stood scowling, his dress shirt unbuttoned. Standing behind him, she slid her arms around his waist.

"You've done this godfather thing before, Burke. Why are you so nervous?"

He sighed. "I'm sorry. I'm just . . ."

She pressed a kiss to his shoulder. "Just what?" She tugged on him until he turned to face her. "Tell me."

He swallowed. "I heard from the prison. He still won't see me."

No one on their team knew that Burke had been trying to visit

Kaleb for two months. He was afraid they wouldn't understand. But of course they would have. Burke needed closure. He needed to understand why the man he'd called brother had turned into a monster he no longer recognized.

"I'm sorry, baby." She put her arms around his neck and drew him down for a soft kiss. "You might never know why he's the way he is, and I'm sorry for that, too."

He rested his forehead against hers. "Thank you. I need to shake this off. I have to be a happy godfather in three hours."

"That baby makes you smile like nobody else. I think as soon as you see him today, you'll be exactly what he needs you to be. You make him feel safe. Just like you do everyone else."

Some of the tension left his body. "You always seem to know the right thing to say."

"My superpower," she whispered.

He grinned lasciviously. "I thought your superpower was the thing you did with your—"

"Excuse me!" a voice bellowed from the open doorway. "Please don't finish that sentence."

They turned as one to find André watching them.

"I don't know," Burke said. "Seems that you barged in on us, so you aren't in a position to be making any demands."

"Your door was open," André said accusingly.

Because Naomi still hated closed doors. Burke had never pushed her to "fix herself," and for that she was grateful. Someday she'd tackle that trigger, but she was still getting used to her new life.

She was one of Burke's full-time investigators and she loved her job. She still filled in at Sylvi's shop, though, whenever her other employee was sick or there was a holiday. This past Mother's Day had been a zoo.

She'd rented a larger house so that she could become a foster parent in the near future. Besides, with Jimmy in prison for perjury and accepting a bribe in exchange for false testimony, Everett now lived with her full-time. He was over at his old house often, though, caring for his half siblings. McKenzie was having a hard time adjusting to single parenthood of three kids under five. Everett wasn't doing it for McKenzie, of course. He was doing it for the kids, and Naomi was so proud of him for stepping up.

Naomi and Burke had decided not to live together just yet. Naomi wanted to live on her own for a little while, but she was over at Burke's mansion in the Quarter whenever she got the chance.

So learning to tolerate closed doors could wait a little longer.

"How did you even get in the house?" Burke asked.

"Everett let me in. Now I know why he was laughing when he told me to just 'go on upstairs.'"

Naomi and Burke shared a glance because André was . . . off. Something was wrong.

"Tell me," Burke said. "Have you come bearing good tidings of great joy again?"

André shook his head, his broad shoulders sagging. "I'm sorry, Burke. I didn't want to do this to you today of all days, but I didn't want you to hear it from someone else or online."

Beside her, Burke straightened his spine. "Who died?" he asked quietly.

"Kaleb. The prison went into lockdown an hour ago. It's all over the news. They're only saying now that an inmate was killed, but we're not giving his name until we've notified next of kin."

Which would be Juliette, although Naomi knew Burke considered himself next of kin as well. Poor Juliette. She'd been a mess since Kaleb's arrest, and Braden and Trent felt so lost. Whenever he saw the boys, Burke was his usual take-charge self, comforting them and giving them whatever help they needed. But then, when he came home, Naomi was always there waiting, because he'd fall apart. He needed her those times.

He needed her now.

He stood stock-still, his only movement the rise and fall of his chest as he breathed, and that was far too shallow.

Naomi led him to the chair, moving her knitting before she gently pushed him to sit. He silently complied, giving her a look of helpless anguish. She kissed his lips, then his forehead before turning to André.

"How did it happen?" she asked.

"Stabbed in the dining hall," André said, coming into the room. "Like what happened with you, except it wasn't just one assailant. A crowd surrounded him and none of the guards could get through. When the inmates stepped back, Kaleb was dead. Nobody will say who did it. At least not right now. But Kaleb had made a lot of enemies in the gen pop in a short time. He tried to be a big man. Tried to step in on the territory of the main dealer inside. He'd already been in at least ten fights. Spent weeks in solitary. It was almost like he wanted them to hate him."

Naomi stroked Burke's hair because it soothed him. "Does Juliette know?"

"Not yet. I'm on my way to see her now. I didn't know if you'd want to go with me, Burke."

Naomi opened her mouth to say *hell no,* but Burke exhaled quietly and stood up.

"Yeah. I'll go. She'll need me." He glanced at his watch. "I have to go straight to the church afterward. It's Jonas's christening."

"Okay," André said. "I'll wait for you downstairs. I'm so sorry, Burke."

Burke nodded. "I know. Thank you."

When André was gone, Burke lowered his head to her shoulder and she put her arms around him, rubbing his back. "I'm sorry," she whispered.

"Me too. But I'm not surprised. I thought this would happen sooner. I knew he'd made enemies. I don't think he ever intended to serve his sentence."

Having taken a plea deal, Kaleb had been sentenced to life in prison without parole. He'd killed so many people—or had them killed, which ended up being the same thing. Wayne Stanley managed to cut a deal for forty years with time off for good behavior. Naomi planned to be at every one of his parole hearings. If she had anything to do with it, Stanley would never be free.

But he'd told the DA where Kaleb and Cresswell had hidden the bodies. Most of the bodies were in pieces—the term still made Naomi ill—because they'd tossed them to the gators. They'd used the bayou around a place Burke owned as their dumping ground. Just another way Kaleb had "gotten back" at Burke.

Divers had retrieved enough pieces of the victims that the ME had been able to identify fifteen people. Some of them were teenagers who'd died as a result of Kaleb's trafficking business. Some were dealers who'd erred. Retrieving bodies gave their families closure, but it would have come at a steep price if Stanley were ever released.

Naomi kissed Burke's temple. "Let me help you get dressed."

"Thank you. I . . ." He shuddered. "I'm glad you're here."

"I'm glad I am, too. Come on. Let me button your shirt. I packed a clean one in case Jonas spits up on you again." It was a common occurrence, but Burke never seemed to mind. "That way you'll look good for the pictures."

He pulled away and steeled his spine. "Button away."

His eyes were dry. But so sad.

Naomi silently cursed Kaleb for getting himself killed on what should have been a happy day. It wasn't entirely sane, but she didn't care.

She buttoned Burke's shirt and tied his tie and buttoned his cuffs before tucking his shirttails into his suit pants. "There. You'll be the most handsome man there."

"Nobody'll be looking at me. They'll all be looking at Jonas and Phin and Cora."

"I'll be looking at you. I'm always looking at you."

He swallowed hard. "You know I love you, right?"

She did, but it was the first time he'd said it. "I know." She cupped his cheek. "You know I love you, too, right?"

He smiled then. "I know. Come with me?"

"Of course. Let me get my purse. I'll have Everett catch a ride with Jace and Elijah." The three had become inseparable and Everett was thriving.

Everett was waiting for them at the bottom of the stairs. He was already dressed for the service, surprising Naomi. "You look so nice," she told him.

"Thanks, Mom." He stepped into Burke's path, making Burke stop. "I heard. I'm sorry. I know you loved him even though he was bad."

Burke shuddered again, blowing out a breath. "Thank you, Everett."

Then Everett surprised Naomi once again when he wrapped Burke in a hard hug. "It wasn't anything you did," Everett said. "Sometimes people are just bad, Burke."

Like Jimmy. Everett was having a hard time coming to terms with his father's sins, but he was getting there. Naomi wiped her eyes because she couldn't stop the tears. She wasn't sad that Kaleb was dead, but she hurt for his family. She wasn't sad that Jimmy was in prison, but her heart broke for his four children.

Burke heaved a short sob into Everett's shoulder. "Sometimes they are just bad." He sucked in a breath and straightened. "Thank you. You helped."

Everett shrugged. "I'm not a dick anymore."

Burke choked on a laugh. "Maybe sometimes."

Everett grinned. "Sometimes. I'll see you at the church."

Burke took Naomi's arm and they followed André to the car.

The Garden District, New Orleans, Louisiana
SUNDAY, JUNE 1, 2:00 P.M.

Naomi had been right, of course. Burke's broken heart began to mend when he held Jonas Montgomery Burke Bishop in his arms. Phin and Cora beamed amid their entire family and all their friends from Ohio.

There were a lot of Bishops. The reception after the christening was loud and full of laughter. *Just what I needed.*

Naomi had bonded with Cora and now Phin's sister Scarlett, which was worrisome. Those three together could get themselves in a pile of trouble, Burke thought. But Naomi shone like the sun. She looked at him every few minutes, making sure he was all right.

He wasn't really. But he would be.

Juliette was definitely not all right. He'd be leaving the christening to go back to her house, where he'd sit with her and the boys. Braden and Trent were in shock, and Burke had hated to leave them, but he'd needed this afternoon with his true family.

With Molly and Gabe, Val and Kaj, Jace and Elijah. Antoine and Joy. Lucien, Chelsea, and Harper, whose grandparents' bid for custody had been squashed like a bug thanks to the attorney Burke had retained. Chelsea was expecting again and André and his wife Farrah had brought their new baby. His family was growing all around him and it soothed his heart.

And of course there was Naomi—and Everett. The boy had quickly grown on him once he'd gotten his head out of his ass and started treating his mother right. Now? Burke pitied anyone who said a mean word about Naomi Cranston. Everett was ready and willing to defend her.

He'd even decided to become an attorney so he could help people unjustly accused like his mother. Who knew if he would actually go that route? He was only sixteen. But that he even wanted to was such a change.

Such a relief.

"How are you?" Stone asked, taking the seat next to Burke. Stone was one of the Cincinnati contingent and Phin's best friend. As per tradition in Cora's church, a male child had two godfathers and one godmother. Burke and Stone were the godfathers. Stone's wife Delores was Jonas's godmother. She had taken to her role with her customary enthusiasm, but Burke knew it was easier for her to hold an infant now that, after several lost pregnancies, she and Stone had finally welcomed their own son into the world.

Burke couldn't be happier for them. "I'm okay, Montgomery."

Stone scowled. Everyone had been calling him Montgomery all afternoon, and he hated his given name. "They could have called the kid Stone. It would have been better."

"I'm just glad they had a boy," Burke said. "Cora said if it was a girl, they would have given her Burkette as a middle name."

Stone threw back his head and laughed. "There's still time. Phin wants a baseball team for a family."

"Wonderful," Burke grumbled, because *Burkette* wouldn't just be bad.

It would be horrific.

Stone laughed again and slapped him on the back. "I like your lady friend."

Burke snorted. "My lady friend? What are you, a hundred and six?"

Phin came over with the baby in his arms and SodaPop at his side. "What are you two plotting over here? You're having too much fun."

Burke held out his arms. "Gimme."

Phin carefully handed over the baby. "Support his—"

"His head," Burke interrupted. "Yeah, yeah. I know." He smiled down at Jonas, who'd been named for his grandfather. "Hey there."

The baby burped and Burke laughed. God, Naomi had been so right. He'd needed his people. He'd needed to hold new life.

Naomi came up behind him and rested her chin on his shoulder. "He puke on you yet?"

"Nope," Burke said, "but the day is still young, isn't it, Jonas *Montgomery* Burke Bishop?"

Stone gave Phin a dirty look. "I really hate you."

Phin grinned. "I know." He sobered, squeezing Burke's shoulder. "We heard the news. We're here, you know. If you need us."

Burke looked up and found that his team had gathered behind Phin. He thought they'd look sad, but they didn't. They just looked like they loved him.

He drew a breath and blinked hard. "You guys are going to make me cry on the baby. Stop it."

"Little salt never hurt anyone," Joy said from the front of the line. "Give me that baby, or there will be hell to pay."

"I'd do what she says," Naomi said with a laugh. "She's badass."

"And don't any of you forget it," Joy declared. "Stop dawdling, Burke Broussard. It's my turn."

Chuckling, Burke gave the baby to Joy, then twisted to kiss Naomi on the mouth. "You are always exactly what I need," he whispered.

She pulled him to his feet. "What you need is some dancing. The DJ's getting ready to start. Come dance with me. It'll do your heart good."

"In a minute." He held his arms out to Molly, who smiled at him. Then Val. Then Antoine, who received a smacking kiss on the cheek. He hugged all his people, one at a time. His family.

And then he danced with the woman who'd healed his heart.

ACKNOWLEDGMENTS

The Starfish—Christine, Sheila, Brian, Kathie, and Cheryl—for the brainstorming. I appreciate you all so very much!

Tracy Bernstein for a seamless transition. I look forward to many more books together!

Andrew Grey for being my word-count partner.

Sarah Hafer for fixing my mistakes.

Sonie Lasker for teaching my characters how to escape from all kinds of situations.

Margaret Taylor for the law enforcement procedural tips.

As always, all mistakes are my own.